STOLEN
OBSESSION

A NOVEL BY

MARLENE M. BELL

Ewephoric Publishing

This book is a work of fiction. Names, characters, dialog, places, and incidents are strictly from the imagination of the author. Any similarities to actual events and locales, or real persons, living or dead, is entirely coincidental and not intended by the author.

Cover design by Vlad & Jade Erica of Steam Power Studios
Book design by Kevin G. Summers

ISBN: 978-0-9995394-0-8
ISBN: 978-0-9995394-1-5 (eBook)

For Patti

Your bleary-eyed, countless hours spent reading Chapter rewrites has made Stolen Obsession a joint effort on so many levels. Bouncing plot ideas between us and the love scenes that made us laugh so hard we cried, are memories I'll cherish always. This novel is a reality because of your steadfast enthusiasm, my friend. I am in your debt.

CHAPTER

ONE

A ground fog shrouded investigators while they unearthed her roommate, Samantha Freeman, from the black dirt of a farmer's field. The August crime scene played out so vividly in Annalisse Drury's head, it made her queasy all over again. She took a shuddering breath and closed her eyes against the vision.

"It's too soon to socialize. I can't stay here long." Annalisse scanned the room full of art collectors and met the gaze of a guest who watched her with curiosity. Shedding the embarrassment with a shrug and a smile, Annalisse considered using a headache as an excuse for a quick escape from the party. She'd rather hang out alone behind the walls of her Greenwich brownstone and dive into a Brontë novel—to an era far from her painful memories. No excuses tonight. She couldn't disappoint her favorite client, Generosa Zavos, who expected her to stay for the grand opening launch of Zavos Gallery in Lower Manhattan.

Annalisse slid next to the window for a break from eavesdropping on guests. She couldn't care less who had the best spa massages in New York or who was having an affair with their hairdresser. She smoothed down her ball gown to overcome the urge to cover her ears from the din. Squeezing back the burning sensation in her eyes, Annalisse peered through the coolish glass pane and into the street. SoHo's boutique district substituted as a catwalk for knockoffs from fall and summer collections during Fashion Week. Rain or radiance, women in split pencil skirts and above-the-waist belts, sporting zippered leather jackets, hit the streets in every season.

A clap of thunder, and umbrellas in blue and black impressively popped open along the sidewalk. The count-the-drop sprinkles had quickly changed to a torrent of water, and the squeals from a power couple caught without cover had Annalisse wishing she were sprinting with them through the downpour.

A lightning flash and another boom shook the window, and she sprang backward into a guest, jolting her from her reverie to reality. Pain rippled through her shoulder as she held on to a nearby drink cart, praying it wouldn't roll away with her attached.

"Sorry, miss. Are you all right?" The tattooed hand of a man in an ill-fitting jacket steadied the cart, then brushed at her bare arm. For an art connoisseur, his dirty nails and sandpaper-rough fingers surprised her.

Annalisse mustered a polite nod as warmth flooded her cheeks. "My fault. I'm truly sorry." She dismissed the incident with a smile.

Sweeping a stray hair away, she glanced at the mahogany long-case clock by the door. Five twenty. For Generosa's sake, she could endure the agony. Mindless chatter swamped her ears, calling her closer to the exit. *Relax. You'll be home in two hours.*

An attendant dressed as a Minuteman in woolen Revolutionary War gear held the door for an endless flow of clients in rain-speckled black ties and designer gowns. Passing yellow cabs swooshed through puddles on the road, transporting the change of seasons to her nose—when rain made contact with warm concrete for the first time in weeks.

New York had hooked her with its claws, drawn her into its global mystique, ideal for an antiquities valuator with her strengths. Even so, she yearned for the sweet grass aroma of first-cut bales of hay, the slipperiness of lanolin between her fingers when she and her aunt sheared the ewes down to their pink bodies, and the steamy piles of fresh horse apples gathered in the corner of a stall, mingled with coppery horse hide. Rural life was freedom, and she intended to retire one day to the serenity of the country. So far, the girl from a Kensington neighborhood in Brooklyn made good, not great, in the big city.

Generosa appeared with two flutes of golden Armand de Brignac. "Drink this, hon." She looked radiant, but concern flickered in her aging, dark eyes.

"Thanks." Annalisse took the glass and sipped the crisp champagne, savoring the fruit flavor and kick of bubbles. "You're wearing the Lagerfeld? It's so chic. That shade of purple is stunning on you."

"Really?" Generosa grabbed a handful of silk at the hip. "I wasn't sure about this shade of violet." She tipped her head and regarded Annalisse. "I can't afford to have you falling ill on us."

Generosa's extravagant Italian accent brightened Annalisse's mood. "The party's a wicked success. And the Revolutionary soldier as a greeter—what an idea."

"Are you feverish?" Generosa leaned closer, touching Annalisse's forehead. "It's warm in here. No wonder I found you near the door."

"Reliving the same terrible day." Annalisse bit her lower lip. "Samantha is everywhere, and to make matters worse, today is her birthday."

Generosa patted her arm and sighed wistfully. "I wish you weren't part of that search team. I remember the day Sam had to swing by the gallery to show me her exquisite horse bracelet."

The ghostly image of the gold circlet of horses made her breath catch. Their glaring eyes and open mouths kept Annalisse awake most nights. Samantha would be safe and miles away from the Upstate Killer if she'd listened to her and had taken the artifact back to the estate sale.

"If only I could've convinced her to give it up." She closed her eyes and opened them as the tear that lingered for the past hour trickled down. "I should've tried harder, and now it's too late."

Her free-spirited college roomie had laughed over stories about curses. She'd said they belonged with Ouija boards at lame parties. Samantha had regarded her bracelet as nothing more than an *inexpensive piece of glitz*, but the string of horses rarely left her wrist.

Annalisse strangled the stem of her champagne flute, recalling the rows of circular burns on Samantha's body when they'd lifted her from the ground. Her rings were caked with mud, and both wrists were bare.

"Happy to see you, Harry." Generosa touched the arm of Harry Carradine, Annalisse's mentor, boss, and the owner of Westinn Gallery.

In his stained white shirt, bold tie, and a pair of suit pants he could've slept in, Harry grunted, barely acknowledging Generosa's greeting. He headed straight for the server with the fullest appetizer cart.

When her boss reached his destination, Annalisse shook her head. "He misses his wife." She sniffed the air. "You went with the coconut shrimp after all. My favorite choice too." Annalisse's mouth watered at the thought of salty ocean and delicate fish on her tongue. She took another sip of her champagne. The dry crackers and a sweet pickle she'd eaten before noon were long gone hours ago.

A twinge zinged through Annalisse's arm, and she rotated her shoulder.

"Something bothering your back?" Generosa gave her the motherly look of concern she'd come to know the past few years—a big step beyond friendship.

"I'm just a wallflower who got in the way." She feigned a crooked smile and focused on the panel of colonial portraits. Their sourpuss faces epitomized Harry's stubbornness over their latest debate about her salary. He'd refused Annalisse's desperate pleas for more hours. Lately she'd resorted to dipping into her inheritance for rent and utility payments. Working overtime once in a while would keep her farm fund where it belonged: in a bank, not squandered on expenses. Her parents would've melted down and insisted she move out of the Village if they'd survived their ordeal and had known of her plight. A chill sent Annalisse's gaze to the grid pattern on the coffered ceiling; the sudden cold felt like a sign from beyond.

"The gallery does look *bellissima,* thanks to you and Chase. Where is he?" Generosa creased her penciled brows.

"Mingling, I hope." Annalisse's gaze swept the crowd upstairs, spotting the pink tie of her escort and coworker, Chase Miller. "He almost didn't make it back after he dressed at his place. By the way, my talk with Harry was useless."

"The old windbag still won't sweeten your paycheck?" Generosa shook a finger at Harry gorging on shrimp. "He'll listen to me."

Annalisse hastened to stop her from making things worse. Too much push from Generosa could backfire. "Thanks, Gen, but I've got this."

Although Harry respected Generosa, he hated being scolded by a strong, opinionated woman. He required a softer touch.

Conversations in the room intensified into a steady hum, while the rustle of fabric and clacking heels joined smatters of laughter, adding to Annalisse's throbbing temples.

"Mingle and take a look at the beautiful showpiece in the case upstairs. I think you'll be amazed. My son brought an exquisite necklace back with him from Greece. Of course, you remember Alec."

Like she could forget Generosa's heartbreaker son with the dimples she'd love to plunge into.

"Is the necklace antique?"

"It's my jeweler's creation." Generosa looked over her shoulder toward four regal men who must have received the same message and arrived in cummerbunds. "The bachelor crowd," she whispered in Annalisse's ear. "Alec's over there. He's not seeing that college friend anymore." Generosa eyed Annalisse with keen perception, her lips curved as she pointed him out and walked away.

Alec Zavos, unattached, lightened the heaviness dragging down Annalisse's thoughts. Even from across the room, he emanated the affluent Zavos aura: the angle of his head when he spoke and his confident baritone laughter.

Watching him from afar made her skin tingle.

A mental picture of Alec on one of his thoroughbreds quickened her pulse. Too bad she'd have to disappoint Generosa in her matchmaking venture. A rich guy who landed on tabloid covers with a different girl each time belonged with someone else, not her.

She glanced at her watch and noted the time, six o'clock. Weaving through the rainbow of mermaid dresses and form-fitting gowns, she glided around the perimeter to the gallery office. To her right were oils of ponytailed militiamen standing proudly in their knee breeches and weskits, boasting impressive tricornered hats and muskets. She nodded to the tattooed man from their collision near the window, receiving his smile. Evening society galas had a way of blending different flavors of the art world together.

Harry, deep in conversation with the spinster sisters, ignored her as she walked by. The identical twins, wearing matching black velveteen gowns with plunging bodices and overstated embroidery, carried the appearance of old curtains draping their shoulders. Annalisse's eyes watered at the heavy jasmine in their dated Chanel perfume. She closed her eyes against the cloud drift overtaking her.

"Slow down, Annalisse," a deep voice said, and a firm grip spun her around.

Alec Zavos pulled her so close that she collided with his muscular chest.

Heat crept up Annalisse's throat as she caught his lapels and squeezed. The sensual scent of smoked woods and citrus flooded her senses, dousing the earlier Chanel. Not having practiced what she'd say to him when they spoke again, she wondered how he recalled her name.

"You'll come out of your stilettos moving that fast."

Alec's inky pupils expanded, and faint laugh lines creased his tanned skin.

That picture of him soaking up rays on the back of a horse ran like a video on an endless loop. He had a business she knew nothing about but wouldn't mind learning if he were by her side. As she fought her ache to belong to someone like Alec, pesky images of his harem flooded the dream and brought her back to reality.

Annalisse pushed away and swiped at droplets of champagne she'd spilled on his jacket. "I'm wrinkling you. I promised your mom I'd be tonight's photographer and need to grab my camera from the office."

"If you hadn't, I would have."

"Grabbed my camera?"

"Wrinkled you in the office. In that dress, you're smoking hot. It's time we got reacquainted since—"

"Gen mentioned your new status."

He threw his head back and let out a sinful laugh.

One that reverberated all the way to her toes.

She smoothed her green gown, trying to decide which was sexier, the way his dark hair set off his amazing eyes or the sound of his throaty voice.

"Mom talks about you all the time, Annalisse. It used to drive my ex wild. If you aren't with someone, would you mind an escort for the evening?"

Distracted by the mention of his ex, Annalisse shifted her gaze toward Harry dangling two shrimp above his mouth with one hand and a napkin stacked with pink tails in the other. He grinned at her, then shoveled the battered delicacies, one after the other, into his round, bloated face. Annalisse considered asking if he felt all right, silently hoping his hair loss and yellowish hue weren't a sign of illness, but thought better of it. After his wife had passed, personal questions were off-limits to employees.

"Hello?" Alec waved a hand in front of her face. "Isn't that your boss?"

Annalisse clutched Alec's arm and lowered her voice. "I'm worried about Harry. He's grumpy and hard to work for at times, but I'd be lost at Westinn without him."

"He seems to be enjoying the shrimp." Alec reached for her glass of warm champagne. "Can I get you a refill?"

"Anna!"

The familiar voice and the flash of a raised hand drew her eyes to the second floor and her friend Chase.

"I'm being paged. Please save me some."

"Save you some what?" He angled a look at her, followed by a slow show of teeth.

"Weren't we discussing champagne?"

"We'll catch up once you check in with the guy upstairs." The muscles in Alec's jaw jumped a couple of times.

Why was he gritting his teeth?

"Give me two minutes." She turned for the staircase, and her heart sank a little. She couldn't remember the last time a guy complimented her on the way she looked, and it felt great.

Lifting her gown and taking two steps at a time, she imagined the places Alec's fantasies went and wondered if someone like her could ever be as carefree as he was. She reached the top of the stairs and scanned for her sandy-haired friend. More guests in damp coats filtered upstairs behind her. Some nibbled hors d'oeuvres and sipped wine, oblivious to the artistry around them. Others browsed the bronze statues, Egyptian masks, and scaled-down sphinxes Generosa had acquired from Africa to enhance the exhibit. Annalisse pivoted when someone tapped her arm.

Chase gave her a toothy grin. "I saw you talking to Zavos. Hope I didn't interrupt anything intense down there."

"You don't like him much, do you?"

"He's all right, I guess."

Chase stood close enough for her to count the freckles on his nose. His trim physique on display in his fitted, pin-striped jacket. For the first time in weeks, he had a bounce in his step. Since his last breakup, he'd become a moper extraordinaire. Her threat to slap a sticker on his back that read Spinster in Training had convinced him to attend the opening because she'd make good on her promise.

"I want your opinion on a bib necklace Gen put in the case." Chase gestured to the display in the middle of the floor.

"Do we have to do this right now?" Without waiting for his reply, she held up her hand. "I'm edgy tonight. Sure, show me."

Annalisse straightened her posture and strolled with him to the center of the room, but her mind was on Alec downstairs.

Chase stood over the glass, shading his eyes with the edge of his palm.

"The gold's eighteen, maybe twenty-two karats. The horses and acorns are scratched, so it's not modern jewelry." He rubbed behind one ear.

"Jewelers can make pieces look old. Is that Gen's new gallery brochure?"

Taking the leaflet from his hands, she flipped to the Adornment pages of the gallery pamphlet and scanned them. On page three, she read: Relive History with Modern Creations ~ Zavos Art Gallery. Illustrations showcased gold bracelets and neckpieces studded in malachite, lapis, peridot, and red jasper. Coin rings in onyx and silver joined the collection of gold. All were a gemologist's dream; reproductions inspired by antiquities.

Annalisse thumbed through every page in the booklet, sending photos to memory. She gazed into the case, grabbed Chase's wrist, and took a hard breath.

"Forget about the jeweler. It's Samantha's bracelet in necklace form," she whispered. The neat row of horses hanging from the collar conjured a scene of Generosa lying in black dirt. "We aren't going through that again. Not with Gen—not her." She grasped the edge of the display as her knees buckled.

He caught her around the waist. "Easy. I wanted confirmation, and you gave it to me. We can't change what happened to Sam. We still don't know who…" The glass pane resonated when he tapped his pinky ring on it.

"Her creepy boyfriend was the last person to see her alive." She clenched her jaw.

"He has an alibi, Anna."

"Not a great one. We had alibis also, but that didn't keep us off the suspect list. Finding her decapitated body in that horrible place—" Annalisse crossed her arms and rubbed. "I still see her arm above the ground… when I can't sleep." Bile rose in her throat, and she gulped. "When did Gen get the necklace?"

Struggling for air, Annalisse backed up. The wide eyes of the horses challenged her equilibrium. There could be a slight chance the necklace was a forgery, even though her gut said otherwise.

"Anna, let's not jump ahead. Gen may have commissioned the necklace from her jeweler."

"Gen never said anything to me, and she tells me everything." Her voice echoed upstairs.

Heads turned in their direction, and several couples retreated down the stairs.

Annalisse lowered her head and calmly whispered, "Bet you a coffee it's the real deal. Why are these nasty horses showing up in New York?" She covered Chase's hand with hers. "Wrap this display. Gen's not going to like it, but we have to shield the public from this evil, cursed thing."

CHAPTER

TWO

Annalisse understood his aura of bewilderment when Chase returned from downstairs with a velveteen cloak under his arm. To cover a display case during a party with guests all around invited questions with no solid answers.

He handed her the folded fabric. "Your funeral."

"Trying to save us from another one. Look, we can verify the authenticity right now if it makes you feel better. Let's check the jeweler's mark on the back." Annalisse fumbled with the button to open the cabinet. "Locked."

She glanced at Chase as a determined set of heel taps marched up the marble stairs, followed by a familiar voice. Jerking her hand from the tab, Annalisse tasted chalk on the back of her tongue.

"There you are. Still glum? Have fun—celebrate." Generosa tipped her head toward Alec on her arm.

As though timed for effect, placid harp music flowed from the main floor. Some vague sense of the angelic realm lifted the hair on the nape of Annalisse's neck. Before her stood Alec, long and lean with a killer smile—and the shadow of a beard from a much earlier shave. An awkward warmth moved from her cheeks and spread the length of her throat to places farther south.

"That's my cue for a do-over." Alec lifted her hand and seductively kissed her knuckles like they'd just met.

Greek men were so romantic.

She felt the urge to curtsy but buried the impulse immediately. He was a stranger she couldn't allow herself to feel anything for and wished she were home, safe from the schoolgirl thuds banging away in her chest. Falling for a man like Alec was dangerous.

Generosa pointed over the brass railing. "Chase, Harry's trying to get your attention downstairs."

"How'd you spot him from up here?" Chase smirked at Annalisse, then sent an uneasy glance toward Alec. "Thanks, Gen. I'll go down. Excuse me. Take over, Anna."

Annalisse nodded as he scurried to the bottom of the staircase. She'd had a lighthearted talk with Chase earlier, and they'd made a pact: he'd start dating again if she would. She would encourage him, but she wasn't ready to date yet. Not since they found Samantha in that field.

"Now, what do you think of the necklace?" Generosa twirled her arm toward the case in a game show host manner.

Annalisse loved the way Generosa's gestures followed her words. A modest woman whose confidence and positive attitude had rescued Annalisse from more than a few scrapes with Harry.

"It scares me, Gen. I'd like your permission to cover it tonight."

"Nonsense, *bambolina*." Generosa escorted Alec to the display.

"It's a bad omen to have one like Samantha wore. Where'd you find it?" Annalisse balled a fist and banged her hip.

The glass clicked beneath Generosa's acrylic nails. "Doesn't the motif remind you of your beautiful horses, son? I know we shouldn't have copied Sam's bracelet, but I had to have one. We added filigree next to the acorns for a modern touch and redesigned it in fourteen karat."

Annalisse peered inside the case, then slowly met Generosa's gaze. "You are one of the most special people in my life, so please don't take this the wrong way. There's no filigree, and it's *not* a recent piece." She lowered her voice. "I beg you—shove it in a safe deposit box. Lock it away—I don't care—but don't tell anyone you have it and never, ever wear it."

"Why?" Alec stepped between her and Generosa.

"The curse this necklace carries—it has the same destiny as Samantha's bracelet."

"Pooh. You're being melodramatic." Generosa waved the concern away.

"What curse?" Alec leaned closer to Annalisse.

With the speed of an open water faucet, Generosa's words ran together. "I know every painting and artifact in this gallery and sell only new jewelry, Annalisse. I've planned this event for months. Must we do this tonight?"

"The ruling Mushasha from ancient Persia had ordered death to the wearer of any collection piece. Samantha bought her bracelet just before she died. Her killing wasn't a random act." Annalisse touched Generosa's wrist. "And I won't stand idle while this necklace hurts you."

"I've never heard of that." Generosa's lips soured into a pucker.

Annalisse's breathing intensified into short bursts. Marble statues on the upper floor mocked her with their stares. If Generosa had copied it, then someone switched her necklace with the original artifact. But taking a fake and leaving the real one in its place was a ridiculous notion.

"Do you have the matching ring too?" Annalisse swayed.

When she stumbled, Alec caught her around the waist, holding her steady.

"I'm good." Annalisse adjusted the foot that slipped out of her shoe. "Champagne on an empty stomach."

"Eat something." Generosa crooked a finger at a server near the staircase.

"The jewelry collection's been missing a long time. For hundreds of years. It's priceless, and now someone wants the pieces back. This display in your shop makes us a... target."

"Maybe you're mistaken and Mom's right." Alec gave Annalisse's arm a gentle nudge.

Annalisse exhaled and shifted her weight from one throbbing high-heeled foot to the other. What she wouldn't give for her sheepskin slippers right now.

"Mom, we're taking you away from your friends. We'll finish this another time." Alec patted his mother's hand, but his smile disappeared.

"Forgive me." Annalisse hugged Generosa and whispered, "I'm being a major pain."

"You aren't."

"Would you mind if I stop by early tomorrow before you open?"

"I'll be here at seven. Alec, take Annalisse downstairs and make her eat something, will you? Have fun you two." Generosa twirled around and grazed the arm of the tatted man from downstairs who'd been near enough to overhear. "Excuse me, Mr. Chesnokov. I didn't see you there. I'm dying to hear what Incan goodies you found on your jaunt to Peru." She took his arm and strolled off.

Annalisse faced Alec with a makeshift smile. "Thanks for saving me from the floor earlier." She tried on her party face, but the exchange with Generosa knotted her insides. The two of them rarely disagreed. "Would you please ask Gen to lock the necklace in her big office vault? She'll do it for you."

His gaze was a blanket of gray flannel filled with gentleness. A look so pronounced and comforting, it melted some of the ice in her veins.

"Sure. Are you shivering? Stick with me, pretty lady."

He tugged her next to him and led her by the arm toward the stairs in a natural flow.

As if she belonged beside him.

She palmed an invisible wrinkle from her gown to remove the stickiness.

"I wish you'd left the necklace in Greece, Alec."

A mere two steps from the stairs, he cinched her closer, single-handed. "A strand of gold jewelry can't hurt us."

"If only you could convince my intuition of that."

He patted her hand reassuringly before tucking it in the crook of his elbow.

On his arm, Annalisse floated down the staircase, her feet more comfortable on the move. Muted conversations intensified when they entered the parade of black tails and banded bow ties. A sea of proper penguins swimming on a floor filled with color. She allowed the healing echoes of classical strings in the background to transport her soul away from the dread upstairs.

Alec left her side and returned with two glasses, handing one to her.

"Be careful. The last time I drank Cristal at the estate, I woke up covered in straw in one of the stalls."

"Drinking and riding—it's no wonder."

"Never mix the two." His eyes teased flirtatiously.

Annalisse suppressed a grin at his trying-too-hard approach. Tonight, with Alec dressed in a slick tux—mimicking so many of his paparazzi shots—she had a hard time picturing him in Levi's and boots, holding a pitchfork full of horse poop.

The wine tasted sweeter with Alec standing nearby. In fact, it went down so fast and easy, some trickled down her chin.

"Darn." She brushed at the drip, looking for a napkin.

He handed her one monogrammed with a silver *Z*.

"Thanks. Klutzy me." Annalisse found a nearby server in a ruffled apron and laid the empty flute next to plates of shrimp and lamb meatballs. The tangy, acid bounce of teriyaki sauce in her nostrils made her taste buds sour. "A fitting place for my glass, between seafood and sheep."

Alec bobbed his eyebrows. "Sheep?"

"Seafood and sheep are my favorite things."

"Interesting." He studied her for a beat. "Let's find a place to sit. Something tells me you aren't used to walking in heels."

"That obvious, huh? Maybe you'd be more comfortable with someone else? I'm hardly your type."

He paused, drenching her with an attentive stare. "What's my *type*?"

She bit her lip and turned away, having said too much. Scanning the room's sparse furniture, an elderly couple vacated a Queen Anne-style settee. Annalisse pointed toward it. "Let's grab that couch before someone else does."

"You're avoiding my question."

"I'm a mess, Alec."

"Hardly the description I'd use."

He walked her to the comfort of the cushions and asked her to save his seat.

Alec left her alone on the straight-backed bench with thoughts of the necklace—and the stark reminder that she was unattached and lonely. Generosa's motherly advice to her was awkward to imagine. How could she make her break from a humdrum, workaholic life? She had responsibilities and several galleries that depended on her expertise.

Annalisse sensed a lull in the noise and peered through the hushed crowd. Gasps erupted as people pressed toward the wall of colonial paintings. She jumped to her feet, searching for Alec's tanned handsomeness somewhere in the formal wear overflow.

"I think he's choking. Call 911!" someone cried.

"Does anyone know the Heimlich maneuver?"

CHAPTER
THREE

Several wild-eyed women stood in a semicircle, their hands pressed against their cheeks in stunned silence. Annalisse broke through an opening in the rigid line of guests, and her heart stopped at the sight of Alec administering the Heimlich to her boss. A cool clamminess rushed her bare neck while she watched Alec's repeated cupped fists to Harry's upper abdomen. Harry's stoic, ashen face left her woozy.

"Alec, let me help you. What can I do?" Annalisse ran to Alec's side.

Harry's immobile weight collapsed on Alec, and he stumbled to keep Harry's body from falling on her.

Alec slowly laid him on his back, emptied of life.

Annalisse's suspicions over her boss being ill were confirmed.

The silk fabric clung to her waistline, while perspiration trickled down her thighs. She sank to her knees and leaned over Harry's paunch, loosened his tie, and checked for a pulse at his neck. Heat from the lingering crowd suffocated her. Open-mouthed, she labored for air.

Westinn's patriarch couldn't leave her yet.

Annalisse clutched his shirt and yelled, "Don't give up, Harry!" She massaged his face and found it corpse-like in temperature. Scanning the room, Annalisse asked, "Is anyone a doctor or EMT?"

Vacant stares met her question.

A reel of her first aid training ran through her head.

Annalisse tilted Harry's head back and looked down his throat, making a finger sweep. "No shrimp blocking the airway," she mumbled.

She checked for a pulse at the carotid again and, one hand over the other, pressed the heel of her palm over his breastbone and pumped in short bursts. Counting to thirty in her head, she huffed after each thrust. The actions made her arms ache and her palms hurt.

"Harry, breathe! C'mon, breathe!"

"Where's the ambulance?" Alec checked the Rolex on his wrist and crouched next to her. "When you're tired, I'll take over."

The irony in the last act for her boss… Harry had forced his employees to take the CPR course with no idea he'd be the one in need.

A lonesome siren's wail pierced her ears when the vehicle stopped in front of the gallery in a myriad of blinding lights. Annalisse glanced through the entrance as the FDNY emergency truck's blazing red-and-yellow door opened.

She turned back to her unresponsive superior and ripped open his shirt, sending buttons flying to the tile before she continued CPR.

Muffled voices, footsteps, and a metallic clank sounded from behind her. Ambulance attendants rushed through the double glass doors, banging their gurney along the way. In the cool relief of the air from outside, she silently said a prayer for Harry.

"I appreciate everyone's concern, but please allow the emergency personnel some room to do their work." Generosa swiped her forehead with the back of her hand. "Hang on, Harry."

The retreating shoes of the gallery guests scuffed the floor tiles.

Annalisse noticed the EMS team paramedic bending down next to her.

"Stop please." The medic laid two fingers against Harry's neck. "I'll charge the AED." He waved to Generosa. "Can we get a tablecloth to block the patient from the crowd? It'll make our job easier. Are you okay to continue compressions, miss?" The crease between his furry brows formed a V while he waited for Annalisse's reply.

She nodded, hardly aware of his question, and resumed the hand-numbing pumps to Harry's chest.

A minute later, emergency services assumed ventilating with a bag while another cut off Harry's shirt, exposing the defibrillator patches they'd applied. Three times they charged the system, and three times Harry stayed unresponsive.

Helplessness washed over Annalisse as Alec helped her off her knees. She turned toward the second floor—eyeing the jewelry case that held the necklace.

An evil force had intervened.

Annalisse brushed at dirt that had migrated into the folds of her dress, then fell into Alec's open arms. A tremor rippled through her, and the room rose and fell in such an odd way that she felt seasick.

"My legs are rubbery." She clung tighter to Alec and tucked her head into his chest.

Although her hands trembled and tears threatened, Harry wouldn't have approved if he were watching. He'd shake his finger at her and say, "If you cry, I'll fire you." With her cheek crushed against Alec's pleated shirt, she allowed the smell of him to drain off the tension.

Alec broke their embrace and gazed at her. "Annalisse, you're as white as the flooring."

The entrance opened, and a pair of uniformed men appeared.

"That's Detective Colum Mooney and his partner. I knew Harry better than anyone here. I should speak to them."

"Grab Mom and wait for me. Please?" He tilted Annalisse's chin so she couldn't turn away. "You need to rest. Did Harry come alone?"

She shook her head and strangled a sob as her eyes followed the yellow-shirted emergency team rolling the oxygen-masked Harry outside.

Once the gallery doors closed behind the gurney, she absorbed who'd stayed behind. Like highway rubberneckers, clusters of party guests spoke in low whispers and pointed at the ambulance as it drove away. The celebration was over, and they didn't belong there, but the officers needed statements and wouldn't allow them to leave.

Within forty minutes, the police completed their reports, the gallery had emptied, and Harry was on his way to the morgue, awaiting the medical examiner. Annalisse dreaded a simple truth—Harry's death would shake her job stability. She'd dared to imagine Westinn as a stepping-stone to one of the renowned auction houses like Sotheby's or Christie's. That hope had all but vanished.

The manager, brother-in-law Peter Gregory, stood next in line to run Westinn. He and Annalisse had a quiet rivalry going behind Harry's back. She had the degree and a greater knowledge of antiques, and Peter had nepotism on his side.

One by one, the crowd thinned, leaving her empty. She forced thoughts of self-pity into regret now that Harry had disappeared from her world. How she longed for the chance to take back the less-than-gracious things she'd said during their disagreements. Her own problems paled against the finality of his death.

Annalisse reached for a fresh glass from a server's cart and poured champagne from a sweaty bottle. Her hands shook so badly, the bottle slipped to its neck. Setting the heavy vessel aside, she wiped her hand on a cloth when a figure caught her peripheral vision.

Alec paced the wall of muted wartime oils, staring at the floor. The man who held unspeakable fortune acted as if he'd lost it all at the card table. Though he hadn't said it aloud, Alec felt her sense of despair even though he barely knew Harry.

If she couldn't convince the Zavoses their threat was real, she'd make off with the necklace and hide it away forever. Annalisse had to save them from themselves.

Alec stopped her near the staircase. "Where are you going, and where's Mom?"

"I left something upstairs. Gen is in the kitchen with the servers, and who could blame her? Your mother's beautiful opening is memorable in a horrible way. I hope she's okay." Annalisse glanced at the brass rail on the second floor. "We'll have to work on a new publicity campaign for your mom, perhaps a relaunch of sorts. We don't want her friends to have Harry on their minds when they enter the shop. You should check on her."

Alec took her hand, spinning her to him. "What about you?"

His caring warmed her.

"You mean other than scared and hot?" Annalisse wagged the flat of her hand like a fan, relishing the breeze.

He smiled with a sparkle in his eyes; she had seen that hint of desire plenty of times. "Does your boss have relatives we could contact?"

Her shoulders forced back, she said, "That would be Peter, his brother-in-law. He didn't come to the party." She sighed. "We'd better tell him. What a way to get what he wants."

"He wanted Harry dead?" Alec asked.

"There's a lawsuit. Peter's left Westinn vulnerable."

With Harry gone, she had no one to protect her from Peter. The Revere silver appraisal lawsuit against Westinn was ongoing. An appraisal Annalisse had nothing to do with yet received all the blame for Peter's bungled mess. Harry had known she wasn't involved in the reckless valuation and had promised to keep her out of the fray.

A stray lock of hair fell across her forehead, and Alec tried to brush it back.

She put her hand over his and pressed it to her face lovingly to let him know she appreciated his touch.

"I should help Gen," she said.

"Let's get some air instead."

"And I need to find Chase," she added.

He sighed. "I have to ask you something, and my timing is awful, but—"

"Ask."

"This thing with Chase, is it serious?"

"He's a colleague." She thought about leaving the description there, but the confusion written on Alec's face deserved more. "Not a date."

21

Generosa appeared in the archway of the reception area and wandered to Annalisse, giving her a longer than usual hug. "It won't be the same without Harry. Let me know if there's anything we can do for you. Anything at all." She dropped the dishtowel she held onto a nearby chair.

"Thank you. I'm here for moral support, publicity, just name it. Like a dazzling Zavos Gallery relaunch mailer for you. We can talk more tomorrow." Annalisse glanced at the service door. "Where's Chase?"

"In the back, a little tipsy, I'm afraid. He's taking Harry's death pretty hard. You and Alec go on. I'll put him in a cab." She flipped her hand toward the double doors. "You know what I always say. When you can't do anything else, make baklava. The rain's stopped; go out for a stroll and eat something." Generosa shared a look with Alec and turned for the kitchen.

Annalisse squinted and blinked at the headlights from a stream of cabs and Ubers outside the gallery. Engine noise and impatient drivers with their windows rolled down amplified the sound bombarding her ears. Exhaust fumes in a rotten egg cocktail turned her empty stomach and took her appetite away.

She touched Alec's arm. "I'm tempted to go back inside and wait for our walk later."

"Would you rather duck into a restaurant?" From behind his back, Alec presented her with a small bouquet of baby pink roses. "Caught a vendor closing early while you were talking to Chase."

Alec stood close, leaning over her in just the right spot to block the mist from her face. His nearness plunged her into a pool of delicious heat.

"Alec, they're so fragrant." Holding the flowers to her nose, the suggestion of springtime refreshed the air, and her pulse ticked higher. "Thank you, kind sir." She offered a slight curtsy. The move she almost made when he'd kissed her hand in the gallery.

He reached for her, and her leather bag slipped to the ground with a splat.

"You're exhausted. What can I do to make this night easier, Ms. *Drury*?" He lingered over the last syllable of her name like she demanded the royal treatment.

Touché, Mr. Zavos. Reaching for her purse, she motioned him toward the building. As she edged against the wall, the horse necklace popped back into her mind. The cool champagne had numbed her thoughts and clouded her senses. She had to stay in control.

Alec followed her to the protection of the building's eaves. The moist ends of his hair glistened with gold from the nearby streetlight.

She reeled from a combination of sorrow, guilt, fatigue—and too much sexual adrenaline from the man next to her.

Somehow, he must have felt that he'd moved too deeply into her space earlier, because he stopped an arm's length away and leaned against the brick, observing her.

"The roses are amazing." She buried her face in the soft petals smelling of sweet nutmeg. "Nothing like a workout, complete with a sweaty dress." She slid layers of her gown between her fingertips and shivered from a sudden breeze.

Alec stripped off his jacket and placed it over her shoulders. His ambiance lingered in the fabric, and the warmth removed the chill.

"For your case of teeth chatters." He offered a slow smile. "Ready for that dry and quiet place so we can talk?"

"Promise me you'll keep Gen safe."

"Always," he said.

"We're in unspeakable danger."

He gushed a bit of air. "Don't worry about the mythical curse."

"It's here, Alec. And if tonight's any indication, we aren't going to escape unscathed."

CHAPTER
FOUR

Alec held open the door to the Amico SoHo restaurant, and Annalisse walked into the frigid waiting area, with her damp gown clinging to moist ankles. She waited a few seconds for her eyes to adjust to the darkness before stepping farther onto the uneven brick floor.

"Thanks for the jacket." She graciously gave him the tail-coat back. "I believe their bar is in the far corner. I can already taste their meat-and-cheese platter."

Instead of answering, he nodded to the host and pointed out the carved wood bar lined with leather stools.

On a short wall of the nostalgia room, hundreds of signed and dated singles from customers were stapled to black paneling. Annalisse lingered awhile and noted some bills that went back forty years, the passage of time evident by the washed-out signatures and size of George Washington's portrait on the front.

A fresh-faced barmaid with ghoulish silver and black skull rings on every finger clicked out Dean Martin's "That's Amore" on a blender of margaritas. She released the pulse button and bounded over to them with a hop-skip, her curls bouncing up and down to the rhythm of her stride. She slid two green beverage napkins stamped with a gold rooster logo across the bar. The bartender tilted her head and analyzed Annalisse first, then shifted to Alec as if to size him up as prime or choice.

"What's your pleasure?"

Annalisse glanced at Alec, and when he didn't reply, she said, "I'll have a Manhattan. Bourbon, not rye."

"Dirty martini, Williams Chase, shaken for me."

"Extra olive?"

Alec nodded at the barmaid, then turned to Annalisse. "A whiskey girl. Cool."

"What about you and your dirty martini?"

"I like dirty things." His eyes shifted in her direction.

Annalisse was about to spear him with a wisecrack, but she didn't trust herself to make a coherent joke.

"It's a blasted freezer in here, or is it me?" She rubbed her arms.

He scooted his stool closer, bringing more heat in.

With a deep breath, she allowed woodsy Alec to explode beneath her nose, but his nearness rattled her. Palpable fear of rejection threatened her want for intimacy with him. A wall of hesitancy stood in the way, with the faces of his past relationships plastered to each dark panel. Annalisse wouldn't be his next short-term conquest; she required more commitment to be satisfied.

The barmaid returned with their drinks; her smile aimed directly at Alec. Multicolored light refracted from her rings into their glasses via the huge liquor display at the wall.

"Could we get an antipasto tray please?" Alec asked as the barmaid devoted a longer gaze his way.

"I never made it upstairs to lift Gen's necklace from the case."

"Chase put it in Mom's safe." He moved one finger seductively down the side of his shadowed cheek and slid closer. "Let's talk about you."

Grasping the highball glass, she sipped her strong drink, trying to ignore his thigh touching hers—on purpose.

"But your mom still has it. Please explain how the necklace landed in Gen's lap. It could be important."

"Mom asked me to bring it for the opening, that's all. She asked, so I brought it."

Cold from the ice cubes froze her fingertips to the glass. "Gen doesn't get it." She cringed inwardly, squeezing the drink until her knuckles whitened. "Neither do you. Samantha and Harry are dead. I think their deaths are related."

"Mom mentioned your friend. I'm sorry for your loss, but Harry choked. I doubt there's a connection."

"Because of the horses. That's why I begged Samantha to get rid of her matching bracelet to Gen's. Those pieces were meant to stay in Iran, old Persia, and worn only by royalty. I don't know how Harry figures into this, but there are no coincidences. There is strength in this particular curse."

She folded her napkin and studied how the emerald-green silk flowed over her lap. Annalisse had battled Gen on research at times, and Alec's stubbornness came straight from his mother.

He hummed in reflection from the back of his throat.

"You and Samantha were close?" he asked.

"Tight. The three of us—me, Chase, and Samantha— since grammar school. She and I roomed together at NYU."

"Are you taking over the gallery for Harry?"

"Hardly." She cupped the glass bottom with both hands as Peter's bald head hit her imagination in a grim picture. "I expect Peter will demote me, and I'll be looking for another job soon." She circled the rim of her glass with a finger. "Admit something that no one else knows about you."

He paused for a moment. "I like the thrill of fast cars, faster airplanes, galloping thoroughbreds—and maybe even a few fast women." He cleared his throat, and his gaze lingered on the bar, as if he'd let too much information slip.

No kidding on the last one. She batted her lashes and took another sip of her Manhattan, but she was still uneasy. "Gen beams when she mentions you. I like seeing her happy."

A huge platter of Italian salami and prosciutto nestled beside pungent cheeses, pepperoncini peppers, breadsticks, and various flatbreads arrived in front of them.

Annalisse slid away from Alec to accommodate the plate of plenty. The mixture of aromas reminded her of soured sweat socks and old frankfurters.

Alec grabbed a slice of prosciutto and washed it down with a big gulp of his second martini.

Annalisse nearly asked for another round but shivered at the memories of her dad's drunken tirades. How her mother pleaded with him to lower his voice during their boozy fights, fearing he'd wake her and little Ariel in their twin beds. Annalisse had lost count how many times she'd longed for sleep to come, sobbing into her pillow. The night her father broke a half-empty bottle of Jack over their glass coffee table—

"You know there's two pieces, don't you?"

Alec's voice broke her thoughts. "Pieces of what?"

"Horsehead necklaces." He looked at her questioningly. "You drifted off a minute ago. Welcome back. The other strand is still at the villa. My dad bought her birthday necklace four years ago."

"Wait." She held up a hand, trying to unravel what she'd just heard. "Two identical necklaces? That's impossible."

"Mom's jeweler has his store near our Signorile car plant in Italy. Sometimes Dad stops in and buys something for Mom when he's there. He probably saw the new design in the case and picked it up. The one in the gallery has to be a copy."

"Alec, the gallery necklace is ancient, not recent. Did your father buy Gen's necklace from the jeweler? Or did he buy her the one in the gallery case? New or old? Which is it?"

Alec played with a slice of bread, then set it aside. "When you put it like that, I don't know. I left one in Greece."

"Did you ever compare the necklaces side by side?"

"No, but I knew they were similar." He wiped his mouth with a napkin. "Ready for the dining room?"

A second necklace made their situation even more convoluted. And dangerous. She twisted her earring and considered how much more Alec knew about the piece in the gallery. She needed Alec's influence on Gen and redirected their talk.

"How long have you been interested in horseracing?"

"Since I graduated from Cornell. Mom's granddad owned a couple of Italian draft horses when she was a little girl in Bari. She talked about them all the time. I've always imagined I'd have horses in a big stable one day. They're cool, noble beasts."

27

He pushed himself from the bar. "Dad asked me to join him in the family business, Signorile Corporation, when he retired from racing stock cars. Building handmade sports cars abroad isn't my thing, but I help him out when I can."

"How does your dad feel about racehorses?" she asked.

"He got used to the idea and even loaned me the money for Brookehaven when he saw the fantastic deal on the property. He chose the name for the farm's stud, Kristol Magic, which made him more invested in the project. The estate is six hundred and forty spectacular acres, fewer than two hours from the heart of New York." He shook his head. "The realtor never mentioned the graveyard in the deal. I found out about it later."

She grabbed his arm. "You have a graveyard? How amazing is that? From which era?"

"If I'd known cemeteries made you giddy, I would've mentioned it sooner."

"That's so awesome. I'd love to see the headstones and research their ancestry for you."

"Most are around the time of the Civil War. Some are older, but there's no way to pin down the exact period since many of the older stones have disintegrated. Some of the stones are missing dates, and other graves are marked only by a brick. One time, I saw Mom taking a rubbing from one of the markers."

"Why would Gen want a rubbing?"

"Who knows?" His grin melted her into the stool. "Mom gets crazy ideas."

Annalisse glanced at the rows of faded autographed photos. Frank Sinatra holding a glass of red wine and Perry Como in his signature spread collar and red cotton sweater. Days of the Rat Pack. Famous Italian men peppered the back of the bar: Jerry Vale, Tony Bennett, and Dean Martin holding a cigarette that's billowing smoke. Recognizable faces from record albums her dad kept beside the stereo turntable near his recliner. Pop, classical, jazz, numerous vocals, and instrumentals floated throughout the Drury household on any given day. Harold Drury had crowned himself the family's music connoisseur.

"Didn't you grow up on a farm?" he asked.

"After thirteen." She sighed. "That's fifteen long years ago. A huge part of me still lives in the Goshen farmhouse, doing chores and throwing hay to the sheep in the lambing barn. I still help out there whenever possible. While I'm with the sheep, my problems instantly slip away. Barnyard aromas have that effect on me." Her words brought back Alec's broad smile.

"I know the area well. You're full of surprises." Alec straightened. "Then you might appreciate this. We broke ground on my vet hospital last week and set the foundation forms near the stables."

"*Your* vet hospital?"

"Yep. When the doors open, I'll be an official certified practitioner for the equine, specializing in surgery." He puffed his chest out.

"You're too hot to be a vet."

Alec laughed, his gaze so deep it reached into her soul.

She covered her mouth, staring at the bar railing. A twinge of ice fluttered her insides and squeezed. *This isn't happening.*

"Annalisse, what's wrong?"

A quick peek at Alec's Rolex made the sensation worse. Her lips were numb, and she took a few moments to focus on the upside-down Roman numerals.

"I have to go, Alec."

"Aren't you hungry?"

If she didn't leave the room quickly, champagne and the rest could end up somewhere between the bar and the ladies' room.

"It's warm in here. I'll meet you outside." Annalisse touched her clammy cheek, certain that she must be chartreuse. She needed outdoor air—soon.

"Right behind you."

She dashed for the exit, jolting a server carrying a tray as she passed.

Out front on the sidewalk, she drew a haggard breath.

Alec met her under the red-white-and-green awning. His expression was one of sympathy, the same look he'd given her after she'd failed to revive Harry.

"You scared me in there. Don't worry. Let's get you in a taxi, and I'll ride along to be sure you're all right. Where do you live?"

"I'm not totally helpless. I'll hail a cab for myself."

Alec stepped backward. "Whoa, there. Beautiful women shouldn't travel alone at night."

"Thanks, not interested."

"I didn't mean... You're twisting my words. It's late and dangerous for a woman alone." He glanced off into space. "How about this? Get a good night's sleep, and we'll start fresh in the morning. Be my guest for a picnic at Brookehaven. What could be more fun than a picnic beside a babbling brook, a cold bottle of chardonnay, and for the historian, a visit to the graveyard with a dashing host? What do you say?" He tossed her an enormous horse-breeder-of-the-year grin.

Annalisse swore she could almost read his gleeful mind. The little boy in him ready to say "pretty please?" at any moment.

"I'm gonna be up for hours notifying Harry's clients of his death."

"Let his brother do that. Take a few days off." Alec stuffed his hand into his tuxedo pants.

Boulders rumbled across her middle in another churn of nausea. She stepped to the curb and waved down a yellow cab.

"Have a good night, Alec."

As the cab sped away, Annalisse glanced over her shoulder at Alec's frame growing smaller in the rear window, watching her drive away. His roses. She'd bolted and left his pretty bouquet on the bar. It was everything she could do to keep from asking the driver to turn around. She wanted to fling open the door, jump out, and run back to apologize for her rudeness.

She touched the door handle, but the image of Samantha, cloaked in dirt and cut to ribbons, kept her inside the vehicle. Her friend had dated a veterinarian who was slime—the stuff that floated on stagnant water. The boyfriend could've murdered her for the bracelet.

CHAPTER
FIVE

Staring through the double doors of Zavos Gallery, Alec took another sip of bitter coffee and gritted his teeth. "I hate the flavor of coffee in foam cups. Couldn't you manage porcelain or even pottery?"

His mom chuckled. "Don't be so persnickety. We didn't teach you to complain about little things like coffee containers. The disposable cups are fine."

"What time did Annalisse say she'd be in?" Alec chucked the half-full cup into the trash and glanced at his watch. "You need a clock in here."

"There's a clock right above you. It's seven thirty. How'd it go last night?"

"I wish I knew."

"Who should I ask?" His mom showed a row of straight teeth. "She's overloaded; give her time. Harry had that girl practically run Westinn by herself."

Heels thumped on the sidewalk, followed by a shadow that broke the sun's glare through the entrance. Alec's heart rate surged when he recognized Annalisse.

"I can ask her myself. Good morning, hon." His mother gave Annalisse a hug and breathed air kisses across her cheeks before she'd made it completely through the door. "How are you? Better after some sleep?"

Annalisse pivoted toward him. "I don't want to interrupt. I'll make myself scarce upstairs."

"Don't leave on my account." Alec tried a winning smile. "Join us."

From the dropped jaw and sparkle in her eyes, he had to admit her utter surprise was hot and sexy. Her comfortable jeans and above-the-knee boots defined every curve and muscle, hidden by her dress from the previous night. Dressing casual made her even hotter.

His mother brushed her hand along Annalisse's cheek. "That won't do. You forgot concealer for those puffy tea bags under your eyes."

"It's Harry. I keep asking myself if I did enough to save him."

"He was gone before the CPR," he offered.

Annalisse pinched her brows together and mumbled something inaudible, then said, "Gen, Chase is on his way to my brownstone. I'll get my photos and be out of your hair. Is the necklace still in the safe?"

"It's in the display case." Alec pointed upstairs.

"I thought it was locked up last night." She flipped coffee-colored hair over one shoulder. "I can't even trust you to be honest."

In no time, she'd slid the tasseled zipper of her purse and pulled out a camera and another object he couldn't make out. "I need to get a good look at the necklace details. After I take a few close-ups, please stow it in a safe, Mr. Horse Breeder." She fired a glance at him that could peel rust from the undercarriage of a car.

"Alec left the case unlocked for you," Generosa said with a puzzled look in her eyes. As Annalisse climbed the stairs, his mother tugged him next to her and whispered, "I see what you mean. What did you say to her?"

"Nothing. We were having a great time, then she weirded out on me."

"Get up there and fix it." She gave his shoulder a gentle push. "She needs our support—excuse me." His mother swiped her phone and answered, "Good morning, Colum. Well, as good as possible, considering." She glared at him and stabbed the air toward the stairs with an index finger.

"Annalisse, wait up," Alec said.

When he joined her at the top of the stairs, she was using an instrument to scrutinize the back of the necklace like a jeweler would.

He swiveled at the sound of Beethoven's Fifth, muffled but recognizable.

"Alec, would you mind grabbing my phone? Please?" Annalisse glanced up. "It's in the side pocket of my purse downstairs."

Alec bowed, followed by a graceful sweep of his arm.

"Smart alec. Pun intended. Never mind, if it's too much trouble." She laughed, trotting around him to the stairs.

Following, he kept pace with her to the ground floor and met his mother, who held Annalisse's cell phone.

"Thanks, Gen." Annalisse touched the speakerphone. "Hey, Peter." She bent over and slid the camera's strap off, handing it to his mother. "Yeah, I'm at Zavos Gallery. Haven't had a chance to tell you how sorry we all are—"

"Who pays your salary? Them? I need you down here... Ann. We have a messy, messy, mess Harry left." Peter's slurred words echoed from the speaker.

"Seriously? Have some coffee and gather your wits. You didn't see how bad Harry was. Our clients will more than understand if we close Westinn for a few days out of respect. There's nothing pressing until Monday."

What followed were words no man should utter to any woman. Alec stepped beside her and motioned for her to hang up with an air slash across his throat.

"Don't take that from him, Annalisse." Alec made his slashing motion again.

"Hang up. Let him sleep it off." By her sharp tone, his mother had lost patience.

"Peter, I can't talk to you when you're like this. I'll be in Monday." She ended the call and slid the phone into her back pocket, her hand shaking. "Sorry about that. There's nothing like talking to a drunken viper first thing in the morning." She sighed, long and loud.

Alec wondered how she'd manage working solo alongside Peter.

"Are you all right?" His mother patted Annalisse's shoulder.

"I know he likes to hit the booze in the afternoons, but he's already gassed. I almost forgot—here." Reaching into her flared jacket, she handed a folded card to his mother. "I found this upstairs, stuck in the cloth with the necklace."

Gen lifted her readers and squinted. "There's nothing on it but symbols. I've never seen this before." She flipped it over, placing the card on the nearest table. "In the case, you say? The writing is Russian."

"At first glance, Cyrillic script. Shoot." Annalisse reached into another pocket and pulled out a driving glove. "We shouldn't be touching it with bare hands." She lifted the card to the light. "I have a friend who's fluent in Slavic languages. I'll send her a text or translate it online. Detective Mooney should test for prints since it was inside *that* particular jewelry case." Annalisse snapped a phone picture and attached the image to the message.

"Gloves? Being a bit overcautious, aren't we?" Alec peered up at bold, black strokes, drawing in Annalisse's sensual flowers in a meadow scent, then he turned to his mother. "I didn't know you had Russian vendors. I'm surprised we didn't notice the card when we were all upstairs."

"It was shoved behind the glass shelf where it meets the corner. Gen, Chase, and I were all over that jewelry display last night. No way was it there."

"Son, when you unlocked the case this morning, was the card there?"

Alec shook his head. "I wouldn't make too much out of this."

"You two figure it out. Colum is coming to the gallery with that FBI woman. Can't recall her name. We can ask him about the card, but I'm sure it's nothing. I have calls to make." His mother looked up as a gentleman in a dark suit entered the gallery.

"Hello, Mr. Chesnokov. I'm surprised to see you early. I thought our appointment was for this afternoon."

The man nodded to Annalisse and found a smile for Gen.

"I was having coffee across the street and saw that you were open. I hope I'm not interrupting family business. Good morning." Chesnokov tipped his short-brimmed fedora, but his eyes strayed upstairs. "I was wondering... may I inspect a few pieces more closely upstairs? I'm interested in your Egyptian bust and a certain exquisite Usekh collar and matching scarab that caught my eye. My partner didn't want to miss them. He insisted that I secure them today."

Alec noted the heavy accent and how the man's tattooed cat with a hat rose on his neck every time his jaw moved. His face was a mesh of speed bumps and chuckholes intersected by scars.

"Kids, if you'll excuse us." She smiled at Chesnokov. "Allow me to get my keys, and I'll meet you upstairs."

Alec ushered Annalisse by the elbow out of earshot and said quietly, "You're pale." The blood had rushed out of Annalisse's face, leaving her almost translucent.

"Why is Mooney bringing that special agent with him?" she asked him.

"What agent? I don't follow."

"The FBI's been stumbling through Samantha's case for weeks, working some organized crime lead. I met with investigators once, and that's all they'd say." Annalisse shook noticeably. "What is she up to?"

"Maybe there's a break in the case."

"Or they're about to question me again. I'm not a criminal just because I wanted Samantha to get rid of her bracelet."

Much about Annalisse twisted his heart and begged him to dig deeper—get a toehold with her. He wanted to find out what had pushed her away last night.

"You can't be a suspect," he said. "They don't even know you're here."

"I found Samantha's decaying body, Alec. We volunteered to search and—unlucky us—Chase and I stumbled over her arm that awful Friday." She put fingers to her temple and swayed.

"Careful." Alec caught her by the waist as she buckled, then he helped her to the small sofa. "Rest here; I'll bring you a coffee."

"Wait." She squeezed a fistful of his shirt. "All we did was find her. We'd never hurt her. I could never—"

Alec felt a tremor as she collapsed against his shoulder and let out a whimper. He rubbed her back and inhaled, aware of the private woman whose hard shell had a hairline crack. He doubted the authorities thought her capable of murdering her friend.

"I'm sure they know that," he said, touching her hair.

"How can you be so nice to me after I was such a brat last night?" She pushed away and swiped her eyes. "Damaged goods. Run, run, run as fast as you can."

"None of us were at our best. Besides"—he pulled her closer—"I crave challenges, live for them actually. What did you find on the back of the necklace? I saw you with your spyglass."

"It's called a jeweler's loupe." Annalisse dropped her gaze and pulled away. "The makers' mark on the back screams authentic old workmanship. Two winged seahorses with green eyes. Modern jewelers don't use precious stones in places that will never be seen because it's expensive. And they're emeralds, not cut glass. I'd stake my education on this necklace being one of the collection pieces. If Harry were here, he'd agree."

"How did Dad find such a piece?"

"How do you know your dad bought what's upstairs? Where is your dad, Alec? I thought I'd get a chance to meet him at the party." She glided a shaky hand down her throat. "If I hurry, I can finish up and leave the gallery before they arrive. I'm not in the mood to talk with Mooney's nosy sidekick."

"Wait a sec." Alec gazed into Annalisse's heavily lashed turquoise eyes. Eyes that could lighten the darkest gloom he could imagine. "Ask me anything about Dad. I could be *your* sidekick." He tried a look of nonchalance and expected her to say something clever.

A dark sedan with blacked-out windows parked outside the gallery.

"So much for my quick getaway." Annalisse tilted her head toward the entrance. "That's gotta be Mooney. I know you don't think the card in the case is important, but I do. Have Gen take inventory in the gallery. Make sure there hasn't been a burglary under our noses—and let me exit to the upstairs while I can."

Her graceful stepping boots were quick and sure. Alec found himself imagining what delights he'd encounter tangled up in that feisty brunette.

Mooney opened the glass door for a woman clad in navy. Bold yellow FBI letters were emblazoned on her arm and chest. With each deliberate stride, her blond ponytail swayed beneath her surprisingly feminine ball cap, casting a shadow on her face from its brim.

"Just the man—and woman—we expected. Hello, Detective Mooney." Alec extended his hand to him. "I see you've brought reinforcements."

"And you are?" The agent's voice was curt.

"Special Agent Norcross, this is Alec Zavos. His mother, Generosa, owns the gallery." Mooney glanced around the room. "Did Gen leave?"

"No, she's with a client upstairs."

Flying soles scraped the marble stairs behind him, and the Russian man named Chesnokov swept by.

"Good day, Mr. Zavos. Let your mother know I'll drop by later. I've been called away on an emergency." Chesnokov lost no time escaping beyond the glass doors.

Alec squinted through the pane at the man in a flat run across the street.

Agent Norcross's eyes were steely in the shade of her visor. "We've received an update and wanted to share it with Mrs. Zavos in person before she hears it on the news."

"What could be more distressing than a dead guy at our opening?" Alec asked her.

"The medical examiner's preliminary toxicology is in, and you should know—your dead guy was poisoned."

CHAPTER

Annalisse hadn't planned to spend her morning hiding from a federal agent. Luckily for her, the client's departure made it much easier for Annalisse to become invisible on the upper floor of the gallery. She crouched and peered over the empty display, mad at herself for her unprofessionalism. Gradually standing to her full height, she brushed off her jeans as an incoming text message tinkled on her phone. Pulling it from her pocket, she had a reply about the cryptic note and waved to get Alec's attention.

"I think we have our translation, Alec."

She dreaded the meeting with Norcross about the note.

Generosa appeared from the stockroom, offering a gleaming smile to the officers and greeted them individually.

A break Annalisse was thankful for.

She hurried downstairs and turned to the detective she liked a great deal. "Sorry to bring you down here on a Saturday." Addressing the FBI officer, she said, "Agent Norcross, why are *you* here? Should I obtain an attorney for more questioning?"

Mooney opened his mouth to answer for the agent, but Norcross stopped him with a lifted palm.

"Ms. Drury, Annalisse isn't it? You were cleared on the Freeman case, but last night's incident shifted our focus in another direction."

Alec and Generosa exchanged blank looks.

"Samantha's boyfriend. I knew it." Annalisse dropped her phone into her jacket, no longer engaged in the text. Her heart thudded. "Have you arrested him yet? Tell me he's in custody."

"I'm not at liberty to answer that, but what I *can* tell you is we think the death of Mr. Carradine may be related to the Freeman case. I do have a few questions involving your position at Westinn Gallery, however. The manager recommended that we talk to you about your boss, the decedent."

"Why? Because Harry choked? Peter's a drunk." Her hands flew to her hips.

"Annalisse, it's an investigation." Alec swooped in and took her arm. "Would you excuse us? Detective, please fill Mom in on what you found out about Harry."

Annalisse went with Alec to the office. "Darn that Peter, siccing the authorities on me. I should've stayed home today."

"Take a few breaths. Stop thinking. Just breathe. Yeah, like that," he said in a soothing voice.

"Hide this." She reached into her jacket and handed him the collar of golden horses. "Now please."

"Annalisse, Harry didn't choke. Someone killed him, or he killed himself."

"He was eating too fast."

"He was poisoned."

"No way," she denied automatically. But his symptoms made sense. His pallor. His hair loss. His erratic behavior. She glanced through the open door as the red-haired detective slid his sport coat off and placed it on a chair. "Don't mention the necklace. Put it away."

"What if it's related to Harry or the card?" he asked.

"Until we know more, let's keep the necklace between us. Gen owns it, so we deal. As much as I hate to, let's get this mini-interrogation over with." She closed her eyes as an image of Samantha's face with a partially burnt cigar in her mouth strayed her thoughts.

"What about the translation on the card?" Alec asked.

"Ismail lives."

"Like the seaman in *Moby-Dick*?"

"Not the same." She smiled at the reference and handed the card to Alec, who held it by the edges. "After you stash the necklace, give that to Mooney and let him investigate. I'll be along once I get a cup of Gen's famous coffee in me. Something to steady the jitters and kill off my caffeine headache."

While she poured herself the aromatic hazelnut brew, adding tons of cream, she waited for the detective to cover his freckled hands with a pair of latex gloves before accepting Alec's card for closer scrutiny.

Annalisse studied the Ralph Lauren emblem on Alec's shirt to keep her mind off the questions to come. Obvious folds marked the aqua fabric, and his jeans had perfect creases down the front. They must have been a new pair or were fresh from the dry cleaners. At that moment, she realized how much she missed being held by a man. A guy she could call hers and cuddle next to at night.

Annalisse walked over to the officer while he bagged and sealed the card.

"This message could just be a prank," Mooney said.

"I'm no detective, but *Ismail lives* means something to someone. Do you know what information Agent Norcross wants?"

"I'm told you have a translation?" Mooney removed a notepad from his breast pocket. "I wouldn't worry, Ms. Drury. Harry was a very quiet man and had few close friends beyond Peter Gregory, who could barely string three comprehensible words together. We'll visit him again when he's sober."

"It's unusual to find him snockered this early in the day, but he's an alcoholic and won't admit it."

Norcross joined them with Alec and Generosa in tow.

Generosa offered, "We counted one hundred and eighty-three guests signed into the book at the opening. Any one of them could've left the card."

"Was anything inside the case missing?" Norcross asked. "Or anywhere else?"

Annalisse replied, "Chase cleared all the jewelry displays after the party. Isn't that right, Gen?"

Generosa nodded slowly at Annalisse. "I don't leave jewelry displayed at night. It's always locked in my safe."

"And you know Chase Miller?" The agent addressed Annalisse. Her honeyed twang seemed out of place, but she had the practiced intimidating look down perfectly.

"Yes. I've explained the relationship. You spoke with him about Samantha that day too, remember?"

"Of course. Yes." Norcross scratched something in her notebook and turned to Generosa. "How about the security system? Any issues when you opened this morning?"

"Colum, you followed us out last night when we closed. Chase set the alarm— Come to think of it, the security panel didn't beep today like it normally does when we unlock. I thought it was odd." Generosa pointed at the alarm panel.

Mooney walked beneath one of the matte black motion detectors near the door. "These units should show an active red light. This one doesn't."

"I'll check the one upstairs." Alec rushed to the bottom of the steps. "Dark here too."

"*Mamma mia*. My system's off. For how long? I'm sure it was working last night."

"Detective, let's bring in a tech team. No one touches anything." Norcross took the mystery card from Mooney, studied it front and back, then stashed it in her jacket. "Filthy Mafia."

"Good lord! Here in my shop? I don't deal with garbage business types." Generosa's shoulders sagged. "I can't tell Pearce. He'll be worried sick."

Alec closed in on Annalisse, sending warmth to her skin.

"How do you know we had a break in, Agent Norcross? Could someone have stayed behind after Mom's party and fooled around with the alarm as a joke? It was nuts around here," Alec said.

"The security company should've notified the station of a breach. He or she may have tried to destroy the security video and found a way to circumvent the alarm and detectors. Gen, we'll need the names from the catering company and all guests who signed in. Including those invited who may not have attended," Mooney said.

41

"None of this makes any sense. Nothing's been stolen. All for a silly note? Colum, really." Generosa was noticeably shaken.

"That's it then. Mom, the gallery closes."

"But, son, that's foolish. It's an insignificant scribble."

"We won't open again until every inch of this gallery's been scoured," Alec said. "We had a death here, and with all that Annalisse told us—"

Both Mooney and Norcross were alerted.

"About the loss of her friend. That's all I meant." Alec chewed the corner of his lip.

"I'd post a security guard too. Your card is more than *scribbles*, Miss Generosa, if I may call you by your first name. We believe Carradine's death was no accident, and the card you found— Let's just say it fits a certain profile we've been monitoring. I spoke out of turn earlier about the Mafia. I'm sorry if I've frightened you." Norcross looked at her watch. "We'll take the card down to forensics."

"Gen, my partner knows a reliable man. Ex-military. He moonlights as security when he isn't working as a private dick," Mooney added.

"I still can't believe Harry had any enemies. That poor, poor man." Generosa swiped an eye.

The detective handed her a tissue from inside his jacket.

Alec pulled Annalisse aside, while Generosa and the officers wandered to the middle of the foyer. "How are you holding up?"

"Fine." She gripped the seam on her jeans to hide the shakes. "Norcross is keeping facts to herself about Samantha. How can we be sure other people weren't exposed to the same poison as Harry?"

"We can't be."

"Shouldn't Gen notify her guests?"

"Of their possible poison exposure?" He dimpled one cheek. "Let's wait and see what develops before we open a legal nightmare. Harry could've been poisoned before he got here."

"True. Blabbing to the world without knowing the facts wouldn't be smart." She glanced at her watch and gasped. "I'm late. Chase is going to send out the military. It's nearly nine. Here comes Gen."

"What a mess." Generosa hugged Annalisse and sniffed. "Alec's right. I'll close the gallery and post a guard inside until this sorts out. This is a good time to go to Greece—and Pearce. I'll schedule the jet for Crete. Pearce has wanted to meet you in the worst way, Annalisse. Why don't you and Alec come with? October is beautiful on the island."

"No complaints here." Alec's eyes gleamed.

Annalisse squeezed her knees together. She didn't trust herself with him on an island in paradise. Although the thought of Alec's warm caress sent a parade of tingles down her spine.

"I'd love to meet Pearce, but I have a job. As thrilling as it sounds to play in the sand and bake on the Aegean, I can't shirk my responsibilities. Peter won't let me off anyway."

"Pooh. I'll talk to Chase. He'll take over your gallery duties for a few days while you relax in the sunshine. I'll fix everything."

"You're so thoughtful." Annalisse hugged her petite frame. In her own way, Generosa filled the motherly affection gap she'd been missing.

Harry would expect her to stick around Westinn and sort out his business. One he never left in Peter's hands, but her tortured mind could use a dose of serenity.

"You *must* come." Her plea came at Annalisse with more emotion this time.

"I'll work on it, Gen, but I have to go. Chase is waiting." She could feel Alec's eyes on her. "Agent Norcross, find Samantha's killer soon—please. I'll sleep better when I know that maniac can't do those things to another beautiful soul." She glanced at the clock, blinking back a tear. "I'm so late for an appointment. Alec, will you walk me out?"

Four uniformed cops filed through the glass entrance.

"Go ahead, son. I have all these nice officers to protect me." Generosa smiled with a quick wink at Annalisse. "We aren't done with this conversation."

Annalisse snatched her tote and waited for Alec. Once on the sidewalk, she adjusted the wide leather straps cutting into her shoulder.

"Darn it. I didn't get a chance to take more photos. A lot of good it did to substitute a camera for my pistol."

"You carry a weapon?" Alec's jaw went slack.

"Yeah, since last year. It took seven months to get my concealed-carry permit."

"Lady, you do amaze."

He held her transfixed in his platinum gaze until he ran his thumb across her cheek, bringing her feet back to earth.

"It's security when I travel alone on appraisals. Perverts can come from anywhere."

"What about now?"

"Are you a pervert?" she asked him.

"Depends." Alec laughed. "No. The answer is a solid no. You don't have your gun with you, so what if you need it before you get home?"

She slid one of the tote straps off and dug into an inside pocket. "This works as backup."

He stepped closer, staring at the pink tube she held up. "Mace?"

"Pepper spray. Fits in my palm and shoots a mist everywhere. That's why I prefer my Lady Smith. Point it and the shot goes where it's supposed to." She slipped the tube back into her bag and hooked the side pocket. "Alec, don't let Gen out of your sight. If you can't be with her, don't wait for Mooney's security; station a bodyguard."

"Is that your head or your intuition talking?" he asked.

"Both. This new wrinkle with Harry and the creepy card feel like we're being manipulated. I sense it. I'll call you if Chase and I dig anything up. If you haven't noticed, Gen is like my own mother. I won't lose her too." She gently squeezed his arm.

Shoving a hand through his wavy hair, Alec's expression changed from pensive to playful.

"Since you seem to have my number, shouldn't I add you to *my* contacts?" He raised a brow and picked up his phone. "Ready when you are."

She turned away long enough to wave down the next cab and give her respiration time to slow.

"There's a good reason I have your number." She stroked the textured side of her purse strap while searching for an excuse, when she spotted Generosa eyeing them. "You know. In case of an emergency. For Gen."

From his crooked smile, she could tell he hadn't bought it.

CHAPTER

SEVEN

Annalisse opened the door of her brownstone to a tempting whiff of cinnamon. She found Chase had already let himself in with the key she'd given him years before. Sunk deep behind reams of paper at the computer, chewing on a bakery roll, he clicked his pen, rapid-fire under his thumb. He did his best work when he turned his retractable pen into a cricket.

He looked up as she entered, and Boris, her orange tabby, jumped off the couch, landing with a four-footed thump. A small tuft of fur floated to the floor in his wake.

"Glad you're still here. Sorry I'm late. We had an interesting development at Gen's gallery, and Special Agent Norcross graced us with her presence." Annalisse set her tote down on the kitchen table, grateful to shed the weight.

"Oh no. What did she want?"

For the next few minutes, Annalisse narrated the latest events to Chase about the message, Harry, and how they'd knock out research for the day.

"Who would've suspected anything as diabolical as poison for Harry? Do they know what kind?" Chase scratched his head.

"Maybe. I didn't ask."

"You're sure about the translation? Can I see it?"

"Here's the text." She grabbed her phone and scrolled to the message. "Check it. It should be easy with the English words to begin with, and then we'll compare the Slavic languages. While you do that, I'll get my laptop and take a look at the pictures from the party. Maybe I'll recognize someone of interest. God knows I wanted to be someplace else last night."

Annalisse opened her laptop, pulled the memory card from the camera, and slipped it into the card reader. Each time she launched the photos, nothing looked out of the ordinary. Party guests smiled and chatted with friends. The gallery's appearance was superb—each painting hung just right against the quiet blue walls.

An out-of-place older couple in kooky hibiscus shirts made their own private dance floor near the harpist, bringing laughter from her. Happy-and-in-love vibes poured from them, fox trotting to a tune of their own. Annalisse went into full-screen mode and carefully studied each image for anything unusual. There had to be something she'd missed, something remarkable her pictures would reveal.

Two men stood with Generosa, and she recognized one of them from today. The thin man with black obsidian eyes was Mr. Chesnokov, and the other in a pinstripe suit hadn't been in the sun for months. His ghostly pallor deepened the hollows and lines in his craggy skin. One man stood rigid and wary, while the other seemed more at ease in his surroundings.

"Anything on your end? Did a search confirm the text?" she asked Chase.

"Ismail has a different spelling. Most of the references belong to *Moby-Dick*, which isn't spelled the same. The writing on the card might be a misspelling."

Thoughts of Alec mentioning the whaling classic brought a little smile from Annalisse. Ismail wasn't a common, modern name.

"Let's switch. You take my laptop, and I'll do some internet searches on the desktop. If nothing else, media articles about Samantha could trigger a memory." She handed him the laptop.

"I left a photo on the screen for you to look at. That man came back into the shop today to look at pieces upstairs."

"Whoever left that note may not have been at the party, Anna."

"True, but we have to start somewhere. It's too coincidental the note landed inside the precise case that held the necklace. Ismail must be a code word for something."

Chase grinned and saluted. "Okay, Indiana."

"Goofball." She jokingly socked him on the arm.

Annalisse sat at her desk and slid the keyboard forward. Clicking through a few websites, she found one with an in-depth history of Persian relics. She narrowed her search to those made in AD rather than BC. "I'm checking ancient Arabia, images first. If we're lucky, we could uncover details skimmed over earlier. If not, I'll revisit my thesis again and hit some college textbooks. How are you doing with the photos?"

"I've looked at them twice already, Anna, but whatever shears your sheep."

"Now you're making me homesick for the farm."

Chase lowered the screen on the laptop and peered over it. "I'm not sure what you want. Give me a clue here."

Annalisse sighed. She'd rather be hanging out with the fall lambs at Aunt Kate's barn. As far away from the necklace as possible. "What about those two guys with Gen? I haven't seen either one in the shop before the party."

"I think one guy is Scandinavian."

"What? Scroll to the picture and let me look." She saved her images website and then sank into the worn cushion next to Chase. "Enlarge just their faces."

The clarity of Mr. Chesnokov's image diminished, but his strong facial details were visible.

"Whew, that's too close. I didn't notice his pitted face, and look at that on his neck." She touched the tattoo on the screen. "It's a silly cat in a hat."

"With a big bow tie and bigger teeth. So what?" Chase asked.

Pushing her tongue to the roof of her mouth, she cropped the cat and examined its pointy ears and cartoonish face.

"This guy isn't your usual art collector. He has dirt under his nails like a mechanic, and the way he's ogling Gen is downright creepy. The *Scandinavian*, as you say, seems pretty chummy with Harry in some photos." Annalisse pointed at the next picture. "See the arm over his shoulder as if they're longtime buddies? I've never seen him at Westinn either. It might be a dead end, but researching a cat tattoo would be a nice break from the necklace. Be my guest."

"So the guy likes cats and works on cars. Why bother?"

"I've seen cutesy cats on women's ankles and shoulder blades, but his is masculine and unusual. Humor me."

Back at her personal computer, Annalisse exhausted the trove of photos relating to gems and necklaces from old Egypt and the Arabian Peninsula, so she used the only link she'd come across for *Ismail.*

"Chase, here it is. How did we miss this? Ismail I was the ruler of Iran during the Safavid dynasty from 1500 to 1524. His family line ruled Persia for over two hundred years." She scrolled further. "During his reign, the palace was burglarized. This is what I recall." Scrolling deeper into the article, her throat tightened. "The horses in gold were stolen when thieves broke into Ismail's palace in Tabriz, taking swords, jeweled knives, brooches, and pottery. I'm quoting here: In the shah's attempt to regain his prized creations, he conjured a curse of violent death on any wearer of his jewels until their safe return to Persia." She slapped the desk. "Alec and Gen should read this."

Chase dragged one of her armchairs next to her computer chair and plopped down in it. "Are there pictures of the missing pieces?" he asked.

"No." As the hair on her forearms stood at attention, she drifted closer to the screen to read the fine print. "Well known to those of the art world as… the Curse of the Mushasha."

Chase brushed against her shoulder. "I don't know whether to be happy or freaked out about the confirmation. I didn't believe the curse part either and gave you a hard time about it, but the curse's history is real. Without actual photos to compare, how do we know Samantha had one of the jewels—and now Gen?"

"The dots are connected because Samantha's bracelet matches Gen's horsehead design. The bracelet was stolen, and Samantha was mutilated prior to burial—a hate crime of the worst kind. The curse mentions a violent death to the wearer. If she was killed for her bracelet, what would stop this person, or persons, from going after Gen?"

"Which puts Samantha's boyfriend in the clear. If she was killed for jewelry, then the animal doc didn't murder her," Chase said.

"How do we know he didn't kill her for it? It's priceless. His veterinary practice is failing, even after he went through the family money. That's why he battered Samantha and started drinking. How many lame excuses did she use when we asked her about the strange bruises? He terrified her into covering for the abuse." Annalisse hiccuped a sob.

"I know." Chase patted her hand.

"Gen is in bad, bad trouble. As long as she has the necklace, and someone inside the gallery saw it—"

"Anna, she insists her necklace is new."

"That's a dead issue. I have proof." Annalisse pulled up the phone images she'd taken from the gallery. "The metal is clearly flawed on the back, and the workmanship is crude, like a handmade mold would look."

"I noticed that on the front side too. Is that an emerald?"

"Yes."

"Elaborate markings and a precious stone worn against the skin. Old craftsmanship," Chase said.

She nodded. "Absolutely right. There's no modern jewelers' mark. It's a time bomb."

"Who's the woman? The ruler's wife?" Chase pointed to the picture on the computer monitor.

"It says Shah Ismail never married. There's mention of his consort, the daughter of Shirvanshah Kha…li…lullah II. What a mouthful."

He tapped the screen on the woman's neck and enlarged it. "Did you notice her necklace?"

Annalisse leaned forward, but the image fuzzed the closer she got. "The thumbnail's too small for detail. That's a hefty collar necklace."

"Search on the woman. Maybe we can find a bigger photo with more detail."

Beethoven's Fifth spewed from Annalisse's cell phone, leaving her cold.

Chase smiled. "Uh-oh, Peter the great."

"From the black lagoon, you mean. Damn, he called me at the gallery."

The tune stopped for a few seconds, then the symphony began again.

"Peter, can't you just leave a message like normal people?" She felt her blood pressure on the rise.

"You'd better see what the ogre wants."

She put it on speaker and answered, "Yes, Peter. What's up?"

"I have a job for you that can't wait," Peter said.

"I told you I'm off till Monday. Can't *you* take care of her?"

"She's a friend of Mom's from New Jersey who asked specifically for your appraisal." Peter blew his nose and snorted.

"Fine, I'll do it for your mom." Annalisse shut down the call and groaned loudly. "Harry would never annoy me on my day off."

"He's not Harry," Chase said.

"No foolin'. When Harry was around, I ignored the kindness he showed every day. We tend to take people's good points for granted, concentrating more on their bad. Remind me not to do that again," she said.

Harry's suspected illness she'd brushed off too lightly. She could kick herself for not helping him more after the devastating passing of his wife, Fiona. If she'd pushed him to get checked by a doctor, he might be giving orders and making her laugh at his bad jokes rather than being dead.

Annalisse shifted her heel away from the blister that had formed inside her boot, feeling the sting of sweaty, broken skin.

"Why meet now, after last night?" Chase asked her.

"The woman believes she has a rare brooch and works during the week, yada, yada. I wish Peter wasn't so hammered."

"He's drunk again? Then I'm going with you."

"I don't need a supervisor."

"Oh, yes you do. Peter's a jerk when he's wasted."

She'd learned when Chase made up his mind, there was no changing it.

"If you insist on playing protector, do me a favor and hang back once we get to the gallery. He makes me so angry when he picks at you over the smallest things. I'm not in the mood for his jabs."

Annalisse walked to the kitchen table and removed the camera from her bag. "I feel naked without my .38 along." She reached beneath the dish towel near the toaster and slipped the snub nose into the bottom of a tote, large enough to be considered carry-on luggage.

"Why's your pistol in the kitchen?"

"Needed room for the camera. It's where it belongs now." She patted the designer leather.

CHAPTER
EIGHT

At ten minutes to eleven, Annalisse tiptoed into a bleak and quiet Westinn Gallery near Union Square, with Chase at her side. Obscure paintings watched their arrival with multiple pairs of uncertain eyes. She lifted her nose into the aroma of the clove soap Harry used when he shaved. His presence was all around her even though he wasn't there. Harry's departure from his beloved art sanctuary resonated in the shadows.

"The place is dark. Peter's obviously more juiced than I thought and wasted our time. Let's go, Chase."

He reached beside the entrance and punched the bank of electric rocker switches to the *on* position, pointing toward Annalisse's office. "I hear voices down the hall."

"Wait in my office. I'll make the appraisal, then we'll go." Annalisse raised a finger to her lips. "Shh. I think she's about to leave. Hurry, I'm right behind you."

"You dare to insult me." The heavyset woman in a black pantsuit shook her fist at Peter. Her charm bracelet clinked at her wrist. "This is a gorgeous rhinoceros beetle brooch, and those *are* rubies. I don't care what you say. Where's your expert? Your mother told me that Annalisse person has talent."

"Miss Whiny Cow, I don't know who told you they were rubies, but at best they're garnets—most likely cut glass. Cheap dime-store trash, and we have no intention of taking it on commission."

Her sprayed hairdo shook above oversize glasses with gold bling on the frames. "I'm never coming here again, you drunkard. Harry was kind, and you… you are doggy doo-doo. Don't you bathe?"

Laughing into her palm, Annalisse bumped Chase's shoulder as the woman's Birkenstocks clunked and swished out of the building.

She composed herself and motioned for Chase to stay hidden near the desk.

"Might need this." He reached into her bag for the pink cylinder she'd hooked in a side pocket. "Just in case."

Annalisse palmed the spray and cleared the dryness in her throat with a mint from her desk drawer, saying aloud, "Peter, was that the woman who needed the appraisal?"

A slight man with a beer belly and a bad comb-over emerged from the corridor. "'Bout time you got here, Ann." He gestured with a jerk of his head. "My office. Now."

She took small steps and conjured the image of Vincent Price in a floor-length cape, one brow lifted, eyeteeth extended over his lower lip. Goose bumps rose on her neck. The distinct odor of whiskey was present when she entered his office.

"Sit down please."

"Wasn't that her? Seems you've handled it— See you Monday."

"My client hasn't arrived. Sssit… down." He swept his arm at a spot in front of his blotter.

Annalisse fisted her hands, squeezing the small tube hidden in her palm. Watching him form words while snockered was a sad affair, if it weren't so serious for the gallery.

"I don't have a lot of time." She plunked into a webbed chair that resembled a backyard lawn lounge from the 1960s, and it was just about as comfortable.

"You need to replace this thing, Peter."

A toothpick in his mouth, he alternated between picks and sucks to the point she had to turn away from the gross spectacle.

"Since I'm running the show now, I have a nephew I'm grooming as my 'sistant. You have *some* appraisal acumen, so I've elected you to train him for Westinn." Peter wandered slowly around his desk, and hanging on to the edge, he closed the door and swayed on the way back to his tall desk chair.

The walls closed in like a jail, and she considered leaving, but she didn't plan to stay long.

"Assessing antiques takes schooling, years of training and practice. I appreciate your confidence in me, but you're so much more adept at valuating than I am. He'd learn the trade better from you." Praising him made her sick, but Peter loved to be flattered by women subordinates. Growing his already inflated ego might move things along.

"Yes, my talents far outweigh yours. Unfortunately, I'm too busy fixing Harry's garbage-fest in progress. This is an order, not a request. Consider my nephew part of your new job description." His authority over her rang sober and direct.

"Your brother-in-law passed away last night. Why not let things settle around here before we start adding employees? I'm sure your nephew could be an asset, but my plate's full with Zavos research at the moment. Gen needs—"

"I don't give a hoot what that snooty *I-talian* wants. You work for Westinn, that's me." The stack of papers on his blotter crinkled beneath his fist.

"Gen has brought this gallery tons of business. Not just hers but a huge number of referrals. Harry appreciated Gen."

"Harry's gone. Done. Soon to be incinerated."

"What a crass comment to make about a relative. Did you hate him that much? Harry cared about his clients, and he respected Generosa Zavos." Her lips trembled when Peter rose out of his seat.

He adjusted his dated bow tie in the reflection of a vintage James Bond movie poster. She beheld his little-man complex in full view. Peter would never be a big man, big hearted, or big anything, except a big, drunken wannabe in Harry's shadow. A sigh escaped her at the realization that Westinn Gallery was doomed with such a detached man at the helm.

Then he smiled wide enough to show a couple of capped silver teeth.

"Perhaps you'd like to join me for dinner tonight? You do eat, don't you?" He grinned, glassily taking her in. "I want your opinion on some changes for the gallery."

"I already have plans."

"I'd advise you to reconsider my invitation."

"Or what?"

Peter clutched the edge of his desk to steady himself. "Missss Drury, you refuse to train or attend a dinner meeting with me. What else can I think? Would a raise in pay encourage?" He wiped spittle from the corner of his mouth.

She wondered if the snakelike hiss before her surname was done intentionally. The phrase *take a leap off the Williamsburg Bridge* came to mind, but she couldn't afford to dish out some of his own rhetoric. Annalisse needed her job until she could find a replacement.

The way he smacked his lips said volumes. The way he ogled her breasts made her feel dirty. Being the head honcho at Westinn Gallery must have tasted sweet to him.

Annalisse stood and crossed her arms, looking at the group photo beside Peter's Online Art Institute honorary degree. It stood out next to the foil-sealed documents lined up in vertical rows.

"When was that photo taken?" She pointed at the wall of shameless Peter fame.

Ornate green drawings were covering the arms of a short-sleeved guy in the picture. Tattooed men made her uneasy for no other reason than the permanent record the drawings made on the skin. She couldn't imagine staining herself forever with artwork.

"Harry's standing with a man from the Zavos opening. It looks like the karaoke bar at Freddie's." Annalisse stared at the familiar face smiling back at her.

"It's a bachelor party. You wanna know who popped out of the cake and lap danced on ol' Pete?"

Annalisse coughed, blinking away that image. "Are the two men with Harry brothers? What do you know about them?"

"Harry had one, maybe both, in here looking at jewelry. Neither have made a purchase to my knowledge."

"The guy next to the tatted-up man; what's his name?"

"Niki-something-or-other."

"Niki first or Niki last name?"

"What's it to ya? Have ya got a thing for Russians?"

The tip of her tongue pushed behind her teeth, and she suppressed an eye roll, but confusion piqued her curiosity. She'd expected the name Chesnokov.

"Last time Niki-boy made an appearance, he got into it with Harry. Sidewalk bums could've heard them yelling from two blocks away," Peter said.

"How long ago was he here? What was the argument about?" she asked.

Peter shrugged. "None of my business."

"I thought everything that went on in this gallery was your business. You must have heard something. The man I ran into has a heavy accent. Is he naturalized or visiting from abroad?"

She made a mental note to add the Madonna and child with a cross tattoo to their research since the photo showed this image.

"Is he a citizen or just visiting? It's very important."

Her wrist rested next to the picture, thumb and forefinger rubbing the spray nozzle until she could smell capsaicin. She caught the action before spraying herself inadvertently.

"That barking dog got run over a long time ago. Who knows if he's a citizen? I haven't seen the vodka flasker lately and don't care if I do. Nikita was Harry's friend, not mine."

It was a wonder how his gracious mother had raised such a lowlife. During Annalisse's apprenticeship, Mrs. Gregory came into the gallery before her disabilities took hold. Too bad she didn't pass on her big heart and classiness to Peter.

"This Nikita vodka person likes jewelry?" She asked her question in another way.

Behind her, his chair squealed, then in less than a second, Peter pressed his groin hard against her backside. His hands were locked around her in a death grip, painfully kneading both breasts.

"Get off me!" She felt one arm release and thrust herself backward, but he was stronger and pushed her harder at the wall.

He'd trapped her between his body and the wall in a human sandwich.

"Drunken freak, let loose!" She twisted and squirmed but made no headway against his surprisingly strong grip.

The photo she'd studied crashed to the tile, shattering glass at her feet.

He managed to work a smelly hand over her mouth.

Annalisse tried to bite him, fighting to breathe through her nose. Blood pounded her eardrums. *Think.*

"Don't fight it, Ann. You said I'm good. Let me show you how good I am."

The vile mixture of body odor and cheap whiskey swirled in the little air she had available to her. She hoped the gallery surveillance cameras were on and recording her assault in progress. Annalisse gagged behind his clammy fingers, too far from her teeth to bite, and readied the tube of pepper spray.

"Anna?" Chase asked, muffled by the distance.

In her jumbled thoughts, she'd forgotten Chase, but the surprise voice from outside was enough to break Peter's short attention span.

Annalisse slammed back against the man's rock of a forehead.

"Ow!" he cried out.

The pressure against her body slackened, and his palm fell from her mouth.

Annalisse spun a half turn and kneed him in the groin with force. "Feel that, you sick jerk."

Peter fell on his side, holding himself, yelping in pain.

Chase flung open the door and ran to her side. "Dang, dude. Zip it up." He shifted his eyes to her. "Did he hurt you?"

"Back away." She checked her aim, depressed the nozzle, and let the cone of mist spread over his balding head and exposed skin, saving a little for his genitals, until the canister emptied and he was a rolling, crying, blathering idiot.

Tossing the pink tube in the wastebasket, she fought against the pepper stench cutting off her air supply.

Peter wailed with both hands plastered over his eyes, writhing on his back and wheezing like an asthmatic in need of an inhalant.

"I can't breathe; you blinded me! You're gonna pay, sister." He doubled over on his knees and spat gobs of yellowish saliva on the floor. His moans echoed throughout the ten-by-ten office.

Chase pulled her by the arm, sending her flying to the doorjamb.

"Back away, Anna! He's trying to get up." He waved a hand through the air and gazed at her. "Man, the fumes are bad. That scuzbag left red marks on your face."

"Call 911 for me, would you? I can't see through the burning haze making my eyes water." She coughed and kicked Peter's loafer. "By the way, I quit."

Chase stepped backward, tapped his phone, and urged her out of the room. "Anyone who makes Anna empty a pepper canister in self-defense doesn't deserve me either. I quit too." He shut the door with Peter inside.

"I'm pressing charges. Don't you worry," Peter blubbered.

Peter's muffled speech was surreal to her ears. Mirthless laughter erupted from her without warning, and in a shaky voice she said, "The way I see it, you should be thankful it wasn't a bullet."

From her office, Chase recited the gallery address to dispatch while the chili burn stung her nose and eyes. She grabbed a handful of tissues and blew her nose, getting some relief.

Chase rounded the corner, carrying her leather tote. "I thought you'd be outside by now. I'll stay here and make sure he doesn't leave before the cops get here." He held out her bag. "I still see the outline of his fingers. Are you gonna be all right?"

She shook her head, on the verge of tears. "I've got to wash up but not here. I'll go next door to the deli and use their facilities. Bringing back a couple of pastrami combos will get the pepper taste out of our mouths." She rifled through her wallet and pulled out a few bills. "Please hang on to my purse for me. I don't trust myself *not* to give Peter a taste of Ms. Smith after all."

CHAPTER
NINE

Standing in the noonday heat outside Westinn with a bag of deli sandwiches tucked under one arm, Annalisse rubbed the golf ball-sized knot on the back of her head. Her mouth still ached, but the breeze soothed her lips. Smiling, she imagined Peter in the bathroom, washing the fire out of his ears and eyes, not to mention what had soaked his crotch. Knowing he'd live the aftereffects for hours gave her some satisfaction.

Detective Mooney's sedan stopped in the road, lights flashing. He stepped out of the car on the passenger side, waving another detective off to park in some unknown space in the Square. A red sports car with the top down flipped an illegal U-turn and squeezed into a tiny spot on the other side of the street. The car wasn't recognizable, but the driver she knew.

It was Alec.

The gallery door behind her opened, and Chase poked his head out, handing her the leather tote.

"What's going on inside?" She shoved the sandwiches inside her bag.

"Pete shot past me to the can. I'd better get back there in case he tries to run out the back exit."

Detective Mooney had hit the pavement running, his red hair glistening in the sun and green tie flapping near his shoulder.

"Ms. Drury, do you need an ambulance?" He glared into her eyes.

"Pride injury only. The jerk inside with his zipper down might need it though."

"My partner's called for a paddy wagon since pepper spray's involved. Squad cars smell bad enough. Are you able to give me your statement now?"

"Annalisse!"

A series of honks followed Alec's progress across the crowded street. As he approached, she noticed his polo tucked neatly into his belted pants, emphasizing a narrow waist.

"What are you doing here?" She glanced at Alec, then strayed to his vehicle.

"I could ticket you for that U-turn back there." Mooney lifted his chin with authority.

"Detective, I didn't know you broadcast your emergencies." Annalisse stepped away from the entrance as a man in a sport shirt and slacks ran behind them, following Chase into the gallery.

"When I overheard the car radio, I recognized the Westinn address. Are those bruises near your mouth?" Alec's steely gaze felt like a hot poker. "Who did that to you?"

Mooney stretched out one arm and shuffled them away from the door. "Stand clear, people."

An NYPD van had pulled up outside with its light bar whirling, and Mooney's partner burst through the entrance, leading a handcuffed Peter Gregory onto the sidewalk.

"John, ride along and take him to the hospital," Mooney said.

"He's declined medical attention."

"Then book him. I'll get statements from Ms. Drury and the other witness."

All signs of fight and drunkenness had melted into Peter's surrender. He stared at the ground and nothing else. His cheeks were swollen badly near his eyes, and his nose needed an entire box of tissues. Strands of gray hair stuck out in all directions on his bald, crimson head and cauliflower ears. For a moment she almost pitied him, but the urge for sympathy quickly evaporated. Her story could've had a different ending without Chase along and his suggestion to carry the spray.

"What happened?" Alec reached toward her cheek, but his eye contact with Chase stopped him.

"I'll give the detective my statement first, Anna," Chase said solemnly.

What a spectacular friend Chase was. The nights he'd given her a shoulder and held her hand when she'd dropped by and couldn't sleep—the annual anniversary of her parents' deaths and after Samantha's ordeal. Annalisse was needier than he was, today being a stark reminder of the fact. Chase's companionship had helped her through every personal trauma since college.

Annalisse clutched Chase's hand and squeezed. "I'll go first; take a break." She flushed, aware of Alec watching her. "Thanks for what you did today. If I'd come alone like I wanted..."

Alec glanced away, clearly uncomfortable with what she'd said.

Once Annalisse realized that he'd come to her rescue too, and three gallant men surrounded her on the sidewalk, she allowed herself to smile at the notion.

"Wasn't that Harry's brother?" Alec asked.

"*Brother-in-law*. Harry would've hauled Pete out on his keister if he'd seen the assault take place, but Anna held her own in there. I'm proud of her." Chase grinned.

"Speaking of which, we should get to it, folks." Mooney drew a notebook from his pocket.

"Right, Detective. If you need anything, Anna—" Alec fiddled with his belt and looked at his shoes, as if on an awkward first date.

Annalisse's chest ached with a private wistfulness. Eventually she'd mess up whatever happened with Alec at some point in their future, so she owed it to herself to binge on his charm while it felt good.

"Alec, don't leave yet. I have sustenance." She held up her purse and swung it back and forth. "One more sandwich, and we'll be set."

"Give mine to Alec. After my statement, I'm going home. I've had enough excitement to last me a while." Chase nodded to Alec near the roadway. "Take care, Anna."

Detective Mooney scribbled notes while Annalisse gave her account of Peter's unwarranted assault, and Alec paced the curb nearby. His occasional wince made her think about what she'd gone through. Reciting the time spent with that horrible man gave her the shivers.

When she finished, she hugged her chest and dug her fingernails into her sweater to hide any obvious signs of the Krakatoa-like eruption she felt coming on—unsure which was more potent, the attack at the gallery or Alec's concern for her.

"Would you like to press charges, Ms. Drury?" Detective Mooney asked.

"I've terminated my employment with Westinn and won't have to deal with him again."

Until she'd uttered the words out loud, the gravity of her joblessness hadn't hit her. She quickly calculated how many months her bank account would last.

"You quit?" Alec's astonishment was genuine.

"Yes, and so did Chase. Would you rather I stick around for more abuse? I've seen more of Peter than I need in a lifetime."

Alec side-glanced at her, then looked at Mooney. "Detective, throw all you've got at him so he can't assault any more beautiful protégées." Alec turned to Annalisse. "The prosecutor may still press charges even if you don't."

"There's a surveillance camera in his office. Every office. I bet the whole thing's on tape," Annalisse said, hanging on Alec's word choice for her.

"If you need more from us in person, give me a call, Detective. I'm driving Annalisse to her home. She hasn't had time to grieve over Harry's death, let alone what happened this morning."

Her stomach let out a drawn-out gurgle, and she smiled. "And food. Wait. I drove my car."

Chase exited the delicatessen and headed toward them.

"I'll take Mr. Miller's statement now. Is the gallery locked?" Mooney asked.

"Let Alec take you home, Anna. I'll drop off your BMW later. Show him what our research turned up this morning."

"Thank you." She pulled Chase into a hug. In a low voice meant only for him, she whispered, "As usual, I owe you big-time. What made you think of the pepper spray?"

"Nice touch, wasn't it?"

She kissed Chase lightly on the temple, once again feeling Alec's eyes on her.

It seemed that Alec stood closer than a bodyguard would stand to shield her from more harm. Near enough to touch her—and she longed for it. Through the electricity passing between them, she sensed his torment over Chase having saved her from Peter, instead of him.

"It's time to allow the detective to do his job. Thank you, Chase. I won't forget what you did for Annalisse." Alec shook Chase's hand in what seemed to her a stronger than normal handshake, then pivoted toward her. "May I escort you back to your apartment?"

"Brownstone." Chase corrected him.

At that moment, a ride in the little sports car with Alec felt foolish when she had her own car.

"Thank you, but I have a way home," she said to Alec. "Please don't bother."

"You heard Chase. We'll take my Signorile." He nodded toward the street. "Dad shipped her right off the assembly line a few months ago. Take a ride with me."

Alec held out his arm, bent at the elbow. So much the gentleman, he was his mother's creation for sure.

And she'd morphed into a basket case when it came to letting a man in; afraid to be hurt again. She was exactly what she'd accused Chase of becoming. A wimpy old maid-in-waiting.

She could never have a life with Alec anyway, so why open a new wound?

"I'm capable of navigating the street without your help."

His shoulders dropped, and he jerked his elbow to his side.

"If you'll just lower your drawbridge over the moat that you've built around yourself… let me show you a little kindness."

CHAPTER
TEN

On the short drive past boutiques filled with weekend shoppers to her place on Bank Street, Alec's behavior froze Annalisse to the supple upholstery. When he'd bothered to talk, curt and formal blasted her side of the car, making her uncomfortable the entire trip. She couldn't blame him. He'd been so comforting since the gallery party, and she'd offered him nothing but ingratitude in return. A sheet of solid ice separated them rather than the beautiful wooden console at her left. In fact, the entire dashboard of Alec's distinctive car was polished to a shiny gloss, not unlike the deck on a fancy boat. The convertible had to be worth more than her annual salary—ex-salary.

"How long should we stare at the dash?" Alec leaned over, squinting into the direct sun.

"Honestly, I've had some body-language training, and yours is a doozie," she said.

Alec's expression hardened and his eyes flashed. "What happened back there?"

"When?"

"You choose."

"You heard everything I told Mooney. Do I have to re-gurgitate it again?"

He exhaled loudly. "Help me out here. I'm trying to understand what I've done to you." Alec rotated his hands on

66

the steering wheel, his frustration evident. "It feels like you're letting everyone in but me."

"Chase is family, and we've been a team for a long time. It's hot, and I'm hungry. Please come inside and help me eat all this pastrami before it gets cooked and goes rancid."

He huffed his disappointment, dismissing her entirely.

"Look at me, Alec." She waited until he finally focused on her. "I'm offering an olive branch. Let's eat, then we'll talk." She batted her lashes flirtatiously. "Promise."

She turned to open her door, and he fondled her arm.

"Before you do." Alec leaped out of the driver's seat and bounded over the hood in one giant vault to the passenger side. "I'm doing this right."

He opened her door, and she slid around, making as gracious an exit possible from a car whose frame sat six inches from the asphalt.

"Give me your key." He held out his hand in a way that suggested he wouldn't take no for an answer.

She dug into her zipper compartment and gave him the fob, house key extended.

With a gentle nudge, Alec guided her up the steps, as if he belonged beside her. He turned the doorknob before inserting the key, and the door gave way.

"Don't you lock up before you leave?"

"I'm sure Chase did."

"Please." He waited for her to enter first.

The door swung in but caught midway on an overturned chair.

"What happened?" Annalisse's head swam as she gazed into the room and caught her toe on the threshold. Unbalanced by the tote on her shoulder, she fell against the jamb, her funny bone taking the brunt when she'd hit the wood squarely.

"That hurt." She cupped her elbow while the pain dissipated. "Who would loot in broad daylight?" Her eyes went from living room to kitchen, checking for anything obvious that might be missing.

"Stay outside while I check the house out, but if you won't, stick close to me," Alec said.

If someone had taken a high velocity fan to the room, it would've been an improvement. Following Alec, she picked her way over magazines and binders scattered along the hardwood flooring. Nothing was in its rightful place.

She was as violated as Peter had made her feel.

He reached for her with his sights still trained ahead. "Stay close." Alec locked his fingers with hers.

"My cat. Boris, come here little buddy. Alec, what if something's happened to him? Boris! Please be hiding where I can find you." She left Alec's side to close the front door and swallowed back tears. Her faithful kitty roommate had been a rescued stray. He'd shown up at the farm as a young kitten, thin and hungry. A pile of trembling orange fur who'd nestled into her palm, his golden eyes unsure of her. She forced back the fear of losing him too.

Tiptoeing around books and papers, she surveyed the damage in the kitchen and went back to Alec. She took his warm hand, and a shudder flooded her body. Home invasions happened to other people in other neighborhoods. She found no logic in the rampage unless the act was a random burglary.

"I'd better look closely for anything stolen," Annalisse said.

"No." He turned to her, his Adam's apple working his throat. His stare went right through her, as if he were trying to read her innermost thoughts.

Neither of them talked in the long pause.

Annalisse was certain that Alec could hear the chugging in her chest, or maybe it was his heartbeats thudding her ears.

Most of her paintings were ripped from the walls, twisted in broken frames, lying helter-skelter on the floor. Chunks of white plaster at the missing nail heads marked the places where they'd hung with care. Every kitchen cupboard and drawer were slid to the stops or spilled out across the tile. Pots, skillets, tableware, canned goods, junk drawer, and glassware—her favorite set of iced tea glasses given to her by Aunt Kate—were among the broken and injured. Not the work of a typical rob-and-run burglar but the handiwork of a creature who preyed on destruction of the psyche.

"Why the demolition? What are they after?" Annalisse regretted having her research out in the open when she noticed her pristine desk—empty. "My identity is on that computer."

Alec broke eye contact, then dropped her hand. "You can't be home one hundred percent of the time. We'll fix it. I'd better check the rest of the house myself." He started for the staircase.

Annalisse set her purse onto the flipped-over cushions on the couch, repositioned them, and stepped through what used to be neat stacks, years of gallery work. A groan passed her lips when she walked to the desk marred with deep gouges, bereft of her monitor and tower hard drive. She looked around the room for her red laptop. It, too, was missing.

"Oh no. Please don't be dented." Her prized possession, a two-foot bronze of a shepherdess with a pair of sheep grazing near her feet, lay on its side next to a toppled plant stand. An expensive work of art from Florence she'd had no business buying but couldn't resist when Generosa had called from Italy describing it. Everyone who knew her understood the love for sheep she held close to her heart. Even if Annalisse had declined Generosa's offer, it was a certainty the bronze would've ended up in her hands eventually.

Alec waited by the stairs and whispered, "Is your bedroom at the top of the stairs?"

She nodded, lifting the mahogany stand upright. With both hands on the base, she lifted the heavy bronze to its rightful place next to the desk—close enough to admire its detail while she worked.

"Don't go up there without me, Alec. I need to see what's missing upstairs."

Standing at the oak banister, he said, "No. You're safer down there. I won't be long, and I'll look for your cat while I'm up there."

"Be careful. We may have interrupted the burglar if he's still here."

Boris had to be scared out of his mind. She hoped he'd found his hiding place in the closet, deep behind the extra blankets.

Whoever destroyed her home had acted with malice. They had her personal data and internet search history, where she shopped online, email correspondence, and business contacts. A privacy breach she couldn't afford, especially while jobless. Mentally compiling a list of possible suspects, obscure names and faces entered her head. With fingertips pressed at her temples, she willed the jackhammers to stop.

Raising her arms as if a make-believe thief told her to, she said, "I give up. Alec, we may as well set a match to this place; it's such a mess."

Alec uttered a sentence upstairs she couldn't make out.

"I can't hear you. Did you find Boris in the closet?"

The sound of shuffling filtered downstairs, then a thump.

"What fell?" She watched an empty landing. The unnatural silence pricked the hairs straight out on her neck. "Answer me."

A mechanical voice broke the silence. "Don't move."

She stopped breathing, frozen in place and afraid to look up but then looked anyway.

A figure in a brownish ski mask and desert camouflage occupied the top of the staircase, holding Alec at gunpoint. One arm cradled Alec's waist, and the other held a black pistol so close to Alec's right ear his curls hid part of the barrel.

She'd expected Alec's expression to be as wild as hers must have been, but he appeared strangely calm.

"I'm all right, Annalisse."

"Shut up." The voice was distorted with some kind of speech-altering mechanism, giving off tones similar to a bumblebee in distress.

The masked person let go of Alec long enough to backhand him across the face.

Annalisse gasped, covering her mouth. Her blood boiled as she watched Alec and the intruder descend the stairs side by side. She suffered in horror several feet from her pistol at the bottom of her purse, observing the figure who held Alec. Had the nasty creep surveilled her? Did the break-in at Zavos Gallery have anything to do with the destruction of her brownstone?

The buzzing voice came again, and an evil glint shone through the eyeholes in the mask. "You run, he dies. Get into kitchen. Let's have a little *zakuski, malysh*."

A breath caught in her lungs.

They were Russian terms she understood.

She'd nearly become a main course in Peter's office—no way would she stand for playing appetizer to another predator.

CHAPTER
ELEVEN

"Back from stairs, *gerla*," the odd mechanical voice said.

When they neared the bottom steps, she noticed Alec's collar beneath his ear was soaked in blood. Gulping back a shriek, she closed her eyes for a split second. If she hadn't asked him up for lunch, he'd be safe and on the way to his estate. With two against one, their chance of survival increased if they kept their wits about them.

Annalisse stared at the handgun pressed against Alec's temple. She said a silent prayer that he wouldn't get shot and could somehow escape the gunman. A whimper tore from her lips when the intruder swept the pistol from Alec and pointed it at her. Taking baby steps backward, she bumped against the kitchen table, jarring her to a standstill.

"Why are you here?" Perspiration raced down her back and into her waistband.

Alec blinked a few times and tilted his head toward the couch, but she couldn't be certain what he meant. Did he want her on the sofa?

She gave a slight shrug and begged him with her eyes to give another sign she could interpret—mouth his words—anything she could understand.

The gunman pushed the pistol behind Alec's ear and yelled, "Quiet!" Through the narrow strip of exposed skin, the man's dark eyes glittered dangerously. "The necklace. Where is it?"

"What necklace?" Alec asked.

"Don't play." The gunman pushed Alec forcefully on the couch. He landed half on, half off the leather tote she'd placed there earlier.

Annalisse released a held breath and clenched her teeth together as the intruder waved his firearm perilously close to Alec's face. Before she knew it, the gun sank squarely into Alec's belly.

She had to keep her cool.

She couldn't lose it for his sake.

"I know the one." Annalisse stopped the guessing game because he held his weapon in checkmate.

"Truth now, or I kill one of you." The man beckoned to her and said, "You. Come."

The burglar stepped backward, keeping the pistol aimed at the couch, and crushed her arm in his grip. Smooth fingers, almost feminine, clamped down hard enough to leave bruises as he flung her beside Alec. The action brought a scratchy sound from beneath the mask; perhaps he had a beard or mustache hidden by the dark cloth.

"Sorry you're caught up in this," she whispered to Alec.

He gave her knee a squeeze and rubbed his thumb over the fabric.

Salty blood seeped from her tongue, and she swallowed. With the security beefed up at Zavos Gallery, the gunman needed their help to obtain what he wanted.

"You have our attention." Alec's hand tensed on her leg.

"Gold horses. Give them."

She glanced at Alec, but his eyes weren't focused on her. His unwavering gaze was trained on the man in camouflage in front of them.

The intruder walked over to the sofa and jabbed the pistol to her forehead, gluing the barrel's opening there.

Motionless, she inhaled the strange odors emanating from the mask.

He bent toward her, his breath full in her face, smelling of pickling spices, long favored by residents of Russia. But his short stature couldn't be Nikita or anyone else from Peter's photo.

He grazed her cheek with his weapon, trailing smooth, cold steel along her hairline.

"Where's Mushasha?" He slid the pistol barrel down her brow line to the bridge of her nose.

"Let me think." For a brief instant, she wondered if this was how Samantha had felt before her attacker burned and stabbed her. Before he sliced her face into strips—all while she was alive, according to the medical examiner.

Alec's hand shifted on her leg, breaking her concentration and bringing her back to the current menace within reach.

Annalisse made slow, even breaths and pulled herself together. She wasn't Samantha, and their situation wouldn't go down that way. Digging her nails into Alec's thigh, she fixed her gaze on the bay window over the man's shoulder—watching—hoping to conjure an unknown visitor to her home.

Her bag tipped over behind her.

Annalisse slowly leaned toward Alec, obscuring her purse because she had a plan.

The combination of Alec's musk and the pastrami on rye from inside her tote had her nausea rolling uncomfortably in her belly.

The eyes in the mask narrowed.

He grew impatient, and she had to stall for time.

"It's in Italy. The necklace is in Italy," she blurted.

The interrogator flipped his wrist, and in the next instant, the barrel struck her brow.

She gasped and shrank, covering the ache with one hand. "Beating us will get you nowhere."

Alec raised a fist, but lashing out wouldn't help them either.

"I'm good, Alec."

Between throbs above her eye and the beginnings of a headache, Annalisse memorized what few details of his appearance she could distinguish.

His ungloved, girlish hands were shaved, and his head formed an egg shape under the fitted mask. No gloves, so he cared little about leaving fingerprints on her belongings.

"Don't hurt her. The necklace you want is in another country," Alec added.

The man grunted. "Liar. The art place."

"What you want is in Italy." Annalisse noted his clipped English.

"Not so," the mechanical voice said.

"The necklace isn't in the gallery. We're telling the truth," Alec said.

A deafening bang took her hearing away.

"I'm shot!" Alec grabbed his shoulder and winced, plowing against the sofa cushion— excruciating pain written in the twist of his mouth.

"No!" Annalisse caught herself reaching for Alec but let her hand drop. She seethed inside as she turned her fury on the gunman.

"We were cooperating," she hissed.

In her peripheral vision, Alec pressed his fingers into a bloody spot on his shoulder.

"I'm going to help him. Don't shoot me. You'll get what you want." She shifted her knees on the cushion and blocked the tote as she pried Alec's fingers away from his shirt. "Move your hand," she told him. "Bite down. This will hurt." Annalisse pushed hard on his wound. Warm blood seeped through her fingers, spreading to the couch. The shot had grazed the top of his shoulder.

Alec grimaced. "Easy there, babe."

She clamped her teeth together but didn't turn around. "All right, Short Fuse; we don't have the necklace. It's not here." She twisted slowly and faced the mask. "He's bleeding, and I need something dry. I'll tell you where to find the necklace but only if I'm allowed to get towels for his wound." She pointed to the kitchen. "You can watch me. Okay?"

Blood continued to flow from the bullet hole, worrying her. One-handed, she grappled with the buttons of his polo to make what she was about to do easier.

Alec held her wrist still and gave a slight headshake. "Let me."

"The angle is awkward. It's better that I bandage you." Annalisse softly grazed the stubbles on his jawline. "Please, just relax."

"If you lie, I'm shooting him in the head." Metallic laughter spilled behind her back.

"I won't let him bleed out!" She turned to confront the black handgun near her face, trying to forget how much trouble they were in. "I never lie."

He waved toward the kitchen with the gun. "Go."

"Alec, can you scoot a little to your left? You've soaked through the cushion."

She cringed at the hitching grunt he made while he shifted, urging him to slide over the purse with directional nods.

When she bent to look at his injury, the bullet had passed through the shoulder seam of his polo. Annalisse felt awful about the pain she'd caused him.

Ignoring the gunman behind them, she noticed Alec's hesitation, and a flicker of satisfaction washed through his eyes. Annalisse brushed his sweaty bangs aside and whispered, "Focus."

Alec coughed, managing a groan from the minor movement.

"Kitchen!" yelled the man.

"Take over, Alec. Rotate slightly and hold pressure, lots of pressure."

With her gut in twisted knots, Annalisse ran to the stove, yanked at three hand towels draped over the oven door handle, then reached for the paper towels.

"Enough," the masked man said.

When she returned to the couch, she placed the roll of absorbent paper in Alec's lap and piled the fabric towels in the corner next to him near her unzipped bag. Using handfuls of bunched paper towels over his wound, she gave Alec a slow, deliberate blink. The bleeding had slowed.

Alec watched her work—best described as all the intensity of a teenager with a painful crush. His chest rose and fell with some difficulty.

"We'll come out the other side," she whispered near his ear, detecting a tremble as she traveled near his wound.

The spell broken, he wrinkled his brow and frowned, placing his hand over hers. "I'll do it."

"Where's horses? Now!"

She could bite through nails at this point. "When he stops bleeding."

He hauled her by the arm away from Alec.

"You stall. No more time. The necklace."

He jabbed the gun deeply into her spine and pushed.

"All right." Annalisse raised her hands above her head and slowly turned toward him. She blocked out every thought except getting to her pistol in the tote. "He needs a doctor, but I can help him temporarily. Killing us won't get you the necklace. He's not stable—so back up and let me finish." She half expected the guy to explode or use the gun again.

Instead, he stepped back and removed the sting from his gun barrel.

With one foot planted on the floor and the other knee in the sofa cushion, she applied more pressure to Alec's shoulder. With the other hand wrapped around Alec, she unzipped the enclosure and dug for her pistol, all the while making small talk to deflect the gunman's attention.

She kicked the springs underneath the couch with the toe of her boot.

"That's a car door." She glanced over her shoulder. "Someone's out front."

The diversion was just long enough to give her a moment to ease the pistol from the bottom of the tote. With a finger on the trigger, she spun on her knee, getting off one shot to his gun hand.

The man screamed, holding his wrist, and dropping the Glock to the floor.

In the weird angle, she'd missed his torso, but she'd injured him.

The intruder weaved toward her desk and stumbled.

She fired again.

The masked man managed to lift her bronze shepherdess and toss the statue through the window. The sound of breaking glass filled the room and shards scattered from floor to flower-bed. He dove through the opening and disappeared.

She reached into her tote to phone 911 as Chase burst into the room, banging the entry door against the stop.

"Anna, this place—your clothes—your head is bleeding. Who was that?" Chase scanned the room, then he turned white when his gaze settled on Alec.

"Did you see him?" Alec asked.

"Mooney's on him."

"I thought you were going home—but you're here." Annalisse felt grateful for Chase's change of heart.

Alec lifted his shoulder and winced. "She could use another shirt since I've ruined her sweater." He tipped his head toward the stairs. "Second floor is a mess too."

She smiled at his thoughtfulness. Alec had suffered a terrible injury in her brownstone, and his first concern was for her.

Annalisse patted Alec's thigh and looked at him for signs of shock or weakness, but his expression was unreadable. "I have painkillers to tide you over, but if you need something stronger than over-the-counter meds, they'll give you way better drugs at the hospital." Rock steady, she reached for his shoulder with a clean towel.

Alec grabbed her wrist and left lingering kisses on her knuckles. "That was quite something you did."

"Mooney called for an ambulance. What's missing?" Chase asked.

She heard Chase's question, but the way Alec's lashes lowered and the sensation of his face against her hand left her speechless.

He slowly grazed her palm against scratchy whiskers, which felt as if they'd lengthened in the past ten minutes.

"You have incredible moxie, pretty lady." He wrenched a purple pouch from his waistband and handed it to her.

From the sharp edges and a clink of the metal behind the fabric, she nearly fainted dead away. "From Zavos Gallery?"

He nodded. "While Mom spoke to the detective. I thought it would be safer at Brookehaven. It's been cutting into me for the past hour."

She laughed nervously. "Poor baby. I won't ask which part of your body hurts worse."

"A discussion for later." A flicker of passion shone back at her, and he lifted one side of his mouth.

His dimples had a way of dissolving the fence she'd wrapped around herself. They were as much an aphrodisiac as they were charming. What a knack she had—the uncanny ability to transport Alec's mind to the gutter. She'd have her work cut out to keep it casual with him, although she'd fought against men with other ideas before. She wanted to trust Alec like she trusted Gen and not become another conquest left in the aftermath of his affections.

Chase whistled softly. "I never thought I'd be grateful for nosy-body Clara next door. She called in the gunshot."

Annalisse dropped the pouch into her purse. "Forget about Mooney thinking we lead average lives. This is our third official call today. He's going to be thrilled."

The detective appeared with perspiration stains on his short red hair, darkened to brown on his forehead. "Who's hurt? Anybody?" His eyes fell on Alec. "Should I notify Generosa?"

"I'll give her a call as soon as I'm patched up." Alec lowered his eyes and shrugged at the floor.

He would delay to the last moment because that's what Gen would do. With Generosa on Crete, she'd imagine the worst and be furious with Annalisse for putting their sacred offspring in jeopardy. Gen was much safer in Greece.

"It looks like the bullet grazed his shoulder. I don't think any bones are involved. What about the shooter? Did you get him?" she asked.

"He left a major blood trail. We've put out a BOLO, and we're watching the ERs in the area." He pulled out a pair of latex gloves. "His pistol?" Mooney pointed at the weapon on the floor.

Annalisse nodded. "Better take mine too." She raised her gun with two fingers. "I fired twice. Got him near the wrist. His slug's in my couch or the wall behind Alec. I'm not sure where my second one went. He moved, and I missed."

"I'll find something for you to wear." Chase trudged up the stairs.

Mooney nodded at her bloodstained sweater and smiled. "It gave its life for a good cause."

The comment brought a laugh from Alec.

"Camo Guy cloaked his voice, Detective. Why go to the trouble to disguise yourself but use bare hands on the weapon? Really bare—like shaved," she said.

"Is that so?" He flipped open his notebook and jotted down a few notes. "For one man without an accomplice, he spent a lot of time trashing the place. Same upstairs?"

Alec nodded. "I interrupted him."

"Found Boris!" Chase shouted from the stair landing. "He's okay."

Annalisse placed a palm on her chest and sighed. "Wonderful. Put him in the carrier from my closet."

"Is this a random burglary, Ms. Drury? What did he say to you?" Mooney asked.

Annalisse exchanged looks with Alec, then twisted her fingers in her lap. "My laptop and computer are missing. That's all I know right now. He must have stashed them before we got here, or he had some help."

Mooney pursed his lips, squinting at her. "I'll ask again. Did he say anything specific?"

By his insistence, the detective must have suspected important facts were left dangling.

"It's hard to know how to answer that. The device made it difficult to translate. Can we do this later?" Annalisse turned toward Alec. "He is priority one."

A siren pierced the silence, and she relaxed a little. Soon Alec would get the help he needed. Flashing lights on the ambulance temporarily distracted her from the conversation.

"I'll call for a cruiser to surveil the area until your window's boarded and add patrols throughout the neighborhood.

Until we've finished the investigation here, you'll have to stay with a friend or relative." He glanced at Alec. "I'm glad your injury isn't as severe as it could've been. You're in good hands." Mooney smiled at her. "When you're able, my partner will take your statements at the hospital." Mooney left them, closing the door.

"Are we doing the right thing... not turning over the necklace?" Alec whispered.

"Giving it to authorities increases the danger to everyone. After what just happened, it's too late anyway."

"We can't keep it in New York anymore. Greece maybe." Alec looked at his watch. "Almost three. Mom's aboard the Gulfstream by now." He rotated his shoulder, inhaling a breath. "Burns like fire. You and Boris should stay with me at the estate." He dug into a pocket with care. "Take my keys and follow me to the hospital. Can you drive a stick?"

"Yes, but we can't stay with you."

"Look around. You can't stay here. I'd take the offer."

She had no logical reason to turn down Alec's invitation. Neither she nor Chase had a job, and her brownstone was a crime scene.

"I *could* go to the farm, but my being there would endanger my aunt." She reached out to the fidgety guy on her sofa. "Stop moving around. You'll start bleeding again." Hesitating at first, Annalisse gently hugged his neck. "Thank you for taking the brunt of my worst nightmare." Without another thought, she kissed his temple, just like she'd done with Chase, and right away regretted the familiarity.

"Minor obstacles." He lifted his shoulder. "The perp called the necklace something. What was it?"

"Mushasha. It's the jewelry collection that belonged to an ancient ruler in Persia. I found solid proof of a curse placed on the pieces, and so far, the curse is winning. My notes were scattered beside the stolen electronics."

"Mooney heard from the medical examiner after you left Mom's gallery. Harry died from radioactive polonium. Harry, my mother, me—and now you—are joined at the hip in this," Alec said.

"The poison used by spies." The mask and Slavic language whizzed through her thoughts. "Russian spy stuff."

A medical team entered the premises in a noisy scrape of shoes hitting the threshold.

"Annalisse, I believe you." He gave her his key fob. "Now, jump in my car, and we'll talk more about your sleeping arrangements after I'm stitched up."

CHAPTER
TWELVE

Alec's shoulder twinged, and he sank deeper into the convertible's bucket seat. He straightened his head and passed a sideways look at Annalisse. Her dark hair blowing away from her face in the breeze flaunted her delicate features. A model's neck, perfect nose, and the most surprising green eyes.

"I should be driving. The hospital should've monitored you overnight," she said.

Since leaving Bellevue Hospital for Brookehaven, the woman next to him hadn't carried off her maneuver of neutrality well. She'd never be a poker player, stealing hungry glances while biting down on her lower lip. The sensual way she touched her earlobe and the occasional swipe of a palm across her throat gave her away. Nervousness caused by attraction—but there was a self-imposed barrier he had to break down. They'd spent the hour with the top down, exchanging niceties like they were strangers, with no mention of their bizarre past forty-eight hours. After what they'd endured, he'd picked up many mixed signals.

"They don't hospitalize people for scratches," he hollered over the wind.

"A bullet wound isn't a scratch."

"Superficial wound then. The nurses were impressed by your first aid skills." He grinned, drawing a smile from her. "I could have passed out from blood loss."

Her face flushed a shade of rose, and she dipped her head, tugging her hair.

"You're handy to have around, Annalisse."

"If I'd left Westinn alone five hours ago, we wouldn't be having this chat. It's nice to have you as a willing ally." Her lustful glance appeared, then retreated.

"I'll admit, it feels strange in the presence of a chick who packs."

Annalisse raised one eyebrow, opened her mouth as if to say something, then stopped.

"Today opened my eyes." He swept fingers through windblown curls, rough to the touch. "Being with you is such a rush."

Ahead, the lavish foothills of the Hudson Valley dimmed in the sunset. Mowed fields and waterways mingled with white birches appeared like Popsicle sticks among the sugar maples decked out in blaze of orange leaves. He loved this part of New York and couldn't wait to introduce her to his retreat in the Catskill Mountains.

For the next twenty minutes, Alec lost count of all the questions he had for Annalisse. He wanted to know every detail about her, but his curiosity would keep. His role as an interrogator would scare her if he poured it on too soon.

"I hope Boris calms down from his big shock. I've never heard him meow so much. I felt awful leaving him with Chase."

"Chase is bringing him here tomorrow, remember?"

"What are we going to do? It's a blessing that Gen's not here." She rubbed her hands down her tempting thighs.

"I'm working on a plan." He downshifted, and the car whined as it slowed at the curve. "There's the estate house on the right. The property covers both sides of the road." Alec pointed toward the grove of trees next to the oncoming fences, recalling the dilapidated state he'd found the property in after escrow closed.

Annalisse drew a long breath. "All this is part of the estate?"

"It's not so large, but the place was a wreck in the beginning. If I'd known the monumental task— I was blinded by its majesty. The owner's real estate gal was one heck of a salesperson." He smiled and pointed to the roof. "Refurbishing the gables and finding the right wood beams took some doing. I thought we'd never finish buying tall windows."

"The Tudor style reminds me of England's Ascott House in Buckinghamshire built in the eighteen hundreds. Tudor architecture is one of my favorites." She pointed to the front of the house. "You're missing a fountain and the swirl of topiaries for authenticity."

"I'll add those to my to-do list. When we get to the house, I'll check in with Helga, then give you the grand tour."

Gravel crackled beneath the tires as he parked next to the huge maple near the house. Brookehaven nestled between stands of hardwoods he'd insisted had to stay in place, adding buildings only where necessary.

Several mares and their foals wandered the grass, finding better spots to graze at the end of the pasture. Soft whinnies and hoofbeats floated on the air.

Annalisse turned toward the fence, her face alight with wonderment.

"On second thought, it's getting late." He checked his watch. "Sunset is at six thirty, so we'd better do the abbreviated tour."

"Your shoulder has to hurt. Can we do it another time?"

"I hardly feel it. Great drugs," he said.

Before he could get out and open her door, Annalisse was standing outside, leaning on the car, arms folded, chuckling at the horseplay on the other side of the rails. Alec rounded the hood slowly, watching her gaze at the foals. Of all the lovers he'd taken in the past, not a single one had haunted his dreams like Annalisse. Since his mother had introduced him to her, an undefined vision kept him from sleeping some nights. He hadn't connected the turquoise eyes he'd imagined with this woman though. The eyes were real, but the association seemed more than that—as if he'd known her in a past lifetime. He believed in having past lives.

The sensitive woman leaning against his car had been changed by recent events. Since Harry's death, her spontaneous laughter had slipped away, and her smiles were barren of pleasure.

Annalisse's sigh brought him back to earth.

"Alec, I envy you. Creatures as glorious as these romping the pastures. That sense of belonging to nature just outside your door."

"I'd like to think we all belong to something... or someone special." He silently hoped that she'd consider dating him. A boyfriend lurking in another town would be a disappointment.

"I wish," she said with sorrow in her voice.

He studied her profile in the Signorile's red paint, pensive, with her lips drawn downward, and wondered what her story was. What demons caused her to distance herself from him yet cling to Chase?

"You're more fortunate than you realize, Alec. In so many ways. Gen... your dad..." He caught her feeble attempt at laughter and the white-knuckled grasp of the leather at the top of the door. "I've never met your father, and yet I'm jealous. Pathetic, huh?" she asked him.

In that moment, he felt her pain altering the atmosphere. Maybe she'd endured too much hurt to ever make a commitment to another human being. If that were true, he'd find small ways to gain her trust.

He touched her arm and forced her to look at him. Her heartbeats pulsed near the hollow of her throat. That tender patch of skin he could rest against and feel beneath his lips. Like he had in his dreams.

"There's a guy across the street who'll lift our spirits. Let's go."

As they stood beside the highway, Annalisse scanned the courtyard-style building in a rock and timber frame. Above the giant sliding doors, a logo with a silver horse galloping out of a crimson letter *B* took up most of the header. Even though Alec told her this was his horse barn—the elite version for professional trainers and breeders—from the road, it could be mistaken for a monster home. Picturesque and immaculate, Alec's facilities dripped of luxury and success. When she'd priced out custom wood barns with tack rooms and grooming stalls for her aunt, they couldn't afford them, so they'd settled on metal prefab buildings. Walker Farm couldn't compare to the grandeur of the Brookehaven estate.

"C'mon, we'll take the speed tour. We forgot jackets." Alec motioned to her with a tilt of his head.

"How did you talk me into this? I shouldn't have abandoned Chase. We left in such a hurry; I don't even have a change of clothes."

And she'd left her brownstone turned upside down, left Boris behind, and law enforcement pawing through every personal item she owned. Crossing her arms, she shivered in disbelief.

"Your house is evidence. They're fingerprinting every inch of it. If you're with me, I can keep you safe. Or you can keep *me* safe." A hint of a smile touched his lips. "I expected this talk on the road. I promise you'll see things my way." He checked the highway side to side and grabbed her hand. "Are you up for a jog? C'mon."

As Alec slid the breezeway doors open and turned on the barn lights, the metal runners squealed a protest.

When she crossed the threshold, Annalisse entered the world of pine shavings blended with horse sweat. The familiar smell, while doing chores at Walker Farm, rushed back to her.

Alec called out to the horses, and the whinnies echoed stall to stall. Glee. The sound of happiness among the horses when a known friend approaches. A brass plate on the first stall caught her eye. It read Kristol Magic.

Annalisse set her tote down and wandered closer to the stall. A hulking stallion pranced toward the bars with his ears at attention and his nostrils flared. He bobbed his head and snorted as if he was bored within his four walls. Other than the small white crescent on the forehead, his coat was the color of burnt redwood. Her aunt called the shade "sorrel for sissies" since it wasn't red enough for a sorrel and too dark to be a true chestnut.

"What a majestic creature." She calculated the stallion's height at seventeen hands.

"Meet the stable's stud Kris." Alec reached through the vertical bars and tickled the stallion's nose. "I've neglected you lately, big guy."

A jockey would get lost on this tall giant. He was a splendid example of a textbook thoroughbred stud, if the colt she'd watched earlier was an indication.

"A lot of breeders wanted him. Kris was slated for a Stallion Season charity auction, but a friend told us about him before the sale. Dad and I took a ride to Blood Rush Stables in Kentucky, and we bought the colt on the spot."

She wandered to the bright-eyed mare in the next stall. "And who's this?"

"Harriet is a dilemma. She hasn't foaled for the past two seasons, and right now she's taking up needed space. We have forty brood mares that all need to pull their weight."

"How old?"

"She's twelve."

"A little young for conception problems. Did she have a bad time with her last foal?" she asked.

"I can't find the logic in it, but I'm late preg-checking mares this time around, so we'll have to see. This could be her shot as a brood mare for us, but she's gentle enough to ride."

A horse of her breeding would be a shame to waste as a plug in someone's backyard. Harriet was the kind of project Annalisse could dig into with gusto. She shoved the notion in the back of her mind for a later date.

The mare pricked her ears forward at Alec's rich voice, then nickered. Her coat sparkled like polished cherrywood with brass highlights, and Annalisse's heart space opened wide.

Wrapping her fingers around the stall bars, she drew in the scent of old pennies and damp peat moss. An unforgettable aroma that she loved.

"May I go in with her?" Her hand gripped the slider wand.

"Watch your step." Alec laid his hand over hers, and together, they slid the door open. Annalisse wandered inside, but he stayed out, blocking the door opening, just in case she required a hasty retreat.

Annalisse reached out carefully so the mare could pick up her scent, then ventured closer. "Beautiful." She carefully rested her cheek against the horse's warm neck, wiping shaving dust from her coat. "Horsehide smells great. What I'd give for my own place someday, but it's too big a dream to hold on to." She glanced at Alec, who'd remained silent; the keen Zavos eyes watching her movements. She hadn't meant to verbalize her innermost thoughts.

Wishing for something Alec already had made her feel ungrateful and pitiful.

"I could spend hours in here with you, but we'd better go, girl." Scratching behind the mare's ear, she kissed her fragrant cheek and whispered, "If I'm still here, maybe we can talk *Dad* into letting you out of your cage. You've gotta be amazing in the sunlight."

Harriet bobbed, followed by an equine's throaty approval.

"See there, she agrees." Annalisse laughed and looked over her shoulder at Alec.

His striking eyes had taken on the color of silver bullion; the shade that daydreams are made of. Each time she looked into them, she felt the heat of a burning candle filled with desire. A thousand women would hand their virtue over, to drown in Alec's caress and gaze into his beautiful eyes just once.

"No argument here," he said.

"What?" A flush raged through her.

"I've never seen Harriet take to anyone like that. She has little to do with me, but with you... she seems... happy. We'd better head back to the house. It'll be dark soon, and I'm getting weak from starvation." Alec held out his hand to her.

Relieved that her last thoughts were her own, she brushed past him for her purse. "I don't feel right keeping this." She attempted to hand over the purple bag with the necklace inside, but he wouldn't take it. "It's safer someplace else, Alec."

"Not in here. We both know where it is." He sniffed the air and hummed through a tight mouth. "Smell that? Helga's beer bratwurst is the best. She's one heck of a cook."

Food. No wonder she was cold and watery at the knees. She'd slipped the pastrami sandwiches into her fridge for Chase and couldn't remember what she'd eaten since the party.

In a surprise move, Alec walked to the entrance and flipped a switch, throwing her eyesight into temporary blindness.

"Hey, are you testing my night vision skills?" She fast-walked to the edge of the breezeway with her teeth chattering.

"Sorry, force of habit. I'm used to being out here alone." Alec stared at the ground.

His starlets weren't invited to the stables, not many anyway. A contradiction to his media photos that she hadn't expected. Annalisse spotted a large concrete pad not far from where they stood. "Are you building another barn over there?" She motioned to the foundation still in concrete forms.

"That's the footing for the clinic I mentioned."

Chills tore at her chest when she recalled their talk prior to leaving the restaurant bar in a huge hurry. Why go into that profession when he had racehorses to manage?

In a matter of months, he'd be a practicing vet who accepted animals to diagnose and suture. She wrapped her arms tighter across her breasts. The comfort she'd felt while being with Harriet floated away on the frigid wind.

"Take my hand, Annalisse. Your teeth are going to chatter right out of that pretty mouth of yours."

She shuddered, envisioning Samantha's string-bean loser of a boyfriend with his sinewy hands and couldn't help but wonder if the creep had ever used that same line on her friend.

CHAPTER
THIRTEEN

Her stomach full of bratwurst and cabbage, Annalisse snuggled into a lounge in a dim corner of the room. Alec's interior decorating taste wasn't like his mother's. The mahogany-stained beams of the vaulted ceiling met blood-red wainscoting on three sides. Such a shame to ruin the authenticity of the oversized room with the crimson, in-your-face color. She found the space overstated and all male. Most of Alec's furnishings, with their fine legs and clawed feet, were spot-on classic with nineteenth-century English Tudor cottages, and she liked that part, but the walls clashed. Though he'd added an unexpected floral here and there, the room begged for a woman's touch.

Alec walked in, sitting beside her on the mint-colored fainting couch.

"Do the drawing room antiques pass muster? I'd like your professional opinion."

"The totally awesome cobblestone fireplace is my favorite part." Logs crackled, and sparks melted into the chimney. She scooted deeper into the seat, allowing the room's ambiance to penetrate. "My uncle was a mason—a wonder with brick and stone. There's an art to crafting a proper draw. Your contractor nailed this one. It must have taken a long time to gather so many colored rocks for an entire wall."

"River rock. I wonder if your uncle would agree with you."

She sighed, staring into the fire. "Me too. Aunt Kate's been widowed for years."

"The aunt you lived with? I didn't know. I'm sorry." Alec clasped his hands together.

Annalisse rarely made reference to her uncle around Kate. Memories of him typically brought tears, so remembrances were left unsaid most of the time. She plucked a piece of lint from the couch and glanced down the hallway.

"I haven't seen Ms. Rissman since supper. Did she go to bed?"

"She's getting the guest room ready."

"Tell her not to go to any trouble for me."

"That's where I'm going to sleep. The guest rooms downstairs haven't been slept in for some time, and I like clean sheets." Alec patted the couch. "You're sleeping in my master suite."

"No, Alec. Give me a comforter, and I'll sleep right here."

"And turn me into a bad host? Not gonna happen. After the day you've had, nothing but the best bedroom in the place for you, sweetheart. My bed's darn comfortable."

Annalisse thought she caught a subtle lifting of his eyebrows—or not. Her lids were so heavy from the last glass of port and the cozy fire that she couldn't be sure of her eyes and ears.

In the hall, the clatter of wooden clogs echoed throughout the artwork-free paneled walls. Ms. Rissman, in a starched frock straight out of a stereotypical British household, appeared behind them. Her rigid white bun was stiff, as if the hairs were trained to stay put without pins.

"Alec, I— Oh my. I didn't mean to interrupt." The housekeeper spun a military about-face.

"Don't leave. Are the rooms ready?" Alec asked.

Annalisse smiled as she swiveled around. "Thank you, Ms. Rissman, but I'll sleep here. It's comfortable enough."

The soft brown eyes below the taut bun looked perplexed. "Does your lady friend prefer the drawing room?" she asked Alec.

"She'll be more comfortable in the master suite if I have to pick her up and haul her there myself."

From the housekeeper's little bunny hop, Alec's pushier side caught Ms. Rissman off guard. Annalisse preferred they talk to her and not around her—almost the way Peter and Harry used to be in her presence.

"Very well. Is your *other* friend coming tonight?" The housekeeper gave Alec a stony look.

"One of the rooms will be for Annalisse's cat so he'll have time to adjust to his new surroundings. Is that okay with you?" he asked Annalisse.

"Sure." His house, his rules. "Chase can hang out as long as he wants, but Boris and I won't be staying long."

"Until we figure this out, please don't think about going back to the city," he said.

"We don't want to be a burden to you." Annalisse strayed a palm over her knee.

Alec exhaled. "Until Mooney says you can return, you'll stay here."

"If there's nothing else, I'll retire upstairs." The housekeeper rolled her *R* heavily.

"Your food was heavenly, Ms. Rissman. Thank you for being so kind."

She nodded stiffly. "My friends call me Helga. You can too, *schatz.*"

Schatz could be a slang German term of endearment. She doubted that Helga would drop a slur toward one of Alec's guests.

"Another great meal, Helga. See you in the morning." His eyes followed Helga down the hall, then he patted Annalisse's leg. "She likes you. That's as fine a welcome as you're gonna get, *honey—schatz.*"

"Ah, thanks for clarifying that." She giggled at herself.

Alec's sandalwood and citrus scent floated in, and she wanted to lean into it. The smell of outdoors soothed her tortured mind. Too bad she couldn't bottle it to open later on, where she'd put it on her nightstand for sleepless nights when she felt alone and forgotten.

"Could I bother you for a throw?" She touched his thigh and leaned back against the chaise, fighting against droopy lids.

"You're tired. I'll walk you to your room," he said.

"No. I'd like to talk awhile. It's so nice here."

She gave in to Alec's nearness and stared at the golden flames licking the coals.

Annalisse shooed away what she thought was a fly and opened her eyes.

When Alec jerked his hand away, she flinched. How long had he stood there—watching her—touching her cheek?

"Did I snore?" she asked.

"You've been out for twenty minutes. I should've let you sleep, but I'd like another opinion." Alec gave her a letter-sized printout.

She rubbed her eyelids and scanned the sheet with the word *Lufthansa* printed in bold at the top left. "Two first-class tickets to Athens? For who?"

"And a hop over to Crete."

Annalisse sat up and stared at the passenger names—hers and Alec's.

"How did you get my personal information?" she asked.

"I called Mom; don't be mad."

"You've already told Gen what happened today? I thought—"

"Not quite everything." His chin dipped. "I left out the part where I got shot."

"Convenient." She glanced at the departure date. "Tomorrow night? Cancel my seat. I can't go without packing and making arrangements for Boris." He'd taken a lot for granted. Her rule was plan first, act later.

His turf. His rules.

Alec lifted his palms to stop her tirade. "Whoa. Mom suggested it, if you must know. From your own mouth, you said they'd keep searching for the jewelry collection. You can't stay alone in a hotel; I won't allow it."

Taken aback by his chivalrous gesture, she asked, "The cost of first-class tickets… I have to think about this." She folded the paper and handed it back.

"We have to fly commercially because Mom has the company bird. Don't change the subject. It's time to tell the police about the purple pouch."

"Let's make a plan before we tell the world about what we *think* is happening. We had a close call at the brownstone, that's it." She folded her arms.

"It's more than that, and you know it."

He'd taken a bullet for her, and ingratitude had managed to poke its ugly head into things. Again.

"Agent Norcross didn't say that Harry had anything to do with the necklace. He and Gen weren't that close. Telling Mooney about the horses or handing over the piece puts us in an awkward situation."

Alec tried to interrupt, but she kept going.

"Don't ask me why I know this. It's just a feeling. For now, your mother's safe, I think. We haven't thought this through yet. Let the investigations play out." She sighed, dropping her head in her hands. "Can we talk about this later?" She pressed her fingertips to her temples and remembered his injury. "How's your shoulder?" Sliding to one side, she patted the cushion next to her. "Let me look. You may need a fresh bandage."

"You'd do that for me?" Seconds later, he was beside her, needing no more encouragement. His Zavos gaze felt sinful and wonderful.

"How could I have forgotten to check you?" Annalisse shook her head. "Stop me the next time I become too self-involved. Lift the shirt," she ordered flatly.

Alec grimaced and pulled the long-sleeved tee over his head, exposing a dark patch of glistening chest hair on an extremely broad chest. All muscled up like guys who worked out.

Why did he have to be so gorgeous? Annalisse considered whether his chest hair was soft or wiry or if he'd hold her tenderly as she had her way with him. Drawn to his charms, she may as well admit it to herself. She tore her eyes from his pecs to his shoulder and gently tugged at the adhesive tape. The neat row of stitches looked fine, but the area around the sutures had puffed an angry red.

"We'll watch the swelling closely. Having been in battle with metal and gunpowder, I expected worse. I'd find something waterproof to put over it in the shower, like a liquid bandage. And finish *all* your antibiotics even if you feel better." His skin came alive under her fingertips.

"Aye, aye, Dr. Drury. Thank you." He saluted her. "Is there anything else?"

Annalisse's face flushed, and she jerked her wrist into a ball, punching it into her lap. Her mind hadn't convinced her body to keep some distance from him or be lost.

With his forefinger, he rotated her chin so she'd face him. "It's just you and me. Relax."

Alec was far too close. Close enough to kiss his perfectly matched, parted lips. She willed herself to stay strong. Next to him like this was too tempting. A shudder shook her body violently.

"Are you afraid of me?" His question came disguised in a throaty growl.

She clenched her jaw, hoping to keep that old hurt from reaching him.

He took her hand and flattened her palm to his chest. "I won't hurt you. Trust me."

She opened her mouth but couldn't speak.

"I'll take that as a maybe." One side of his mouth lifted into a sly smile.

Her head swam at his touch. With Helga gone, she could allow herself to taste want, defer her loneliness; Alec could wash so much sadness away, even if the dream wouldn't last. No, she couldn't, not with him. As much as she wanted—needed—to feel a man's arms around her, this one could damage her heart in an unspeakable way. The risk was too grave giving in to a charming, handsome Greek. Her throat tightened, and she swallowed.

Annalisse slipped her hand from his and drew back from no-return territory. "I'll get your shirt." She jumped for his polo at the end of the chaise and wobbled backward, grabbing the edge of the seat.

Alec caught her waist with one arm. "Gotcha." He eased her back onto the couch and pulled her closer again.

"Please don't trouble yourself." She struggled against him.

His lips thinned and his eyes flashed dangerously. "You're in my house, and whether I trouble myself or not, that's up to me." Then his expression softened. "My bedroom's at the end of the hall. If I know Helga, she's already turned down the covers for you."

"In a while." She curled up and wriggled her toes into the soft cushion. "Now, tell me about the ocean that surrounds Greece and what the people are like. I've imagined sugar sand shorelines and bouzouki playing in the distance." She closed her eyes and pulled up the afghan, taken back to settling in for one of her mother's bedtime stories, next to her sister. How she'd missed confiding in her younger sister.

"We both need sleep, and there's lots to do before we leave." He paused. "Aw, a few more minutes won't kill us."

She winced, and her eyes snapped open.

"Sorry. Poor choice of words. Relax."

Her last firm memory was his molasses-colored hair reflecting the glow of the fire as he talked, as she imagined him beside her, his exotic heat spooned against her back.

CHAPTER
FOURTEEN

Annalisse awoke to the snap of a log in the fireplace, more compact but just as grand as the hearth in Alec's formal room. No longer lying on the green chaise, she roamed her hand along a cool, silk coverlet on a king-size bed. She glanced at the empty pillow next to her and halfway expected to find Alec sleeping.

"Silly. If he asked me to trust him, he'd be a perfect gentleman," she mumbled.

As hard as she'd tried to convince herself that she didn't need him, he'd made himself indispensable since the gallery party. The tug-of-war between his tabloid reputation and the way he'd lifted her spirits was exhausting to work through. She reminded herself that every guy had weak areas—especially how to be kind once the novelty cooled from a relationship.

Alec as a veterinarian had poked holes in his desirability already.

Birds chirped outside, but no sounds came from inside the house. Alec's digital alarm clock informed her that it was Sunday morning, seven thirty. Much too early to shower and risk waking the household. She hadn't brought a change of clothes anyway.

At the foot of the bed, a neatly folded flannel gown smothered in yellow and pink roses awaited her. Too prim to have been left behind by an ex. How many women had slept in the suite and never left the room long enough for the barn tour? Touching the soft, brushed cotton, she caught the scent of Helga's fabric softener. Annalisse looked at herself in his cheval mirror at the foot of the bed, finding the same clothes she'd worn yesterday. Why expect anything else? Alec wouldn't take advantage of a sleepy, slightly drunken guest.

Scrunching the comforter between her fingers, she studied the black hide rugs scattered about and the profusion of live scheffleras in metal baskets near the windows. The plants stood as a silent tribute to the cattle remnants strewn along the floorboards.

Being in Alec's bed had such a languishing effect, ratcheting her pulse rate a tiny bit. He was so gentlemanly yet so hard-body hot it sent the war between her mind and body's needs into overtime. Staying with Alec alone risked exposure to a complete breakdown of will because her desire for him would eventually win the day.

The squealing of wheels not quite in sync approached the door, followed by three soft knocks.

"Annalisse." Alec opened the door a crack. "Are you decent? I have breakfast."

Giving her no time to answer, he entered like a butler, pushing a cart bearing a silver cloche and pitcher of orange juice.

The smoky aroma of bacon carried her back to weekends at the Walker farmhouse, with Kate at her cast-iron skillet and humming a country tune. On the next burner, sunny-side-up eggs popped, splattering grease on the stove, and in the oven, homemade biscuits made with fresh-churned butter slowly raised to amber puffs on the baking sheet.

"Hello?" He waved a hand in front of her face.

She smiled. "You've brought back sweet memories."

"Helga wasn't sure what you liked, so she punted. Eggs Benedict, fruit, hash browns, scrambled eggs—" He lifted the dome to reveal heaven on a platter.

"And bacon." She pored over the extravagant goodies on the menu. "Helga's an angel and a mind reader. I was ready to check under the cowhides for meat scraps. After Helga's late feast, I'm surprised I can think about food, but in your presence, I'm always hungry."

"Is that right?" He raised a brow.

She pursed her lips from the verbal slip-up. "Hungry for food, I mean."

"We'll see." Alec sat on the edge of the mattress. "Slide on over." He looked toward the door and said, "C'mon, Boris."

A flash of ginger color darted through the opening and hopped onto the covers. Boris bumped his head against Annalisse's arm while he shook the base of his tail in joy.

She dove into his fur and kissed his neck. "When did you get here, little man?" Annalisse rubbed his slick coat, warming both hands in the dense softness. "Chase is here then?"

"Sleeping. He texted me after we ate last night to say that he couldn't stop Boris from howling in the carrier. I didn't want to worry you, so I kept it to myself. Don't be angry at me. They got here about eleven."

"Poor Boris." She gave the cat a crumb of bacon, then turned to face Alec. "I must have been more pooped than I thought. How did I get into your room?"

He playfully flexed his muscles beneath the flannel shirt he wore. "I carried you."

Annalisse had been cradled against the expansive chest, his warmth had soaked into her skin—and she'd missed the whole thing.

"Eat up." Alec checked his watch. "We have to get moving if we're going to make the flight. I figure we have two hours on the road and at least two hours in security."

"Honey, lest we forget, I shot a man yesterday. It's unlikely that Mooney would allow us to go abroad. Besides, I don't have clothes or my passport."

"Mooney's kept me in the loop. So far, the shooter hasn't been admitted to an ER or clinic anywhere. Ballistics has your pistol, and they've verified your permit as well as our story. As far as the detective's concerned, he's treating your break-in as an armed burglary-slash-self-defense shooting. Neither you nor I are a suspect. Agent Norcross recommended we stay clear because—" Alec stopped short.

Annalisse's throat tightened. "Because why?"

"You'll"—he quickly amended—"*we'll* get in the way."

"Why am I not surprised? We didn't exactly hit it off when she interrogated me about Samantha's death. Shoot. My passport's probably stolen with the rest of my important papers."

"The gunman went through the nightstands and flipped your mattress but hadn't touched the dresser and closet when I showed up. I asked Chase to pick up your passport from the Bureau before the ride to the hospital."

She dropped her jaw. "You were planning to take me to Greece before the ambulance ride?"

"Planned, no. I'd considered it." He patted her leg. "With no evil intentions. Chase packed a few clothing articles for you before Mooney taped off the scene. We can hit the mall in Monticello on the way to JFK or shop in Athens to pick up anything else you need."

"I haven't said I'm going yet. Why not stay here?"

"New York's no good; you've been right about your intuition. I promise to be a better listener in the future." Alec ran a hand through his hair. "There's nothing like the feeling of being followed... and hunted. The shooter had connected the necklace to you because of your affiliation with Mom. It's entirely possible that he waited on a side street and followed us to the hospital. He could be outside right now—staking out the estate. We didn't exactly cover our tracks."

"Thanks for the visual," she said with a sigh. Those exact thoughts had run through her head yesterday. Stay in New York or go; their dilemma hadn't changed. "If that's true, won't we lead them to your parents? We're going to hide out at your island villa for how long?"

"Detective Mooney has contacted his friend. He's offered the family two fully vetted bodyguards until the danger's passed. Once they're set up, we'll fly them over. We should be fine on Crete until they arrive."

"I'm not family," Annalisse reminded him.

"Better together than apart."

Annalisse smothered a giggle. In the middle of a serious moment he could joke around with slogans. Another thing she liked about him.

"What?" He joined her levity with that killer smile of his.

"That's a good title for a country song."

"Man, you're so— Eat please," he said.

"That bears some explaining." She jabbed his side playfully. "I'm so what?"

Alec cleared his throat and folded his hands.

She knitted her lips together to suppress the impulse to smile, pleased with herself at tongue-tying him for a change.

"And the answer is…" She bumped her brows.

"You're such a fox, and you're haunting me, okay?"

His statement turned off the humor. She'd expected a joke, not honesty.

Alec grazed her cheek with a finger and pulled her chin around like he'd done the night before so she couldn't look away and hide her blush.

"Until the other night, we barely knew each other. How am I haunting you?" she asked.

"I've seen you every night—for months." He blinked twice, with pure longing etched on his face. "I'll bring in your suitcase. You'll find fresh towels in the cabinet above the sink. Help yourself to a shower."

Alec speared her with a wounded glance, then left the room.

In his dreams? She'd spent but a few minutes with him here and there at the gallery, and he'd never let on. Or maybe he had, but she'd been so engrossed in one project or another, she hadn't noticed. Her whole body tensed, and chill bumps raised small peaks over her skin. She'd lost precious time getting to know him if an overture from Alec had flown by. What else had she missed lately?

Annalisse's reflection in the huge framed mirror brought her back to the present. She groaned in disgust as she visualized unfamiliar dark smudges below her eyes and hollowed-out cheeks in a less than fetching chalky gray. In the past forty-eight hours, she'd transformed into a ghost of herself.

She stroked Boris's fur until he turned over on his back, waiting for a tummy rub. At least she still had his love.

"Do I tell Kate about our trip, Boris? Who knows how long we'll be gone?"

He purred louder, but her options were limited. If Kate knew about the shooting and Harry's death, she would insist they stay at the farm. Even if she could help, Annalisse wouldn't endanger the only relative who meant the world to her. She'd send a text before they boarded the flight and withhold everything about the real reason they were flying to Greece.

As much as it scared her to the marrow, she had to allow a chance for romance to bloom in order to function normally again. She wanted desperately to be needed by a man like Alec. How she'd get over her fear of flying was a different story.

CHAPTER

FIFTEEN

The Lufthansa lounge inside terminal one at JFK was nearly empty. On the big screen television near the bar, a comedian blathered sit-down humor to a lounge empty of travelers, perhaps because late-night departures weren't as popular with the public. Through gigantic windows, blue taxiway lights and bright rotating beacons blurred Annalisse's tired vision.

She sat by herself, drinking a flat Coke without ice, not that thirsty, just bored and apprehensive for the trip ahead of them. A clock bearing the Lufthansa logo had ticked off fifteen minutes since Alec had left her to check on their flight status. In his absence, their plane had already suffered a gate change and two boarding delays. Flying over the Atlantic overpowered any happy thoughts she could gather about visiting beautiful Greece because she was a chicken and scared to death of falling out of the sky.

She'd flown on very few commercial flights in her appraisal career. When asked to buy a plane ticket, her hyperventilation each time had given Harry pause. He'd kept her in-house for appraisals, with an occasional driving trip between appointments.

Her last travel disaster was a one-way flight from LaGuardia to Boston-Logan to meet a client with a set of rare William Wegman Weimaraners. She'd clutched her knees, on the verge of throwing up the entire time, praying the plane wouldn't hit the ground in a heap of twisted metal. During the rental car ride back to New York, she'd vowed never to fly again.

Until Alec wrangled her to the safety of Greece.

The most idiotic move for her acrophobia. Anyone who hated elevators as much as she did had no business sitting in the lounge, waiting for an aircraft departure.

An older couple in military green loungewear entered and sat at the corner bar, fondling and kissing like newlyweds. A man who had his arms covered with tattoos seated himself a few chairs away from them. His fingertips thrummed, and he glanced at the clock often, making Annalisse wonder if he'd missed his flight or waited to be called for a standby seat.

The greenish tattoo ink made it hard to decipher shapes and text from his distance away from her. From the size of his biceps and the skull chain he wore around his neck, she suspected he'd parked his Harley motorcycle in long term.

As a means to pass the time, Annalisse took her tablet from the tote and ran a general search on tattoos. Nikita's cross and the cat with bow tie and hat had to signify something to those men. She started with gang and prison tattoos since full-body art was popular with the incarcerated, and their tattoos were well documented for prison identification records.

Pages and pages of prisoners tatted with various symbols and phrases gave her plenty to consider. Four examples of common cat tattoos splashed the screen when she searched the description of what she'd noted on the art collector.

"These tattoos signify the personification of the thieves' fortune. The cat is one of the oldest symbols of the underworld," she mumbled quietly.

As she typed in the description of the Madonna and child tattoo, Alec rounded the corner, holding his carry-on bag.

"You could've left your carry-on with me, Alec. How's our flight doing?"

"The plane had mechanical problems, but they think it's fixed. According to Lufthansa, we should board in thirty minutes."

"Broken plane, lovely." Annalisse spun her pearl ring, the one that Kate had given her, around the middle finger.

A girl doused in Shalimar with dishwater-colored hair appeared from nowhere and asked Alec if he wanted drinks or food. He ordered his usual dirty martini, and the attendant hurried to the bar with wings on her feet.

Annalisse leaned over and whispered in his ear, "What's your secret? I've been here half an hour, and she didn't offer *me* anything." The loudspeakers crackled, and a woman announced in English, Greek, and then French that Athens flight 321 was boarding.

"That's us." Alec waved off the server when she returned with his drink. "Thanks, no time." He pulled out a tip and handed it to her. "Can't wait to see the folks, but I hate the long ride."

"You have no idea. I hope there's plenty of booze in first class," she said.

Alec studied her curiously and helped her from the chair.

The tattooed man with the skull around his neck also stood and strolled to the terminal without any luggage. He passed on Annalisse's left, making no eye contact with them or other travelers. On an overseas flight without a cabin bag felt odd to her.

By the time they'd reached the gate, the thrifty traveler had already handed his boarding pass to the attendant, but before heading down the jetway, he turned, exposing the tattoo on his neck: the scales of justice, uneven, minus Lady Justice.

All the tiny hairs on Annalisse's arms prickled. Lady Justice came from ancient Greek and Roman mythology and represented mortal or divine justice. She took a giant breath, handed her sweat-coated pass to the woman, and stepped onto the jet bridge.

Once she and Alec had stowed their bags on the Airbus A380 and buckled their seat belts, a female attendant clad in a sharp navy suit and wild gold scarf greeted them. The quiet blues in the cabin should have calmed Annalisse, but her pulse raced instead. She pushed against the headrest, counting to ten while squeezing the life out of the armrests.

"Hey." Alec covered her hand with his. "You're not afraid to fly are you?"

"Yep. You guessed it. Long trips in metal tubes aren't my forte."

Alec laced his fingers with hers, smiling as he did. "You should've told me. The takeoff is the hardest part. Squeeze my hand as hard as you want."

"We aren't taking off yet." She unlocked herself from him and jerked that hand into her lap.

He turned toward his window and, just as quickly, swiveled back in glaring eye contact. "Don't believe that garbage in the tabloids about me. It's salacious and false. I'm not that guy, and I'll prove it to you if you'll give me the chance."

The most honest response she could give him would be to admit her fears of commitment with certain men and how unworthy she felt in his presence. But this wasn't the time.

"Fine, don't answer," he grumbled. "If I've done something to offend you, I hope you'll eventually tell me, or this is going to be one crazy, long flight." Alec's gaze held hers firmly.

Annalisse had so many reasons to hold back, but none would be good enough or make sense to him. Alec grew up with the class and privilege most people aspired to. Her life had been fractured by family, then no family, and eventually living with distant relatives who toiled in manual labor. He wanted for nothing, and she couldn't move past that fact.

Annalisse closed her eyes to the texture of the seat straight ahead and the unoccupied seats to her right. Dozens of voices melded into garbled confusion, like the rear of the plane wasn't attached to the front, barring the occasional swish of shoes on the carpet as an attendant passed. She glanced down at her seat belt, then swiped both hands over the armrests as blotters.

"If you must know, I'm afraid. Gen's close to me, but you're a stranger. How I got myself here, on a plane that's making me physically ill, I'll never understand. It's been awful the past couple of days." Annalisse's lower lip trembled. "I don't want to break down, Alec, so let me catch up. You're the bright spot in everything since the party, so thank you for that."

Sympathy drifted into Alec's expression.

"The hesitancy I'm reading in your body language isn't about me then?" he asked.

"I didn't say that."

Turning to the cabin wall again, he calmly muttered, "Chicks. The more complex, the harder they are to figure out."

She laughed, coming so close to comforting him with a touch, in awe of the chiseled lines of his profile, but stopped herself from sending a mixed message. The real Alec was still a question mark to her. Many handsome guys were stuck on themselves, but this one, not as much as she'd imagined. Although he conveyed confidence, he'd placed the needs of others in front of his own.

"It might be nothing, but I've noticed a lot of strange tattoos on people lately. Mr. Chesnokov at Gen's gallery had a cat on his neck, and I think I saw him again in a picture in Peter's office. His arms are tatted up too. It might be the same man, but I didn't get a good look at his neck. Peter called the guy in his picture Nikita," she said.

"Two guys or one?"

"The man in the picture had a lot of ink on his arms. The suited guy we met at the gallery feels all wrong, but his face resembled Nikita's. He might be a relative."

While the last three hundred passengers settled into their seats on the upper deck, Annalisse recited what she'd uncovered in Peter's office, from Nikita's Madonna to the cats researched from the internet.

"Once we're airborne…" She slid an arm over her stomach to comfort the nervous shakes. "If I can concentrate and not think about the plane, I'll keep at it. From what I've found so far, the tattoo themes look to be thievery; acquiring wealth by stealing it."

"Or the tattoos could be a cultural thing," Alec said.

"Possibly, but I have a nagging suspicion that it's much more. I'm still baffled by how the necklace ended up in Gen's hands. Your dad, I know, but there's a gap—information is definitely missing."

Softly he covered her hand with his in a light touch, as if he couldn't get too comfortable, in case she pulled back.

"Sleuthing is your calling. When you're thinking through evidence, your cheeks bloom a pretty shade of pink." He smiled and shifted closer. "I know you're worried, but we'll figure this out."

"How can you be sure?"

"The bad guys are in New York, and we will be an ocean away in Greece," he assured her.

"They won't stop that easily."

"I didn't say they would. Our time on Crete will give us a chance to regroup and decide how to deal with the necklaces, plural. And Mom should have a say." Alec lifted his phone and read a text. "Mooney. Our shooter came out of a clinic in Bushwick, but he escaped being picked up."

"Brooklyn?"

Alec checked the text again. "He said he'll be in touch."

"Ask Mooney to run a background on Chesnokov and Nikita. We don't have any first names. Chesnokov wanted something upstairs in the gallery and vamoosed in a hurry when the cops came in." Annalisse shoved an image of Samantha back into the recesses of her mind. "Let's talk about the necklace you took out of the gallery."

Alec stiffened and avoided her question with a one-shouldered shrug.

"You left it at the estate, right?" she asked.

"I couldn't."

Her eyes widened, and a weight dropped on her chest. "It's with us?" Staring straight ahead, she sank backward. "I thought if we were followed to Brookehaven, maybe they'd stop the pursuit and…" She pressed fingertip perspiration into her jeans and dug her nails in.

"Break in and steal it?" he asked.

"Leave us alone. The necklace is goading us—just daring us to do the wrong thing. I know it's selfish because Chase and Helga are there, and I wouldn't want anything terrible to happen to anyone, but evil hangs over us." She rubbed her temples. "And my head hurts—is it possible to get a bottle of water?"

"I'll flag someone down."

"I hope you're wrong about being followed or watched. When we land, you *have* to call Chase. Warn them not to answer the door unless Helga knows them and to watch for unusual cars parked near the house," she said.

"Already have. Chase knows his way around security. I quizzed him about his training and picked his brain over the safes he'd installed at Mom's. I've also called the security company Mooney recommended. They're sending over armed reinforcements, so we're covered in that department. Chase will stay at the estate until we get back, and he's promised not to allow Helga to leave the house alone. Anyway, we're probably the targets, not them."

"Nothing like having a bull's-eye painted on my big, wide backside," she said.

His tempting mouth crooked.

"Go ahead. Say it." Annalisse laughed, fumbling with her seat belt as she realized she'd given carte blanche to the guy who liked dirty things.

"I'll skate on quicksand when I'm sure you'll drag me out," was his answer.

Glancing toward the center aisle, she glued her eyes to the carpet so that he wouldn't catch the flush traveling from throat to cheeks. She'd bruised his ego badly and presumed a lot from what she'd read about Alec in published rumor rags. The tabloids were filled with flamboyant gossip to sell papers, not print the truth. She *was* attracted to Alec; the attraction was stronger than with any man before him. What a magnificent job she'd done—stonewalling the potential for an awesome relationship with a hot celebrity most women could only fantasize about. She'd leave out the *stonewall* part when she texted her aunt.

"Shoot, I forgot." She reached into her tote stowed beneath the seat ahead.

"Whatever it is, we'll pick it up in Greece."

"I'm supposed to drop Kate a note, or she'll worry. Do I still have time before we take off?"

"They've already closed the doors and are about to tell us to turn devices off. Later, you'll be able to plug into the internet and send her an email."

"Okay. She's going to fret about the flight and my phobias though."

But deep down, Kate's heart would somersault when she found out Annalisse was traveling with Alec.

Being homeless and unemployed was unthinkable, but at the moment, she was both. Annalisse had planned to phone gallery contacts in Midtown and New Jersey next week, but Generosa's suggestion at the gallery stopped her. The last time she'd taken a vacation was sheepshearing at the farm two Marches ago. Three days of backbreaking shearing, hoof trimming, and bagging wool in raging temperatures. Some vacation.

Her today world included Alec as a dazzling distraction, clouding her thoughts when they were in so much trouble. Annalisse had to knuckle down and concentrate on how to keep Generosa—and everyone enveloped by the necklace—safe. With Samantha, Annalisse had lost the luxury of time. And Samantha's boyfriend, Ryan Petrov, fit the suspect narrative with her friend as well. His flimsy alibi made him a person of interest but not enough to hold him in custody, according to Agent Norcross. His Russian last name was a concern but no more than a whole army of tattoo-covered men around Annalisse lately.

"Won't your aunt feel better if she knows you're with me?" Alec asked.

"That's a loaded question. If Kate knew your mother, she might." She laughed.

"You don't give in that easily, do you?" he asked.

"Convince me. Lord knows, I want you to."

Giving her hand a squeeze, he leaned over and whispered, "I accept your challenge." His face was close to her cheek, suspended there, lips parted.

Annalisse turned to him, feeling the heat of his breath on her skin. Little separated her from bliss. She gripped the armrests and waited for him to move.

"Babe," Alec grazed his lips against her cheekbone. "When you're totally ready and not before."

Like an intoxicant, his scent made her somewhat drunk. She wanted to imagine what he'd do to her behind closed doors but stopped the stream in its tracks. Not with him so close and ten hours in front of them. Annalisse tucked those thoughts away and withdrew a notepad and pen from a seat back pocket. She wrote: *Stowed the necklace in luggage?*

She handed the pad and pen to him.

He shook his head and scribbled: *Not in the checked bags. Where?* she asked him.

My carry-on.

A male attendant decked out in a deflated yellow life vest stood at the front of the cabin. Annalisse followed his animated emergency how-to instructions on life vests, exits, and seat floatation devices, but little registered. When the well-practiced speech ended, she squirmed deeper into the seat. The necklace in the carry-on compartment added extra weight to her flight fears.

Annalisse shuddered as the jet turbines whined for take-off. When the brakes released, the aircraft tires methodically bumped over the runway. She gripped the seat, and Alec covered his fingers with hers. The plane's nose pitched skyward, and g-forces pushed her into the cushions.

CHAPTER

SIXTEEN

Annalisse's calves throbbed on the climb up the hill to the Zavos villa, past the dozens of tiny hilltop homes along the jagged island seascape of Crete. Bougainvillea bushes shook paperlike blossoms at her, all purple and red with tiny white stamens. Standing beside Alec, she turned her face to the breeze and raised her sunglasses against the ocean's glare. One whiff of their sweet perfume mingled with sea brine was enough to recharge her. She'd had a workout on the trek to Alec's family villa but welcomed the breathlessness and sore muscles just for the view. For a few days anyway, they'd relax in Sitia's surf and block out the danger lurking back home.

Alec knocked on the cobalt-colored door of the villa and paused; the only sounds around them were breakers tumbling in succession onto the shore.

"Huh. I didn't expect a ghost town at nine in the morning." He swiveled and stared at the waves. "Ah. The yacht's not in port. They're sailing." He turned the knob, and the door gave way.

"Unlocked? That's not like Gen."

"It's a close-knit community. No one worries. We'll make sure the doors are locked and windows are secured from now on. They probably left us a note inside. Luciana must be shopping." He ushered her in ahead of him. "After you."

Annalisse wondered who Luciana was, but herbal petals of yellow chrysanthemums and a medicinal smell of rosemary sprigs sucked her into the bright living area. Right away, the difference between the villa's modern surroundings and the Zavos Gallery bombarded her. The villa decorator bore no resemblance to the woman with an appetite for history, as if two separate individuals had decorated, and this one intended to have a place of serenity.

Annalisse twirled a three-sixty. "Cool. So apropos for a beach house. Refreshing and lovely, just like your mom."

"I wasn't sure that you'd like it with your love of antiques. I'll get our bags. Crash anywhere you'd like."

The room had an understated color palette of white on off-white with touches of blue and yellow. Overstuffed linen sofas and chaises were scattered around the nubby carpet. Driftwood shapes with starfish and giant clamshells—simple sculptures on top of tables and glass counters. Through the bay windows facing the ocean, fishing boats anchored in turquoise water bobbed visibly as waves licked at the shoreline and deposited their foam in perfect time with a distant call of seabirds. Pale blue sheers billowed from windows without screens to hinder the stunning view. Simply gorgeous.

A winded Alec wiped his feet on the mat and shifted the bags through the entrance, largest first. "That was quite a haul. Your suitcase is heavier than it looks. You sure you didn't buy out the entire boutique?"

"Courtesy of the awesome use of your credit card. Thank you." She meshed the slick sheers between her fingers and pulled them aside, refreshed by the breeze. Annalisse kicked off her shoes, removed her sunglasses, and sank into a lounge as soft as a marshmallow. A conspicuous sheet of parchment in a shade of brilliant daffodil rested on the side table. "My legs are Jell-O." She leaned over for a view of the ornate handwriting and immediately recognized the flourish. "Here's Gen's note."

Alec closed the door and wandered to the table. One cheek dimpled, and he curved his lips, nodding. "It's a setup from the matchmaker. She wanted our first day in Greece to be special, so they're staying on the boat till tomorrow. She sent our housemaid on a short trip too. They want us to sail with them tomorrow. Would you like to go?"

She chuckled at his wiggling eyebrow and his arms imitating waves. Her impression of his mother's note hadn't come across as matchmaking. On the contrary, it was sweet; so much like her friend to let them chill out in the villa after the long flight. Depending on how much Alec had told his mother about the brownstone or the incident with Peter, Generosa would look for ways to take their minds somewhere else.

"I've never sailed before. Show me the rest of the house before I collapse and get lost in the pillows." She held out her hand. "I may need help digging out."

He gave her the gentlest of tugs, taking a step closer in the process. "You are obscenely irresistible."

Her fingers trembled in his. Alec's upper lip had beaded with sweat, and a sexy light beard had deepened his aristocratic features.

She sank deeper into her fantasy, and a warm sensation curled throughout her chest and radiated downward.

His fixed stare drew her to his mouth like a magnet.

She wanted what he offered and leaned in.

An odd chime rang three times and surprised her back to reality. Annalisse saw disappointment on his face.

"I set that ring for Chase, so I'd better get it. I have an international calling plan and wasn't sure that you had one."

"It's one in the morning in New York." Her chest heaved. "What's wrong now?"

Alec swiped his phone. "Hey, Chase; you're on speaker. We just got to the house. Are things good there?"

"Yeah. Other than Helga taking a couple of calls on the house phone, no trespassers, so we're cool."

"Who called the estate?" Alec asked.

"Ya got me. I listened until I realized she was just yakking with one of her friends. Ladies gossip; you know how it goes."

Annalisse recalled how often Chase accused women of being snoops by nature. Most of the men she'd come in contact with in her job were the worst gossips ever, Chase included.

"How's Boris?" she asked.

"Spoiled as ever. Helga's feeding him leftovers as treats, so he'll be royally messed up by the time you get back." He laughed. "Did you check email yet? I couldn't sleep until I talked to you."

"Not a note from Peter, I hope."

"No. I forwarded a message from Agent Norcross in case she didn't copy you. They've turned up something on Samantha."

Alec motioned her to the sofa, then sat on the arm.

"Fill us in." Her feet wouldn't move.

"They found a thong stuck in the brush a half mile from the field where Samantha was found. A female jogger noticed it at shoulder height, stuck in some vines. She got scared, took a picture, and turned it in to the Orange County cops. Ryan verified it had belonged to Samantha."

"Ryan? He could've planted it to get the heat off. They checked those woods weeks ago," Annalisse said.

"Norcross's email said the DNA confirms it. There was additional DNA evidence though. They found blood other than hers."

Alec gave her arm a gentle squeeze. "Please sit before you fall down."

Landing on the lemony cushions, she crossed her legs at the knee. "The blood's Ryan's, right? They tested it, and what? Chase, is it his?" She bounced her calf, kicking her toe in the air.

"Not her boyfriend's. He's type O and this blood is AB negative. Petrov's off the hook for now."

A cold shiver coursed from her low back to the base of her neck. "I was so sure he'd killed her." She swiveled toward Alec.

"Since when?" Alec slid to the couch, pleading further. "Why him?"

"Ryan was cruel. It broke my heart when she stayed with him," Annalisse said.

There were so many tearful conversations with Samantha during her two years with Petrov. Her friend had endured his physical abuse and threats to euthanize her golden retriever. Annalisse had offered Samantha and her dog sanctuary at the brownstone on several occasions, much to Boris's distaste. As hard as those moments were, she wished she could do them over—have another chance to convince her friend that Ryan was no good. Another opportunity to change Samantha's fate.

"Look at the email after some rest. You sound dog-tired. I'll check in tomorrow. Have fun and don't worry about us. Eat a ton of seafood for me, Anna. *Ciao*."

They were still for a moment before she said, "I'm dumbfounded."

"I can see that," Alec said.

"Whoever killed her probably did it for the bracelet, which is still missing, by the way. But if Ryan's involved, I couldn't figure in the jewelry, other than its melt value. I assumed that he had motive to finally finish her off because they fought so much, but the bracelet part always perplexed me. Ryan could have taken it in a fit of rage, but why? Unless he'd planned to divert attention from himself by making it look like a burglary gone out of control. If that were so, why leave her rings behind?" Annalisse put her head in her hands and closed her eyes. "We know less now than we did weeks ago."

Alec's thumb gently massaged the base of her neck. "I know that losing your friend is a terrible thing to deal with."

"They had a rotten history, Samantha and Ryan. She came over bruised and cut up a lot, but she felt trapped that he'd hurt her worse if she left him."

"I'm sorry," he said with a sigh.

"Every inch of me believes Samantha was murdered by the same person who wants Gen's necklace. The bracelet hasn't turned up in New York or Jersey pawnshops. Whoever has it hasn't sold it in the States that we know of."

"Mom has refused to talk about the day you found your friend. Was she really buried?"

Annalisse sighed. "Yes, tortured first, then buried. Whoever—whatever maniac did that to her spent hours at the scene. The medical examiner said most of her wounds were sustained while she was alive, and finally, strangulation before decapitation." She shivered, dropping her head toward her lap.

Alec patted a spot on his shoulder. "Lean back. You're shaking so hard the sofa's moving."

"Not against your sore shoulder." She laughed feebly and pulled her legs up to the cushion beneath her, resting her head against the crook of his arm. She wanted the weight of the past twelve hours to dissipate, Alec's body felt comfortable and right.

"The authorities will find your friend's killer, and we'll get to the bottom of who's terrorizing us."

"Yeah, but they're way ahead. We have what they want, and they already know who we are."

CHAPTER

SEVENTEEN

The sweet aroma of lavender filled Alec's nostrils, while something soft yet prickly tickled his face. He opened one eye to find Annalisse resting against the crook of his arm. Visions of the lavender fields of Provence roamed his thoughts as he twiddled the dark strands of her thick, fragrant hair. He winced at the pain radiating from the stitches mending his gunshot wound. They'd napped in the corner of the sofa for what felt like hours, but he didn't care. She was with him, touching him, in a restful, deep slumber.

Alec kissed the top of her head and tilted backward to straighten his neck and shift himself to a different angle. From where the ballooning curtains floated, an odor of rotten fish reminded him of death from the sea—times ten.

Carefully sliding Annalisse so he wouldn't wake her, he stood and headed toward the windows to find the source of the foul air.

"Where are you going?" Annalisse sat up, rubbing her eyes. "How long were we out? Ugh. What's that smell?"

"Could be a beached monk seal," he said. "We've gotta shut the windows." He cursed himself for being lax about their safety. Literally anyone could've walked in while they slept. Alec's heart jolted when he got to the armchair. "What's this?"

He reached down and picked up a spiral conch shell with a sheet of paper underneath.

"Remind me to never try conch." She waved a hand beneath her nose. "How did *that* get in here?"

"Stinks, I know." He read the one-word note. "Thieves. It says *thieves*." In a quick step to the door, Alec unzipped the smallest piece of luggage and found the purple satchel. "I left everything open while we dozed, but the necklace is safe."

He rolled the carry-on into the first bedroom and came back to find Annalisse fidgeting with her phone, the note in her hand. Beautifully tousled with a look of bewilderment, she could bring a man to his knees in her current state. His fingers itched to bury themselves in the silky tresses when—if—they got that far on this trip.

"The note's in English," she said, barely audible.

"This is hardly how I imagined our first day on the island. I planned to take you to a great Mediterranean restaurant for their seafood specialty, but shellfish might have to wait for another occasion." Alec smiled, expecting a zinger comeback, but she let out a pitiful sigh instead.

"You know what the note means, don't you?" She turned toward the window as a large wave curled and crashed onto the shore.

"We do Italian?" he asked.

Annalisse put her hands on her hips, flashing green eyes at him. "We haven't escaped anything by coming here."

"I'm sure we can find a place that serves Greek lamb."

"Seriously?" She smacked her forehead flat-handed. "Are we still talking about food? We have no firearms and no way to defend ourselves if need be. Did you check outside for the person who left the shell?"

They weren't without weapons. Unbeknownst to her, his second Glock lay in a drawer near the TV a few feet from her. It had to stay behind when he'd returned to the States via the airlines on his last trip overseas. If he'd had a pistol with him at Annalisse's brownstone, their situation might have ended differently, though not necessarily better.

He rolled his shoulder and winced as the clock on the side table chimed three. "I'll look outside in a minute. Follow me."

"Where?"

He led her into his mother's bright white kitchen. Pulling out a painted chair for her, he took one at the opposite end of the table.

"Let's calmly think this through." Alec folded his hands and laid them on the glazed oak table, committing her heart-shaped face and sensual mouth to memory. "I'll give Mooney an update, then wait for him to advise us."

"Alec, we aren't safe anywhere."

He couldn't ignore her quaking voice and how she bit her lower lip when she was unsure.

"Do you think the guy who shot you followed us here?" she asked him.

"What if there's someone else who's always known we had the necklace?" Alec pursed his lips. "Dad gave it to her a while ago."

Annalisse lifted her nose and sniffed. "That nasty shell. The room needs a serious airing out." She glanced down the hall. "How many bedrooms are here?"

"Three."

She wrapped a few strands of hair around her index finger and twisted it nervously. Desire filled her eyes and just as quickly disappeared. Fleeting curiosity. The same light in her he'd discovered in the drawing room in front of the fire, on the edge of his bed, and again on the plane. A physical attraction she went out of her way to hide from him.

"The lady's disappointed," he said.

"Three's a good number."

"That depends on how many get used." He tilted his head, smothering something else he'd preferred to say.

"Do you have a notepad?"

Alec noticed one attached to the refrigerator, but before he gave it to her, he scribbled: *A strange time to make a grocery list.* He slid the pad and pencil across the table.

Annalisse wrote: *Could this house be bugged?*

He wrinkled his nose at her offbeat question, then considered it. Nothing was an impossibility. He reached across and wrote back: *It's possible.*

Put the necklace in a safe. Now.

Alec scraped his chair on the tile and jumped up.

"Wait!" Annalisse beckoned him to her side, then pointed to the notepad where she'd written: *What about hidden cameras?*

"Whoa, food deprivation is weirding us out," he said aloud.

Lock it up, and let's go outside.

Annalisse pushed her chair from the table and stopped short.

Alec read while she scrawled a short paragraph about the necklace, then he nodded. "There's sentimental value. Mom won't part with anything Dad's given her."

"Even if it kills her?" she asked.

"Mom's *una testa dura.*"

Annalisse questioned his Italian with thoughtful eyes, begging for a translation.

"She's hardheaded. But yeah, even if she thought it might kill her."

CHAPTER

EIGHTEEN

"I'm as stuffed as the braciole we polished off at the restaurant. Why didn't you save me from my third helping?" Annalisse stood in front of the full-length cheval mirror and rubbed her stomach bump that hadn't been there before their Greek-Italian meal.

"I wouldn't dare get between you and your fork." Alec studied her in the mirror's reflection. "My mother would be proud. She makes her own mean version of flank steak, pro-sciutto, and cheese."

"No more food talk please." She grimaced, feeling dessert rise in her throat. "I can't remember the last time I felt this miserable after dinner. We've been sitting on hard chairs for two hours, and I should move around, but my feet are killing me." Annalisse slipped off her flats and crept to the recliner, dropping slowly into it. "Ah." She pushed into the soft leather that carried a peppery scent different from Alec's.

"How about a romantic stroll on the beach?" he asked.

"Not unless you have a burning desire to see my meal a second time." Annalisse glanced at the still-packed pair of suitcases. The clothes inside were no doubt heavily creased. "When I'm with you, I'm changed. Normally, I would've un-packed hours ago."

Alec drew her away from normalcy. From planning every moment and contemplating her future in such intricate detail she couldn't possibly make a mistake, to winging it hour by hour. Her everyday habits hadn't made any difference when it came to him. She'd allowed Alec to take the lead away from her since Harry's death. In fact, after losing two people close to her and resigning from Westinn, she'd regressed to an awful place of insecurity, not unlike how she'd felt when she came to live on the farm with Aunt Kate and Uncle Ted in her teens.

Alec's two-toned whistle and sweeping arm wave jarred her from the memories.

"Where'd you go?" He knelt on one knee in front of her. His patient gaze was so mesmerizing, all she could do was stare into the steel abyss.

He looked like a stereotypical guy about to propose on one knee. Crushing the vision, Annalisse squished the pillowed armrests and attempted to stand.

Alec grabbed her wrist. "Stay here."

"I need a hot bath, badly. I should unpack too."

"Ever do anything you shouldn't?" His strained jaw muscles twitched to the rhythm of her own.

Alec rose and helped her out of the chair but stayed glued to his spot on the carpet.

Toe to toe, she swam in his sinful gaze. His lashes were dark and curled at the ends, shadowing his eyelids. Their lips were inches apart.

Annalisse waited for him to shift aside so that she could pass, but instead, his immobile body dared her to touch him. A tremor came from nowhere, filling her with a devastating need for human contact. She drew her eyes to the button details of his shirt, wanting to unbutton and let herself go.

Alec smoothed her hair behind an ear, then grazed his lips near the lobe and whispered, "When I'm with you, I forget to breathe."

"That can be a problem." She'd experienced the same difficulty but refused to admit it.

"Occasionally."

His playfulness blew her composure out to the sea. If she allowed his charms to enter her heart, she'd be happy for a little while at least. With one hand caressing his rough cheek, she gave way to tension-releasing laughter.

"What am I going to do with you?" she asked him with the most genuine smile she could summon.

"Anything you'd like." He returned her repartee. "For the lady's enjoyment, you'll find a nice, full bath down the hall, in the second room on your right. I'll wheel in your suitcase in the meantime. When you're done, I'll take a shower in the master." He paused. "Unless you'd like to conserve water and share yours."

"In your dreams, hon." She repositioned one of the sweaty, dark curls stuck to his forehead.

"Annalisse, you're already there." He kissed her hand and added, "Go, please. Before I change my mind and jump in first."

Refreshed from her shower and dressed in the green linen sheath she'd picked up in the Athens boutique, Annalisse wandered the bedroom's perimeter. The queen-size bed featured chintz pillows with a Greek key design in navy and white, drawing her fingertips to trace the interlocking spirals in the fabric. Nightstand lamps with tiny shades on bronze rods and a pole lamp with the same Greek emblem stood in the corners. Instead of a headboard, white canopy sheers were attached to the wall behind the bed in an ultrafeminine touch she'd viewed in designer-home magazines.

Annalisse opened the door and poked her head out when Frank Sinatra's voice launched into his rendition of "All the Way" from down the hall. She found it unique that a guy Alec's age would listen to the oldies of her parents' era.

"Your turn," she shouted over the music. "The shower's free. Alec?"

The master bedroom door clicked open, and he walked out in an unwrinkled pair of chinos and a T-shirt. His hypnotic sandalwood scent that drove her crazy drifted down the hall almost immediately. A wonderful guy like Alec was close enough to reach for—right in front of her—no waiting.

"Shower's free," she repeated.

"When I heard the water shut off, I got in." He nodded, giving her the once-over, spending a tad too much time on her bare legs. "I wasn't sure about the dress on the rack, but on you, that color is dazzling. I approve."

Strangling a sassy comment, Annalisse reminded herself who'd paid for the awesome spree in the boutique. A luxury she'd rarely afforded herself in New York on her meager Westinn salary. Past salary. She'd let him *approve* and compliment her looks anytime.

Nelson Riddle's orchestra and Sinatra's familiar croon brought goose pimples racing up both arms. Without warning, her throat tightened, and her eyes blurred with tears. Family scenes in her past had a way of making her long for the old days.

"Sinatra's voice is like no other. My dad was a fan of Ol' Blue Eyes." Her father used to hum this tune as he read the morning edition of the *Wall Street Journal*. "You're full of surprises. I didn't peg you for an oldies sort of guy." She laughed, swiping a tear. "Aunt Kate dragged me to an Arthur Murray studio for dance lessons when I graduated from high school. She'd insisted that I would get a boy to notice me if I could dance the foxtrot."

"Notice you? How could they miss you? Ready for that stroll on the beach?" He gestured toward the quiet roll of the surf against the sand. "We have it all to ourselves."

"Perfect. But let me hear the rest of this song first," she said.

"I'll do you one better. Let's go out on the veranda, and I'll crank the speakers outside. It's one of Mom's CDs. Hope you're just as cool with Mel Torme and Bobby Darin; they're up next."

Annalisse found herself tapping a toe to the beat, taken back to an earlier time when the Drury household was the only home she knew.

Alec stopped at the sofa table, pulled out a side drawer, then untucked his shirt. In one quick movement, he slid a black Glock down the back of his waistband.

"You *do* have a weapon after all." Annalisse twirled her pearl ring while the pistol disappeared beneath his shirttail. She took a deep breath in relief. "I feel better."

"Good. It's time that I get back into the habit. Me and this Glock have been friends for years, especially after Dad and I were robbed on the Athens Metro. We haven't taken it since. At the time, neither of us were armed; it hadn't crossed our minds. The economy stunk back then, and with the explosion of Syrian migration, it's worse now." He fluffed his shirt around his waist. "People may own shotguns on the mainland, but the Greek government's not hot on its citizens carrying pistols. There are heavy background checks involved, and thankfully, Dad has some pull."

"I didn't know that," she said.

Alec tapped his waistband. "This goes with me everywhere except the boat since Dad has a sweet little nickel-plated snub nose he keeps on the yacht. The Glock can't be taken on airline flights since 9/11."

"That's why you didn't have the Glock with you in New York."

"The last time I came to Greece, I flew commercial. Due to TSA searches, I won't put it in the checked baggage ever."

She peered through the sliding door to the veranda. "The moonlight's dancing on the calmest ocean. Manhattan lights, take a number." Annalisse tugged at the glass slider and stepped onto the slats of the creaky porch, allowing the salt air currents to curve around her. "Brr. Cooler than I thought."

Alec tapped her shoulder and held up an open-weave sweater.

"Mind reader." Annalisse shuffled into the armholes, and the chill subsided. "That's just enough. Thank you." She leaned on the wrought iron rail, allowing the full moon to work its magic. "What a beautiful view."

"Ever lie in the sand while a wave washes over your body?" he whispered from behind.

His warm breath and sexy reference sent a shudder through her.

"It's intensely pleasurable." Alec spun her around by the waist and took her hand. "I know of an instant warmer-upper. Show me how good you are."

"Excuse me?"

He placed her squarely in front of him, his arms outstretched in ballroom beginning stance. "Mom taught me the foxtrot. Dance with me."

"I thought men like you didn't exist."

"Wanna bet?" he asked.

Before she could blink, Alec swept her across the painted boards while Frank sang "You Go to My Head."

Annalisse's mind filled with poignant memories of her parents' laughter at taped television reruns of *The Frank Sinatra Show* from the 1950s. The last line of his show when Sinatra said "May you live to be a hundred, and may the last voice you hear be mine" was one of her favorite expressions growing up.

At the violin crescendo and Frank's fading voice, Alec leaned into the small gap between them and let out a theatrical growl. "Nice fit." He pressed her against him so tightly she grew aware of every hard and soft spot on his body. He caressed her hair and said, "You're light on your feet."

Her imagination ran an image of Alec touching her, tasting her. Everywhere.

Annalisse's airway clogged with something similar to a spider's web, and she pulled back, avoiding his eyes. The coincidence of his choice of music matching her childhood days in Kensington confused her.

"How did you know Sinatra's music had special meaning for me? It's like you can see right into my past."

"ESP." He grinned and lifted her chin. "I didn't know, but I want to. Your parents must be a lot like mine."

She broke away from him. "How?"

"They produced a smart, sexy woman who makes me feel alive." He paused. "You hold your own under tough circumstances, and you're moral and caring with the same old-fashioned values I have." He fidgeted with his collar. "Mom suggested that I take you out months ago. I'm sorry that I dismissed the idea." He gently tugged her against his chest, and his voice softened. "She also mentioned that you were an honest-to-goodness angel. No one could be that—"

"What? Just because your mother likes me, I can't be real?" Annalisse had no idea Gen had praised her like that. She broke out of his arms and dropped into a chaise. "Sit, Alec. There are things about me that you should know." She waited for him to take a chair a few feet away and said, "I'm virtually alone. Well, almost."

"No, you're not. I'm here." He smiled, then sobered when she didn't smile back.

Annalisse folded both hands and bowed her head, rewording her jumbled thoughts so as not to sound too pathetic.

"Annalisse, what's wrong?"

"My father *used* to listen to Sinatra."

"Okay, so his taste in music's changed."

"Not that." She swallowed. "My parents are dead, Alec. So is my sister, and I'm to blame."

Alec got up, and in wide strides across the porch, he sat beside her. "Oh, babe, I had no idea. How long ago?" He wrapped her in the cocoon of his arm, taking the edge off the chilly remembrance.

"Fifteen years this past August."

"I'm so sorry. Here I am jabbering on about—"

"I should've told you before."

"Are there other siblings?"

"No. Just me and Mom's sister, Kate, with the farm. Kate has two adult children who live in other states."

A minute of strained silence passed, then Alec slid his arm from her waist and grabbed the cushion.

"Why are you to blame?" he asked.

"We lived in a nice part of Brooklyn where Dad was a dentist." She drew a haggard breath. "It was one of those freakish, horrible accidents that happen to other people. A gas main exploded, wiping out neighborhood homes. Eleven people died in the fires burning for days. Mom, Dad, and Ariel were inside our house, and I was at Walker Farm, playing. If I hadn't gone to the farm—" She choked on a sob and bent in half, holding herself with both arms.

"We don't have to talk about it."

Annalisse rocked, trying to block all thoughts except Alec. He was such a good listener. Genuine too, as if he truly wanted to hear from the space case next to him.

"I begged them to come with me to the farm that day, but I didn't try hard enough. My love for animals always came first. I should've been there." She closed her eyes and squeezed back the tears.

"Then you wouldn't be here on this pretty evening." Alec wiped the drop trailing down her chin with his thumb. "I'll take you inside."

She reached for his leg. "Not yet. The past can't be changed, but we have some say in what happens now."

"Yes. As long as we're in possession of the horses, we have to be smart. I spoke to Mooney when you were in the shower," he said.

"And?"

"The gunman from your townhouse has vanished."

"You think he's here, don't you?" She felt a pang shoot through her chest.

"No, I don't. Not yet. Unless he was on our plane…"

"Then who wrote that note?"

He shrugged. "Camo guy meant business. A transition from Russian notes in the gallery to ransacking and shooting, then back to an English note doesn't jibe with me. When Mom gets here, we'll convince her to turn the necklace over to the cops."

"It's too late, Alec. Someone on this island believes we either have the Mushasha jewel or stole it. Calling us thieves isn't a prank, not when we understand the reference." She shivered, tugging at her sleeves. "I regret keeping the whole truth from Mooney. Family, friends, those we can't go a day without, are who matter most."

"The detective talked to his partner, and he's secured one guard, Steve Jacobs, as security for us. As soon as he can arrange with the Greek government for firearms, he'll be on his way to Crete in the company jet."

Annalisse stood, stretched, and yawned. "Jet lag has me in its clutches. I could sleep through tomorrow afternoon. This is perfect sleeping weather." Her eyelids were heavy. "Would you mind if I grabbed a blanket and sat here for a while?"

"You're worried about sleeping inside?" he asked.

Her laughter was tinged with unease. "No kidding. Now all we have to do is stay alive long enough to get the bodyguard here. Is the guy any good?"

"Let's hope we don't have to find out."

CHAPTER
NINETEEN

Alec in the villa kitchen piling slices of french toast high on a platter—the view floored Annalisse. She'd imagined bachelors who had housekeepers never made their own breakfasts, but Alec was at home in front of the stove. Cinnamon and the sweet smell of vanilla on golden, egg-battered bread filled the small space with nirvana. What a catch he'd make for someone of his tastes who wasn't adept at being domestic.

"I hope you're hungry. Bacon's next on the menu." Alec bumped his brows with intimate knowledge. She'd inhaled Helga's breakfast in his suite like it was her last meal, although Boris helped a little.

"You're spoiling me. Why didn't you wake me earlier so I could help you? I can't believe I slept on the veranda all night." Waking to the fuzzy warmth of the blanket and quiet slosh of the waves at daybreak was a marvelous feeling. "What time did you put the blanket over me?"

"I dozed off myself. Around midnight, I think." He laid strips of thick bacon into a skillet, wincing at the pop and splatter of grease on his shirt and arm.

Crisping pork slices. She tasted the smoky goodness on her tongue, and her mouth watered as she watched Alec's practiced fingers maneuver his spatula.

"Where'd you sleep?" she asked him.

Alec's lips curved into a lecherous smirk. The gleam in his eyes, followed by the waggle of brows, unnerved her.

"With me? No way."

Her lounge wasn't large enough for both of them comfortably. It would've been a snug fit, and she would've noticed his body pressed against hers, his arm draped over her as if it belonged there. That she would've remembered.

Annalisse gripped the table leg and took a swig of lukewarm coffee. "You went to bed, right?"

"I slept."

She squeezed the table ledge. "I got that part."

"Outside."

"Beach or someplace else?" she asked.

"Orange or grapefruit juice?"

Why play coy with her? Annalisse closed her eyes to recall the last moments on the chaise before she fell asleep. Cool winds and Mel Torme in the background. Alec's mellow voice that dripped sensuality on each syllable. A tingle pulled up the stubble on her bare legs, and she rubbed the chill from her calf, glancing down at the shift she wore after her shower. She lightly passed her hands over her hips, skimming the crisscross grain of the fabric. Had he done the same with his hands last night?

Alec's laughter echoed off the walls. "Don't you remember?"

Unspoken words were logjammed in her racing mind. She had to look foolish, rubbing herself down in front of him. "Did you slip something in my drink at dinner?"

Alec turned off the burners and calmly sat in the chair next to her.

"Pretty lady, you have to learn to trust me." He did that tongue-against-the-roof-of-his-mouth thing like his mother and folded his hands on the table. "No. I would never slip a mickey in your drink. You faded after our talk. Remember? Mooney's guy? I considered waking you, but you looked so peaceful, I couldn't. Bathed in moonlight—you're a treat to behold; such a fox." His eyes lit up briefly, then he blinked.

"A cute term I haven't heard in a while." She managed a half smile for him. "Thank you for leaving me there." She swiveled toward footsteps in the hall and shifted her eyes on him. "Who's here?"

A sun-kissed Generosa in bright culottes, tank top, and ballet flats tiptoed into the kitchen. "If all you did was sleep, I'm disappointed." She wagged her finger at Alec. "You'll have to do better than that, son."

Annalisse and Alec jumped to their feet.

"Gen! When did you arrive?" Annalisse picked at the nubby sweater of Generosa's she'd worn since the night before. Alec's mother must have walked past Annalisse while they'd slept on the veranda, oblivious to another presence at the villa.

"Too soon, it seems." Generosa shook her head at Alec. "Fly, my darling potato. You aren't the romantic your father is, *passerotto*." Generosa air-kissed Alec at both cheeks.

The lingo left Annalisse wondering about the significance of the comment and if Alec had planned to make a move on this trip but had lost his nerve after their talk.

"Come here, my dear. We've finally gotten you on Crete."

Annalisse gave her a firm hug and kissed her cheeks. "The island is lovely, and so is your home."

"Ready to sail?" Generosa sniffed the air. "I smell Grandpa Tony's french toast recipe. Alec, go check on your father. He got sidetracked by a neighbor's sorry boat motor. Annalisse, have you—" Her eyes studied Alec's nervous fingers that wouldn't stay still. "We've interrupted something by showing up this early, haven't we?" She tilted her head, sending the Zavos gaze at her, then Alec.

"Alec's made breakfast for us." Annalisse was thankful Alec's choice of menu had masked last night's fishy stench from the conch.

A phone rang from inside Generosa's culottes. She drew it out and studied the number. "Hmm, it's New York. Excuse me, kids. *Ciao.*"

"Annalisse, eat before it gets cold. Help yourself. I'd better check on Dad." Alec swept toward the door.

Her hunger gone, Annalisse got up from the table and moved to the love seat with a lemon-yellow afghan thrown over the back. She gnawed one of her cuticles and watched

Generosa's eyes flash and lips thin at her conversation with the unknown caller.

"You might be able to get away with that kind of talk with other people but not with me. Never call me again, do you hear?" Generosa slapped the phone screen.

Annalisse waited for Generosa to stow her cell phone shakily in her pocket, then asked who the caller was.

"You must get away from that deranged beast of a man."

At least three came to Annalisse's mind. "Which one?"

Generosa pinched the bridge of her nose, creasing her forehead.

"Peter's sending a consortium from the Appraiser's Society to my gallery. *My* gallery. They're going through every item you've valued for me. He said he's having your certification removed. Do you know what's going on? Doesn't he know you're here?"

"He's out of jail then." Annalisse muttered.

Generosa's hand flew over her mouth, then dropped. "Jail?"

In watered-down fashion, Annalisse explained Peter's assault, stopping short of the incident at her brownstone. She'd let Alec pick the time and place to go there.

"Don't give that dirty fool another thought. He's not worth it," Annalisse said.

Generosa fixated on Annalisse like she was an exquisite antique, then patted her hand. "You're right, *bambolina*. I'm glad you weren't alone with that... person. And Chase quit too. What a shame. Harry would be so sad; God rest his soul."

"Chase and I will make do."

"Of course. Make baklava," Generosa said.

"You always say that. What good is making dessert?"

Generosa's eyes glinted, little fireflies captive in their brown velvet cages. "No." She giggled. "When life throws *merde* your way, turn it into honey and phyllo dough."

She knew what *merde* meant since her friend had cussed only once in her presence, on the occasion of a rare French barbotine vase slipping out of her hand. Fragments of fragile kaolin clay petals had scattered under display tables and into tiny crevices where tile met the gallery wall. The irreplaceable vase was ruined. Generosa had cursed with such ferocity, Annalisse translated *merde* for the heck of it, even though a child could've figured it out as a pile of poop.

Annalisse laughed and kissed her cheek. "You're an awesome lady."

"Our yacht, the *Gen Amore*—now she's awesome, as you say. You kids are going to have so much fun on the water. The Aegean's peaceful now. Not so touristy near the shorelines. Do you get seasick?"

"I've never sailed before."

"Then you're in for a treat. Pearce and Alec love the water. You will too, sweetie. Let's get breakfast moving along and pack a few things. We'd like to be on the boat by noon."

Reaching across the coffee table, Annalisse grabbed her silent phone. "I haven't checked messages since we left New York."

"Go ahead. I'll fix you a plate," Generosa said.

"I'm not exactly Ms. Popularity these days." With her lips pursed, she swiped the screen. "Four new emails in the past two days. Chase's message. My aunt replied. That's good." She nodded and scrolled farther. "No Peter. Not today. Delete."

"Wait. See what he wants."

Annalisse clicked on his message and groaned at the all caps.

YOU ARE DEAD MEAT.

She shouldn't be surprised he'd threaten her from across the Atlantic. Sending email was easy, cowardly, and so *Peter*. For now, she'd ignore his threat.

CHAPTER

TWENTY

Waves spanked the thirty-nine-foot hull of the *Gen Amore*, rocking the Zavos vessel anchored in the Sea of Crete. The afternoon sun blazed overhead as Annalisse inhaled salty brine and studied the picture-perfect yacht Generosa had described dozens of times. Small enough for them to sail without a crew and large enough for Pearce and her to be intimately comfortable. The teak marine deck gleamed between twin masts, and navy-trimmed sails crackled from above. Wooden chairs were placed alongside lounges covered in striped cushions and square azure pillows. A fashion statement by the same designer who had decorated the yacht to match the island villa.

Sitting next to Generosa, Annalisse watched the rainbow windsock twist and swirl its streamers above their heads. She hadn't counted on such a cool breeze and shivered in her one-piece swimsuit that exposed too much skin. She set her mimosa on the side table and wiped her freezing fingers along the chair slats, dissipating some of the moisture.

On a diagonal from them, the men chatted, with Alec and Pearce gesturing with their arms as they talked about current events. It was easy to conceive how Generosa had fallen for a man like Pearce Zavos, currently barefoot in bermuda shorts and richly tanned everywhere. If Annalisse were several years older, a single man with Pearce's attributes would've been irresistible to her too. Pearce was the mature version of Alec, with the same muscular physique, light eyes, and wavy hair graying at the temples. Where both of Alec's cheeks were dimpled, Pearce had a single dent near the corner of his mouth and a supercool cleft chin. Annalisse was a sucker for actors with cleft chins. They were aphrodisiac city.

Without a doubt, Pearce had to know the answer to how he'd ended up with a relic from the 1500s and why two identical horsehead necklaces existed. Brushing off the notion a viable evilness had chased them to Greece, Annalisse planned to catch Pearce alone and ask a few generic questions any antiquities appraiser would ask the buyer of an important artifact.

"We're a long way from shore. Shouldn't I know how to use the ship's radio?" Annalisse tossed her question out there.

"Gen knows, but I'll show you too, if you'd like." Pearce smiled. "Finish your drink. There's plenty of time for how to use the radio and flags later."

"Mr. Zavos, how did you and Gen settle on Sitia when the entire island is so lovely?"

"First, please call me Pearce." He paused a few beats before answering. "I met Gen in Italy at the wedding of a mutual friend. Since her family fished the Adriatic, Gen admired the homes on the ocean. She's an excellent swimmer, you know— loves the water as much as she loves me." He winked at his wife. "My family vacationed in Sitia when I was a boy, and I promised myself that one day I'd buy a home that faced this sea. Gen was ecstatic about the idea."

"After Dad retired as a stock car driver in North Carolina," Alec added.

Pearce lolled his head back and watched the sail's flap cutting the air. "I had to think about Alec. When I had a close call on the track, we decided it was time for me to get out."

Alec shifted in his seat and looked at his mom. "Will Luciana be gone long?"

"She's due back tonight."

"The time to ourselves gave us a good excuse to run an errand in Heraklion City," Pearce said.

"Who's Luciana?" Annalisse slid her sunglasses on top of her head.

"Sorry, hon. Luci is our villa maid and the daughter of a longtime friend. We wanted lots of playmates for Alec, but it wasn't to be." Generosa gave a wistful sigh and looked at Pearce. "God has a habit of testing us."

Her heart wrenched at the truth in Generosa's words, for Annalisse understood the pain in her voice. Little on earth hurt as badly as losing a child, her aunt had reminded Annalisse years ago.

Generosa had incredible mothering instincts, but Annalisse wasn't hardwired for kids. Small babies were too dependent, and their shrill cries made her nervous. Short of a miracle, having children wasn't in Annalisse's future, but she admired those who had the patience for kids.

"What's wrong?" Alec looked at his father, who'd started and stared at a section of water.

"Hand me the binoculars. Hurry." Pearce pointed to the pair on the table next to Alec.

Annalisse observed a tiny black dot speeding toward them that carried the faint hum of a speedboat with it.

Pearce spent seconds with the binoculars, and for Annalisse, the wait for him to say something felt excruciating. She stood alongside the men to get a better look at the boat.

"Ladies, get below. Now. And take the keys to the yacht with you. Hide them someplace where no one will find them, and hide yourselves," Pearce said.

"Why?" Generosa asked.

"We may be getting unwanted guests."

"You can forget it; I'm staying here." Generosa planted hands on her hips in revolt.

"Same goes for me," Annalisse added.

In less than a minute, a black boat filled with dark men closed on the *Gen Amore*. A red flag with a symbol fluttered ominously on the bow of their low-profile craft.

"Gen, go. Hide that key." Pearce hissed through closed teeth. "If you won't stay down there, then come back, but hurry." As if he'd changed his mind, he gave the binoculars to Alec.

"I'm going below with your mother. Watch but do not engage; wait for me."

As the strangers steered closer, Annalisse noticed they were shaved bald, without beards, except for one person. A blue-and-white *keffiyeh* covered his head and most of the face from the bridge of his nose down. Her hands twitched, evoking the man from the brownstone, whose eyes were the only thing visible beneath his mask.

When the couple returned topside, Annalisse whispered to Generosa, "Where'd you hide it?"

"In a small vase. They'll never find it."

Annalisse sought out Alec and asked, "Any guesses who they are?"

"Not sure. Turkish maybe."

"Are we accepting more refugees on Crete?" Generosa stepped toward Pearce.

"The men have rifles, which doesn't bode well for us," Pearce said.

Annalisse's stomach roiled with a vengeance. Against multiple weapons they were all in deep trouble and wouldn't be able to keep the men at bay for long—unless Alec's dad was a well-trained sharpshooter.

"Did you leave the Glock on the island?" Annalisse asked in Alec's ear, knowing he'd done exactly that by the way he held his mouth. "Why don't we pull anchor and run?"

"Ladies, listen. They're closing fast and we can't outrun them. No matter what, don't lead them to the key. On the black market, this yacht's worth plenty. Say nothing. Do nothing," Pearce said.

"Pirates." Alec spat a quiet curse at the deck.

Annalisse and Generosa chimed together, "Pirates?"

"Or they could be refugees." Pearce added the option, but Annalisse couldn't imagine refugees would be heavily armed. When people left their countries, most came with children and the clothing on their backs. Four men with guns weren't seeking asylum.

Annalisse's french toast was dangerously close to making a deck appearance.

Pearce slid a small pistol inside his belt at the back of his bermuda shorts and dropped extra ammo in a pocket.

Alec hadn't reminded her about the extra risks of sailing in the area. She'd forgotten how many were fleeing the region. She envisioned a world map of Lebanon, Syria, Egypt, and Turkey bordering the eastern Mediterranean Sea. Émigrés fleeing bombs and homeland wars would possess rougher physical characteristics. The men in the boat had a smooth bone structure and rounded features.

As the boat sloshed water to the starboard side of the yacht, a male with two missing fingers hailed them.

"Do any of you speak English?" Pearce asked, three decibels louder than usual.

They glanced at each other and laughed. "We speak English good."

"What do you want?"

The thinnest in the group, with arms and legs tattooed, brandished a sinister AK-47 with a pistol grip at them. He held his weapon like he'd comfortably used it before.

Annalisse calmed herself, curious about the men's tattoos. She noted their red shoulders from hours on the water, worsened by the ocean's glare. They weren't muscular men, rather a ragtag crew of stringy characters with lifeless eyes and broken teeth.

"We need gas. Pay in gold."

"No need for guns." Pearce pointed to the man's rifle. "I'll give you what you want." Then he added under his breath, "I have plenty of lead."

Annalisse's heart stopped when Alec jerked her behind him and whispered, "Shh."

"Take the gas and leave." Pearce's tension wafted the deck.

"We come on boat. Put rope down so we board. Now!"

During the back-and-forth, the two most sunburned marauders had slipped into the sea, clinging to their boat hooks, only feet away from the *Gen Amore*'s hull.

"We don't want trouble. Stay in your boat. I'll give you the supplies." Pearce hugged the brass rail, his voice even and stern while he convinced the men to stay with their boat.

An object burned her lower spine, and Annalisse saw a shadow cross the deck.

"Alec!" she yelled.

The butt of a rifle struck Alec at the base of his skull, echoing over the water.

He collapsed in front of her in a motionless heap.

Two goons, wet with salt water, stood close enough for her to smell their dense body odor—so powerful the ocean water hadn't washed it away. Annalisse gulped to keep down the vomit surging in her throat.

Someone yanked her hair hard, jerking her backward, stinging the scalp where fingernails dug and scratched.

Annalisse scanned for Generosa and Pearce, but the sun's blaze overhead blinded her.

"Let me go. I have to help him." Annalisse gritted her teeth and hitched forward while sending an elbow backward at her captor. She hoped to catch him off guard with the seesaw action and land near his genitals.

He yelped and released her.

Annalisse grimaced and grabbed her painful scalp, feeling hair missing, then scrambled toward Alec's still body. His breaths were shallow ones, but he was alive.

"Where is boat key?" an accented voice asked her.

Annalisse shook Alec by the shoulders. "Wake up!" She rotated around and blurted, "I don't know where the key is." Her attention immediately went back to Alec. "Please open your eyes, hon."

"Get away from them!" Pearce screamed.

Generosa shouted, "Watch out, Pearce!"

Pearce fired his weapon twice, taking down the man nearest him and one more nearby. A lake of blood spread onto the deck planks under the fallen bodies. For an instant, Annalisse took comfort in Pearce's marksmanship, but two men still remained.

She hovered over Alec, willing him to respond as she massaged his body.

A scuffle from behind her made Annalisse swivel. She watched helplessly, unable to assist anyone without her trusty Lady Smith.

"Quiet!" A man with a facial scar tied Generosa's wrists together, and once secured, he held the barrel of his weapon to her temple to accentuate his demand of Pearce. "Drop your gun. Do it now, or your woman dies."

The man in the *keffiyeh* who'd pulled her hair grabbed the dead man's abandoned rifle and slammed the stock into Pearce's face.

Generosa uttered a bloodcurdling scream.

Pearce's cheek opened. Blood flowed from a wound so deep the white of his cheekbone showed beneath the flap of skin and muscle.

The sight brought Annalisse to tears, and she closed her eyes.

A shot rang out.

She ducked, covering Alec with her body.

Pearce lost footing in the blood of the dead men, and his pistol skidded along the slippery deck. Swaying, he dropped to his knees, one hand holding his profusely bleeding cheek.

"Where is it, you self-righteous slab of dung?" The disguised man shoved his rifle at Pearce, speaking crisp American English without an accent like the rest.

Pearce's eyes glazed over, then narrowed. "What the… Val?" He'd recognized the voice of his attacker.

Pulling the cloth higher on the bridge of his nose, the gunman threw his shoulders back, sucking in a gut Annalisse hadn't noticed earlier.

"I'll give it to you." Generosa struggled against the rifle buried in her side.

"No, Gen!" Pearce shook his head as he yelled, "Don't!"

"But—"

Gunfire resounded in multiple rounds in a war scene on deck as Annalisse pressed herself harder against Alec's body.

Generosa shouted for Pearce and screamed again.

Craning her neck, Annalisse regarded Generosa's condition, then shuddered at what she encountered where Pearce had folded himself over. The top of his head was gone. Bloody tissue peppered the rails and the deck; the smell of gunpowder and iron permeated the humidity, engulfing her. In the horror, time stalled, and Pearce's bullet-ridden body thudded to the boards.

"Pearce!" Generosa sobbed into her bound hands.

Both lowlifes laughed, and the one holding Generosa pushed his rifle fiercely at her. "Quit squawking."

The man in the makeshift *keffiyeh* moved near Generosa, spat, then whispered indecipherable words to her captor.

Annalisse placed a hand against her chest, fearing she'd be next. Pearce's last message to them faded in and out. Light-headed and shaky, Annalisse fought a total breakdown for the sake of Generosa and Alec since she alone remained free to plot an escape strategy. Her scalp on fire, she cleared away the fear welling inside her. Alec had mentioned the boat had bad cell service, and she'd had no instructions on how to use the ship-to-shore radio, but she would try it.

"Stupid woman. Give key." Generosa's captor slapped her open-handed, strong enough to plant a pink blotch on her blanched skin. She stiffened and mumbled three quiet words Annalisse couldn't make out.

Annalisse held Alec tighter. She couldn't help Pearce, but she might be able to see where his gun landed. Her tears fell as she pinched Alec hard on the arm, trying to get a reaction.

Turning her head, she caught the glint of the little pearl handle. The pistol was an arm's length away. There were two, maybe three shots left. She stretched her fingers to their limits. Either the gun had grown feet, or her mind couldn't judge distance correctly.

A black boot stomped on her forearm.

Annalisse bit the inside of her cheek when his heel twisted near her wrist. "Get off. You're breaking my arm!"

When he removed his weight, she pulled back, holding her throbbing wrist, and then rolled against Alec.

The man's kerchief had slipped below his tiny, feminine nose.

"I'd stick to your artsy-fartsies if I were you." His words were muffled behind the cloth he wore, and he followed them with a raspy laugh.

He knew her.

Something dark came at her, ramming her head with the speed of a rocket. She saw white dots beneath closed lids, then blackness.

Annalisse awoke to searing heat and colored halos around her. She closed her eyes against the glare and opened them again. The drums in her head pounded, and she rose on sore knees, rubbing small circles on her temples.

With a sudden rush of adrenaline, she remembered the yacht and Alec beside her, only to find that Alec hadn't regained consciousness. Remnants of cabin decor cluttered the deck like the aftermath of a knife-fight free-for-all. Cushions were slashed and their sails were in tatters. Intact sails that had managed to weather the tears snapped in the wind overhead, cracking the air. She laid two fingers on Alec's throat and verified a pulse.

Annalisse watched the waves' motion that went on for miles. She saw nothing but water and surveyed the deck for Generosa or other human beings. Seeing no one, she took the stairs belowdecks in the hope of finding her waiting, maybe tied up, but instead found the berth and galley matched the topside nightmare of shredded cushions and broken equipment.

"Gen? Are you here?" She scanned bunks and the floor for any possible hiding place, opening every door that she could find. "She's gone." A pang of remorse for not helping Generosa escape the men struck her so hard she had to grab a cupboard to steady herself. Annalisse ran up the cabin steps, taking two at a time, and skimmed the sea once more for the intruders' boat or a glimpse of the orange culottes Generosa had worn before Annalisse blacked out.

Choppy crests of translucent blue clunked against the side of the *Gen Amore*.

"Please be alive, Gen. I'm so sorry." Doubling over, Annalisse fought back her fear for Alec's sake. She cleared cobwebs from her head in order to recall Pearce's words about flags. She'd read about nautical flags having meanings to sailors on other vessels. "How can I locate them in this mess?" Flags were a means of others finding their yacht.

Inside the cabin once more, Annalisse rummaged through sliced bedsheets and anything fabric. She checked underneath the beds and dragged out a two-by-three-foot white square with a red *X* splashed rivet to rivet.

"I don't know what the *X* means, but it can't hurt." She checked under the beds for any other signal flag just in case.

Back on deck, she searched for a place to mount the flag and decided to hang it on a mast with what was left of the sails. Her head ached, and she held it to quell the spinning there and in her stomach.

Pearce's body, as well as the dead raiders, had vanished, leaving a huge amount of drying blood on the deck. She wiped her forehead with the back of her hand and stared at Alec. How would she explain his father was dead and his mother might be too?

"Alec, please wake up." She wobbled a few steps and squatted to massage his reddened arms. "You're frying." Reaching for a section of sailcloth, she covered him against the searing sun.

A faint buzz penetrated the sounds of sea birds and waves. "An engine! Hold on, Alec."

She squinted at a growing speck of white in the distance. She called out, "Help us please!"

Annalisse kept waving until the boat drew alongside.

CHAPTER
TWENTY-ONE

A moan took her attention from the water in the Aegean.

"Alec, you're back." Annalisse crouched beside him, sliding one hand under his head. "Take my hand. Go slow."

He touched his forehead as she carefully raised his torso.

"Big-ass headache," he said as he made circles on both temples.

Sitting upright, he rubbed the next spot that hurt him. "How did I get the goose egg on my skull? I feel like a broiler chicken on the rotisserie." He shuffled to his feet. "Don't feel well." Staggering, he lunged for the arm of the deck chair, his face a ghostly white.

"Small steps. Sit here, and I'll bring you some water."

When she returned, she asked him, "How much do you remember?"

"Just a minute." He guzzled the bottle in a matter of seconds.

She handed him another. "Drink slowly. You've been unconscious for a while, but some nice fishermen moved you into the shade. We're being towed back to Sitia."

He took a long swig and wiped the side of his mouth. Alec looked at their surroundings with glazed-over vision. "Fishermen towing us? Why? The yacht is ripped up." He shook his head. "Who did this? What happened?"

"Sit back please, Alec."

His eyes widened as he scanned the black pool on the deck. "Is that dried blood?"

"Do you remember boarding the *Gen Amore*?" she asked.

"Yeah." Comprehension dawned on his face. "The speed-boat. Those men. Are Mom and Dad below?" Alec grabbed her wrist, the plea in his voice mirroring his expression.

Annalisse choked back a sob and held him tenderly, her own body trembling. For his sake, she had to keep herself together and not break down. How would she do that? The horrible exchange between Pearce and the turbaned guy—all that blood. And how would she tell Alec that his life had changed forever?

Limp with exhaustion, she sat down on a torn cushion next to him and began to explain to Alec, who was in stunned shock, what had happened to his parents.

When she'd finished the heartbreaking narrative, he wiped his eyes and shivered outwardly. "Tell me I'm going to wake up. That this is my imagination…"

Annalisse felt his gut-racking hurt along with him. She understood all too well. He needed to know that things would be all right, even though they wouldn't be. Not for a long while… or never. She pushed aside the fact that Generosa was still missing.

"Alec." Annalisse knelt before him, waiting until he gazed at her through his tears. "I'm so very sorry." She rested her cheek on his thigh to dam the salty burn of tears spilling over.

His trembling hand caressed her hair lightly, then he wept uncontrollably on her shoulder.

The sight of such a strong, confident man buckling in anguish destroyed her. She could bear her own grief but not his. She embraced him and gave him a quick, motherly kiss on the temple, tasting perspiration and despair as if they were one.

After a time, his shudders subsided, and he guided her to his mouth for a sobering kiss. All at once, he drew back as if his internal light bulb had switched on.

"They took Mom?"

"Yes, that's my assumption." She stared in another direction to hide the doubt in her eyes.

"You aren't sure." He clasped his hands. "Did you see them hurt her?"

"No. Not like you, and not like—"

"Dad," Alec whispered. With palms together, he lowered his head to them, then met her eyes. "Oh, babe, you witnessed it all, didn't you?"

"Yes." She had to turn away or lose it in front of him.

"My brave ray of sunshine." He reached up and brushed her hair back, then traced the left side of her face. "Did you know you have a knot on your noggin?"

She pulled away and felt the bump. "Whacked with his boot, I think. A small price—" She kept the rest to herself.

"Why'd they leave us alive?" he asked.

"There's no way to know. Your dad fought like a tiger after you went down. He killed half of them. Without him and his pistol, I'm sure we'd all be dead."

Alec took a deep breath and leaned back. "If they wanted the boat, why take Mom? Why tear up the yacht?"

Annalisse unfolded herself and stood, grunting and brushing her knees. He'd eventually come to the same conclusion that she had. The attack wasn't about the yacht.

She rolled her shoulders and changed the subject. "We'll both need plenty of aloe cream when we get ashore."

"I pity the fools in charge of watching Mom." He ran a hand through his hair and forced a sad smile. "She won't be an easy captive."

"I heard something between the men and your mom, but before I say more, I want my thoughts clearer. Right now I'm not sure what's real and what I may have dreamed when I blacked out." She pointed toward land. "Finally, shoreline."

"Help me up." Alec reached for her hand.

"Listen." Annalisse pulled him with her to the railing. "Is that a party on the beach? A crowd has gathered. Look."

As they approached the shore, they witnessed hordes of bystanders in shorts and bright bikinis sprinkled along a thin white beach, their murmurs carrying on the wind. An area was roped off close to the pier. People in dark uniforms formed a half circle in front of curious sunbathers standing at attention.

"Greek Hellenic Police. Something's brought them to the beach. I wish I had Dad's binoculars."

"The fishermen must have called ahead," Annalisse said.

He nodded. "That's it. And there's an ambulance parked down there too."

"My word! It's a body!" A woman cried.

Annalisse brought her hand against her mouth. "Did you hear that?" She turned to Alec, but he wasn't beside her anymore. "Alec?"

TWENTY - TWO

At the villa, the sea had changed color since their arrival on Sitia two days earlier. The sparkles of awe-inspiring waves that had raised her spirits were gone, taken over by foam dissolving into nothingness on the sand. She turned her eyes from a place marked by stones where Pearce's body had washed ashore at high tide yesterday. The stark moment Alec saw for himself what the thugs had done to his father had ripped a deep gouge in her heart.

"May I get you someting, miss?" a voice asked in a sing-song lilt.

Annalisse jumped and turned around. "Luciana." She patted her chest. "I didn't think anyone but me and Alec were in the house."

The housemaid she'd met briefly the night before stood behind her, hands in the pockets of a stained muslin apron. Her hazel eyes were sorrowful.

"Sorry. Gennie say to work Wednesday." Luciana worried her hands. "How is he? Awake?" She glanced down the hall to where Alec slept fitfully in the master suite.

"Not yet."

The maid jingled what sounded like keys in her apron. "Do I stay wit you since Gennie and Pearce—"

Luciana's *h* dropping grated on Annalisse's nerves. Without Alec's parents around, having this meek person waiting on them felt unnatural—like a constant irritation they could do without. But Luciana was the Zavos family maid, and unwelcome annoyance or not, Annalisse had to bend.

Wincing from sunburn, she asked the maid, "Do you live here full time?"

She shook her head. "Down road. Not far. Are you leaving soon?" Luciana drew her bushy brows together questioningly.

"We'll be staying as long as Alec wants."

Luciana scrunched her nose as if she would've preferred a different answer. The thirtysomething woman shuffled stiffly to a chair and slid it closer to the wall. Sweat rings darkened the armhole seams of her yellow cotton shift. The gap between Luciana and the table was remarkable, and she'd made a point to be unfriendly to a new woman in the Zavos villa.

"Your accent is beautiful, Luciana."

"Tank you." The maid fiddled with her apron, then popped her hands in her lap. "Are you rich too, miss?"

Taken aback by Luciana's question, Annalisse tightened her lips and ignored it. The frankness was unexpected.

"Gennie and Pearce have nice tings. Alec like nice tings. My family no afford fancy tings."

"You must be Italian, like Gen."

"*Si.*"

Annalisse rubbed the scabbed patch of scalp and looked down at her legs, sure to peel in a couple of days. In her french-fried state, she would've preferred to hang out clothing-free. Fabric felt like one hundred grit sandpaper on her skin. The shorts and gauze blouse she wore were the lightest things Alec had purchased for her.

"The DePalmas and Bruccias are farmers and fishermen." Luciana added context with a bob of her head.

"Who?" Annalisse asked.

"Gennie. She's a DePalma."

"That's Gen's maiden name?"

Luciana nodded. "My mother was a Bruccia."

Alec rounded the corner in bare feet and a striped terry-cloth robe, nonstandard attire from a rich bachelor's closet. She wondered if Alec wanted to be closer to Pearce by wearing his robe. Alec's beard shadowed the hollows of his cheeks, and his eyes were smudged with grief.

Annalisse jumped off the couch, ruffling her peasant blouse at the bottom, and met him halfway. "Good morning. I peeked in on you a few times. Did you get any sleep?"

He swept a hand through his hair and grimaced. "Hardly. I feel like I've been through a brawl with a troop of gorillas. Any news from the coast guard?"

"I'll be in t'e kitchen." Luciana hurried past Alec as if breakfast was burning in the oven.

"You *were* in a brawl. How 'bout an omelet or a Danish?" Annalisse switched to a subject other than his mother's disappearance.

"Too queasy. I should be out there with the guard, looking for Mom, but I can't bring myself to get back on a boat."

"Then don't, hon." She touched his arm. "I'll bring you an awesome painkiller for body aches. I was afraid to give it to you last night. You were saying things that scared the crud out of me."

"Stay here." Alec reached out and pulled her to him, taking her waist in both hands. "Medics checked us both out. The aches are the easy part." He sighed. "All night I imagined Mom's voice and Dad's—pleading with those lowlifes." He rubbed the back of his neck, then sifted a couple of fingers through her hair. "I also thought about how an angel brought you to me. I've put you in danger by bringing you to Greece."

"Walk with me please?" She searched him for a glimmer of the old Alec. "Let's sort out what we know, if you're up to it."

Passion seeped through his robe and penetrated the gauzy material to her breasts. She placed her arms around his neck, and on tiptoes, gazed into the most captivating eyes she'd ever known. His body sprang to life—he wanted her, and she needed him—more than she dared to let on, but their timing was way wrong. They were both too emotionally drained after what had happened on his yacht. And they weren't alone.

Alec leaned in, the desire in his eyes unmistakable as anything else.

"Pretty lady." Words that dripped from his tongue like sweet honey.

She loved it when he referred to her in such a formal, refined way, as long as *he* uttered the words. Hot waves of wanting this man threatened to engulf her. She tugged at his sleeves while he kissed the corner of her mouth. So gentle. So perfect. As though she might break. Annalisse moistened her lips and kissed him more deeply, tasting his voracious mouth until she was breathless.

Panting, she rested her forehead on his chest, and when Alec pulled her closer, she groaned. His faint woodland scent dueled with the cedar of his robe in an intoxicating potpourri. Eager to explore more of him, she had to stop herself.

She tapped her fingertips on his terrycloth lapel and whispered, "Make baklava."

A memory of Generosa's face, lit in perfect delight and framed in a pageboy the last time they had a private talk, stood between Alec and Annalisse, prompting her to shed an unwanted tear.

He made a wistful sound, tucking her beneath his chin. "You're tempting me into places I'd rather be." He kissed her head. "A conversation for later. It's only been a day, but I miss them so much."

"Gen's out there, and we'll get her back."

He kissed her lips again, with tenderness, and held her in the protection of his arms. "I believe you."

"C'mon." Annalisse wrapped an arm around him and led him onto the veranda.

A cool breeze lifted her blouse, and she shivered. Annalisse ignored the sunburn sting when she snuggled next to Alec and allowed his warmth to penetrate her. She looked down the hill at native stone pavers sprinkling the walkway in a beige mosaic puzzle. She grasped the painted rail and luxuriated in the parting of clouds to sunshine.

Alec left her and sat on the chaise, patting the spot next to him. "I'd like to know what you overheard on the boat."

"I don't want to hurt you all over again," she said.

"Not that. What you heard and aren't sure about."

"They're just suspicions. Feelings, mostly."

"I trust your feelings," he said.

"Careful saying that." Annalisse smiled slowly.

In the most delicate way possible, Annalisse conveyed facts to Alec as she understood them and her worst fears surrounding the necklace. All hypotheses, crazy or not.

He kept his reactions subdued and refrained from interrupting until she'd finished.

"Man, that's unreal. The guy in the cloth knew Dad and recognized you?"

"It felt that way to me. When your dad said *Val*, he must have realized his killer or thought he did. *Val* was the last word Pearce spoke."

Alec shook his head. "I don't know any Val."

"Don't think about it now." She rubbed his neck and shoulders, carefully navigating around the stitches until his muscles relaxed beneath her fingertips.

"Does your heart feel that Mom's a hostage and still alive?" he asked her.

"Yes."

"Why didn't they ask for the necklace? And why haven't they contacted us?"

She wasn't sure how to answer without upsetting him further. Annalisse paused long enough to weigh her thoughts, then gave it a try.

"The guy in the head covering didn't have an accent. He's a mismatch with those sleazebags. Too polished when he gave out orders. We have what they want, Alec. Gen doesn't. They searched the yacht for the key and probably the necklace, but it's all speculation since we were both knocked out when they tore the yacht apart. I assume they took Gen with them for a reason, like her knowledge of the jewelry or ransom."

"I want your complete, honest opinion." Alec reached for her hand.

Annalisse held her breath for what might come next.

"Would they?" Alec dropped his gaze. "Hurt Mom?"

"Would you want the wrath of that little spitfire on you?" She laughed, noticing a flicker in his eyes, and eventually he grinned. Alec had the same boyish smile she'd witnessed from Pearce on the *Gen Amore*. "Gen's too important to abuse her. They need her alive." When his eyes widened, she added, "And unharmed. I also believe our relic is keeping her alive, if it's their endgame."

"That's it." He rubbed his temples. "Time to 'fess up about the necklace. Mooney has to be told."

"Only Mooney." She glared at Alec.

"Mooney and FBI Norcross. He'll bring her in on this because he has to. You have a stake in this too. Beyond Mom and Dad." He'd lost all expression when he name-dropped his parents.

That day in Kensington—how she'd felt when she heard the news that her family had perished—rushed between them like a blowtorch. Alec had a bumpy road ahead—changed forever by the private terrors they'd endured.

"As much as I hate it, I know you're right. Norcross's smug, Southern drawl is just hard to be around. She probably says the same thing about me."

"The US Embassy and our ambassador in Athens know about Dad and about Mom's missing status. It's probably world news by now, but I told the ambassador not to give out any names. Since my parents are US citizens, Ambassador Holden's getting the FBI involved."

"Is it good to have a lot of agencies crawling around? What if they feel threatened? Small steps, Alec. Talk to Detective Mooney. I trust him." Annalisse smiled, recalling the detective's many visits to the gallery. "I've seen the Detective and Gen together. He has a soft spot for her."

Alec furrowed his brows.

"Not that kind of a soft spot. Mooney and his partner are friends of hers. The precinct treats her like royalty because she donates to 9/11 police and fire charities. Everyone loves Gen; who can resist her?" She swallowed against the tightness in her throat and leaned into his shoulder. "I wish we were years from now with your mom sitting right there." She pointed to the chair beside them. "No more mysteries, no more deaths, no more necklace."

He gazed into the ocean for a time, then asked, "How did you do it?"

"A broad question."

"How did you move forward from losing your parents? It might help me."

"Handling loss is deeply personal—a one-person journey." She drew a long breath and sank into that deep well—the place she couldn't go often. This time for Alec. "Funerals are the hardest for me. I have to force myself to go, and I can't attend many of them except for friends who're superclose to me, which is awful, I know. I'm criticized for it, but I'd rather remember them as they were. Luckily, Kate took me in after the explosion, or I could've landed in foster care." Annalisse gave his knee a squeeze. "Your headache has made your eyebrows grow together from wrinkling your forehead so much."

He sought her hand and raised it to his lips.

Touching the new lines on his face, her mind relived the weeks following those three agonizing funerals. She'd hugged so many strangers, her father's clients and her mother's friends, until her arms ached. Watching Ariel's classmates from school was the worst part. Kids were outwardly sobbing as adults passed out tissues in the pews, mourning the upbeat little girl who'd cherished her friends and made everyone laugh at her silly jokes. Her sister's short existence—taken from the earth before she'd lived a full life. Annalisse missed Ariel every day.

At least Alec was spared his father's final moments. She hoped he'd never ask her to recite the painful details for him.

"I couldn't handle this alone." His sorrowful eyes met hers. "I feel like my guts have spilled out for everyone to see."

"Grief fades, but you'll have days where it's hard to rise out of bed. I spent too long blaming, and that was a mistake." Annalisse had opened a door she badly needed to walk through and might never get the nerve to ask again. "There's something I'd like to ask since you brought it up on the flight."

His worry lines disappeared, leaving his beautiful eyes boring a hole in her.

"The tabloids paint you as a player. Should I be worried?" she asked.

He skimmed his thumb over her pearl ring but remained silent.

"It's none of my business." Wishing that he wasn't a womanizer wouldn't make it so.

"Nothing I say will convince you otherwise. There's more to me than what you'll read in print. I hope you'll stick around so I can show you who I am." He'd handily avoided a direct answer.

The connection she'd felt growing between them abruptly snapped. She got on her feet and nervously smoothed the wrinkles out of her blouse, buying him a little more time.

Alec grabbed her wrist and drew her down to the chaise. "I was married once."

"Uh, I'll get those pain meds. Let me go." Her lungs deflated, and she needed air.

His grip on her said otherwise. "No secrets; I want you to know."

She'd presumed he led a carefree bachelor lifestyle; it hadn't occurred to her that he could be a divorcée or a widower. Generosa hadn't brought up having a daughter-in-law during small talk. But if a young wife had passed, he'd know about death firsthand.

"We were married during our second year of college. At first everything was great, until she got pregnant, then lost the baby in the second trimester."

"I'm sorry to open old wounds. You don't have to say more," she said.

"We were having a boy." He stared straight ahead. "I immersed myself in my studies, and Tina quit school, crying incessantly. I thought she was healing, then I found her fiddling with baby things in the nursery we'd spent months working on." Alec bit his lower lip. "I pleaded with her to get help, but Tina blew a gasket. She'd gotten hooked on coke."

"That's rough."

He laughed humorlessly. "Rough was finding them in our bed, Tina and her drug dealer. She was so blasted out of her mind, she didn't even know I was there, observing, listening to her say things she'd never said to me when we were... making love."

Annalisse let out the deep breath she was holding. He'd known another kind of grief. Crouching in front of him, she tried to find the right words. "My mom used to say, 'Great life if you don't weaken.' I was too little to understand back then, but life's disasters do make us stronger."

Annalisse felt his cool hands cradle her face, and he kissed her eyelids closed, one at a time—a gentle sweep of butterfly wings on her lashes.

"Babe, all that trash in the rags is made-up sensationalism to sell papers. Rely on your intuition and don't overthink it." He brushed his lips in a caress near her collarbone and pulled back, watching for a reply she didn't have.

"Will you finally take something for your headache, stubborn man?"

He managed a crooked smile. "Okay. I'll call Mooney and my folks' attorney, Ralph Farley. See if he'll make time in his schedule. We should know what provisions Dad made for the family following his death."

CHAPTER
TWENTY - THREE

Ralph Farley's office in Heraklion City carried a hint of medicinals, the kind Alec worked with when he'd practiced during his veterinary internship in Youngsville. It reminded him of a cross between mentholated balm and watered-down vanilla. Ralph's office could've doubled as a cool backdrop in a dramatic Scorsese film. Dark mahogany furniture, a highly polished speckled granite counter, and cave-brown plaster walls were broken by white molding against floor tiles in the same gravestone shade as the counter.

Alec reached for Annalisse's hand. "If I failed to say it before, thank you for coming along."

"I want to be here. Where's his receptionist?" She tossed aside the taxidermy magazine in her hand. "Your lawyer must be a hunter."

"Yeah, I got that sense too," Alec whispered, looking at his Rolex. "Our appointment's not until two. We're early."

"Maybe I should wait in the lobby or sit in the car while you discuss personal matters with him."

"If you're uncomfortable, but I could sure use your support. Never, ever, did I expect to be discussing Dad's last will—so young. I'm only twenty-nine." He swept his hair back, recalling Annalisse's younger age when she'd lost her parents.

"Forgive me. That was rude and unfeeling." Alec fretted over her leaving when he wanted her with him in the worst way.

Across the room, a door creaked open, and a preoccupied, middle-aged man with round spectacles stepped out while perusing the contents of a pale blue folder. A ballpoint pen was stationed over one ear.

Alec cleared his throat. "Mr. Farley."

The attorney whipped off his glasses, sending the pen to the tile. "Oh, hello there. My admin's on maternity leave, so I'm a bit lost without her." He picked up the pen and opened his office door wider. "Please come in."

Alec glanced at Annalisse and beckoned her with his eyes. Though she hesitated, she joined him, taking his hand. Several times in the past few days, he'd witnessed her unselfishness and admired that about her. Not many women would put themselves in front of a loaded pistol to save another person. Twice. With no regard for the danger.

Farley's office blew Alec away. Taxidermic birds, half-realistic and half-mythical, overran the attorney's space. Some were on stands facing each other in a battle for the prime spot on a wooden ledge as two-headed fawns and flying monkeys mocked the rest with their ominous grins. No wonder his waiting room reading material covered the art of preserving dead animals.

Ralph ushered them to a pair of plain, straight-backed leather chairs. His traditional green-shaded lamp and desk blotter gave Alec hope they were in the presence of a bona fide legal practitioner.

His eyes traveled the rows of wood shelves. "Quite a menagerie, Ralph."

"A great icebreaker. People who come to me are not in happy land, as a rule. It gives them something else to discuss. How long has it been, Alec?" Ralph reached across his desk and shook Alec's hand.

"A long time."

Ralph offered his hand to Annalisse. "I haven't had the pleasure. Ralph Farley."

Alec jumped in. "Annalisse is a good friend of the family." He ignored her jaw drop. "She was visiting when this happened."

Ralph arched his brows. "Ah, to be young again. Very, very lovely. Nice to meet you." He turned again in Alec's direction. "My deepest condolences to you both. When you called this morning—I'm still in shock. What a terrible tragedy. Are you well? Not injured?"

"We were lucky." Alec shrugged. "A few flea bites, but we're okay, considering."

"We'll find Gen," Annalisse said tersely.

"I truly hope so. Your parents were just here on Monday. It was such a treat for me to see them together. Pearce was a good and decent man, and I will miss him and his comical stories." His long teeth gleamed through a wide, genuine grin.

"My folks came here?" He shot a quick glance at Annalisse, who looked as surprised as he felt.

"Yes," Ralph said.

Leaning against the chair back, Ralph picked up a legal-sized envelope labeled Zavos, Pearce and Generosa. "Right on top of my stack. Generosa made a few minor bank account changes on her trust this week. I'm sure you're aware that your parents have separate assets. They filed separate wills."

"Sounds about right," Alec said.

Ralph pulled pages from a portfolio and studied one particular sheet with keen interest. "Pearce's will is straightforward. I'll give you a copy to take, but here's the gist: all personal assets and the family business of Signorile Corporation are to be left to you, Alec. Distribution of your father's assets are immediate."

"Me? Not Mom?"

"You." He paused, adjusting his readers that had slid down his nose. "We calculate his net worth to be about two hundred and sixty million dollars, including the business and bank holdings in the US and Europe."

Annalisse's expression went blank.

"I had no idea how successful Dad was." Alec's pulse quickened, and he scooted forward in the chair. How would he manage a portfolio like that? Worse yet, the entire weight of the corporation rested on him alone. His own affairs, shoved aside once he took over for his dad, without a chance of resurrecting the veterinary practice. Forced into the family business he'd tried to distance himself from. Was this his dad's plan all along? He clasped his fingers and worried his palms together. *A ridiculous notion.*

"I can see this is a shock. Understandably so. Since you're here, I have Generosa's will." He raised the file folder with hesitation. "I'm prepared to discuss it with you since she gave me permission to explain her wishes should the need arise. I don't even know what compelled me to ask her the other day. Anyway, would you like me to share your mother's holdings with you as well?"

"But she's not dead." Annalisse widened her eyes at Ralph, then narrowed them at Alec before catapulting to the door, tote in hand. "I'll be outside."

"Mom won't mind."

"I do." She softly clicked the door closed without a look back.

Alec stared at Ralph, but parts of him ached for the woman who'd left the room.

"What happened on the *Gen Amore* has taken a toll on both of us. She loves her too," Alec said.

"Of course. We can do this another time so you can be with your girlfriend." Ralph glanced at the door.

"I'm here; let's do this." Alec massaged the armrests.

"Fine. Generosa's estate remains in stasis until we can determine her status."

"We'll stay until we find her. Whatever it takes."

"Absolutely. I meant no disrespect."

"I'm not familiar with international law in these matters. At what point, if the worst happens, do circumstances change? I'm not saying this right." Alec tried again. "Mom missing versus considered deceased, I mean."

Ralph nodded. "A fair question. Under Greek law, a person is missing for one full year. Your mother held a dual citizenship, but we must abide by the laws of Greece in this case.

After one year, if Generosa remains missing, the court may be petitioned for a certificate of death in absentia."

"Okay. Go ahead with Mom's side."

"Please keep this in the utmost confidence." Ralph looked at him over his glasses. "Her estate is best summed up by her most recent savings account statement." He shuffled through the folder and removed an envelope. "It seems Generosa isn't fond of the US banking system." He chuckled and continued, "She wired money here often. I've taken the liberty of converting euros to dollars. It's written in bold." Ralph reached across his desk and handed him a folded document.

Alec's jaw dropped at the figure, and he scrubbed his brows with thumb and forefinger, staring at the document in disbelief. Antiques and jewelry were more of a lucrative business than he could've imagined. There were so many numbers in front of the decimal point he took a few moments to calculate.

"Almost eight hundred million? Is this right?"

Ralph smiled. "The numbers look fake, but banks don't lie. Generosa brought me that statement when they came in. No stock market holdings, secret offshore accounts, IRAs, just what you see there. Quite amazing."

"Just? Mom didn't need any other investments. She'd make a dent in the Greek national debt."

"Keep in mind, until she's officially declared deceased, those funds remain in her accounts."

"Did Dad know about this?"

"I don't know the answer to that. They were as close as any two people I've known, so we'd have to assume so, but there's no way to know for sure. Please have your trust and will updated once you get back to the States. It avoids probate. Governments love to get their hands on private money. Greece especially. I'll forward Pearce's account numbers and banking information for your financial planning. If the banks give you any problems with wiring funds or account access, feel free to call my office." He stretched out his hand and took Alec's with the force of a small vise. "Alec, I wish we were meeting under different circumstances, but it's good to see you. Allow me to make a copy of Pearce's will. I'll keep Generosa's information should the need arise." He paused, sending a blank look to the folder. "When you find her, I'd like to hear."

Alec gave him a subdued smile and shot a sideways look at the door again. It had been selfish of him to bring Annalisse along.

"And take care of that beautiful gal." Ralph gestured with a tilt of his head. "I'm glad she's here for you."

"Me too."

CHAPTER
TWENTY - FOUR

Annalisse jumped when Alec's phone blared a series of ear-pounding bongs. The noise reverberated off the cloth interior of the Zavos family Mercedes and jangled her thoughts.

"Really? I think I left my wits on your floorboard." She laid her hand against her chest and patted a couple of times.

"I didn't want to miss Mooney's call. I'll change the alert. Why don't you check in with Luci? Then we'll grab a late lunch," Alec said.

Annalisse nodded, grateful to be out of Generosa's cramped, classic sedan made for tiny people. "Take your time. I'll pour us a couple of glasses of lemonade." She snagged her purse and got out.

Since their return from the attorney's office, she and Alec had talked in the car, soft top down, for half an hour in the driveway of the villa. She suspected Alec wanted to keep the maid from overhearing his personal business, and no one could blame him for caution with a girl like Luciana inside. When Alec mentioned the family finance discussion with Ralph, Annalisse promptly changed the subject back to finding his mother. His family's wealth was a sore reminder of her living in the worst place in the country to be jobless. She couldn't think about how she'd pay her bills at home.

When she reached the house, mandolins and accordions erupted from inside, rattling the windows and vibrating the deck beneath her feet. She peered into the glass sliding door and viewed Luciana, poised with a mop on the kitchen tile, swishing like a belly dancer to the ruckus.

Annalisse dragged the slider open, covering one ear with her palm. "Hey! A little loud, isn't it?" The accordion was one of her favorite instruments because it reminded her of Italian outdoor cafés or Parisian coffeehouses, but playing it loud enough to break the good china went too far. She looked around the room for the sound system and switched it off.

The maid stopped her gyrations and asked, "What happen? No power?"

Annalisse shook her head. "That racket is peeling the paint off the walls."

"I like."

"I'm sure you do, but I doubt Alec will. We're in mourning and would appreciate quiet."

Luciana swept her hairline with the edge of the apron, jerked a nod, and under her breath muttered, "You tink you better tan me."

Her words were faint but clear enough. Although Annalisse couldn't read her face, apparently Luciana disliked her presence in the villa. The most likely possibility was that Luciana had a crush on Alec. He was her only concern, not his dead father or missing mother. The maid's resentment added unnecessary stress nobody needed right now. Annalisse could take care of anything Alec required without going through a third party.

"Luciana, since I'm here, please take a few days off. Maybe do some shopping. We'll be fine." Annalisse pointed to the door, trying to muster a pleasant smile. "We'll call you when we hear from Gen. I promise."

"Alec needs—"

"Alec needs rest and no interruptions."

"Can't I say someting?" Luciana asked.

"We'll call you."

The mop handle clattered to the ceramic tile. The maid turned toward Annalisse, and with a snarl, tipped over the bucket, spreading gray water in the middle of the kitchen.

"What a hateful thing to do." Annalisse ran for the mop, her temper on high.

"Alec says. Not you."

Annalisse strode to the love seat with the dripping mop in hand, plucked the maid's straw bag from the cushion, and tossed it at her.

"Leave. Before I strap you to this mop and fly you to Oz."

Luciana stamped across the thin layer of dirty water, sending droplets everywhere. As she passed Annalisse, she hissed like a feral cat, her upper lip curled, exposing a set of less than pretty front teeth.

Once the maid slammed the door, Annalisse's frazzled nerves diminished. "Best get to it." She took off her shoes and tiptoed into the mess with the mop.

She ran a clean mop over the entire kitchen on the second pass, then rolled up the hems of her soggy slacks and looked for any water she'd overlooked. Fortunately, the mess hadn't drifted into the white living room carpet.

Checking the path from kitchen to carpet, Luciana's shoes had left behind smudges on the white fibers, but while wet, a dry towel cured the problem. The tile had turned Annalisse's toes into Popsicles, and she headed for the bedroom to warm up and dry out. She wondered what Alec would say about Luciana's flight from the villa. Annalisse envisioned Luciana riding her mop through the air and chortled at the thought.

After she changed into a light dress, she went back and poured two glasses of lemonade, setting one on a coaster in the living room while taking a long swig from the other. Alec hadn't returned from his long call with Mooney, but his absence gave her plenty of time to regret sending Luciana away.

The door to the villa opened, and Alec walked inside, making a beeline for the glass of lemonade. Annalisse imagined the sweet tang and taste of salt on his lips while he gulped.

"What?" He wrinkled his nose. "I guess you'll tell me later." He took another long drink. "I saw Luci stomp out, and I tried to get her attention, but she ignored me."

Luciana must have concluded Annalisse was Alec's steady girlfriend, and her word was as good as his. Girlfriend. Ha. She hadn't been anyone's girlfriend in ages.

"I sent her home." Annalisse explained the confrontation from start to finish. "I had no right to, but her attitude made me so angry. I should've talked to you first." She turned away as her skin flushed hot. "I'm going outside."

Annalisse walked onto the veranda with her hands balled into fists. When they found Generosa, Alec would have to explain what she had done. Luciana might find another job in the meantime, and it would be *her* fault for letting her go, no matter Annalisse's intentions.

Alec came up behind her and spun her to him.

"You have a habit of leaving me behind." He hugged her gently, cascading his scent around her. "Be careful. You'll give me a complex." Alec found her lips and urged her into a slow, smoldering kiss, then broke it, saying, "Thank you for what you did with Luci."

She pulled back and studied his facial expression for clues.

"Luci needed to go. Mom's opinionated, which I've gotten used to, but Luci likes to play my parents against each other." He smiled sadly at her. "Mom's ties with a best friend were the glue that held Luci here. When Luci's mother died, Mom felt the obligation to take care of her daughter."

Annalisse could understand that, knowing Generosa. What she'd give for some of her natural wisdom right now. When it came to affairs of the heart, Generosa was always spot on.

"Your maid can't stand me." Annalisse rested her cheek on his chest and murmured, "I'd be happy for just one lousy day without drama. I thought I could handle the attorney business earlier. Please forgive my walkout at the office." She burrowed deeper into the curve of his shoulder.

"It was a lot to ask of you." He gently rubbed her back.

"Mooney's call went long," she said, hoping for the details.

"Our *detective* is not happy that we kept him out of the loop about the necklace. He knew we were hiding facts and so did Norcross."

"I saw it in his eyes at the gallery and again at the brownstone," she added.

"This investigation is bigger than the necklace and what's happened to us. The FBI's taking over the local probe, and he said to be expecting the Feds' arrival on Crete soon."

A procession of tingles charged down the length of her back. Having the authorities watching them meant zero privacy while she and Alec were on Crete. But at least they were alone in the house for now.

Staring out to an unknown spot in the sea, he was still and silent before he spoke. "Our bodyguard will be here this evening." His phone chimed. "Just discussing you with Annalisse, Detective. I'm putting you on speaker, and she's with me."

"Special Agent Norcross finally got a hit on Chesnokov. The name's an alias. He and his brother are here on expired visas, and that could be why he left the gallery in such a hurry." Mooney paused for what felt like forever. "Since Ms. Drury sent us in that direction, you should know, they're tied to the Chechen Mafia and extremely dangerous. We've put APBs out on them."

Annalisse gasped. "And Gen's been friendly with him."

"There's no way Mom is knowingly making deals with the Mafia."

"We're looking into more, but Agent Norcross wanted me to relay that much. If you see Chesnokov, *do not* pursue him in any fashion. Notify us. It's good that you're both out of the country with security," Mooney said.

The note under the conch shell and Mooney's advice convinced her that someone of interest to law enforcement had already followed them to the island.

"What about the thief who shot me at the brownstone?" Alec asked.

"Unfortunately, no one has seen him. We aren't entirely sure there's any connection between him and the brothers."

"How about the men on the yacht? Are they also Chechens? Does any of this bring us closer to finding out who has Gen? We believe the necklace is what these men who killed Pearce and took Gen were trying to recover," Annalisse said.

"It's too soon to tell who these operators are and how they're all intertwined. The agents assigned to your case may have more details. It's everything we can do to keep up with unfolding events in New York. We know that Chesnokov moved in from San Diego—too bad they didn't stay out West in someone else's jurisdiction."

"We appreciate the information, Detective, and we'll be extra careful. If anything else breaks, please notify us immediately. Thanks." Alec touched another phone icon.

"A text came through from Agent Matthew Brennan while Mooney was talking. He's been assigned to us."

"That was fast."

"Yes, and he's already on Crete. Here's a follow-up email from him." Alec walked over to the lounge, staring at the screen.

She leaned against the round metal rail and watched the amazing man in front of her work their situation with a determination she admired. But his face painted the story of a tortured man, aged by a decade since they'd stepped on the plane in New York.

Alec's lips curved upward, dimpling one cheek. "His note reads like he's the Dirty Harry type; strictly the facts, ma'am. He wants to meet us at a café in Agios. Whew, that's a long way down the coast for a meeting." Alec scrolled the email and recited a set of numbers out loud. "I'm calling him."

Annalisse noticed her overstuffed tote bag outside the sliding glass door. "How could I have left that there?" She must have dropped it in a hurry when she ran inside to shut down the crazy music.

As he dialed Brennan's cell phone, she snapped up the tote and emptied it of all lotions, lipsticks, sunglasses, and receipts, making a quick tally of her wallet and passport in a side pocket. Everything seemed in order as she'd left it. "No wonder it weighs a ton. Huh, that's weird." She found an odd-shaped note and tossed it on top of the pile. "Must be a coupon from that little gift shop at the Athens airport."

The bold symbols in superb penmanship caught her attention, but she couldn't recall how the slip got inside her bag.

"I left Brennan a message." Alec walked over and sat next to her. "Are you ready to see more of the coast? It should be a nice drive. Annalisse?"

With a shaky hand, she showed him the scrap of colored paper. "Alec, Slavic writing. I don't know how it got into my purse."

"Take everything from your purse and zip-bag it separately, including the leather tote. They might be able to get prints off the leather." Alec glanced at his watch. "We're about an hour's drive from Agios Nikolaos. I'll try Brennan again and let him know our ETA."

"He'll be able to translate the note?" she asked.

"If spy flicks are realistic, they'll send an agent who knows the area." He gave her a huge smile. One she hadn't seen enough since the party. "Text it to your translator friend in New York. It's late out there but worth a shot."

Alec's phone rang. "Zavos." He paused, edging back to the chaise, his smile fading. "Yes, this is he."

Annalisse froze. The conversation was one-sided, and by the slump of Alec's shoulders and the twist in his mouth, he didn't like the news.

"I didn't catch that. Can you repeat it?" Alec held pain in his eyes as he stood mute, then his voice softened. "Thank the coast guard for me. I appreciate their help." Alec's moan was gut-wrenching.

"They found Gen?" She couldn't keep fear from entering her words.

He clasped his hands and lowered his head. "Pray that Mom's being held inland, because it's the only good option we have left. The coast guard's ending the search."

CHAPTER
TWENTY - FIVE

In the shade of a mature bougainvillea, tired raspberry blossoms rained down on Annalisse's shoulders as Alec made a reservation with the maître d'. Archaic buildings in rows blocked what little heat radiated through the mottled clouds above. She pressed cold fingers against her neck for warmth and regretted leaving Generosa's sweater draped over a chair at the villa.

"If my Greek is correct, we can seat ourselves," Alec said, anxiously checking his watch for the fifth time. "I hope Brennan didn't change his mind."

She managed to laugh at the hairy restaurateur in a mint-green shirt and black vest, standing beside a Greek sign that she presumed read something like Wait to be Seated.

"Do you have any idea what he looks like?" she asked.

He shrugged. "Got me. I thought he'd beat us here. What's so funny?"

"You with sign language. I didn't watch you with the headwaiter, but I'll bet you nailed it." Annalisse covered a snicker by dropping her head and turning away.

"I saw that. If someone tied my hands together, I couldn't speak." His self-deprecating humor and laughter felt genuine.

"I'm awful… picking on a handsome guy with such great hands." She paused long enough for him to see her smirk. "Gen does the exact same thing; poetry in action. Are we supposed to wait on the street with so many tables inside?" Annalisse rubbed her arms.

Alec pulled out her wooden chair. A poster of shelled clams and mussels on a bed of rice leaned on a rustic easel beside the entrance. The scent of the lunch special, grilled seafood with oranges and olives and a hint of buttered bread and pungent cheeses, drifted through Café Gleekos' coved entrance. Her mouth watered in anticipation.

"I'd love to see a menu." She scanned the cobbled street for anyone remotely spyish, then glanced at her own watch. "Almost four. Are we at the right place?"

"How many Café Gleekos' in Agios can there be? He'll be here."

Across the table, Alec fiddled with a cloth napkin, oblivious to the chill. Wistful and slightly sad, with blue blotches below his eyes, he had more wealth than most people could spend in a lifetime. And a loss that he'd never get over in any lifetime.

She appreciated his selfless concern for others that far outweighed the dollar signs attached to his family name. Not once had he referred to money or what he could make of himself with more of it. Annalisse's early impression of the Alec from the media had gigantic flaws in it, but that still left the larger question of his dad's wishes.

By leaving his fortune to Alec, Pearce had disregarded Generosa for no reason Annalisse could comprehend, but she had to know her husband's plans. Alec's new financial standing would bring a torrent of beautiful women. Wanting him for the money. And personal gratification.

The money would be an afterthought. Annalisse fixated on his brawny shoulders. He'd obviously found time in his schedule for exercise. And his hair—the way the ebony waves curled just above the ear—enhanced the silver flecks in his eyes when he looked at her. His gaze had melted her more than once since the party. That Alec was heir to a fortune wouldn't stay secret for long once Pearce's name leaked out to the scavenger press corps—the media who adored all things Alec to sell their newspapers and attract new subscribers.

After this trip, her so-called vacation, she'd resume appraising but somewhere other than New York. New Jersey seemed a good place to start. A new state and a new city, working alongside clients she'd grown fond of through Harry's connections. She'd find a small apartment to extend her inheritance until she'd gained a foothold and earned a decent living as a freelancer.

Alec repositioned his knife and fork, adrift in thought to some faraway place. The charmer across the table would focus on his dad's business once they found Generosa and departed from Greece, if they were lucky enough to find her. Her heart clenched, knowing her record for past relationships was abominable. Would she send Alec packing too?

A tall man with buzzed auburn hair and laughing eyes, accompanied by a guy with a cool arrogance, stopped beside their table. "Zavos?"

Alec nodded. "Agent—"

Laughing Eyes cut him short with a tip of his gray wool fisherman's cap. "Matt. Nice to meet you. This is Flynn. We hope you haven't been waiting long. I got carried away jogging—lost track of time."

"I envy you. I don't have the knees for jogging," Annalisse said.

Matt and Flynn pulled out their chairs.

"I have to; doctor's orders. It helps to run with a partner. Personally, I despise running." Matt turned up his nose.

His hands were freckled, and he wore a simple gold wedding band. For some reason, Annalisse hadn't expected to find a married man in the spy business.

"I'm surprised to see two of you." Alec's chair cracked as he rocked backward.

"How was the drive up? Any problems finding the place?" Matt asked.

"Why couldn't we meet in Sitia?" Alec brought the chair back down with a snap.

"I should've explained." He shot a glance at Flynn across the table and lowered his voice. "In case you're being watched. You didn't notice anyone tailing you here, did you?"

Alec shook his head.

Matt sat back and gazed down the street. "God, I love this place. Beautiful Mirabello Bay. The best seafood on Crete. Right, Flynn?" He directed the question at his silent partner.

Flynn set his square jaw as if he was afraid to speak. "First time here."

"The smells are sinful. Let's flag down a waiter." Annalisse put her napkin on her lap. "The restaurant was a great idea."

Matt gave a well-practiced, official grin. "Sure thing. I'll get some menus. They're in Greek, but I can translate if you don't speak the language."

He twisted his over six-foot physique at an awkward angle. As he turned, Annalisse noticed a long white scar under his chin to the side of his neck. It forked near the jugular like he'd been cut twice in the past.

During the forty minutes it took them to finish their meals, a trickle of guests came and went from the café. Matt's insistence on being outside for privacy had worked since no one liked their food to get cold while dining. She'd eaten fast just to stay warm.

Matt wiped the corner of his mouth and turned to Alec. "I've been in touch with investigators in SoHo. The Bureau's on it now. I wasn't sure if they told you."

"Detective Mooney mentioned it."

"There's one thing you should know." A corner of his mouth curved. "We're CIA—covert."

"How'd you get here so fast?" Alec asked.

"We were already in Athens."

"Have you heard about the brownstone shooting?" She glanced at Alec. "And the rest?" Annalisse twirled a few strands of leftover linguini on her plate.

"We've been briefed. Polonium is certainly something we don't hear about every day." Flynn pushed his horn-rims higher on his nose.

"Agent Flynn or just Flynn? What do we call you?" Alec snapped.

Annalisse cringed inside at his irritated tone. For the CIA to send two guys to Crete supported Mooney's stark warnings.

"Just Flynn will be fine." He gave Alec an amused look.

Spies were as cocky in person as depicted on television. She liked Matt, but Flynn's silence and attitude unnerved her. He might be the kind of guy who had to grow on a person, but she hoped he wouldn't stick around long enough to find out.

"Have you spoken to Detective Mooney today? He—" Alec jumped when Flynn dropped a fork on his plate. Perhaps on purpose.

"We know what you know… and more." Flynn's clipped words had shut Alec down.

To break the tension around the table, she dug into the gallon ziplock bag inside her leather tote and handed the note across the table to Matt. "I found this today in the bottom of my purse. We both handled it."

Matt frowned as he studied the writing, then nodded. "Chechen, like the first one. The letterbox was right about receiving another one. Inside your purse, huh?" He lifted one ruddy brow and took another bite of shrimp saganaki. "Interesting."

"More like scary, and this one too." She gave him the scrap that said *Thieves*.

"It's the network. Spooks see it all, miss." Flynn wiped a speck of sauce from his chin with a napkin. "We're dealing with a crime family who're lethal as a viper's fangs. Do you have security?"

Alec looked at his watch. "He's expected in a few hours."

"How many are on the team?" Matt asked.

"Isn't one guy enough?" Alec turned slightly gray.

"What about the blue note from my purse?" Annalisse tapped the table with a fingernail.

"It says *the curse spares no one*." Matt rubbed his index finger across his lower lip. "Palace intrigue."

Alec covered her hand with his and pressed his lips into a scowl. "We'd better divulge the rest."

"Are you certain Gen isn't mentioned?" she asked.

"I'm fluent in several Russian dialects, spoken and read. This note undeniably warns of a curse. Shed some light on what you know about this so-called curse, Miss Drury." Matt

177

glanced at his partner and back to her. "Mind if I smoke?" No sooner had he asked, he'd already pulled a Camel from the package in his breast pocket and tapped the filter on the table.

"I'm still trying to decode spooks and letterboxes. It's all Greek to me." She realized what a lame pun she'd made and avoided Alec's gaze.

Matt bent low and whispered, "I'll try to keep the lingo to a minimum. A letterbox is a go-between, and the spooks are us." Matt waggled his thumb between himself and Flynn. "What else do you have for us?"

Alec told the operatives about their suspicions over the necklace while she listened, pushing shrimp shells and leftover octopus from the rim of her plate.

In return, Matt explained how their surveillance team, which he called a hunting pack, had picked up evidence from informants. But his sketchy data about what they'd uncovered left her with more questions.

Annalisse mulled over Matt's inconsistencies and forced herself not to interrupt, even though she was dying to do so.

"The briefing's over. Miss Drury, do you have something to add?"

"It's Annalisse, and yes, we'd like some clarifications please."

"Shoot," Matt said.

She caught herself from jumping in and turned to Alec. "Go ahead."

"Do you believe these notes are connected to the men on our yacht?" Alec asked.

"Now that we know there's an artifact involved, they could be. We'll require you to turn over the necklace. It should be secured."

"Dad's killers never asked for the necklace," Alec said. "And what about Harry Carradine, the poison victim? He's tied to this how?"

Matt set his cap by his plate, exposing a military buzz cut. "We believe Mr. Carradine was being coerced, bribed, or perhaps shaken down. We found several communiqués from a man using an alias, looking for jewelry he thought was in Generosa Zavos's possession. What you've explained is consistent."

"You mean Chesnokov? So when Harry wouldn't—or didn't—deliver the jewelry, they poisoned him?" she asked.

"Chesnokov contacted you?" Flynn whispered. "What did he say?"

Matt raised a hand to stop his partner. "We also know Mr. Carradine owed money to a bookie. Lots of money. Our FBI liaison is moving in on the bookmaker."

"I didn't know Harry bet on the horses, did you, Annalisse?" Alec asked.

"Not to my knowledge."

"We don't know it's the ponies. Sports is more likely," Matt said.

"Let's get back to my mother, shall we?" Alec narrowed his eyes at Flynn.

"We've picked up chatter that's uncovered who the main players are, tracing their communiqués between Turkey and Manhattan. I assume the necklace is hidden on Crete?" Flynn waited for confirmation.

"I have it in a safe, but it stays with me for the time being," Alec said.

"That's a mistake, Mr. Zavos," Matt said earnestly. "Please reconsider. We have the means to secure it. On a side note, I spoke in person with a Mr. Gregory from Westinn Gallery."

She groaned at the idea of Peter knowing their whereabouts. "The ogre rears his bald head again."

"You *are* the same person who worked with him? Mr. Gregory was—let's say—ambiguous. He couldn't be bothered with the death of his brother-in-law. As a matter-of-fact, he seemed more interested in you, Annalisse." Matt glared at her. "Odd fellow, but he's somebody's kid. We aren't done with him, but judging by your comment, he's been a nuisance. What can you tell us about him?"

"He's a rat who bites. Forget about him. Has any of this brought us closer to finding Mom? Are you certain she's alive?" Alec muttered a curse.

"During the fingerprint sweep of your gallery, the FBI recovered two high-value matches through AFIS with ties to the syndicate—drugs, heists, mob hits; a long list. Grifters with bad attitudes and short fuses. We have one in custody being questioned, but the other's still at large."

"Colum Mooney has kept details from us. But why single Mom out?" Alec asked Matt.

"They followed the biggest score. Tangos—sorry, thieves and assassins—are driven by greed. Drug deals, robberies, jewels, antiquities, murder, anything. The payday at the end is what matters."

"Whose prints came up at the gallery?" Alec asked.

"Two brothers. One of which left this calling card." Matt turned his head, and the forked scar showed again. "Pavel Andreyev. He sometimes goes by Nikita."

Annalisse sucked in a breath. "I know that name. His picture's on Peter's wall."

"Mr. Gregory?" Matt widened his eyes. "We'll get back to that. The Andreyev boys report directly to a rogue named Viktor Titov. He's known for big scores and even bigger daggers—slashing throats from ear to ear. Alec, if your mother took that necklace from him, Titov won't stop till he gets it back. He'll scorch earth for a priceless, stolen possession. If your mother's alive and he's tied her to the necklace, she's—"

"Gen never *stole* a priceless treasure from anybody, so don't go there." She shot a hard look at Matt. "Who's the man you have in custody?" Annalisse suspected what he might say, having mentioned Nikita and Flynn's reaction to her knowing Chesnokov.

"Yuri Andreyev. He goes by several aliases. You mentioned one of them—Chesnokov. He also goes by Maxim Andreyev."

"He's Nikita's brother, isn't he?" She recalled the faces were similar in the photo. "Twin brother?"

"Yes. They impersonate each other," Flynn said, raising both brows.

"Here. I almost forgot." Alec leaned to one side and pulled out his wallet. "I found this in Dad's files."

Annalisse gasped and asked, "When did you have time to do that?"

"Last night when I couldn't sleep." Alec slipped out a page folded in quarters and handed it to Matt. "I don't know if this helps, but it looks like some kind of a receipt paid with dinar. Dad left most expenditures to Mom. It's what made this so unusual. Mom handles the finances, but he did give her the necklace for her birthday. Take a look at the date."

Matt unfolded the sheet and examined it. He nodded. "Kurdish."

"Pearce bought it in Iraq?" Annalisse asked.

"It's not that simple. The handwriting's very poor. It's hard to know the exact region since the Kurds range from Iraq to Turkey, Syria, and Iran. When we ousted Saddam, the Iraqi museums had been stripped bare. Artifacts were stolen and re-sold. Your necklace could've been one of those relics. A thief may have sold it to Mr. Zavos without knowing its history." Matt said.

"Dad wouldn't go to that much trouble when Mom had her own jeweler. I don't buy any of this, Matt."

"The receipt is small potatoes, about three hundred dollars. If your father knew the value, it was a bargain."

"Yeah, some bargain." Annalisse laid her napkin next to her plate.

"I need to see the horses, this Mushasha piece, for myself. If your mother was kidnapped for it, we'll know soon enough. But I'll take your purse and the rest with me." Matt accepted the tote as she passed it over, empty.

"There's something else." Alec glanced at Annalisse sympathetically. "Mom has a health condition. She looks outwardly fine, but she needs medication for Gaucher disease."

"Gen's sick? Oh, Alec." She squeezed his hand. "I didn't know."

"Only the family knows." He turned to Matt. "We've run out the clock, and Mom's situation is serious. She takes pills twice a day."

"Pills that she doesn't have," Matt added.

"What happens when she goes without her pills?" Annalisse's pulse pounded at her temples. Generosa might be captive in some wet cargo hold or dirty cave with no food or water, hurting—or dying.

His eyes flashed with tears. "Mom's bones ache, she tires, and bruises easily. She felt bad for years before they diagnosed her. Gaucher keeps blood from clotting, so she has to be careful with cuts."

Closing her eyes, Annalisse steadied herself. Generosa had hidden her disease well. When they reached the villa after their meeting with Matt and Flynn, she'd check the medicine cabinet for Generosa's prescription meds and keep those pills with her at all times.

"Matt." Annalisse glanced at Alec then back to the men. "Do we have enough leads to find Gen quickly?"

Matt took a long drag on his cigarette and blew smoke to the side. "If you're asking if we'll find her alive, I hope so. Yuri Andreyev appears to be cooperating. It's been twenty-four hours, and our ops team is in the region. But until we determine where she's being held, if she's being held, every day that passes without word goes against us." He bent low and leaned across the table. "Before we finish, I'd like to hear what you know about Yuri Andreyev. Alec, you have my direct line. If I'm compromised, Flynn will contact you."

Annalisse pinched the seam on her jeans to give herself something to do. "I don't know how to put this, so I'll just toss it out. Matt, can we trust you? Gen's life and our lives depend on strangers—three-letter agencies—running a dangerous rescue operation. Speaking for myself, I'm scared to death." Annalisse couldn't bring herself to look at Alec, but he must have had similar thoughts. She relaxed a little when he grasped her fingertips below the table.

"We're the best there is, if that helps," Matt said.

"Out of curiosity, did you ask for this assignment?" Alec's gaze dropped to Matt's neck.

Matt showed them his official smile and lit up another Camel.

"Who's sitting on the steps?" Annalisse shoved her sunglasses on top of her head, training her eyes on someone who looked remarkably like Luciana seated at the villa. The girl's elbows were plastered on her knees, her head bowed. "That's your maid, isn't it?" She sighed in dread. "I can't believe she's back after her stunt."

Alec wound the Mercedes into the slanted driveway and parked. "Let's see what she wants."

Allowing him to take the lead, Annalisse walked a few paces behind. Luciana jumped to attention, wiping her eyes. The same eyes that devoured Alec with a look of lust and, not surprising, crocodile tears. Annalisse repressed her satisfaction at seeing the maid groveling at Alec's feet.

"Alec. I must say someting. Please. I want work here. I did terrible ting. So sorry for what I did. Don't fire. Please?"

"Let's go inside and talk," he said to Luciana.

He'd fallen for the act.

Annalisse stayed to the rear and wrinkled her nose at the maid's red dress with the pungent scent of damp clothes left in the washer too long. Generosa must have handled that household duty herself since she never had a wrinkle and loved a touch of fabric softener.

Once inside, a gust of wind pulled the door out of Annalisse's sweaty fingers. The slam could've been heard on Greece's mainland.

Alec spun around wide-eyed, took a breath, then pivoted toward the maid.

"Luci, I'm only going to say this once. My… friend spent an hour in the kitchen mopping up after your tantrum. That won't happen again."

Luciana nodded slowly.

"I'd like you to apologize. To her." He pointed at Annalisse.

"It's not necessary, Alec."

The apology about to tumble from the maid's mouth meant little, but Alec's stilted reference to being a *friend*, she hadn't anticipated. The reference left her doubting her chances of winning over a man who'd seemed genuinely interested in her.

"Missy?"

Annalisse glared and gritted her teeth against further snarky remarks.

"Miss, forgive please. Big sorry. I love Zavos family. Crete my home now. Let me work here. Please?"

Annalisse was unexpectedly moved. On an island built for the tourist trade, an out-of-work maid's only options were to find another family or work in a hotel. Or, in Luciana's case, return to Italy.

"We're all too emotional right now. Please work this out with Alec. If you'll excuse me." She glanced at him and hurried to her bedroom, leaving the door open a crack.

"Luci, here's the deal. I'm going to pay you six months in advance to stay at your place. Use that time to look for a new job."

"You pay me, and I work here, not home. I work here."

"No. When Mom returns, we'll bring you back, *if* you still need a job."

"Please, please let me stay. I belong here wit you."

"Luci, wait here." His footsteps quieted, then he asked, "What's your monthly pay?"

"Eight hundred euro, but I no take."

Peeking around the doorjamb, she witnessed Alec returning to offer Luciana a handful of multicolored bank notes.

"No. I no take from you."

"Luci, it's done. Thank you for your service and friendship to my parents. There's extra in there for you."

Luciana squealed and parted with the word "*Ingrato.*"

When the maid left, Annalisse entered the hall. "Did she just call you an ingrate?"

"She said ungrateful."

"But generous." She wiped her forehead with the back of her hand. "I'm so sorry to have caused her dismissal. More turmoil we don't need."

"Shh." He drew her into his space.

She read so many contradictory emotions on him. Sorrow, hope, trust, and desire blended together behind his intense scrutiny. Gently touching the rise near his collarbone, she felt his pecs flex when he breathed. She wanted Alec's come-and-get-me signals to mean something more than casual lust between them. Finally alone with no fear of Luciana's return, if he kissed her now, she'd be cooked—set the table.

"Pretty lady, I'm happy Luci's gone. We won't be in Greece forever." The lilt in his voice had nothing to do with Luciana or Greece.

"Should we…?" Annalisse's thigh touched his. "Change the locks?"

Alec grazed a palm down the curve of her hip. "That's not what I thought you were going to say." He intimately stroked her hair. "Luci can't get into the safe. Don't worry."

"Gen's life depends on the necklace and her meds, so when we find her…" Her trembling added to the crazy thumping of her heart.

"We'll be careful." He bent excruciatingly close to her mouth.

His nearness sent her desire into overdrive; she was breathless and hot with anticipation, but she couldn't—they couldn't give in while they were in so much peril.

"My shoes have worn blisters." Annalisse broke their embrace and kicked off her loafers, settling onto the love seat.

Alec stayed put, stoic and unreadable. Not quite unreadable. He dropped his head and closed his eyes, breathing in and out slowly, making no effort to move or hide his attraction to her.

When she couldn't interpret his emotions, a tiny bit of her ached. His expressive eyes were her window into what made him so magnetic and enticing. She hadn't noticed other men yearning for her as Alec had on more than one occasion. She'd felt his attentiveness going far beyond the superficial.

Patting the cushion next to her, she managed an empathetic smile. "Sit here. We've had a few horrible days and possibly more to come, but I can't imagine spending them with anyone but you."

He laughed as he sat beside her. "It's a good thing my ego's in check."

"That's twice today my attempt at humor has bombed."

His grin dimpled both his cheeks. "It's charming."

"I'll keep the day job. I mean, what used to be my day job. You know what I mean." She half closed her eyes, counting the beats in her chest. "Since the party, I hardly know the real *me* anymore."

Alec scooted over, leaving a small gap between them, and patted a spot high on his thigh.

"Rest your head. There's no place we need to be right now." He lifted just enough to extract his wallet, jangling his keys when he dropped them on the glass table.

Her mind raced with multiple options. Should she keep sending mixed signals and wonder about him forever or be honest with herself? Knowing the answer, she guided him nearer, wrapping her arms about his neck.

"I'm not tired, Alec. Not even close."

The silver diamonds of his eyes shone back at her. He parted his lips and stared in astonishment, leaving her in total control. A good thing for her because if he'd taken command of the moment, she'd likely lose her nerve.

Annalisse shoved all scenarios aside except for his lips. She wanted more of that mouth and leaned backward, pulling him in with her kiss and biting his lower lip softly on the retreat.

He groaned in pure passion, and holding her face in his hands, he mashed her into a caress that went from hard to savage as he stifled another moan and pulled her inward to new depths.

Sugared ice pulsed through her body.

Tearing her lips away, she nipped his ear lobe and whispered, "I don't normally act this way."

"It's new for me too."

Right. Like you've never known other women.

She hated tired lines. The kind he'd undoubtedly used on the harem before her. Their pleasurable moment destroyed, Annalisse pushed him away and rose from the couch cushion.

"What?" he asked.

"Don't say that on my account. I'm not a ditsy fool."

His gaze hardened on her like iron. "Will you please have some faith in me? Who did the number on you?"

"Don't spout lines that aren't so," she said.

"I haven't."

"Then what's new about this?"

"You are."

Annalisse shook her head, unsure if her frustration was with him or botching what might be the best thing that's happened to her. Ever.

A sigh came from deep in his chest. "Don't flash those wicked green eyes at me until you've heard me out. I'm taking *us* at a slower pace so that we don't mess this up. I want the chance to get to know *the real you*, as you say, but only when *you're* ready. We take this to the next level on your timeline, not mine. What do I have to do to convince you that my intentions are honorable and not lascivious?"

Their few innocent kisses so far had been instigated by her, and with his explanation, she understood why. He'd planned to wait and not push her into a more serious relationship. To him, she was damaged. Alec had a past, as did she, and what they created together would be theirs alone.

187

"I'm more than a conquest?" she asked.

"Yes," he whispered. Alec drenched her with the stare that reached into her deeply. "Mom knows me, and she's noticed you too—the most awesome creature to bump into me in a very long while."

She relaxed the tension in her muscles as he covered her hand with his. The desire on his face turned her into a puddle of want. Leaning against his shoulder, she closed her eyes, consumed in the frosty rush left by his sensual long fingers touching hers.

"Umm." She breathed, bending him down to her mouth once more, where she tasted the salty perspiration above his lips.

Alec stiffened and pulled back from her. "I've imagined sweet and slow for us, but you'll have to help me with that, babe." He traced a line on a patch of bare skin visible from her blouse. "That sunburn from the boat looks mean. Are you hurting?"

"Right now I wouldn't exactly call it that." She raised a brow. "If you'd asked me yesterday—"

Before she could protest, Alec stood, watching her silently, as if assessing her innermost thoughts. She visualized a fatal gratification in his arms—one she could never come back from and be the same.

Annalisse followed his lead from the sofa and lovingly embraced him, savoring how good it felt to be in his powerful arms. His nurturing warmth left a wide-open door to intimacy beyond her wildest dreams—with an incredible man—who wanted her.

"I'm heading for the shower." *Before I throw myself at you or throw up on the floor.*

CHAPTER
TWENTY - SEVEN

Once he'd closed the bay window and sheers, Alec flicked on the living room fan.

"Clothing optional," he said toward her bedroom in jest.

Alec began to pull his polo over his head, debated the action, and stopped. He'd taken on her challenge happily since he'd surprised her at the opening. She'd been genuine and unpretentious—and self-reliant to a fault, which frustrated him to no end. But with her past, he realized why she was made that way. When she'd performed CPR on Harry, stood up to Peter at Westinn and the brownstone gunman, what she saw and did during the boat attack—he knew she was different than any woman he'd met. And when she felt comfortable enough for a deeper relationship with him, he'd explore her at greater depth.

Annalisse appeared at the end of the hallway, hair tied up, in his dress shirt, tails barely covering her thighs. She looked so young and inviting, it took his breath. He hadn't expected her—like this—so soon with all that they'd been through.

"The shower felt wonderful once I got past the sunburn scald." She rolled her shoulders, lifting the hemline even higher, exposing more skin.

After their talk, the sexy woman coming at him at full speed, ready for anything, was a total shocker. Her newest challenge nearly stopped his heart dead away. She'd worked him into a frenzy with so little effort on her part. How would he control himself when he'd promised to take things more slowly with her? While he stared at the amazing woman from feet away, the thought of her long, gorgeous legs entwined with his, he groaned involuntarily. She must have misunderstood what he meant by waiting for the right moment.

Annalisse faced him, daring him to touch her, or at least it felt like that to him.

"I've been thinking… with Pearce, and knowing your mother is still out there, I'm having a bad case of the guilts. Should we get involved in a satisfying tryst when so much is at stake and bombs are lighting up around us?"

He couldn't fault her considerations, but his response came too late.

"And *you* aren't the type I usually go for," she added.

"I've gathered that, so enlighten me. What category do I fit into?"

"Dirty minded and a little malnourished." Stone serious, she grasped his arm near the elbow and jiggled.

He grinned. "I'll give you the first part, but I've never been called malnourished before." What started as a laugh came out in a piglike snort instead.

Her mirth filled him with contagious joy, and he instantly joined her in the ice-breaking laughter.

After the lighthearted minute passed, he guided her to him. Close enough to taste her toothpaste breath and feel the bang of her pulse.

"Let's reserve judgment on all the above." One shirt button stood between them, and he quickly undid it. Pulling apart the cotton, he was overcome, like he'd been so many times in her presence. He released the barrette corralling her hair and fluffed the layers around her. Drawing a long breath, he allowed her fresh, floral scent to settle way back into his nostrils.

"What flower is that?" he asked.

"Lavender and honey."

He sniffed again, kissed the hollow of her neck, then growled, bringing a stifled giggle from her.

Annalisse pulled him down in a shuddering kiss and glided one silky leg up the side of his slacks.

"Are you sure about this?" He'd felt obligated to ask, even as his body craved the excitement of their first time together.

Her sultry gaze spoke of sinful wishes. "I won't break."

"Not what I asked." He smiled, sliding his hands to the curve of her small waist. Her skin vibrated under his fingertips, and the mysterious eyes in the night that had haunted him for so long finally awaited him—flooded with pure, wanton desire.

Filling his lungs with her perfume, he lifted her lithe body in his arms and walked to his parent's master bedroom, pausing uncomfortably at the threshold.

He'd hesitated too long not to be noticed by her.

"It's okay, Alec." She rearranged his collar and swiped at a trickle of his sweat that slid from his temple. "Put me down."

He obliged her wishes and set her on her feet, feeling like he'd failed her in the worst way possible.

"I totally understand and agree; we're being disrespectful of two wonderful people by letting our passions get the best of us. If you'll give me a minute, I'll go and change." Annalisse turned away from him.

He caught her by the wrist and shook his head, directed at himself more than the beautiful woman making a retreat.

She soberly confronted him.

"Annalisse, I want you in the worst way, but I can't force you to my will and won't under any circumstances. If this thing between us is real and going to blossom, we have to learn to trust the other person explicitly and have zero misgivings. Complete and total faith in each other. I'm not sure you're there yet."

"And neither are you. What you describe takes time. You've suffered a terrible loss, and it's wrong of me to treat this trip like a carefree vacation. It may have begun as such, but that changed once we sailed. How I wish I'd known your father before… I should've been able to help—" Her voice broke, and she bowed her head in reverence.

In front of him, she fell apart, and it had everything to do with his messed-up, kid-glove treatment of her. She'd been strong yet delicate in the face of remarkable challenges, showing true courage where others would've collapsed under the weight. If they were to move into a future together, he had to fix his approach. He'd made her sad and regretful when he wanted her to believe in him.

Gathering Annalisse in his arms, he hugged her tightly to his chest, stroking her dark hair as he had in his dreams of the green-eyed temptress.

"You're unlike anyone I've known," he said, kissing the top of her head. "And you know what else? We belong together."

"Is that right?" She poked his ribs gently, causing him to smile. "How did you come to that wild conclusion, Mr. Zavos?"

Raising a brow at her cute formality, he whispered, "Because, Ms. Drury… pretty lady, I'm falling for you."

She abruptly spun about, searching his eyes. "Don't joke around."

"Then you leave me no choice." He took her hand and strolled with her to the guestroom doorway. "How can I set your mind at ease?" Flipping her lustrous brown hair over one shoulder, he added, "Here's my advice: quit overthinking and concentrate on what you want. Right now."

She gazed at him with the same mix of emotions he'd seen since the gallery party. He sensed hope and doubt that she deserved to be happy—with him.

He'd remedy that.

Lifting her once again in his arms, he walked through the threshold, and this time he shut their door with his bare foot.

Seconds became minutes while Alec's pulse slowed, and he caught his wind. He watched Annalisse's eyelids, shut tight as if she were listening to her own heart. Turning on his side, he drew a line down the sweaty center of her body. He felt elation at the promise of so many possibilities with Annalisse once they'd rescued Mom. A double knot tied in his chest. He wouldn't believe that his mother could be dead.

"She's not," he mumbled.

"Did you say something?" Annalisse opened one eye, crinkling the corner of her mouth. "I need another shower."

"*We* need a shower."

The image of his dad holding a pair of binoculars, then pleading with the scum to leave them alone, formed on the plaster-and-beam ceiling. Alec tried to recall his last memory before being beaned on the back of his head.

Dad had settled for nothing but perfection his entire existence.

I'm not a perfectionist.

Annalisse flipped over and propped herself on an elbow. "There's a worried guy where a happy man used to be. What are you thinking about?"

"Dad. Mom. Prescription meds. This whole business." Alec rolled back to her. "We needed a nice—uh—very nice diversion." Sending a finger down her cheek, he added, "I hope this hasn't muddied up our pond."

"I've been knee-deep in that pond long before you no-ticed." She tapped the end of his nose. "A caramel macchiato with a whipped cream chaser." Nuzzling his neck, she feigned a swoon.

He blinked, rising on his elbows. "Do you feel like going out for a coffee?"

"No." She smiled demurely. "That's you. The type I usu-ally run from."

"I'll take hot and steamy over dirty and malnourished any day." He licked his lips and growled, then planted a wet kiss on her.

"Me too."

"Have I lowered the barrier between us—just a little?" he asked her.

"Pierced right through it." Her smile disappeared. "Thoughtless choice of words. Matt and Flynn understand the urgency of finding Gen soon, don't they? She's in God knows whose hands, treated like God knows what. I've tried not to dwell there, but waiting on the sidelines is killing me. Your dad—her state of mind. She witnessed it all." Annalisse cradled his face in her palms. "How are you? Really?"

193

Laying Annalisse on the pillows, he clicked his tongue behind his teeth, deep in thought.

"Nothing like throwing ice cubes at us on a sizzling evening. Good job, Drury." Annalisse grimaced and shook her head.

"Au contraire. You're saving me from myself, babe. I mean that. But your case of the guilts is rubbing off."

Annalisse ran a fingernail around his ear. "Right this minute, Gen's silently cheering us on. Waiting for us to extract her and bring her home."

He nodded and played with a strand of hair that had fallen over one eye. "You do know her. We'll hear something anytime now."

Alec's phone vibrated on the nightstand. Intuitively, he'd gone back into the living room while she'd dozed and had retrieved it earlier.

He reached over and looked at the ID. "Huh, it's Chase." He swiped the screen. "Hey, Chase."

Annalisse pointed to the bathroom, slipped one arm in Alec's shirt, and slid off the mattress.

"Alec, is Anna close by?"

"She can be. Want me to get her?"

"No. She'd better hear this from you."

CHAPTER

TWENTY-EIGHT

"Hold a minute." Alec jumped into his trousers, jogged down the hall, phone in hand, then flew beyond the sliding glass doors in the darkness. "What's up?"

"It's been… interesting, but first my condolences. We're sorry to hear about your dad… and Gen. Anna sent me an email early this morning." Chase's words were sobering.

"Thanks. We haven't given up on Mom."

"She kinda grows on ya." His chuckle had a tinge of sorrow. "You have to find her. I never met your dad, but Gen's touched so many of us."

Alec's swallow scraped the dry spot in his throat. "The moment we get word, we'll let you know. Thanks, Chase. I don't mean to rush, but—"

"I came home from the hospital a little while ago."

"You were sick?"

"No. Helga is still there. They pumped her stomach, but they think she's out of the woods."

Alec felt his blood pressure climb. "You've gotta be kidding. What did she ingest?" Alec turned over Helga's usual lunch and dinner menus in his mind.

"Don't worry. She didn't overdose. She was poisoned though, and so was Boris."

He sighed in angst. "The cat too?"

"Yeah. The vet hospital pumped the little guy's stomach, but he'd digested more of the poison than Helga. He's not so good."

Annalisse's special buddy. *Losing him is going to kill her.*

Alec plopped on the chaise and adjusted the phone. "I'm relieved to hear Helga's recovering, but something happening to Boris will devastate Annalisse." Jumping up again, Alec paced. "Can Boris pull through? How were they poisoned?"

"Boris is… the furry fart is as much mine as Anna's. I want *you* to tell her about him. I can't handle her breaking down."

"Gee, thanks. So, what happened?"

"We got a delivery on Monday. Lilies and tulips along with a box of brownies. Not the homemade type. These were foil packaged and they were big suckers. Helga cooed over the flowers."

"She loves tulips. But they're not in season to my knowledge."

"Anyway, she showed them to me and set aside the brownies. The note was from you, Alec."

"Obviously, I didn't send her anything. Tell me about the note."

"Something to the effect of how you missed us, junk like that. You know, a sugary note."

Alec hummed at the back of his throat. "I don't do sugary with the housekeeper."

"Yeah. I figured that, now that this happened."

"I take it the brownies were spiked?" Alec asked.

"That's what I think. I didn't touch them. Helga offered one to me, but I passed—adds to the love handles. I gave the box to the hospital so they could compare it to her stomach contents. Gross. Helga didn't get into the brownies until yesterday with Boris's help."

"How did Boris—" Alec nodded. "I remember now. You said Helga was feeding him people food. Doesn't she know cats and dogs can't eat chocolate?"

"I didn't know that."

"One of the first things we learn in vet school."

"Vet school? You? I'll bet that's going over well with Anna." Chase whistled.

"Why is it so inconceivable that I could be a veterinarian? Annalisse almost had a cow when she learned about it. You'd better spill the information. It might shed some light on things."

"Doctor Death traumatized Walker Farm because that guy killed more animals than he saved. Having had so many bad experiences, Anna learned to care for the stock herself. I even saw her set a broken leg on a lamb once, using pipe-wrap foam. It worked too." Chase's silence went on for several beats. "Alec, did I lose you?"

"I'm here. I was thinking about the vet's name. *Doctor Death.*"

"That was Anna's nickname for him. She didn't tell you? Anna has a… distaste for veterinarians. She always puts off taking Boris in for his shots. Samantha's boyfriend, Ryan—"

"Is a vet." Alec finished Chase's sentence and muttered, "That explains it."

"You got it. Anna hates the knife-happy jerk who has a fixation with scalpels."

"Samantha's death is still an open case. That's why Annalisse pegged Ryan to her friend's murder, and she ran for a cab outside the restaurant and weirded out when I mentioned setting up a clinic."

"Ryan's a bad dude. A sicko, if you ask me." Chase's voice had climbed a few octaves.

"Did you see the floral delivery or notice anything unusual at the time?"

"Helga said the white van looked like a standard florist's truck. The guy wore street clothes. When we talked about it today, she also mentioned receiving a phone call before the flowers arrived."

"From who?" Alec rubbed the bridge of his nose while pondering suspects.

"Helga said a man was looking for *the boss.* Those were her words. He mentioned being an employee of your gallery and wanted to know when the Zavos shop planned to open again."

"Mom hired a part-time girl for Saturdays. She knows not to discriminate and takes applications from men, but she won't hire them for the floor. She says the ladies tend to be more personable with customers. Now men as gallery security, no problem. Did he say he was security?"

"I don't think so. He sounded more like in the retail part. When Helga wouldn't divulge any answers, he pushed harder for information and asked how you and Gen could be reached."

"What day did the call come in?"

"Monday. Helga didn't tell me about it until today."

Alec sighed. Two days ago. The day before they'd sailed.

"Helga told this person we were in Greece?" Alec asked, flashing on the yacht in his head.

"I think so. Trying to be helpful; you know how she is."

"Okay. The call and delivery were timed together." Alec's gut turned inside out.

"Alec, she thought the stuff was from you. It was an honest mistake."

Annalisse had mentioned the Val guy and assumed that his dad knew him and seemed to know her. It was possible that the same man could've called the estate. Maybe one of the brothers if the caller had spoken with an accent. Chesnokov from the gallery could've found out that Mom had left New York but not known her destination.

"How soon will Helga be released?" Alec asked.

"They may keep her another day or two for observation. Once they feel confident the poison is out of her system, she'll be able to come home. I'll watch over her."

Alec nodded and sank back into the lounge. "Boy, am I glad you're there, Chase. Thank you for managing the catastrophe for us. Did the security company ever make good on sending a guard to the estate?"

"Yeah. Some guy in a rent-a-cop uniform came to the door and introduced himself. From what I saw, he looked legit."

"Text me the guy's picture, name, and any information you have on the security company or any paperwork they left for me. I'll verify everything with Detective Mooney."

"How's Anna holding up?"

Alec smiled. "She's doing better. Awesome, as a matter of fact."

Chase's laughter made Alec's grin widen.

"I'm not going to dig into that. Anna's pretty amazing; treat her right."

"No accepting *any* deliveries. Okay?" Alec picked at the fabric on the lounge.

"Yep."

"Estate security should be barring any salesmen and deliveries from the premises. I'd like you to answer all household calls from now on. Helga won't like it, but we need them screened. I'll keep Boris's mishap to myself for now until Helga's released and you have an update on the cat. Hopefully he'll improve, and I won't have to deliver more bad news."

"I think she'd want to know about Boris, but I'm not there. You know best."

You'll have to trust me too.

"I'd better go." Alec glanced into the living room and saw Annalisse repositioning the cushions on both sofas. "I'll check in with you later. Please let Helga know that we're thinking of her, and I'll call her soon."

"Take down whoever is doing this, Alec."

"Count on it. They've messed with the wrong family."

CHAPTER
TWENTY - NINE

Annalisse headed for the veranda but changed her mind. Observing Alec through the glass, his frowns and hands slicing the air weren't signs of good news from home. Once they located Generosa and caught the man who'd killed Pearce, she'd turn her cruddy existence into something fantastic. The man outside who kneaded her heart into mush and sent her blood racing like one of his sports cars had given her solid encouragement to stop doubting and feed their relationship with the zeal it deserved.

A cluster of framed photos drew her toward the kitchen bookshelf beside Generosa's ample collection of cookbooks. Annalisse wandered there to take her mind off whatever Chase had to say.

Dozens of family pictures were grouped together, with the oldest in the rear and most recent out front. Annalisse studied the smiling threesome in the eight-by-ten-inch frame made up of tiny clamshells and woven satin ribbon. Generosa, Pearce, and Alec stood with pride beside the *Gen Amore* in what appeared to be a boat building yard. Huge blue girders carved out berths between the yachts in varying states of assembly. Alec was in his teens, boyish and gangly but handsome even then. The Zavos clan had pure happiness in their smiles. Pearce had his arm around Generosa, with Alec on her other side, sandwiching her in a petite mom embrace. Alec's dashing grin, pasted on for the camera, warmed Annalisse's insides.

Not unlike the family she had—all gone. Annalisse clutched a fistful of linen on her chest as she remembered Ariel and her parents' picnics underneath trees and watching the horses at the fence during Walker Farm weekend outings. Playing on the wooden swing set built by her uncle during the off-season and their horseback rides under the watchful eyes of her aunt meant more to Annalisse than boys' charms and chaperoned school dances ever did.

Scanning plain pewter frames, she found one shoved all the way behind the rest. It was small and oval among the rectangular pictures. There were four people sitting on a beach, but it was rocky, not like the one in front of the villa. Annalisse pulled out the snapshot for a closer look. In addition to Generosa and Pearce with their little Alec, a woman sat at arm's length from the family with her mouth in a grim line. She seemed there in body only, her mind someplace far away. In her midtwenties, the beautiful brunette had flowing hair all the way down to her back. There was something familiar about the sad face, but Annalisse couldn't place it.

"Mom and her photos. She shows them to everyone who visits." Alec rounded the archway, his face as glum as the woman in the photo she held.

Annalisse replaced the frame and moved the others to their respective spots.

"Are you all right?" she asked him, noting that he'd put on a shirt.

He cocked his head and made an awful try at a wink and smile.

"I miss seeing you in my dress shirt. It looked better on you than it ever did on me."

Hardly. She tugged at the sleeveless tunic she'd changed into while Alec was on the phone.

"I'm starting to understand your hand signals, heaven help me." She bumped her brows. "How's Chase?" A flush of heat moved from her neck to her cheeks. She could devour him on the spot.

"There's been a small mishap at the estate. Helga's in the hospital."

"Oh no. Is it serious?"

"She ate something that didn't agree with her. Chase called to give us an update. He got your email about Dad and the rest. Thank you for sending it."

"He and Boris are doing good?"

Hesitation triggered a spark in his pupils, then died.

"Airs above the ground. Don't worry," he said with a swipe, as if swatting a gnat.

He was trying to be clever with the use of horse terminology.

"Why don't I believe you?" she asked.

Alec twisted his Rolex around. "The company jet should be on the ground by now. What's taking that bodyguard so long?" His palm met his pocket, and he took out his phone. Staring at the screen, he pinched a pair of lines between his brows. "Matt says there's been infrequent chatter about an American woman being held. You know what this means?" His grin began small and spread into a dimple eruption.

"Gen!"

"Matt wants to meet us on the beach. Tonight."

"Here?" Annalisse's heart kicked into second gear. "I thought he didn't want to meet near the villa. Why the change? Are we safer here?"

Alec's eyes were glued to the phone, scrolling down as if Matt had written a book.

"He's in Sitia and wants us outdoors for some reason. He's telling us to keep the door to the villa unlocked. Flynn's with him."

Matt's latest instructions weren't consistent with the others. Their current situation must have changed radically since the luncheon at the café.

"You're certain that message is from Matt? Would he tell us to leave the villa open after his warnings during lunch? Be careful, Alec."

"Unless he's been compromised—it came from his cell." Alec went to the sofa drawer and slipped his Glock into the slash pocket of his pants. "Can't hurt to stay armed." He grabbed her hand. "Let's move. If there's news on Mom, I want to hear it."

Her feet bonded to the floor, she glanced down the hall where she thought Alec had stored the necklace and other valuables, then shook off her nagging suspicions.

Shallow waves chilled her ankles under the haze of a monster moon that hung almost close enough to touch. Annalisse scanned the horizon's pitching shadows of light and dark, feeling like an anchored ship in a gale, helplessly battered breaker after breaker, on its way toward crashing against a rocky cliff. She stepped back from the sea when the surf drifted out and curled her toes in the warmer sand. Squeezing Alec's hand in hers, she carefully leaned on his bad shoulder, letting his strong maleness sweep away her concern over standing in the open.

"We're so vulnerable out here." Annalisse glanced toward the villa.

"I won't let anyone get to you. Matt said he'd flash a penlight so we'd know it was him. My instinct says things are about to move fast."

"It had better," a soft voice said from behind.

Annalisse whirled around and gaped at Matt's dark eyes beneath his fishing cap. He wasn't smiling.

"No need to scare us half to death. I just left my heart over there, flopping in the surf." She pointed into the moonlit water near her feet.

"Don't ever turn your back to what's familiar. I could have signaled with a light, but you wouldn't have seen it."

"All right, Brennan, you've made your point." By his tone, Alec's temper had flared.

"Flynn's checking out your villa," Matt said.

"Right now? Why?" Alec glanced up the hill to the house.

"The letterbox referenced what we believe is inside the building. Flynn's making a sweep."

"What does that even mean?" Annalisse asked.

"Checking out the premises. We want confirmation it's *our* woman in the communiqué. Our Turkey team is confident Mrs. Zavos—or another American woman—is being held in Bodrum on the Turkish coast. A place called Saint Peter's Castle. We have to assume that it could be your mother." He turned toward the ocean. "I'm waiting on a recording from our mole inside Titov's pack. He's been unable to confirm it's her." Matt stared at Alec. "I hear it's grainy, but if her voice is on it, we know you'll recognize her."

Matt hadn't mentioned an operative on the inside, and Mooney kept things from them too, so it must be the way they functioned undercover. A fraction of her tension ebbed from between her shoulder blades. She silently recited a prayer for their protection to Archangel Michael.

They stood for a few minutes with no sound except the lapping surf and an occasional interruption of a monk seal's croak.

"We just wait?" Alec dug a toe into the sand and kicked at the mound. "If you have a man near Mom, why can't you bring her home?"

"It's complicated. The team wants not only Viktor Titov but as many of his gang as possible. Deciphering the mole's recording is the key to our operation. We're told that our man inside back masked in case his identity was compromised and his tape found. He ran a message backward over the normal recording to mask another message."

"You mean subliminal stuff like what the Beatles were accused of doing in the sixties? Man." Alec took his hand out of hers and shoved it through his hair.

"Exactly. The clip is short. Electronic intelligence will decrypt it quickly."

"How does your mole work inside?" Alec asked.

"I can't get into ops with you, but we suspect there's an internal struggle going on. From Andreyev's interrogation, a power struggle between Titov's players."

"Did Chesnokov make bail, or is he still in custody?" she asked.

"No bail."

"In the meantime, Mom's suffering without her meds. How many of your people are working in Turkey?" Alec asked.

Annalisse noted Matt's longer than usual pause.

"We have it covered. I hesitated to bring this up before, but I need to know. Alec, are you willing to do whatever it takes—get big money together fast—if we need it?"

"I can wire over to my account in Greece, but it might not be enough without Dad's funds."

"We need our plan to work. Badly. I ask you again, will you turn over the necklace to us and let us do our job?" Matt ran a hand over his scar at the same time his phone tinkled. He plucked it out of his jacket, nodding. "The email with the recording. They were able to clean up about thirty seconds. Two people talking. One they believe is the captive. I'll listen first."

"No." Alec snatched Matt's phone and opened the file.

Backing away from Alec, Annalisse watched for a reaction when he lifted the phone to his ear. He squinted at first and then straightened up and grinned broadly.

Alec tossed the phone back to Matt. "Thanks. I'll sleep better tonight. That's one very ticked-off lady. There's no doubt—it's Mom." He jumped next to Annalisse, giving her a peck on the cheek. "Can we pinpoint her exact whereabouts from this, Matt?"

Tears of delight flashed, filling her lids. "What did she say?" She tugged on Alec's sleeve. By the time she'd asked, Matt had already replayed the recording for himself.

"It wasn't an interrogation. The guy speaking had an accent similar to Chesnokov's. I heard Mom in the background ask where they were. I think he said *French Tower*."

Annalisse made a mental note to search that term.

"You know Mom; she doesn't cuss, but when she's really mad, I've heard her rip out some good ones in Italian. It's not every day one hears that from a proper lady's mouth."

Matt shook his head and laughed as he put his phone back.

"I'm afraid to ask." She glanced at Matt, then Alec. "Well?"

Alec pulled her to him and hugged her hard enough to squeeze air from her lungs. "I'll tell you later. It's Mom."

Her body warmed in an instant.

He trembled, squeezing her a second time.

She laughed and cried all at once, rubbing Alec's back in small circles. The vermin who'd taken Generosa hadn't broken her will. She pitied the people who held her captive.

"I hope I never see Gen that angry," Annalisse said.

"It's not pretty." Alec's voice wavered, and he sniffed back what she knew to be tears. Good tears.

Annalisse's attention moved to Matt's windbreaker, where he'd quietly removed a small pistol from a shoulder holster. In the dark, she couldn't read him, but something had spooked him.

Matt swung around, his handgun stabbing the air. "Stop. Right there." The threat in his voice held venom.

Alec broke the embrace and jerked her behind him.

A bulky, tall, easy two-hundred-and-eighty-pound mountain of brawn stood face-to-face with Matt.

The big man held his hands high in the air. "Steve Jacobs. I work for them." He lifted his chin toward Alec.

"He's our bodyguard, Matt. We've been expecting him." Alec reached out and shook Steve's hand. "We'll rest easier now that you're here."

"Hand me your credentials." Matt opened his palm.

When he was satisfied, he holstered his weapon with a snap, then lit up a cigarette and inhaled long and deep in his signature toke. "I'll round up Flynn and crash for a few hours. We'll meet up and compare notes at 0500. Then depart the fix in the helicopter—sorry, that's pilot slang for leave the area. When we arrive in Bodrum, we'll get you situated in your hotel. Get some sleep; it's a long day tomorrow."

"You're shoving us in a helicopter with you—just like that? I don't know. Alec, what do you think?"

She'd never flown in a propeller job, the worst, most insane idea ever. Her mind sped at the thought of being in the air so close to the ocean for hundreds of miles. She shuddered and held on to Alec's arm for reassurance.

"How safe is Turkey right now?" Annalisse asked Matt.

The gleam of Steve's teeth in the night gave his face a strange cast. "By the way, Mr. Zavos, I should mention there's two of us."

"Two? Mooney tossed it out in passing once, but I thought he'd changed his mind. He didn't confirm this with me." Alec muttered something intelligible.

Annalisse would give the detective an earful for taking charge without Alec's approval. Where was the other bodyguard? If that person had walked in on Flynn, she hoped they were still breathing.

"I can't stay awake twenty-four seven. Red figured it was best," Steve said.

"You mean Mooney?" Alec asked.

"Yeah. Sleepy security won't collect a paycheck for long."

CHAPTER
THIRTY

The flight to Izmir in the Airbus helicopter over the field of Aegean azure took under two hours. Annalisse had only looked down once, when Alec asked her to, which suited her acrophobia fine. Even with clunky headphones and bad transmission, their second bodyguard had helped to pass the time with his tales of the Arabian Peninsula and its culture.

Most of all, Annalisse welcomed Alec's need to touch her, to hold her hand as a lifeline. She could focus on him instead of the mountain of despair in the wake of New York and the yacht. Alec's world had burned the instant Pearce died, and his problems dwarfed hers at the moment. So much heartache had layered Alec's personality already, it scared her to think what losing his mother might do to him.

Annalisse walked across the desolate tarmac to the rental car and gave her suitcase over to the bodyguard, Chet Wabenetter. His steadfast blue eyes and silver ponytail were in quirky contrast to his three-piece suit and shiny Florsheims. Chet reminded her of an old hippy who got lost on his way to Woodstock but had made some effort to fit into the security stereotype. She recalled the scene prior to leaving the villa and the fatherly way he'd spoken to Alec. With his wrestler physique and calm, buttery voice, he wasn't at all the same as a dry-humored Steve Jacobs.

Steve had her constantly on edge. His repeated knuckle cracking scraped the length of her spine with the sharpness of a pickax. Behind his wraparound sunglasses, his eyes remained a mystery, obscured further by his glacial rigidness. She shrank from men she couldn't read. Ryan Petrov back home was one of those men. When they were on the road to Bodrum, she'd insisted that Steve remove his glasses so she could get a look at his features.

Annalisse wandered away from the vehicles, breathing in the dusty air and absorbing the landscape. Block wall ruins and excavation sites dating back centuries were visible near the edge of the private heliport. She was dying to investigate and stepped beyond the blacktop into more historical territory. Annalisse thought of the Anatolian peninsula from early Turkey before it became part of the Roman Republic, mid-first century BC. How different the untouched land must have looked in the years before the birth of Jesus of Nazareth. She smiled, conjuring familiar appraisal research for Harry. And Samantha's laughing eyes when they'd worked together. Thoughts that made her homesick and sad at the same time.

"Don't go out far, miss." Chet reached for her arm. "Stay close to the group."

By the time they'd neared the hangar, Matt waved to the pilot and stepped out of the helicopter, followed by Alec. They were too far away to hear the conversation, but the men exchanged objects, shook hands, then jogged over to the jeep.

"Steve, you and Chet take our guests to the Bodrum Cave Rock Hotel and drop them off. Surveil first, inside and out." Matt barked orders like he was used to taking the lead.

"Yeah. Anything else?" Steve threw back his shoulders.

"Hotel's on the main, inside city limits. Can't miss the blue-and-gold structure. It looks like Scheherazade's palace. Me and Flynn are meeting the team for a briefing, and we're late already." Matt paused and looked at Alec. "I booked adjoining rooms for you and your lady friend. If you'd like to change when you get there—"

"Adjoining's fine." The sharpness of Annalisse's words belied how she felt. She longed for Alec's body, his hands exploring her. Heat splashed her cheeks, and she turned away.

"The stuff's loaded." Flynn joined them.

"What do we do when we get to the hotel?" Alec addressed Matt but moved beside Annalisse, resting his hand reassuringly on her back.

"Speak to only Steve and Chet. They'll handle the hotel folks once you're checked in." Matt looked at his diver's-style watch and tapped the dial. "Alec, call my prepaid phone should you get contacted by any of the cast."

A pang of regret hit Annalisse as Matt and Flynn got into a low-profile luxury car. She wondered if Turkish airports offered fancy rentals with metal-flaked paint and lots of chrome or if the CIA took care of loaners. The nasty flesh-tone jeep behind her screamed *I'm-a-rental-car*.

"Let's move out." Steve twirled above his head in a lasso arm gesture.

"What about the pilot?" Annalisse looked back to the helicopter.

"He's flying to Ankara for the night. Let's get you inside, Ms. Drury."

Chet seated her and walked to the other side, seat belting himself to her right in a cloud of fabric dust particles. Steve sat in front as official chauffeur with Alec as shotgun.

Annalisse was edgy. They couldn't get to their hotel room soon enough for her.

While she clicked her belt, the turbine engines of the helicopter spooled in a high-pitched whine.

"I guess he's leaving too." Annalisse twisted her neck for a view of the helicopter's tinted windows. "Such a nice man." She glued her eyes to the skids and waited for liftoff.

Steve cranked the jeep's ignition.

Annalisse turned forward.

Boom!

A horrific noise shrouded the sound of their engine.

An unseen force jolted Annalisse. She grabbed her seat with both hands and screamed.

The concussion from an outside blast shook the jeep, rocking it side to side.

An orange glow came from the helicopter.

"Down!" Chet barely got the word out when a second explosion shook the vehicle. He fell over Annalisse, crushing her body with his massive torso, shielding her head and neck with his arms.

Annalisse stayed folded over, her heart banging in her chest.

Shards of rubble pelted their car as if they were in the middle of a war zone.

The windowpanes on the right side cracked, and Chet's window shattered.

"Can't breathe!" Gasping for air, Annalisse coughed while she pried at Chet's arms.

Chet abruptly lifted and brushed something away from her forehead. "You're cut."

"My ears are ringing." Annalisse seesawed her jaws, trying to pop her ears, and touched her temple with a shaky hand, pulling out a glass sliver.

Alec bolted up, unsnapped his shoulder belt, and lurched halfway over the seat. "Annalisse, talk to me." He reached out, coughing hard.

She unbuckled to meet him, grabbing his fingers. "I'm fine. Are you hurt?"

Alec shook his head and then glanced at Steve, who'd remained in a trance, staring through their rear window.

Annalisse craned her neck and squinted through the spider-webbed glass for any movement. The orange outside their car had turned into black smoke, ballooning high above flames licking at the frame of what used to be their ride from Crete.

"Someone needs to help that poor pilot," Annalisse said as Matt's sedan pulled beside the hangar.

Matt ran close to the fire with his arm shading his face, then jumped away.

"I'm going." She strained for the door handle, but Chet grabbed her arm.

"Stay inside." Chet glared at her with the intensity of someone who meant what he said. "It's too late to help him."

"Then break out that window. I can't see." Annalisse's heart sank when Chet ignored her request, wordless and tight-jawed.

"Steve, shut off the engine!" Alec bellowed, looking over his shoulder. "Matt's coming. Sit tight, everyone."

She trembled so severely that her teeth cracked against each other. In a herculean effort, she fought back tears from her stinging eyes, putting her head in her hands until she heard a vehicle approach.

The sedan screeched to a halt near the jeep's driver's side. The Mercedes had heavy pockmarks where metal fragments and hunks of the helicopter had gouged the doors. She rolled down her window and took in a putrid gulp of jet fuel—and other odors she dared not think about. Her tongue swished against grit in her mouth.

Covered in soot and bleeding from head and neck, Matt got out and ran to Steve's door. Flynn's window was missing, and his right arm was wrapped in his jacket like a stuffed sausage, but he'd stayed inside. Annalisse noted Flynn's sooty face where he had taken off his glasses—his raccoon-like grimace and closed lids told the story of his pain.

Matt slapped the jeep's roof. "Move it, Steve! Get these people gone. I'm taking Flynn into Izmir to get a hunk of steel out of his arm. I want you outta here before officials arrive. Someone wanted our pilot dead."

"Or us." Bile rose in Annalisse's throat. If they'd spent a few extra moments on their flight, the sharks would've had themselves a complimentary meal.

"Matt, hold the chitchat for later, okay?" Flynn twisted, elevating his wrapped arm to the headrest.

"I've alerted the team. Punch it. When I know more—" Matt cursed, slapped the jeep's top once more, and scrambled to his side of the sedan.

"Damage control." The green tint of Steve's glasses reflected in the rearview mirror at her, then he faced Alec. "Check yourselves. If you need medical attention, yell out." He looked over his shoulder at Chet.

"Nothing I can't do myself." Chet took off his jacket and shook it.

Annalisse saw a thickness beneath Chet's pastel shirt, no doubt a protective vest.

"Alec?" Steve asked.

After wiping down both arms and legs, Alec said, "All good here. Just drive. Don't you care about any of us? You didn't even undo your seat belt after that explosion. Get in the game, Jacobs. You're supposed to secure us against *every* contingency."

"I'm wearing Kevlar." Steve's self-centered comment made Annalisse cringe.

"Whoopee-do for you. Where's our vests?" she mumbled, and Chet stole a glance at her.

Alec swung around and looked at Chet.

"Thanks for taking care of my girl. We're happy *someone* has our backs."

Her stomach sloshed when the jeep pulled onto the airport road. They were alive by the grace of God, and she made a promise to herself they'd stay that way and wouldn't leave Turkey without Alec's mother.

"Ready, Wabbie?" Steve stretched one arm across the top of Alec's seat and puckered his lips, lifting his glasses for an instant so he could make unhindered eye contact with Chet.

"What's a *wabbie*?" Alec's tone was harsh.

"I think he means me," Chet said.

"Rhymes with Kee-mo-sabbie." Steve snickered, oblivious to the fact that no one else was amused.

"The name's Chet. Chet Wab-en-net-ter. I don't like nicknames."

"C'mon, are we in amateur hour? A man dies, we're almost blown up, and you fools are cracking jokes." Annalisse groaned. "You're making my headache worse."

She could have gone the rest of the day without petty male egos bouncing between the front and back seats. No way was this arrangement going to work. Her stomach did another pirouette at the thought of the pilot's charred remains in the burned wreckage. She looked at Alec, who'd hunkered closer to the door.

Steve shrugged. "He didn't feel a thing."

"This stupid conversation is plenty painful for me. Can we not talk for a while?" Annalisse's head throbbed.

"Pull over, Steve." Alec pointed through the windshield at the dirt shoulder on the road.

"No time," Steve barked.

"Make time. Now! There's a turnout ahead."

Steve swerved the jeep off the road into a patch of weeds. "What?" He turned the ignition off. "This isn't wise. Matt said to get you inside the hotel."

"Alec, what's wrong?" Annalisse unbuckled her seat belt and slid forward to the edge of her seat.

"Steve, outside. You too, Chet." Alec's seat belt retracted, and he opened his door.

Steve yanked off his Ray-Bans. "Are you a freakin' moron, Zavos?"

"This won't take long. I should've checked you guys myself last night. You froze when our helicopter exploded, Jacobs. Chet reacted. Someone torched that bird, and for all we know it might have been one of you. Get your wallets out and step away from the vehicle."

Annalisse opened the door on her side and walked to Alec, giving him a sideways hug.

He kissed the top of her head. "We're okay." He drew back and swiped his thumb across her forehead. "Are you cut anywhere else?"

"I'll check when my adrenaline rush settles…" Annalisse gave him the shortest, best answer she could manage.

"Don't you trust Brennan?" Chet's dejected eyes looked at Alec, then fixed on his shoes.

Steve handed Alec his wallet, and Chet gave his to Annalisse.

"I don't know what you expect to find." Steve rested against the jeep, folding his arms.

Annalisse grudgingly opened Chet's wallet and scanned his driver's license and credit cards—his name neatly printed on them. Outside business cards from others were hidden inside the fold. He was sixty-one, single, and lived in Connecticut. The cards ranged from television repair to a computer store. Nothing she saw concerned her.

Annalisse tucked the business cards back and folded the thin leather in half. She smiled at Chet and handed it to Alec. "Seems okay."

Alec gave Steve's wallet back to him and flipped quickly through Chet's before returning it.

"Alec, please get into the jeep; we're targets out here." Chet slipped his wallet into the front pocket of his suit jacket.

"For whatever it's worth, I've had nightmares of being burned alive. That's why I froze back there. I'm sorry." Steve's soft hazel eyes weren't as foreboding as she'd imagined. He had a kind face that displayed plenty of confusion.

Was he an ex-military veteran who suffered from PTSD? A wonderful touch, Detective Mooney.

Back on the road, the jeep bouncing wildly, small talk had ceased. The silence was so cold, a jacket would've helped her arms. Now that no one in the vehicle trusted each other, their pilot had died, and one of the CIA operatives had injuries, their odds of getting Alec's mom back were worrisome.

CHAPTER
THIRTY-ONE

A bellhop in purple velvet trousers and shiny gold vest opened the door to the hotel's Byzantine Suite.

"Thank you," Alec said. "Drop the bags here."

"Would you like to see the other room?" the boy asked.

"We can find it, thank you."

Alec handed the young man a couple of dollar bills, which he quickly shoved into a pants pocket, then left the room.

"What's with all the eerie grottos and blue lights in the hallways? This place feels like a brothel, not a five-star. Were those live cobras in baskets at the check-in?" Annalisse stifled a shiver. "We'll need our bodyguards posted in the hallway just to keep rogue snakes from slithering into our rooms."

"You know what they say—we aren't in Kansas." Alec dropped the contents of his pockets on the bedside table and reached behind him for the Glock.

"Which man's outside the hotel?" she asked.

"Chet."

"Please call Mooney again about Steve. I'm worried he'll freeze up when it counts. If he's dealing with PTSD—"

"Mooney's partner sang Steve's praises. We might be hypersensitive right now."

"People dead, kidnapped, shot at, and blown up does that to a person." She'd let her mouth overtake her brain again. "We don't need another rundown of events. I'm so sorry, Alec." She dropped to the bed. "Why weren't you told about Steve's problems and Chet added to our security detail?"

"It probably slipped Mooney's mind. He moved fast with the Greek government, considering their firearm laws. They'd never get weapons onto a commercial flight. Customs agents meet private jets on the tarmac and check the luggage inside the plane. Mooney must have some pull."

"Do you trust Matt and Flynn to help us?"

"Yes."

Annalisse gazed around the unusual space at its coved corners and doorway arches. A big red door cut the middle of one wall to her adjoining room. This hotel room consisted of plastered ocher walls and dark inlaid furniture. Turkish rugs in reds, blues, and beiges stretched on a hardwood floor, flanked by the red satin king-sized bed. A tapestry kingfisher with an orange breast and brilliant blue feathers hung above the padded headboard. Glass sconces threw light on the ceiling and walls in a garish hue, broken only by the plaster's shadowy crevices.

"We were almost killed today." She'd found it hard to push away that fact.

"Try to forget about it."

"Who blew up the helicopter? Why do that if they thought we had the necklace with us?"

"It was our ride back to Crete. Titov's group might not want us to escape." Alec whisked away a fly. "We have to be extra careful from now on—where we go, who we speak to, and how we get around. I sure hope Flynn's okay. He looked bad."

"Matt left us in such a hurry. Even with bodyguards, this creepy hotel is an easy target," she said.

Alec distributed the suitcases in the closet and pushed the door closed. "I'm out of my mind with worry about Mom. It's Thursday already. I want control, but the CIA's taken over, and I'm not crazy about being in Turkey either, but hearing Mom on that recording—we didn't have a choice." He walked to her. "I know the helicopter ride was rough, but I couldn't leave you at the villa."

Annalisse glanced at the red door, then back to Alec, curious about what he'd discussed with Matt by the helicopter.

"We've been wandering without a compass since Dad was murdered. Someone knows we're here. The explosion made that clear."

"What did you say to Matt before the helicopter blew up?" she asked.

"He wanted to be sure that I had Mom's necklace. I actually brought both of them."

"Why?"

"The artifact doesn't belong in criminals' hands. I thought we might use Mom's copy."

"No." She shook her head and lowered her voice. "Professional thieves know the difference. We couldn't pull that off. Have you looked at the necklaces side by side?" Annalisse patted the bed and bounced.

"They're together in a hide-in-plain-sight locked container."

"Leave them there as long as possible." She bent to his ear and whispered, "How soundproof are these walls? Can Steve hear us?"

"Hard to know."

Grabbing a notepad and pencil from the night table, she wrote: *This is habit-forming.* She drew a smiley face. *The Mushasha is cursed. Use the real deal to negotiate for Gen.* She handed the pad to Alec.

Laying the pad down, he nodded and mouthed, "Okay."

"I could use a nap. Through there." Annalisse pointed at the red door.

"Sleep's way down my list." He slid his thumb over her lower lip and whispered, "Wanna check out the shower in the bat cave behind us?"

His silliness made her laugh, or maybe it was the teeny crow's-feet crinkling at the corners of his eyes that drew her into their bottomless depths. She was glad he wanted her with him.

"Do we have time?" she asked.

In response, he gently unfastened the first two buttons on her blouse, pressing his mouth to her bare skin.

She slid her fingers behind his head, undulating to the warmth and pressure of lips.

A quiet knock came from behind her, and she jerked and looked up. "What's that?"

"Must be the prepaid phone Matt gave me."

Alec stretched out across the satin bedspread and opened the phone, resting on one elbow. "Zavos." Long pause. "Sorry. I won't use my name again on this rig." Alec squinted and shook his head while Matt spoke unintelligible. "Now? C'mon, really?" He sighed. "All right. I'll meet you across the street in five." Alec flipped the phone closed and looked at her with an apology written in his eyes.

"We haven't even unpacked, and I was looking forward to lunch on the pier. I'll get my shoes and go with you."

"You can't," Alec said coldly. "Matt asked that you stay here."

"Why?"

"In case we get word on Mom. There will be instructions."

"Can't Matt come to the hotel?"

"No. I'm meeting him and the FBI liaison. Matt could be recognized out in the open. He has a black Escalade waiting."

"Did he say how Flynn is?"

"He's been admitted. His arm's broken in two places."

"We're losing precious time." Annalisse grimaced.

"We won't let that stop us."

Alec dragged her against him on the bed and kissed her breathless. The taste of him—the steady beat of his pulse as it became part of her own made her squirm, thigh against thigh.

Alec moaned and rolled away, leaving a cool place between them. "We can't do this now. You have no idea how much…" He stared a hole into the bedspread.

Then he released a soul-searching smile at her.

Alec stood, and with robotic stiffness, he stepped backward, then burst into subdued laughter, thumping the crown of his head on the plaster.

"Shh. What?" She laughed along with him.

He whispered, "I need to wait for things to—normalize. Minx." Alec closed his eyes and took deep breaths for what seemed like eons. Walking back to her, he planted a peck on her nose.

"Don't forget your stuff on the table," she reminded him.

"Right."

"What's that little black thing there?" She motioned to a matte black object.

"It's for you from Matt. Put it somewhere on your person, not in your purse." Alec handed her a key. "Watch this." He flicked out an extension. "The blade's short but sturdy. It's a decent self-defense tool. I'll be back as soon as I can. Text me if you hear anything."

"If you're being sneaky, put Matt's phone on vibrate or you'll have everyone within earshot looking for a door." She showed him a quick flash of teeth. "I'll be here. Hurry back."

Alec nodded and closed the door with a click.

Shoot. She'd forgotten to ask if Chet was going with him.

Taking her laptop out of the suitcase, she plugged in the power supply and took out a lined pad. Annalisse researched Bodrum's Saint Peter's Castle for the next hour and read every trustworthy article from its history dating back to 1404. Its five towers had housed prisoners in the years prior to World War I. A prison. How appropriate.

Castles were notorious for secret hiding places and small passageways, but those kinds of details for Saint Peter's weren't online. She learned of its green volcanic stone blocks and columns chosen from a nearby fourth-century-BC mausoleum. She found plenty of recorded history outside the castle but little on the internal workings. Studying tourist maps and overviews of the castle grounds, she saved photos to the hard drive and sent mental pictures to her head before closing her laptop.

Annalisse worried about Generosa, languishing inside the castle's block walls. Whether she had enough food, water, and care was a big question mark. Annalisse had refrained from asking Alec any questions about his mother's condition, but after forty-eight hours without her meds, she had to be feeling Gaucher's effects.

Annalisse jumped when the hotel phone buzzed next to the bed.

She scrambled to pick up the receiver and asked, "Alec?"

A recognizable voice said, "I'm in the tower of the big castle. I stole one of the phones—heard where you were—come quick—I'm alone. Don't tell anyone, just get here. Hurry!"

Her heart stuttered in a fury of beats.

"Gen! Where do I go? Which tower? Are you guarded?"

The line clicked, and the call ended.

Annalisse slammed the earpiece down. Alec had the necklace locked up somewhere. Running to the door, she opened it and peeked outside. "Steve?" A stained and vacated chair had been placed against the wall. "Great, taking a break when I need you." She shut the door to regroup. Dirty chairs and snakes— Who picked this place?

She checked her contacts for Alec's number but found only Generosa's. Glancing at the black key on the nightstand, she recalled Alec's recommendation. Annalisse dropped the key in the breast pocket of her blouse, pacing frantically, trying to sort out her best options. Matt's key could fall out of her blouse, so it went into a jeans pocket instead.

Scrolling her contact list, she found Chet's number and hit the Call symbol. His phone rang only once and went to his message. Everyone had taken a lunch break, it seemed.

She glanced at her Seiko. Twelve twenty. Generosa called about five to seven minutes ago. How did she know to call *this* hotel?

"Worry about that later."

Earlier, when they'd driven into the city, she'd noticed the castle jutting into the bay on the way in, not far from the hotel. Bodrum Castle opened to the public daily, except for Mondays, as a historical place of interest. Thursday, the place would be crawling with people visiting the shipwreck and underwater museum inside. She could disguise herself as a tourist and look in all five towers, spending the most time in the castle's French Tower because of the mention on Matt's recording. Annalisse had sent the location of that tower to memory from the castle maps online. She wished that Alec hadn't been called away and hoped he'd forgive her should things go badly.

Alec's meeting couldn't have come at a worse time.

Annalisse fell on her knees and clasped her hands, asking for guidance. To ignore her friend's pleas was impossible, yet to leave the safety of the hotel alone—

She took a final look around the room, grabbed her purse, and took out the suite's key card. Annalisse looked for her passport, then decided against bringing it. Shoving a handful of greenbacks and lira into her jeans, she stowed her wallet in the bag and put it back into the closet with the cases. She glanced at the pad where she'd written a note to Alec and tore off the page, shredding it into pieces. Tossing the scraps into the wastebasket, she went over the game plan in her mind and strolled to the door, entering the wasteland of sculptured blue carpet. Annalisse punched Steve's telephone number and received no answer for her trouble.

"Good luck collecting your paychecks, boys." With a sigh, she pulled the door closed and hurried to the open elevator door, smacking the fat button for the first floor.

Annalisse halted at the reception desk, as far away from the snake baskets as possible.

"Would you be so kind and call a taxi for me please?"

A woman in a bright set of sleek pajamas smiled sweetly. "Certainly."

"Now please."

"Of course. Wait outside, and I'll dispatch one right away." She pointed to the double doors. "They won't come inside."

"Thank you." Annalisse felt naked without her purse and fondled the bills in her pocket. She had no idea if she'd brought enough cash to pay for the ride. She pushed on the long bar that led outside into dampness and smells of cinnamon and curry. She glanced at her watch again. The roadway teemed with compact cars swerving to keep from hitting each other, as if the roadway had no rules. She slipped her phone into a front pocket and waited near the corner of the hotel for a cab. Preferably a yellow one with the word *Taxi* on the side.

A white minivan slipped into one of the reserved spots near the curb. Taksi was spelled out on the roof sign. A second van pulled in behind it, screeching to a stop.

She raised her hand and waved to the closest van. "Taxi!" Annalisse stepped forward.

Someone strongarmed her backward from the sidewalk and shoved her to the blacktop. Her jaw hit and she tasted asphalt, jarring her teeth.

"Don't fight me," a gruff voice said. "We can do this easy—or not. Your call."

Annalisse screamed, raking the ground with her fingernails. "Get your knee out of—" Gauze material covered her face and she coughed.

A hand clamped over her mouth.

She tried to scream again, but her head and neck went numb, like they had drifted apart from her torso. Her body floated away, then there was only darkness.

CHAPTER
THIRTY-TWO

"Where's your CIA partner, and where are we going?" Alec asked Matt as the coast road whizzed past them at a good clip.

"We're going to the amphitheater near Gumbet. A secure place where we can talk."

"The entire area looks deserted. I thought Bodrum was a tourist trap," Alec said.

Matt took a draw of his cigarette and blew out rings. "It's the off-season for tourists. But if you look closely, you might catch a skinny-dipper or two struttin' their stuff on the beach."

"Get serious."

"We want these guys, Alec. This is the closest we've ever come to destroying this network from the top."

"So Mom's just an afterthought?"

The Escalade slowed at an exit, and Matt parked on a dusty hillside overlooking a wall of stone steps and an arena in a half circle, reminiscent of Roman amphitheaters. Alec imagined this coliseum in its heyday—in the desert, filled to capacity with an audience cheering on their favorite fighters. Now the amphitheater was nothing more than ruins filled with cracked pillars and scattered stones on a wide, empty stage overlooking a paved modern road.

"This is the place." Matt smiled through the windshield at the awesome view of the bay.

The point at the end of the peninsula was home to gigantic walls of stone and masonry with red flags flying at two ends. Waves crashed against the ocean side to the west; the perfect area to defend a castle from sea as well as land.

"Is that *the* Bodrum Castle?"

"Special Agent Norcross, you remember Alec Zavos." A small arm whipped over the front seat, her business card in hand.

Alec flipped around.

Crouching in the back seat, Norcross studied him with intense catlike eyes. The agent's hair was covered by a navy cap like she'd worn at the gallery. He had to admit, the casual look suited her.

"Take this, darlin'. I neglected to give you one the other day." She shook the business card at him. "The office number is on the front, and my personal cell's written on the back."

Alec shook his head and took her card. "Why the theatrics? Couldn't you just tell me she was here when I got into the Escalade?"

Matt smiled. "She—Agent Mickey Norcross—wants to fill you in on what's happened in New York."

"You can call me Mick." She hung over Alec's seat back. "Sorry for the secrecy. Since the helicopter blast, we've lost the element of surprise."

"No foolin'. What happened back there?"

"Your mother and the little necklace you neglected to mention to Mooney are crucial to the entire operation. We have to move fast, faster than we'd intended to." Matt cracked a window for the fingers of smoke filling the interior.

"No complaints here. So you're part of the rescue, Agent—I mean, Mick?"

"Course, sugar. You have the necklace with you, right?" she asked.

"Matt does," Alec said.

"It's with me. Until this thing goes down, it stays with CIA."

"We arrested Maxim Andreyev trying to board a plane to Europe. He may have introduced himself to your mother as a *Mister* Chesnokov." She paused, and satisfaction flickered across her face. "I see you're acquainted. Andreyev is cooperating with New York's finest since we uncovered his expired visa. Way overextended—to the tune of sixteen months. He's posing as an art dealer but has deep ties to the underworld from Moscow to Turkey. We believe he typically works with his brother Pavel."

"How do you know they're involved with Mom—and Dad's death?"

"Maxim was turned loose on the East Coast to dig up what he could on a relic—your horse necklace, we can assume. One piece of new evidence came to light recently on the Samantha Freeman case that led us to the Andreyevs, but there's not enough to convict either brother of her murder."

"She had the matching horse bracelet, and since Mom's necklace appears to be from the same collection, why wouldn't Samantha's killer be the same person who's after the necklace?"

"Maxim took a polygraph. He passed with flying colors. We don't believe he killed Ms. Freeman. He had orders to hightail it overseas with the necklace, but instead, he subcontracted Mr. Carradine, the deceased, to conning it from your mother. When Carradine refused, he paid with his life," she said.

"Maxim didn't kill Samantha but did poison Harry?" Alec asked.

"Maybe him, maybe Pavel—maybe neither. We aren't sure. The poison used can take time; it's tricky stuff," Matt said.

"How could anyone know Mom had the necklace? It was only on display during the gallery party for a few hours. Maxim or his brother had to know about the necklace well ahead of time to use a long-acting poison."

Her ponytail bobbed up and down. "Apparently your mama wore it to a charity ball several months ago. Maxim had attended that gathering and made the connection. Mr. Carradine, being a good friend of your mother's, was a reasonable choice for the Andreyevs to acquire the necklace, but Carradine's loyalty to Mrs. Zavos threw a wrench in their plans."

"Maxim blew up when Carradine wouldn't steal the horses, but killing him was never part of his plan. Stealing, yes, but popping someone, no way. That's Pavel's specialty." Matt spat the man's name with disdain.

"We believe Maxim could've hired others. The necklace wasn't going into any museum either. Maxim and Pavel were promised a cool quarter mil each for it."

"Paid by the ringleader, Titov, or the guy who shot me in New York?" Alec looked at Matt.

"Viktor Titov. According to Maxim, the *crew* was called to Turkey."

Mick's arm shot over the front seat, and she tapped her wristwatch. "You fellas best get going. I've got *commander homework*." She curved her fingers into quotes.

Matt gave her an eye roll and grumbled, "Bossy."

"I heard that."

"How long is this going to take, Matt? I left Annalisse alone quite a while ago."

"She's got guards. I scoped out a section of the theater earlier. We'll be able to talk there." Matt peered into the back seat. "Stay low."

"As you say, sugar."

Alec slid out of the Escalade and waited for Matt near the hood.

"She's cute—if she wasn't so irritating." Matt directed him to a set of broken steps at the top of the half circle near some shrubs. "This won't take long. I want to run the operation by you, so once we go, nothin' drops through the cracks."

The humidity felt like a sauna at maximum heat. Alec's mind kept wandering between his mother and the hotel room and *her*. He followed the man in the fisherman's cap to the highest point of the amphitheater. Parking himself on the top step beside Matt, Alec skirted the thorns of a fruitless, wild lemon tree. Even without the lemons, the leaves had a heady citrus fragrance.

"How do you plan to get Mom out of that place?"

"Before I start, there's one more thing I didn't want to mention in front of the agent. Chet is one of us."

"He's not security?" Realization dawned. "Mooney knew. It's big of you to tell me. The surprise extra guard thing never felt right to either one of us."

"Mooney was already sending Jacobs, and we felt it was to our advantage to plant one of us with the two of you. Chet asked us to keep his cover between me and Commander Hilliard. He's highly qualified. You're in good hands."

"That takes care of Chet, now tell me about Mom."

"Our operatives are at the castle, and we're going in soon." Matt tilted his head toward the main highway. "The castle has two obvious entrances. Mrs. Zavos is being held in the French Tower, the biggest of the five towers, near the back wall facing the sea. Our inside man gave us solid confirmation. Your mother is rarely left alone, but usually a woman cares for her. On occasion, a man."

"A woman should be easy to overpower. Has anyone tried?"

"The mole inside has limited opportunities to get us information. Castle tours run every day but Monday. Like I said before, tourists are at a trickle but still around."

"If there are tourists, how are the kidnappers hiding Mom?"

"The tours are self-guided on the grounds only. The tower premises are closed to the public. We don't have your mother's exact coordinates inside the tower. I know waiting is difficult, but until they contact you with demands, it's all we can do."

Alec whispered, "What if we're wrong about everything? Dad's gone. Mom's sick, without medication. She has to be in so much pain right now. Can't we put a plan together to rescue her at night? How do we know there's running water or even lights in that—"

Twigs snapped behind Alec, and he whipped his head around.

Something cracked down hard on the back of his neck.

Water flooded Alec's nasal passages, choking him.

He sputtered and coughed, opening his eyes. He lay on a hard surface, what felt like brick or concrete, with his hands bound behind him. The stench of mold stung his nostrils, and his head pounded.

Alec glanced around his dark surroundings. Matt, also bound, bled from his nose and mouth. He was out cold—or dead—about six feet away. They were lying in a long stone hallway—then it came to him. The ruins.

Out of the corner of his eye, Alec saw something whizzing toward his head. He rolled and dodged it. A boot struck his chest. Another kick plugged him in his side. He felt a couple of ribs snap, and he gasped for air. Alec closed his eyes against the radiating pain.

Something cold and hard burrowed into Alec's forehead. He opened his eyes and found himself staring down the barrel of a pistol.

Beyond that, a man watched them. The severity of his black garb was broken only by a sliver of white bandage peeking from his sleeve.

"You have my attention." Alec groaned and tucked his knees.

"Good sleep?"

"Is my friend dead?"

"No, but he'll wish it so."

A larger figure loomed on Alec's left but stayed in the shadows near Matt.

"You've got us. What do you want?"

Again, a boot came at Alec's head. Unable to get out of the way, searing agony split his temple and he dry-heaved. The boots were probably steel-toed.

Footsteps shuffled backward, followed by laughter. "We tire of your games. The Mushasha belongs to us. Your woman spits like a camel and cries like a goat; *suka* feel like the rest. She was made to obey."

My woman—Annalisse or Mom? A shudder swept through his body. It was stupid to leave Annalisse at the hotel, and he regretted it. Alec rolled onto his back and felt for his missing Glock, waiting for the clammy sweats to pass.

I'll shove that smugness right down your throat.

"She enjoyed it when we took turns at her."

"Who? Tell me which woman!" Alec wriggled his wrists. They felt taped together.

"Freeze! FBI!"

Shots rang out in the tight space, and Alec pressed against the floor in as low a profile as possible, clenching his teeth, eyes scrunched closed.

Footsteps echoed, and he heard a dense thud.

Alec opened his eyes.

His tormentor had disappeared.

The big guy in black who'd watched Matt lay crumpled in a heap.

"Alec? How bad are you?" Mick crouched over him with concern on her face. "Can you move?" She slid a blade through the bindings on his wrists.

"Yeah." He grunted when he attempted to rise. "I... can move."

She rotated one arm, then hissed, "Thank goodness for Kevlar."

"You got shot?" Alec asked the agent.

"Twice. In the vest."

"Mick, check on Matt; he's hurt worse than me."

She went next to the prone body and checked for a pulse. "He's alive." She jumped up and kicked the other man sprawled on the floor. "One in the noggin. He won't be visiting his mama anytime soon." She jiggled Matt's boot. "Matt Brennan. Matt!" She crouched near his head. "Matt?"

"Toss some water on him from that bucket over there. It brought me out of it."

Mick grabbed the container by its edge and threw the contents at Matt. He came to, sputtering water and an assortment of obscenities.

"Good." Mick knelt down and cut him free from his tape.

"I feel like hamburger. The only thing that doesn't ache are my toes, but I can't feel them." When he tried to rise, he fell back and moaned.

"Stay put, darlin'. Get your bearings. Don't hurry." Mick helped Alec to his feet.

"My pistol's gone," Alec said.

"Standard procedure. I'm going outside to secure the area. Stay with Matt, and I'll be back as soon as I can."

"You're the only one with a weapon." Alec searched his pocket and came up empty for his phone.

"I'll have to carry you down the hill one at a time, unless you can walk."

Alec nodded, holding his throbbing ribs. "I didn't see what they did to Matt, but he looks worse than I feel. I'll help you with him."

Matt was wiping his mouth and trying to sit up again. "I can manage."

"What did you get out of 'em, Zavos?" Matt asked.

"I'm pretty sure he's the same guy who shot me in New York."

"Yeah?"

"Norcross showed up while he was saying things about a woman or women who were raped. I couldn't tell if he was talking about Mom, Annalisse, or both. He mentioned the necklace and had a bandage on the same wrist where Annalisse shot the gunman at her brownstone. Same build, same height." Alec's breath caught on a shooting pain, and he hissed through his teeth. "It was a bad decision to leave her alone at the hotel, Matt."

Matt winced, holding his midsection gingerly.

"The perps must've been acting alone. I don't see anyone outside the theater. Can you walk, Matt? I sure hope so, because I darn sure can't carry you both," Mick said.

"I'm mobile. Between you and me, we'll make do," Alec said.

"I can walk on my own."

"Sure you can, big, bad Ops Man. I won't tell the chief a peewee agent saved your butt." Mick hit a speed dial number.

"Mick Norcross. I'm taking Brennan to a hospital." She paused and shifted her weight from one foot to the other. "Yeah, he's serious. Which hospital's closest to the amphitheater? University. Got it. Details forthcoming. Gotta split. Meet me at the hospital in twenty. Matt's out of commission, along with Flynn, so run it past Hilliard. Thanks."

"How long have we been here? You have to drop me at the hotel on the way," Alec said.

"You're getting checked out too." She bent over the dead man. "This boy in black ain't so pretty up close."

Alec watched the agent rifle through the man's black garb. The corpse had a five-inch gouge across one cheek. The smooth scar from a knife wound.

"One of yours?" She held two phones into the air and a short pistol.

"Mine." Matt pointed to the larger phone.

"The one that got away has mine." Alec wrapped Matt's arm around his shoulder while struggling through pain worse than his gunshot.

Mick grasped Matt's other arm to steady him, and together, they lifted Matt to his feet.

"Keep this." Mick shoved the dead man's snub nose into Alec's hand. "A twenty-two's probably not what you're used to, but it'll pack a punch if you're close enough."

"What about him?" Alec looked toward the dead man.

"Varmint food. Let's go."

CHAPTER
THIRTY-THREE

Alec waited until Mick drove in behind the valet area of the hotel and swung his door open before she had time to put the Escalade into park. He shut the door, watched the passenger window descend, and leaned into the cab.

Mick tossed a flip phone to him. "Use the dead guy's. I have a feeling this thing's gonna get hairy pretty darn fast. We need a way to contact you."

"Annalisse has a phone."

"No. Use that one. Just don't answer it unless the call comes from me." She spouted the telephone number to him. "Anyone else, let it ring. It won't be long before someone finds the corpse we left back there."

"Norcross, enough!" Matt yelled from the back seat.

"No moves until we give the go-ahead. If they contact you—call me. Wrap up your ribs." Mick glanced at Matt and squealed into traffic.

The putrid odor of curried meat saturated the air. Alec leaned against the hotel wall to curb his reflex to vomit. Muddled images and agony buzzed Alec's head as his shakiness increased. Meeting Matt across the street without Annalisse and a guard was reckless and stupid.

Alec yanked the heavy hotel door, doubling over, then raced through the lobby past the front desk. Both elevators were in use, so he took turns hammering the buttons with his fist.

"Mr. Zavos? You are Mr. Zavos?" A woman in blue silk tapped his shoulder and shoved a letter at him. "I'm to give this to you."

One of the elevators opened, and a young couple in swimsuits with beach towels around their necks stepped out laughing.

Alec took the letter and hurried into the elevator.

He tore the short end of the envelope and found a piece of paper barely legible. He read: *I have your woman. Wire 5 million to this account by 5 PM. Call when done. When funds are verified I release her.*

Alec gasped, scanning the bank codes and other wire numbers listed.

"Which woman? Call who?" He pounded the flat of his hand against the elevator door. "C'mon, open."

A woman's muffled scream filtered into the compartment as the doors opened.

Alec ran down the hall toward a maid near a small closet. She turned to him, her wide eyes glazed in fear, and pointed into a supply room, jabbering in a melodic language he assumed was Turkish.

"I'm in a hurry."

The woman shrieked again, pulling Alec inside a small cubby full of sheets and towels.

On the floor, Steve Jacobs lay on the carpet with a bloody hole in his temple.

Alec cursed and touched Steve's neck for a pulse. "Jacobs, I trusted you." Alec thought about Annalisse and jumped up. If they took out Steve, they have her. "Don't stand there, get help."

"Olu zaman?" She stopped and stared back at him, her mouth open. *"Olu?"*

"I don't understand you. He's dead, and I need room 212 unlocked."

She covered her face with both hands, sobbing like a child.

Alec shook her arm harder than he'd intended and checked his watch.

"I'm. Alec. Zavos. A woman is missing, and I forgot my key." He dragged the maid down the hall, past Steve's empty chair, to room 212 and tapped on the lock. "Please. Open it." Pounding on the door with the flat of his hand, he called, "Annalisse, open the door, babe."

His worst fears realized, Alec laid his cheek against the cool metal.

"Sorry to do this." He reached deep into the largest pocket near her waist.

"No!" She struggled against him, batting away his hands.

Alec plunged for the plastic device against the seam.

The maid had the card tight in her grasp.

Ripping it from her fingers, he shoved it into the door slot.

"Annalisse?" He bolted into the room and searched the bath and adjoining room. He sniffed the air for any clues. Lavender, he imagined, floated through his nostrils.

The maid yelped from behind him, her face in a grimace, and an unsteady hand pointed at the switchblade thrust into the middle of the mattress. The knife pinned a note to the bed.

"Get to the desk. Now!" Alec slashed the air with his arm, and she fled. He raced across the floor to the bed and tore away the page. It read: *Bring Mushasha horses to French Tower St. Peter's Castle. 6:00 tonight. Woman for the necklace. Come alone, or you get her in pieces.*

He dropped to the bed, stunned by the words. He read the note again and, comparing it with the first note, found handwriting differences. "Did they mean Mom or Annalisse? One note for each?" He muttered, rubbing his forehead. "One says five p.m., the other six." He looked at the nightstand clock. Five after three. Maybe enough time to wire the money, but he didn't have five million in his personal account. Dad did. Ralph could help, but his number was in a phone that he no longer had. Alec dropped both notes on the bed and rubbed his palms helplessly down his face. The ransom had to be for Annalisse and the necklace for Mom. Were they working together or separately? He didn't know—didn't care. If he blew it, both could be lost.

Alec's side burned and his head hurt so badly his vision suffered, but he had no time to nurse his painfulness.

Think rationally. Mom needed meds, and he trusted that Annalisse could and would hold her own until he arrived. He scanned the room for an internet search tool and spotted her laptop still in sleep mode. Hitting a key, Bodrum Castle's visitors map flashed on the screen. If she'd tried to investigate on her own—he couldn't go there and slumped into the chair. "Babe, what did you do?"

Alec searched for Ralph Farley's website and punched the office number into his phone. Waiting for the ring, he held his thoughts in check should Ralph not pick up. A man answered.

"Ralph?"

"This is he. Who's calling?"

"Alec. Alec Zavos. I have an urgent situation in Turkey and need assistance."

He explained his request for funds from his dad's account and waited for Ralph's recommendations.

"A dilemma. I fear the bank will require you personally to extract that amount from your father's account. There may be another way. Let me work through two possibilities, and we'll go with the best one. Where do you bank?" Ralph asked.

"Key One Bank, Monticello, New York."

"And the bank in Wales? I need that also."

"I'll text it over from the note. A million thanks, Ralph. Do what you can. I have one call to make, and I'll get back to you, say… in ten minutes. It's all I can spare."

"Fair enough. Talk soon."

Alec stood up and carefully wriggled out Mick's business card for his next call.

"It's Alec. I have their instructions, and they've killed one of our guards. Get to the hotel with my mother's necklace ASAP. Matt has the lockbox. In ten minutes, fifteen tops. After that, I move on my own. I'll wait outside the hotel."

CHAPTER
THIRTY - FOUR

Annalisse opened one eye. She felt hot, and her head was a bowl of mush. The wall—or the ceiling—circled her like a carousel.

"I'm gonna be sick." She popped open the other eye, and the effect worsened. Shadows fuzzed together, spinning with minds of their own. "Stop." Her hands were stuck together in front of her, bound at her wrists when she lifted them to her eyes.

The last time her world had rotated was after graduation and too many frozen mojitos, but there was something different here. She closed her eyes and tried a deep breath, but her lungs wouldn't cooperate. Annalisse cleared her throat and concentrated on getting her eyesight back and breathing normally.

Focusing on her bondage, she found that zip ties held her hands and feet. She curled in a fetal position, straightened her arms, and tried to pull her wrists apart, but her meager attempt was useless.

Annalisse coughed. "I'm dizzy. Body, wake up." She rolled onto her side, using her elbows to sit upright. Hugging her knees, she shut her eyes against the nausea.

The brackish atmosphere smelled of mold and decay. Annalisse rested her chin on her knees while studying her wrists and ankles. "Who tied me, and what is this place?" She looked at the floor, then the ceiling. "The room's made of stone blocks. Darn hard stone blocks." She winced and forced nasty vomit down in a gulp. "I know I'm in Turkey with Alec, and we were in a hotel." Her lips tingled from the awful memory of the arm around her waist and gauze over her mouth. "I was drugged. No wonder I'm sick. Gen—I was going to get Gen from the castle. Alec, you'll never find me, but I hope you find your mother."

A rush of tears stung her lids, and her sobs echoed in the room. She'd never see her aunt and little Boris again, and her heart clenched. No Alec. No Chase. She sniffed, wiping her nose across her knee. Nothing but chiseled stones and a film of dust all around. She could be near Generosa or, worse, stored in some ancient ruin in another part of Turkey.

Annalisse squared her shoulders. "All right, *Art Lady*." She smiled at the vision of Alec saying those words to her the first time Gen had introduced them. "You're not a baby. Find a way outside and find out where you are. Get your personal GPS online."

Turning on palms and knees, she pushed with her hands and managed to stand. She visually ensured there were no wounds other than her wounded pride. The call from Generosa had been designed as a ploy to draw her out from the hotel. Without bodyguards and Alec gone, that plan had worked beautifully, and she'd fallen for the ruse.

Light filtered in a crack straight down the stones on one wall. An opening to the outside would make her escape possible. She hopped closer to the ray so she could examine herself more closely and check out the cable ties.

Sweat beads crept down her skin underneath her blouse, then dizziness hit Annalisse again, and she swayed. She shuffled to the wall and rested her head against the cool stones, feeling better. For a brief moment, the fog parted enough so that she could consider her dire situation. Recalling a self-defense video she'd watched, Annalisse lifted her wrists, and with her teeth, slid the zip tie around, aligning the lock connector with the middle of her hands. She steadied herself against the stone, concentrating on how to release herself in her weakened condition.

With all her strength, Annalisse raised her arms high and crashed her wrists against her midsection. The ties held. She lifted her hands higher over her head, held a breath, and whacked her wrists harder on the down stroke, swinging her elbows out like chicken wings.

The bond snapped, and the tie lay at her feet.

"Yes!"

She rubbed her wrists, then felt her bare ring finger. "Did he take it?" She crouched and strained her eyes to focus. "Find something sharp for the ankles, then look for the ring." She squinted in the dark, handling stone after stone. Handmade blocks with no sharp edges on the wall as well as the floor.

Remembering the tool Matt had left for her, Annalisse felt her breast pocket. She leaned against the wall, her spirit dampened.

"That's right. I moved it."

She sagged with relief as she dug into her pocket and pulled out the key with the tiny knife. In no time, the sharp blade slid through the tie above her feet.

She sighed, snapping the key and knife together. "Ingenious little device. Thank you, Matt. Okay, find the wall with the door. Please let one of them be an outer wall."

The silvered beam of light drew her there, and she ran her fingertips slowly down the crack. Beneath one hand was stone, under the other, softer wood that she could dig a fingernail into. Working her way up, then down, she encountered two metal hinges with two screws in each. The hinges were securely embedded into the stone. She grazed her hands along the middle of the door and found a knob or lock. Annalisse wrapped both hands and turned, feeling resistance. She'd been locked inside.

Using the key knife's larger end, she tried the key head in the screw slot on a hinge. "Too big." Annalisse tried the knife end. "I'll never get it without breaking the blade. Only as a last resort." She nodded. "When I get out of here, this is going to be a barnburner of a tale to tell my clients."

Annalisse wandered the wall with the door, relying on her hands instead of eyesight to feel for any unusual textures or bumps in the stone. She turned along the next wall and proceeded slowly from the corner, dragging her fingertips across the rough surfaces. Unfortunately, there were no changes in the stones. She could try breaking the door down, but it was huge, and she couldn't risk a broken arm or fractured shoulder. Wall three had the same landscape, but near the corner, one rectangular stone protruded farther than the rest. Her heart flittered as quickly as a hummingbird's wings. She felt its corners and noticed more space around that particular stone.

Placing one hand on either side of the stone, she pressed her hands down, jiggling up and down and side to side. The sideways motion loosened dirt and mortar. Her efforts were spurred at the thought of a hiding place in the wall. She worked the stone out a few inches and felt the top, sinking her fingertips into a hollow. Annalisse wiped perspiration from her forehead and worked the block in earnest until she could reach inside and feel around.

There were objects, cold to the touch. Her fingers traced round edges and sharp points like a silverware drawer of sorts. Annalisse worked a fork and spoon out and ran to the metal screw, using the spoon handle first, then the spoon itself. "Too blasted big." She dropped the spoon and tried the tines on the fork. They barely fit into the crevice.

Annalisse removed screws on the top hinge and swung it over. Carefully she removed the screws from the bottom hinge and flipped it. Sliding the fork into her back pocket and concealing it under her blouse, she pressed a shoulder to the door, pushing a few inches at a time until the wood parted from the stone far enough to slide through. She looked around one last time, hoping to see her ring.

"There's no time."

Bright light singed her eyes, and she covered them until her pupils adjusted. She slowly slid the big door back into place behind her and stepped around the building. A small sign near a wrought iron rail read Italian Tower 1405. Aha! One of the Bodrum Castle towers. She still had a chance to rescue Generosa.

Chatty voices in the distance drifted in on the ocean breezes, and she ducked behind a hedge until an older couple passed. Annalisse closed her eyes and envisioned the plat for the French Tower from her internet search. Its outer walls stood tall to her left, a mere few steps away. She inspected the grounds for more visitors as she waited for the couple to meander past the French Tower. From the position of the sun, the castle grounds would close soon. Gripping the rail, Annalisse catapulted across the dirt trail, through the off-limits tape barrier, and up the set of steps that led to the tower.

Crouching low at the French Tower entrance, Annalisse flipped the iron lever up and tiptoed inside another set of stone chambers, only this tower was larger than the one she'd left, and it had short, partitioned interior walls.

Inside, the light was no better than in the Italian Tower. She pressed against a wall, giving her eyes time to adjust to the darkness. Her mouth watered from distant food aromas of beans or some kind of vegetable cooking. Wide steps wound to an upper level at one niche and a shadowy hallway at another. Annalisse crept toward the opening on the short wall and held a breath while snaking into the other chamber. At first blush, the room appeared vacant except for a table and two chairs in the middle and a cot by the wall closest to her. A cot with a pile of blankets in one corner. She couldn't imagine anyone able to sleep in such a dank space.

The blankets moved.

Annalisse recoiled, then flattened herself against the wall.

Once more, Annalisse peered at the cot.

Someone underneath shimmied a section of the blanket away.

Annalisse wanted to run, but she fought the urge and delayed her escape.

Shiny silver gleamed on the cot. A dark-haired person was taped to the cot by their wrists, sitting—gagged—and blindfolded.

Taking the key from her pocket and exposing the knife, Annalisse held it out and tiptoed toward the cot.

The captive had tiny feet.

A tear stung Annalisse's cheek as she hoped against hope. The prisoner she'd found with her head hung down and shoulders slumped had to be Generosa.

Slowly Annalisse crept along the wall and bent close to Generosa's ear, whispering, "Shh. It's me—Annalisse."

Generosa raised a knee and mumbled under the gag.

"I'm removing your blanket first, then the tape. You have no idea how happy I am, Gen." Annalisse's words caught in her throat when she thought about Alec.

Slicing through wrist and ankle tape, Annalisse peeled off the remnants and went to work on the blindfold over Generosa's eyes so she wouldn't give them away.

Generosa's tears cleared a path down her dirty face, and she clutched Annalisse's arm. Her eyes crinkled joyously.

"Once I free the gag, take my hand. I'll help you. Can you walk?"

Generosa nodded.

Annalisse untied the fabric coiled around Generosa's head and finally slipped it up and off.

Annalisse hugged her small, quivering frame and pressed an index finger to her lips, mouthing, "Shh." She rotated for another look around, but the room was quiet. She pulled Generosa to her feet and observed the black shroud she wore.

"*Bambolina*... Thank you. Is Alec outside?"

"Squeeze my hand, and don't let go, no matter what." Annalisse guided her around the corner to the entry room and stopped. "Are your clothes underneath that?"

Generosa nodded.

Annalisse pulled at the sash and watched the heavy fabric hit the stone.

Generosa's orange culottes stood out like a flare, but it was too hot for the abaya and too late to cover her up again.

Annalisse whispered, "Stay close." Having no guards about was fortunate for them, but she'd stay cautious.

She helped Generosa through the big door and closed it quietly. More people in clusters milled around the base of the tower. A young woman with a small child waved at them.

"I didn't know we could go inside. Leave it open please," the woman said.

The shock stopped Annalisse midstride. "Keep to the grounds. I work here."

Generosa quirked up one corner of her mouth.

"Let's go. We have to get outside the gate." Annalisse bent low and tucked Generosa's tiny frame beneath an arm, pulling her down the steps.

Generosa stumbled and let out a small cry.

"You okay? Need a breather?"

"Keep going," Generosa said.

"Wrap your arm around my waist and hang on."

Annalisse barely felt her feet as they quickstepped beyond the Italian Tower and ducked behind a bush next to the building. Generosa labored with her breaths. In the sunlight, her usually perfect pageboy hung in rattails, and shadows ringed her eye sockets. The outdoor heat and extra movement would deteriorate Generosa's already poor condition.

Annalisse again consulted the castle map in her mind. She steered them left toward the seaward side of the castle and its main entrance to the east.

Generosa stepped carefully on the balls of her feet.

"I'm sorry I don't have something to give you for the pain." Annalisse stopped to observe her. "Can you go a little farther?"

"I want out of here."

"Me too." Annalisse offered a smile. "We're gonna make it; I promise."

She and Generosa would have to stay clear of the main walkway, skirt past the two halls with the artifacts and shipwreck museum, and hang near the brush for cover. By her calculation, the moat and outer entrance were at their far left.

"Ready?" Annalisse gave Generosa a sharp nod, then reached for her hand.

"How did you find me? Where's Alec?" Generosa rubbed her elbows and made a painful face. "Darn Gaucher."

Annalisse looked at Generosa sympathetically.

Ahead, a welcome figure approached them.

A sigh of relief passed Annalisse's lips. "Chet." She pulled Generosa closer and picked up the pace.

"Who?"

"He's one of our bodyguards."

Chet gave her a weird smile. His upper lip curled, leaving traces of uncertainty in her mind.

"Fancy finding you here, Ms. Drury. And who's this? Mrs. Zavos perhaps?" He angled his head and looked at Generosa with curious eyes.

"Help us get out of here before we're spotted." Annalisse reached for Chet's arm.

He sidestepped her hand, and his smile became wolfish, as if he were about to gorge on his next meal. He pointed a pistol at Annalisse and extended his other hand.

"I'll take the necklace."

CHAPTER
THIRTY - FIVE

Mick Norcross scowled at Alec, then screeched the Escalade out of the hotel's visitor parking lot. "Where to? Get me up to speed."

"How's Brennan?" Alec waited for Mick, who stared at the access road, ignoring his question. "Agent?"

Mick drew a long breath and skimmed her palms over the steering wheel. "He didn't make it, darlin'."

Alec's mouth dropped in disbelief, and his heart sank.

"I was helping him out of the back seat when he collapsed. We got him on a stretcher, but he was already gone. EMTs worked on him—tried to revive him—"

"Pull over. There!" Alec pointed to a bank of shops with tapestries hanging out front. He gritted his teeth for fear his mouth might spew distasteful opinions he'd regret later.

The Escalade came to an abrupt stop, and Mick turned off the ignition. "Do you really want to do this now?"

"We have a minute. What about Matt?"

"He had major internal bleeding. When they lifted his vest, the bruising was off the charts. I didn't know, Alec. I'm sorry. He was too messed up." She straightened her cap and looked out the windshield. "Tell me what you have."

Alec recited his conversations with Ralph and told her about the notes.

"Your lawyer has ways to get that much money together so soon?"

He shook his head. "I don't think two hours is enough time." He glanced at the dash clock. "Less than that. My dad's account has the money. The problem is I can't officially get to it yet. It's hard to imagine him gone for two days. It feels like a lot longer."

"Money deadline is five, and it's almost four fifteen."

"Ralph came up with another plan. Our only option is to fake it. Since the ransom note said to call when the funds were wired, maybe he doesn't have online access to check his account in Wales."

"The perp's going to take your word the money's in his account? Uh-uh. Not buying it."

"We expect him to verify. If he does, Ralph has the assurance of the bank manager that his people will lie to him about the balance. They'll give him some excuse, explaining why he can't visually see the new funds in his account."

"Sorry, hon, we have to expect he has some computer and banking savvy."

"Same difference. If he checks his balance on a phone or any other device, when his account doesn't show the money, he's sure to call the bank and hear their spiel."

"Or he'll kill Annalisse, and it's over. Where's he holding her?" Mick asked.

"Don't know."

"How do you know she's alive?"

"Why kill her? What would he gain?"

"It's too big a gamble. I'd turn it in your favor. You have everything to lose without knowing where she is. Call and make him put her on the phone, or set up a staging area where you can see her before you transfer the money." Mick leaned against the steering wheel and glared at an imaginary spot on the windshield. "You know there's no money. He doesn't. It's too risky not to know where she'll be before and after the wire transfer."

"I'll phone him and arrange something. I should've thought of that." Alec looked into the back seat, then checked the floorboard in front of him. "Where's Mom's necklace? In back?"

Mick averted her eyes. "I... uh, don't have it."

"No way. How are we going to get Mom at six?"

"Matt left it with the commander. We'll get it."

Alec's guts burned. These agents and operatives were screwing things up.

"What's this rescue operation called? Keystone Cops?" Alec shook his head, wishing he'd held his tongue but part of him was glad he'd said it. "Sorry, Mick." He pulled out the pair of notes and analyzed the writing again. "Any chance the guy holding Annalisse is holding Mom?"

"JDSR." Mick shrugged.

"Huh?" Alec had all but lost faith in the whole lot of them.

"JDSR: Just. Doesn't. Sound. Right. Otherwise, why not ask for money and the necklace at the same time? Unless they're trying to throw us off, making us think there's two operations at work. Make your call, Alec." She pointed to the phone in his hand. "Find out where your girlfriend is. You've assumed she's close by. She may not be."

Alec tapped in the numbers he'd found on the ransom note and put the call on speakerphone.

A man with no accent answered on the first ring. "Is it done?"

"I have it ready. Let me talk to Annalisse."

"After the transfer."

"No transfer until I speak to her," Alec demanded.

"Not possible."

"You've killed her?" His heart beat faster.

"She's very much alive. A pretty thing too." The unknown on the other end smacked his lips.

"I need proof she's alive—and good faith on your part. Why can't I talk to her?"

In an annoyed tone he said, "Pearce spawn, expect a call from me soon."

THIRTY - SIX

Annalisse walked in front of Generosa, holding her by the arm. Then as a team, backed into a stand of oleanders, as far away from Chet as possible.

"You aren't a guard," Annalisse announced.

Chet laughed and shifted the pistol to Generosa. "The necklace? You have it?"

Generosa, her face twisted in questions, gawked at Annalisse with a pair of wide eyes.

"We don't have it, but I know where it is." Annalisse tugged Generosa closer. "Gen needs a doctor quickly. As soon as she gets one, I'll get it for you. Just don't hurt us."

An odd sound like a firecracker split the air.

Chet tumbled backward, hitting the dirt with a dull thud.

"Gen, we can't stay here." Annalisse turned, taking Generosa with her. "Keep low, and I'll get his gun."

"Don't bother. You're two seconds away from a bullet. Move, make a peep, and it's over," a male voice ordered from a side path.

"Frank." Generosa stopped abruptly. "Annalisse, stand still. He'll kill us like he killed Pearce."

From behind a long-leafed tree, a man with thin lips and a stony gaze stepped out, waving a rifle pointed at them.

Annalisse glanced quickly at their surroundings. People's voices rose in the background, but none of the visitors were close enough to see them.

"How many more do you plan to kill?" Generosa asked, surprisingly strong and fearless.

"Frank, or whoever you are, Chet's bleeding in the weeds. Someone's bound to find him and report it." Annalisse's pulse quickened as she wrapped her arm around Generosa's shoulders. "Haven't you done enough damage to Gen? Let her go. If you're after the necklace, take me instead. Alec will bring the Mushasha and trade it for me."

He stared at Generosa, then her. A gleam of teeth spread between whiskers that hadn't seen a razor in days. "On a tight schedule. Turn around and go back."

"Back where?" Annalisse had been in this evil man's presence on the yacht, and he *was* the same guy Pearce had called by name before he died.

He shoved the weapon at her and looked at his wrist. "Italian Tower. Fast." He grumbled something and yelled, "Now!"

Annalisse studied Frank and wondered how this puzzle piece fit. Matt had made no mention of a Frank in any of their discussions. Chesnokov's brother, Pavel, in Peter's photo had plenty of tattoos, but Frank's hands and neck showed no artwork, and he had no accent.

Annalisse stopped by the door she'd escaped from and held a breath. If he opened the latch the normal way, the door would probably fall in since the hinges were undone on the stone side. All she could do was hope the door was wide enough to stand upright and not fall on them.

"Open it," he said to Annalisse.

"I'm not strong enough, and neither is Gen. You have to do it." Annalisse moved herself and Generosa to one side of the massive door.

Frank tugged at the latch, and the wood groaned.

In the next second, Frank fought the door panel with both hands, clanging his rifle against the weighty panel.

"Ugh, you did this." He groaned while he pulled the heavy door back into place by the massive latch. When he'd finished, he grabbed Annalisse and flung her off the top step. "Shut up. Stay against the side of the building. Run, and I shoot the widow."

As Generosa struggled against his hip, Frank dragged her down the steps like her weight was inconsequential.

Though Annalisse's teeth ached from the landing, she was concerned about Generosa's welfare.

"Don't hurt her. She's been through enough."

"Worthless females." Frank pulled out a roll of duct tape and squatted next to Generosa. He motioned to Annalisse. "Get over here, girl, and tape her. Hurry!"

Annalisse got on her knees and took the tape from his hand, halfway tempted to throw it at him if it wouldn't get her shot.

"Tape her mouth first, then hands and ankles." Frank directed his gun at Annalisse. "Do it, and when you're finished, tape your ankles."

He grabbed the roll from her after she'd secured her own ankles and wrapped her wrists with the sticky tape.

Something sharp punctured Annalisse's backside, and she leaned forward slightly. She'd forgotten about the fork in her back pocket until the tines had pierced her skin.

After Frank completed the tape job on her, he took out his phone. "Let's see how important you are." He dialed and listened. "Hang on, Zavos." Frank whispered to Annalisse, "I'm giving you five seconds. Kissy-kissy." He shoved the screen against her ear.

"Are you okay, Annalisse?" Alec's voice brought her instantly to tears.

"I have Gen inside the castle. Italian—"

Frank jerked the phone away. "Your proof. You have ten minutes to make my account heavy." He snapped the phone shut and checked his wristwatch.

The same telephone rang, and he frowned at the caller on the ID.

"Valenti." He paused to listen. "What's *he* doing there?" Another pause. "Where's the woman, and where's Tippy?" He nodded. "I see. Right away."

He shut the phone and spat next to Generosa's feet. "You've caused me a lot of grief. They know you're gone, so come on." He reached for Generosa and hissed. "I don't have time to untape you. See what you made me do? I don't need you anymore, but *he* does." Frank looked over his shoulder and whispered, "Make yourself small." He shoved Annalisse hard at the shoulders.

Walking up the main path to the towers was a woman in a headscarf, lecturing a slew of middle grade chattering kids. From the number of students, they appeared to be a tour group on a school trip. Annalisse glanced into the sky and guessed the time to be somewhere between four and five by the sun's position. Castle walking tours closed at five. Their rescue opportunity might not come again, and hopefully, he wouldn't dare shoot into the children.

"Help us!" she screamed.

Frank slapped Annalisse's face and slammed her head into the ground. "Shut up."

Her cheek throbbed and she swallowed a mouthful of dirt.

The woman guide yelled out in what sounded like Arabic.

A minute or so passed, and all noise had stopped.

Frank looked at his wristwatch; a regular habit.

"You came close to dead. Don't move." He laid his rifle beside him, then taped her mouth and licked his. "Wish we'd had time. Move from this spot and you die." Frank swung his weapon between them then disappeared around the front of the tower.

He was either heading back to the French Tower or hiding Chet's body.

Reaching into her front pocket with a pinky finger, Annalisse dug at the key and worked the blade out carefully with her fingertips. She then sliced the bond at her ankles and got on her feet. With Matt's little black key firmly in her grip, she raised her arms above her head and pounded her wrists hard across her hips. The tearing tape zipped in Annalisse's ears, and she peeled it away against her jeans, finally removing the tape across her mouth.

Generosa's wide eyes glistened, and her head bobbed.

Annalisse gently eased the tape from Generosa's mouth.

"Shh. The CIA should be outside, and Alec's there too." She silently hoped what she'd said was true. Annalisse scissored through the duct tape around Generosa's wrists while giving instructions. "This castle is built in a square. That wall"—she pointed ahead—"leads us to the main entrance. When we reach it, follow it left." She indicated directions with a tilt of her head. "Whatever you do, don't stop; always keep going. I'm right behind you. Don't drop back to watch me—and push on until you get through the main gate."

"Where do I go outside?"

Annalisse squatted next to her and cut through the tape holding Generosa's feet together.

"The special ops guys know what you look like, and you're wearing the same clothes from the yacht, so that helps." She mustered a believable smile and helped Generosa to her feet. "Now, run like crazy and stay against that wall. If Alec isn't outside, he's at the Cave Rock Hotel just inside Bodrum city limits. Not far. Are you good to go?"

Generosa nodded. "Cave Rock Hotel. Bodrum, Turkey? I thought so."

"Find Alec there if I'm not out soon." She dug into her jeans and found the lira deep in her pocket. "Here." She placed the bills into Generosa's hand and curled her fingers over the money.

"I'll wait outside for you. I won't leave you here," Generosa said tearfully.

Annalisse nearly sobbed on the spot as she whispered, "Please, Gen, run for the wall." Her chest heaved from a force so overpowering she lost her balance. "We go for the castle entrance."

My brownstone for a CIA helicopter right now.

Annalisse slipped the key knife into her pocket and trotted behind Generosa, who jogged at a good clip, considering how awful she had to be feeling.

Generosa momentarily glanced over her shoulder, then made a hard turn to the left.

Giant rows of stones were ahead, a hundred feet high at the crest. Five more steps and Annalisse would arrive at the wall. Her head was splitting, and bitterness splattered the back of her throat with each attempt she made to swallow. The effects of the unknown drug furled into unrelenting cold sweats and a bad case of the shakes. On every footfall, Annalisse expended more energy, but she drove herself to their goal.

At the wall, Annalisse turned left as Generosa had but lost sight of her. She wasn't surprised, however, with all the dense underbrush scattered along the narrow path.

Annalisse found a small hedge dense enough for cover and ducked into the green foliage and sweet nectar, hoping to find a hidden water faucet or a drinking fountain nearby. The temperatures inside the shaded plant area were cooler, giving her some relief.

Crunching leaves pricked her ears, and she held her breath. *Please be tourists who can bring help.* She sat on her heels and crouched, peering through an opening in the branches.

Her head jerked violently back, pulled by her hair. With her face tipped upward, she stared nose to nose into the fiery glare of Pearce's killer. His earthy mouth odor reeked of a fresh wad of chewing tobacco.

Annalisse interlocked her fingers and pressed down on his hand. She had to stop him from jerking her backward, so she rocked forward and fell on her knees. "You're breaking my neck." His grip stayed firmly in her hair, but she kept pressure on his hand and managed to stand, one foot at a time. "Let go of me. I won't run."

Before he had a half second to digest her words, she spun, kicked him in the groin, and punched his face before he could buckle.

By the time he hit the ground with a grunt, she had six yards on him.

She tried to forget he had a weapon as she ran for the wall.

Bolting down the path and through the brush with her legs acting like rubber bands, she forced herself to take longer strides while dodging blooms and weeds. Generosa was nowhere in sight, but Annalisse kept running.

To Alec.

To the men of the CIA.

A jarring sensation hit in the middle of her back, then her neck. Every muscle cramped up so tightly that she couldn't move anything. Pain electrified her body, and her mind went blank. Annalisse must have landed on the ground when a hard object struck her ear, shutting down the sound. The object came again, and everything went black.

THIRTY - SEVEN

From Alec's vantage point in the Escalade's front seat, he noted nothing unusual as he scanned the castle's visitor parking. Two cars alone were parked outside the office building. Bodrum Castle was nearly empty, with the exception of a school bus parked sideways across six spaces.

He shook the container in his lap, taking solace in the rattle of gold inside. Mick had retrieved it from Commander Hilliard at the castle mile marker on D330 Highway. Hilliard's skyscraper stature and the way he strutted like a Texan with the wrong hat had triggered a smile from Mick, but Hilliard seemed savvy about his business. Alec hoped so since Annalisse's ransomer could be the same man who'd murdered his father. Why else would he have called him *Pearce spawn*?

Alec worked his throat, partly for his dad and in guilt for Matt Brennan's death. He vowed to get his mother and Annalisse back and put an end to their nightmare for good.

"If the dash clock is right, it's quarter till, Mick. Do you think he's called the bank yet?"

Mick shrugged, watching through the windshield. "The school picked one heck of a day to visit."

"Why not go in now?"

Mick looked down her nose at him. "Think about what you just said. We couldn't risk your mama or those kids in the cross fire with a premature assault. We want Titov and as many of his disciples as possible alive. Your necklace is our best shot at crushing their operation. I know it's hard, hon, but be patient." She patted his hand.

"Annalisse is in there too. When her captor gets his money, what happens to her then?" He twitched his lips. "How are they running their operations while castle tours are ongoing? The museum people have to know."

"Department of Tourism isn't on board. The custodian here insists the towers are locked up tight, and they don't believe us. If you want my opinion, they're scared to death that we're right about everything. We advised Turkish Tourism in writing of our undercover operation weeks ago. Stubborn mules."

"Go over the plan again so I fully understand."

"The Wales bank will call me when your man checks his account. And when he does, he'll think his money is there. That's when we go inside—after the schoolchildren leave, of course. It's four forty-five. They have to come out soon."

"Just you and I go in?" Alec asked.

"You go first, and I follow, covering you, in case you're being stalked. Titov wanted you alone, so we have to make it look that way."

"How do we know Annalisse will be released when the funds are transferred?" Alec made air quotes. "If she's not, what then?"

"She said Italian. She must mean that tower." Mick pointed over the dash. "Her guy wants money. Other than pure spite, I can't see why he'd harm her. If it gets hairy, you'll drop in behind me, and we'll rehash our plan. Military ops go in and cover us once we enter. By that time, the castle will be closed to the public."

"And Mom? Supposing we aren't spotted by Titov's thugs—which is a big if—I go to the French Tower to make the necklace trade an hour later?" Alec shook his head. "I don't see how we carry out two different plans without being seen."

"Titov and the man who's holding Annalisse might be working together. Double-teaming on the ransom. Or Titov is directing the process by himself. For himself."

"It feels like the ransom may be an afterthought, but I'm not the expert. By now, we can expect plenty of publicity about Dad's death. It wouldn't be a shock if the family money proved too great a temptation," Alec said.

"Hilliard wants our operations run simultaneously. We're going on the assumption there are two separate entities. One grabbed your mama, the other, Annalisse. Once we're inside, this is raining down like a Georgia gully washer." She fluttered her hands from the headliner to the seat. "We secure Annalisse first. Then you make the jewelry switch for Miss Generosa. If you're there before six o'clock, Titov will just have to get over it." Mick pointed a nail-bitten finger. "They're coming out."

Alec's anxiety soared as the children trickled out of the castle in small groups. He strained to see every detail.

"Once the bus leaves, we go." Mick released her seat belt slowly.

Alec did the same.

A flash of orange and white jumped from behind the group and ran toward the bus.

"Who's that?" Alec stabbed the air with one finger. "The teacher? No! It's gotta be Mom!" Alec's heart leaped as he tried for the door latch, but Mick forced him backward.

"Stay inside. You're too important to take a slug in the back now. We'll get her." She pulled on her ball cap and tucked her ponytail underneath. "Scooch down, sugar. We'll mosey by like we belong here and pick her up." She started the ignition. "When we secure her, we drop her off at the doc's. Then... showtime."

Alec rolled down the window and stuck his arm out to draw his mother's attention, keeping his body low in the seat.

"She's seen us. Stay here." Mick swerved into a shaded area near the entrance, parked, and shot out the driver's side with the SUV running.

Alec watched apprehensively.

Mick supported Generosa, hurrying her back to the Escalade.

"Mom!"

With his mother safely in the back seat, Alec leaned over the console and gave her a long, teary hug. He realized how much he'd taken her for granted, frail and delicate as she was, and promised himself he'd never do it again.

"Son, you feel so good. But we can't leave Annalisse in that snake pit. They'll hurt her like your father. She told me to keep running— She… she didn't come out with me." Generosa covered her face with both hands and sobbed. Grabbing his hand, she pleaded, "That dear girl got me out of there. We have to go back."

Alec couldn't remember the last time his mother cried. Like an impoverished child—her matted hair, dirty face, and hollowed-out cheeks sickened him.

"Did they hurt you?" Alec touched her neck and shoulders, scanning for bruises or sores.

"I'm tired and achy, but that nice young man, Tippy, watched over me."

Alec watched Mick's tight-lipped smile. "Is Tippy a friend of yours?"

"You could say that. Mrs. Zavos, we're getting you into our doctor's hands. He'll fix you up."

Generosa opened her mouth to protest, but Alec cut her off. "Mom, you remember FBI Special Agent Norcross. The FBI and CIA are working a plan together to rescue you… and Annalisse. Now that you're with us, it should be less complicated. Right?" Alec swiveled toward Mick for her reply.

"We won't know until we get inside."

THIRTY - EIGHT

"Stop manhandling me!" A strong shove sent Annalisse stumbling forward.

"Sit over there. Don't cause trouble, or it's zip ties." Frank Valenti pushed her at the cot in the corner cell where she'd rescued Generosa. "You'd better hope your boyfriend comes with the necklace."

A squatty man with an eye patch and a long dagger on his hip sauntered in, followed by a person she recognized.

"Seriously?" she said in disbelief. "I just figured this place hadn't been aired out since JFK was president. How could I forget your foul stench?"

Luciana towered over her. Finding her here should've come as a shock, but her presence explained a lot of things.

An alarm beeped, and Frank checked his wristwatch.

"What's that?" The little man squinted his good eye, setting his mouth into a snarl. "Time to let this one go too? If Zavos doesn't think enough of her to bring me the Mushasha—I should kill you right now. Why *is* the girl here if you didn't plan the Zavos woman's escape? Are you working with Tippy?" He spit out his words.

"C'mon Viktor, you know me. I'd never let that cranky woman go before we got the goods. *She* screwed this up." He thumbed at Annalisse. "Where's Tippy anyway? He was watching the old coot."

Luciana gestured indifferently. "In there."

"A stoolie. He won't be helping anyone again." Viktor barked. "If you hadn't left—"

"I gotta make a call." Frank moved several steps toward the door.

Matt had mentioned a Chechen ringleader during the meeting at Café Gleekos. The one-eyed man had to be Viktor Titov—who spoke excellent English with only a hint of an accent. She wished Matt had warned her how unsettling this man was in stature as well as armament. *Fond of daggers and cutting throats* floated back to her from their conversation.

Annalisse waited for Frank to look up so that she could address him.

"How do you know Generosa Zavos, and why did you kill Pearce? Did you kill Samantha too? Or maybe it was you." She kicked her foot in Viktor's direction.

"Shut up, *Americana* wench. You no speak here." Luciana crossed her arms.

"No one leaves, Valenti. Sergei is guarding outside. What call's so important?" His words were frosty, and by the way Viktor fingered the hilt at his waist, he had shed some patience. "We all stay until the Mushasha is returned. Six o'clock."

"Will someone answer me?" Annalisse looked at the two-foot blade encrusted with rubies and other gems. "Is that part of Shah Ismail's jewel heist too?"

Viktor rubbed the hilt while a single eye settled on her breasts. "I can arrange a closer look."

"Why did you join these people, Luciana? Gen helped you."

"Help me, bah. Big joke. Cheap pay—treat me like beggar. When Pearce show me necklace, Viktor proud husband— proud I find it. Too bad my fater not kill you in your house." She showed Annalisse her terrible teeth.

The camouflaged gunman was her father? Without a doubt, Luciana had orchestrated the brownstone break-in from Crete and sent the Andreyev goons or others to the grand opening, without a care for the family who'd taken Luciana in when her mother had passed.

"*You* had Pearce murdered? And Alec's ungrateful?" Annalisse shook her head. "You're the poster child for greed." Annalisse stood out of reach of Viktor's dagger and got into Luciana's face. "Why didn't you steal the necklace from Pearce *before* Alec brought it to the gallery opening? No one had to die, you idiot."

"I'm tempted to supply the means and let you two go at it." Viktor drew his dagger free of the scabbard. "Sit before I cut out your tongue."

Annalisse moved backward against the cot's frame and sank onto the creaky springs.

Viktor lit a cigarillo and tilted his head in satisfaction.

Behind his back, Frank tapped on his phone. He'd chosen an odd time to make a call. Facing the door, his phone pressed to an ear, he seemed preoccupied—

"Is that Zavos?" Viktor turned in Frank's direction.

Frank whipped around and smiled. "Excellent, excellent." He ended the call and dropped the flip phone into his pocket.

Annalisse watched Viktor and Luciana warily. In the back of her mind, she had questions about Frank, like the real reason he'd targeted Pearce and how he'd known her identity on the yacht. Had he killed because of something she'd done? Shooting Pearce that way felt cold-blooded and personal.

Now that she'd appraised them all together, Frank still wasn't a logical fit in the gang. With a shrug, she shook off the thought and studied his small features. She thought she'd remember a contact who looked like him but came up with a blank.

Frank addressed Viktor. "Zavos won't come inside the tower. He wants to make the exchange in the open. He refuses to hand over the piece until he sees the girl."

"You talked to Alec? He's here?" Annalisse's heart soared. "Let me go, and I'll bring you the necklace."

"We aren't fools. I set the rules. Tell him no." Viktor stepped away from Luciana.

Annalisse fought the overwhelming urge to curl up on the cot and scream. More would die because the people in this room were nuts.

"Why not let him see her? Haul the girl outside." Frank dabbed at his forehead with a sleeve. "Zavos won't walk into an ambush. I wouldn't either."

The power struggle that Matt had mentioned played out in front of her eyes. If Alec stood his ground with the necklace... She gazed at her surroundings and shivered. Daylight and her freedom were a few strides away... on the other side of that door.

A muffled pop echoed from the castle grounds outside.

Annalisse froze.

CHAPTER
THIRTY-NINE

Alec crouched at the west wall of the Italian Tower and watched Mick make her way to the entrance. His cell phone was on an open channel, and thanks to a spy app, they could hear each other at a distance. At the parking lot's perimeter, a CIA listening post monitored the wire he had taped to his chest beneath his flak vest. Stiff Kevlar that hurt massively where it touched his taped-up ribs.

"This big sucker's been tampered with. There's nothing holding it in place. I can squeeze through and check inside. Just so you know, I got a feeling she—" Mick's transmission skipped out. "Stay down; I don't plan to—"

"Watch yourself." Alec's enthusiasm for finding Annalisse drifted. The kidnapper might have told her to lie about her location. He balanced himself on his heels and picked at wads of cleanly cut duct tape in piles near the stone foundation. Just like Mom had said. They'd been there.

He whispered, "Found where they were. Lots of duct tape on the ground." Alec paused. "Mick?" He heard a clunk. "Mick, talk to me." He lowered his head. "Agent Norcross doesn't answer. We need help."

Alec slowly crept to the end of the wall.

A metallic odor reached his nostrils.

Mick lay sprawled on the steps, her neck slashed, eyes fixed.

He shrank back, shaking from what he'd seen. Alec surveilled his immediate area carefully. The quiet held, but they'd lost their advantage. Whoever had reached Mick found out that he hadn't followed the rules to exchange the necklace. He was early—and exposed—and he'd put Annalisse at greater risk.

How foolish to come out here blind and trusting—without knowledge of Annalisse's whereabouts after the fake bank transfer. The kidnapper might've figured out the ruse after all. Alec closed his eyes for a moment to think. If things had gone well, Annalisse would've been released. The kidnapper must have checked his account by now.

"Anybody? Mick's down. I'm on the west side of the Italian Tower," Alec whispered, staring at the time on his watch. "I've got twenty minutes before—"

Something hit him.

"On your belly."

Mashing himself flat as ordered, Alec groaned at the rib pain. He held his arm against his bruised side, hoping the steel-toed jerk from the amphitheater had committed enough violence for one day.

A hand checked pockets and waist, finding the pistol Alec had hidden.

"Get up." He kicked Alec's ankle.

Alec got to his knees, still holding his ribs. "I have a delivery to make. Are you in charge?"

The bandage around his wrist confirmed the identity of the gunman from the brownstone and theater. *Aren't you dead?* Alec had a fuzzy recollection from the corridor at the ruins.

"Where is it?" his attacker asked.

"Do you have Annalisse? Ugh." Alec struggled to his feet and leaned against the wall. He clenched his jaw when he recognized his stolen Glock in the gun hand.

"I'm sending her there." The gunman motioned with the pistol to the sky above. So sure of himself, he'd let his eyes follow the barrel.

Not today. Alec kicked toward the shooter's groin.

The report of a rifle cracked the air.

Alec recoiled, and watched the bandaged gunman crumple on his side in the dirt.

A bullet had destroyed his attacker's head, spewing an arc of blood on the tower wall and on Alec.

He dropped to the ground.

The man had died before Alec had connected with his kick.

"If you hear this," he whispered hoarsely, "someone's taken out the guy who ambushed me and Matt at the theater. The Italian Tower was— We were bait. Annalisse has to be in the other one, or she's dead. Get your butts up here. You've got two dead people already, and I don't plan on being the third."

Spotting his Glock, he snagged it and the other pistol he'd hidden, then low-crawled along the shrubbery bordering the path. Annalisse needed him, and alone, if necessary, he'd try himself to save her.

But he had to locate her first.

Leaves shuffled, the sound light as robin's feet. Alec squatted for deeper cover, watching the paths. A sleek streak of fur rounded the corner close to the wall. Alec relaxed when he found a ferret moving about.

The animal came up next to Alec's feet.

"You can't be wild." He smoothed the ferret's fur and ran his hand over the webbed collar with a receiving device.

A slip of paper dangled from the ferret's collar.

Alec removed it. "Read me," he read. "What the…?" He ran a hand through his hair and opened the note.

Team 100 yards out. Round tower behind you. Thermal images inside French Tower show 4 people. Outside clear. We're monitoring and moving in. Head that way. Don't announce yourself until we give the signal.

"What's the signal?" Alec set the ferret down and spread out the map of Bodrum Castle to calculate his distance from the biggest tower. If he stayed to his right and followed the Italian Tower's walls, he should meet the north side of the French Tower and find the main entrance—and Annalisse.

The ferret rolled over on its back, and Alec rubbed the soft belly fur. "Agent Ferret, let's get that pretty lady."

CHAPTER

FORTY

"I could use a bottle of water." Annalisse felt light-headed and weak. "Air would be nice."

Frank paced and angled closer to the door. His flat profile cast a shapeless shadow on the wall. "I'll check on Sergei." He stole another look at his watch.

"Fool. That wasn't a gunshot. Sound amplifies inside these towers. It's probably a backfire. Sergei's good." Viktor's sentence was meant to convince, but it hadn't stopped the stubby fingers from dancing over the dagger's hilt.

"My fater outside. Let me go, Viktor." Luciana tugged at his sleeve.

"We should've kept Sergei at the parking lot. What if Zavos is stupid, and he's locked off the grounds? Shouldn't one of us check? What if he's popped Sergei?" Frank asked Victor.

"Then he's one less man I have to pay."

"It reeks in this dump. I'm going." Frank opened the door.

A shard of light filtered into their dungeon.

"Leave and you forfeit your fee."

Luciana touched her husband's arm. "Don't need him. Once we have necklace, no one can hurt us. We step on *Americanos*." She wrinkled her nose and showed Annalisse her eyeteeth.

Annalisse imagined Luciana in her first life as a vampire. *Alec, don't be dead.*

Annalisse took no comfort in being left out of Matt's planned operation, but at least Generosa had enough time to escape. She allowed herself a beautiful daydream where Generosa and Alec had a glorious mother-son reunion. A shot of positive inspiration—Generosa's happy face and Alec's grand smile as he hugged her close. How she wished she could've seen it.

"Tie her," Viktor said.

"With what?" Luciana splayed her hands.

"Use those cable ties." He pointed to the foot-long strips on the table. "Valenti should have done it earlier. I don't trust her blue eyes."

"They're green, and how does Valenti know Mrs. Zavos?" Annalisse asked.

"Shut up." Luciana grabbed a thick pair of plastic ties and swung them at her.

"Do it." Viktor stood beside Luciana with his dagger raised, its beveled edge pointed and sharp near the blood groove.

"Hold toget'er." Bending over, Luciana grabbed Annalisse's wrists.

Annalisse kicked her as hard as she could in the shin.

"Ow!" Luciana lifted her foot and rubbed the ankle. "Kill her. T'row her in back with Tippy. See how she like to bleed."

"Woman, tie her." Viktor tossed his billowing cigarillo on the stones.

Bound at her wrists and ankles, Annalisse worried through various escape scenarios. She didn't know how well armed Alec would be when he got there, if he got there, or if Frank would return with more help. Viktor—or even Luciana—might have another weapon. Best case, the CIA might assault the tower, but dodging cross fire wasn't a comfort either.

The door creaked and slowly opened. Light and fresh air—the smells of freedom—flooded in, giving her hope.

Frank entered, pole-rigid with a stilted gait. Behind him, Alec squinted into the dimly lit room.

Unable to pull her eyes from Alec, Annalisse jolted when a stubby arm tugged her around the waist, almost toppling her.

"Zavos, drop the Mushasha, and I let the girl go. Shoot him. I don't care."

Annalisse twisted against Viktor but couldn't squirm free.

Alec looked at Annalisse. "Be careful. Are you all right?"

Viktor drew the long dagger with his free hand and held it against her throat.

She sucked in a breath and stiffened away from the icy blade.

"Don't do it, Alec. He killed your dad," Annalisse said bluntly.

"Cut her, and you'll never see the artifact." Alec shoved the Glock deeper into Frank's back. "Move it, Valenti."

He knew him.

Lightning quick, Frank stomped on Alec's instep, causing the men to struggle on the floor. The Glock tumbled across the stones, landing yards from Annalisse's feet.

"Rich pig!" Frank hollered; his knee pressed into Alec's chest. "I'm going to kill you, then rape your girly." He wrapped his hands around Alec's neck.

Unable to help him, she witnessed Alec prying at Valenti's fingers for a breath of air. In a massive effort, Alec kicked upward and kneed Frank, twisting him to the floor underneath him, allowing Alec to pound him mercilessly with his fists.

Luciana let out an animalistic shriek, then wrenched the dagger out of her husband's grip.

Annalisse raised her arms and banged her wrists against Viktor's arm.

The zip tie had been applied the wrong way and slipped out easily.

She spun away, reaching for the fork in her back pocket.

With the massive sword above her head, Luciana lunged at Alec.

Annalisse launched herself like a projectile and jabbed the tines deep into Luciana's body once—twice—three times.

Luciana screamed, dropping the dagger and grabbing her side.

Annalisse rolled toward the Glock as Viktor fell to the floor, stretching for the pistol.

Annalisse brought her legs down hard on his head, slipping off the ankle ties that Luciana had also applied wrong, then secured the Glock for herself, slamming Viktor in the temple with the barrel.

Beside her, Alec and Frank pelted each other, trading blows and grunts. Alec sat high on Frank's belly with gravity at his advantage.

"CIA!" A pile of dark gear with legs clomped into the room in a rush.

Annalisse shuffled to her feet, holding the Glock steady on Frank's widened eyes. "I'd love to shoot you for the pain you've caused the family, Valenti—Frank—or whatever you call yourself." She reached out her empty hand. "Alec, I'm right behind you. Reach back."

Alec stumbled to her side. One of his legs buckled and he tripped, holding on to her. "Gonna need help." He draped an arm gingerly over her shoulder, supporting himself. "I thought I'd lost you."

She grazed her lips against his stubbled and bruised face, tasting sweat, and pulled him out of the way of the operatives encircling them.

"Tell me Gen made it," she begged with a lump in her throat.

"We've got her." Alec smiled so wide that his dimples made a shaky appearance.

"You need a doctor." Annalisse studied his swollen face. "Does Matt have the necklace?"

"Mom gave her blessing to melt it down for scrap."

He removed a tin holding the gold from his pocket and handed it to her.

"Another time." She threw the metal case against the wall, and it hit with a tinny rattle. The most beautiful noise she could imagine. "It's someone else's curse now."

Luciana in handcuffs, accompanied by a guy in camo, reappeared from the back room, her gaze fixed on Viktor.

"Tippman's back there. Deceased," the man shepherding Luciana announced.

"Titov!" A big blonde wearing a helmet aimed her pistol at Viktor.

"About time. Couldn't you hear what was going on?" Alec's voice dripped with disgust.

"We told you not to move until we gave the signal. Your wire device had shut down." She nodded toward Frank on the floor. "If we'd acted too soon, we risked total chaos. As soon as we were sure—"

"Sure of what? A firefight taking place? When Valenti showed up outside the tower, I did what I had to: *your job*."

An operative in the group lifted Frank to his feet, but with serpentine speed, Frank grasped a small pistol from his boot, burying it in the CIA man's neck. Frank stripped him of his assault rifle.

Annalisse huddled next to Alec, edging their way to the exit.

The female agent spread her legs in an active shooting stance. "I'll take you out. I swear it. Let him go." She spewed the words to Valenti from behind her teeth.

"Outside. Now!" Frank screamed. "Girly at the wall and Blondie, drop 'em or I'm plugging him at the count of three. One... two—"

"All right!" The blonde held both hands up. "Everyone outside."

"Zavos and the girl stay," Frank said.

Annalisse envisaged the ways Frank could torture her and Alec. What they would endure for minutes or even hours, but Annalisse kept a death grip on the Glock she held.

"Give me the gun," Frank snarled at her.

Alec fumbled with something against her side. "If you're bent on doing this, Val, then tell me why. My dad took you on when no one else would. When he retired, he made sure you had a job at our plant."

"Yeah, crummy charity from the high-and-mighty Pearce. He bit it on your fancy boat, and I'm a little richer." He

270

smiled as if he'd been possessed by a demon. "And now you're getting—"

A pistol shot cracked, and Frank's head jerked back.

Annalisse screamed, and the room burst into bedlam with all agents pouring back in. When she finally understood what had just happened, she turned to Alec in awe.

"That's an amazing thing you did." She rested her head against Alec's.

Alec showed off the pistol from his pocket. "Camo guy's gun came in handy. I'd like mine back please." He grinned sheepishly. "I don't trust those twitchy fingers of yours." Alec gently accepted his Glock from her.

The stout blonde walked up, and with a stern look, she said, "We had a sharpshooter on him. It would've been nice to take him alive."

"Too bad; I wanted it finished." Alec shifted his weight and grimaced.

"It seems to me you ought to be thanking him," Annalisse snapped.

The woman relaxed a bit and smiled. "The agency is grateful we didn't lose more men in there. Can you walk? Hilliard would like a word, and Detective Mooney would too."

"Mooney's here?" She glanced at Alec. "Who's Hilliard?" Annalisse lost her footing and fell against Alec. "Frank drugged me at the hotel, and I'm so thirsty."

"Right away." The agent pointed to a tall man in a dark suit. "Alec, please escort Ms. Drury to Commander Hilliard. He won't keep you long. The doc's on his way to check you guys out."

"He drugged you?" Alec kissed her hair. "I'm so sorry, Annalisse."

At the bottom of the steps, Mooney waited with a triumphant smile.

"Thank God, kids. What a relief." He assessed Alec and made a face.

"Detective, you're the last person I expected to see here," Alec said.

"The Freeman case broke wide open. Chesnokov gave up Frank Valenti to save his brother's sorry hide. Norcross and me, we came over together." He dropped his eyes to the ground. "She was a darn good agent. I'm gonna miss her."

Annalisse inhaled quickly. Norcross was dead? She wondered if Frank had taken her out or if one of Viktor's men had. Either way, she regretted that the agent hadn't stayed in New York.

"Alec, Miss Drury, a little of your time please."

"Commander Hilliard," Alec muttered in her ear.

"We'll touch base later." Mooney gave them an empathetic look and disappeared into the darkness.

The commander radiated authority. "Our new recruits. Well done. Well done."

The commander must have noticed the eye roll she couldn't suppress.

"In bad taste. My apologies. I wanted to thank you both personally." He looked at Alec. "Titov et al. in custody. All in all, a decent conclusion."

"How's Mom?"

"Fine, fine. Some dehydration, but she's responding well to meds. Excuse me." He looked at his phone. "Hilliard." A long pause. "Still here. Okay, make it fast." Hilliard stowed his phone in his jacket. "We'd like you to look at some personal effects. You knew the man you shot, correct?"

"Yes." Alec winced and steadied himself with the help of Annalisse's shoulder.

The blonde returned and handed a bottle of water to her, then Alec.

"Commander, here's his wallet and a black-and-white we found in his breast pocket." She waited for him to pull on a pair of latex gloves, then handed him the bagged evidence. With a gloved hand, she gave him a cell phone. "You'll find this interesting. Look at his photo images."

Hilliard stared at the screen and shook his head. "He had a fixation on this woman."

"Yeah. It's the same one in the Polaroid."

Hilliard dug out the driver's license and flashed his penlight at it. "Frank Dino Valenti. Is that your man?" He asked Alec.

"It's him," Alec agreed.

Taking out the faded photo, Hilliard held it for them to view. "Know her?"

Annalisse stepped closer to study a picture taken decades earlier. Dark hair in a beehive hairdo. She stifled a gasp when the woman's identity registered with one out of the past. Heavy eyeliner and hoop earrings from the flower power days, but it was still her.

"Unbelievable! It's Harry's wife. Is there anything on the back?" Annalisse asked.

"Fiona, 1972." Hilliard moved in with Frank's phone. "I'll scroll, and you tell me if anything pops out at you." His fingers slowly swiped picture after picture.

Fiona Carradine was in all of them. Alone mostly, but sometimes seated across from Frank at a table; they were holding hands. Copies of old Kodak film photos, and from the big prints she wore and equally big hair, the earliest of them were taken during the late sixties, early seventies. The last photo was a newspaper clipping of her obituary notice where Fiona looked more like Annalisse remembered from her frequent visits to Westinn Gallery before she got sick.

"He took a lot of time memorializing her on his phone. How did Frank know Harry's wife?" She glanced at Alec and counted back the years in her mind. Frank's photos with her were taken long before Harry and Fiona married. Frank could've held a grudge toward Harry for their union, if Frank had loved Fiona.

Hilliard scrolled past the obituary to the next shot, a field of soil with a body so grotesque Annalisse had to turn away.

"I'm sorry you saw that," Hilliard said.

"I know her too. That's my dear friend, Samantha Freeman. We found her body there." She closed her eyes to block out the vision. "He took it before she was—decapitated and buried." Her throat closed and she turned away.

"Commander, give us time to digest this," Alec said.

"Of course. Agent Mason will take you to our medic."

The floodgates opened, and Annalisse cried, barely aware of Alec's arms around her or anyone nearby.

"We'll fly home after we bury Dad and when Mom is up to the trip." Alec smoothed her hair and kissed her forehead. "Just a few more days…"

Annalisse wiped her runny nose. "Frank was finishing vendettas by tying up loose ends. Fiona and Frank were pretty chummy in those pictures. I wonder if Harry ever knew about him?"

"That one, we'll never know. Take us to Mom, Commander," Alec said.

Hilliard guided them toward the medics standing by.

CHAPTER

FORTY - ONE

Boris's purrs vibrated under Annalisse's palms while she stroked his bony back, reflecting on the sensation of a lapful of warm love. Boris had won his hard-fought battle against a poison that had left him thin and weak, but he was alive with a good prognosis.

After an extra week on the island for recouperation and Pearce's funeral, she'd watched Crete's coastline disappear through the window of a jet. They'd laid Pearce's body to rest at a bittersweet and private graveside service following their return from Turkey. The full effect of Pearce's death upon them, Alec and his mother were so grief-stricken, they'd delayed the flight home to New York a few extra days. Generosa wanted a huge memorial service for Pearce in Manhattan once she'd fully recovered and could endure another emotional event. This time in the public eye.

The terror was over, but Annalisse's jobless future felt far from hopeful. Still, she remained upbeat and full of love at Brookehaven, snuggled into the curve of Alec's arm.

On the opposite couch, soft snoring filtered from under one of Helga's hand- stitched rainbow quilts. The sight of Generosa curled on her side with only the top of her head visible brought a smile to Annalisse's face. She followed the gentle rise and fall of the patchwork and tensed against her chill bumps. After all their recent turmoil, history and artwork appraisals held no appeal to her.

She leaned against Alec's good shoulder. "We could sure use a vacation from our vacation," she said quietly, massaging circles into Boris's neck with two fingers.

"Our little jaunt to Greece wasn't enough for a while?" Alec chuckled. "Anywhere you want to go, as long as it's not Crete or Turkey." He swept the corner of her mouth with his thumb, and she lifted her lips to his.

The stairs to the upper floor creaked, and Annalisse smiled at the huge pair of terrycloth slippers, then into Helga's mischievous face.

"Helga, I miss your clunky, wooden shoes," Annalisse whispered.

"I don't want to wake her. Look at the little bug. She's pooped. Has Chase come in yet?"

"Where is Chase? I haven't seen him since breakfast." Annalisse glanced at the wall clock.

"I sent him on an errand." Alec looked at her. "He should be back soon."

"I'll make some coffee and boil some water for Mrs. Zavos's tea when she wakes up." Helga tiptoed into the kitchen as quietly as her heavy feet could carry off.

Annalisse shifted Boris to the couch cushion and reached for Alec's hand, unsure whether she should bring up Pearce so soon. She stole a quick look at Generosa.

"Was your father aware that Frank had felt insignificant?"

"I don't know." He gave her hand a little squeeze. "Dad liked you a lot." Alec's Adams apple bobbed, and he turned away.

Her heart wrenched in her chest. "Did Luciana ever say that her father was Sergei? I still have dreams about that pile of sleaze tearing up my brownstone and shooting you."

"No one spoke of Luci's father. It's like he'd never existed. Her mother was an unwed girl, banned from the community and her church. Dad always thought Luci kept things from us, but Mom— Man, I wish they'd had that discussion about Luci long ago."

"I saw a sad woman in that oval frame in Gen's kitchen—taken on a rocky beach."

"Yeah, I remember the photo from Italy. Mom's sentimental about it. When her best friend died, a little of Mom went with her."

"I'll always wonder if Harry was killed for the necklace or because of his wife."

"Mooney thinks both. Since Viktor Titov's arrest, Andreyev explained how they exploited Valenti's large debts and his old connection to Harry's wife. They found out he'd had an affair with Fiona while she was his VA therapist after Vietnam, before she married Harry. Valenti was an easy, emotional mark. He'd blamed Dad and everyone else for his miserable life while living with a sister who had a bad heart, awaiting a transplant he couldn't pay for. She died while he was in Turkey."

"Poetic justice." She fought the desire to grieve for a woman with a brother like Frank.

"Thanks to Ralph, we pulled off the coup of the century. Remind me to come up with something special for him. He helped me bring home my two favorite ladies."

"His office could use another taxidermy specimen." She tilted her head in quiet laughter.

"Silly." Alec jiggled her against him, then winced. "Ugh. Ribs. There are so many ways I'd like to show you my gratitude, babe…" His eyes sparkled with lust and other hungers.

"In the meantime, I have a few less strenuous ideas," Annalisse said.

"In that case, I should go upstairs." Generosa flipped the quilt off and watched them, stone-faced. "To be in young love again. If it's all the same, I'd like to stay." She laughed and fluffed the quilt squarely across her lap.

Annalisse had no idea how long Generosa had eavesdropped, but she didn't mind. Generosa's pale cheeks and sunken eyes were a stark reminder of how close they'd come to losing her. Her personal doctor had her on enzyme replacement therapy, and she'd improved a great deal since leaving Crete.

The serious issues between her and Generosa had to be addressed before she returned to the city. No better time—before she talked herself out of it.

Helga brought in a tray with a flowered teapot and set it beside the sofa. "Mrs. Zavos, would you like some tea? Or maybe a stout cup of Rissman's special coffee?"

"Thank you. In a bit."

Annalisse patted Alec's thigh and kissed him deeply, ignoring his surprise. She didn't care who saw them or what they thought about her open affection for the guy sitting next to her.

"There's something I have to do." She shifted Boris, who'd returned to her lap, and she crossed the room to sit beside Generosa. "Gen, I can't tell you—" She coughed through her clogged throat. "Wow, this is hard. I'm so sorry for starting the gallery mess. I destroyed your husband's life and nearly yours. If I'd only shut up about taking the artifact from the case, they would've stolen it, and none of this would've happened. I'll be looking for another job in Jersey soon, but I hope that one day you'll be able to forgive me."

"Don't even go there, Anna." Alec squeezed in beside her.

"Oh, *bambolina*, you weren't the one. Harry was. When I left you and Alec at the jewelry case on opening night, I knew you were right but didn't want to make a scene in front of guests. The original necklace *was* there. Harry saw it, too, and pulled me aside when I got downstairs. He told me to lock it away. He was so desperate for me to do it; he'd begged me that night. Poor man."

"How did Harry know?" Annalisse asked.

Generosa jerked her chin once. "A while back, I made the mistake of my life wearing Pearce's gift at a cocktail party. Plenty of people commented on the striking collar necklace. Harry said Pavel—Mr. Chesnokov—wanted to buy the necklace or have him steal it, promising him a sum of money. But Harry wasn't that kind of man." Generosa patted her hand. "I shouldn't have copied it, but the piece was stunning. When I flew back to Crete after the opening, Pearce explained how he'd made the purchase. He didn't know its history until I told him what you said."

"Matt with the CIA came to the same conclusion." Annalisse sank deeper into the sofa, thinking about Matt's can-do attitude and his cool fisherman's cap. "You would've liked him. Multiple necklaces threw a wrench in Titov's plans—and Luciana's."

"She's a sneaky… I can't say it." Generosa drew her lips tight.

The sound of tires in the gravel driveway brought their discussion to an end. All eyes turned to the door.

"We don't get visitors on Sunday." Helga moved the blind at the window, then studied Alec.

CHAPTER
FORTY-TWO

Annalisse recognized Chase's double knock and couldn't help but grin. He was hardly a visitor.

Alec hadn't left her side for longer than a few minutes since their return to Brookehaven, making it difficult to answer all of Chase's questions. They were personal questions about Alec she knew he'd wanted to ask. With so much churning emotion, she was grateful for the extra time to pull her thoughts together.

Helga opened the door wide and gave Chase a bear hug, patting his back familiarly.

He stepped inside, bringing the most welcome sight Annalisse could imagine.

"Aunt Kate!" Annalisse leaped to her feet with arms outstretched.

"Lovely to see you. Come in please." Helga backed away and went into domestic mode. "Hello. Welcome to the Zavos estate."

Her wispy aunt, clad in a new pair of jeans and broken-in Western shirt, pulled Annalisse into an embrace so strong it took her next breath.

"Lambie, I've never been so worried." Kate's lips on her cheek felt desperate. "You didn't answer any of my messages. I knew something was off, so I called Chase. When he told me what you'd endured—those men and the shootings—the boat, I imagined the worst. Shame on you for not calling me."

"Ms. Walker, blame me." Alec held out his hand. "I haven't allowed these beautiful women too far out of range. I'm Alec Zavos."

Kate shook his hand, then drew him in for his peck on the cheek. She lingered near his neck a beat longer than the norm.

"You certainly are. You smell good too." Kate looked him up and down, brushing at a curl that fell from her loosened updo. "Yes, indeed, I approve." Kate shot Annalisse a smile as she felt one of Alec's upper arms.

The room erupted into carefree laughter.

Alec smelled heavenly and made her feel even better. For hours, on the flight back to New York, she'd dared to consider what a future would be like with Alec, even though they scarcely knew each other. But alongside him, in this magnificent place, he felt right deep within her soul.

Alec backed up a step and gawked at Kate.

"Don't stare, son." Generosa waved from the couch. "I'm Gen. Nice to meet you finally. Annalisse has told me so much about you and your lovely farm. But I have to say what a striking resemblance Annalisse bears to you. And please forgive Alec's manners."

"Mrs. Walker, would you like some refreshment?" Helga asked.

"Please don't fuss. These tired bones are grateful to stand. Chase needs an upgrade from that teeny can he calls a car." She kneaded the back of her leg.

"I'll add that to my growing list." Chase gave Annalisse a smug look.

"My condolences on the loss of your husband, Gen, and your father, Alec. Cherish each moment, for tomorrow's foretold to but one." Kate bowed her head and closed her eyes.

"Well said. Would you excuse me, ladies? Chase." Alec motioned to him, then walked down the hall.

Kate examined the foyer's artistry and Old-World decor that Annalisse loved too. "I see someone else collects history.

No wonder my Annalisse is so taken, or maybe it's his handsome bod that put him over the top."

"Seriously?" Annalisse wanted to shrink into the darkest corner of the living room and disappear. "Do you always have to be so blunt?"

"It's what you love about me." Kate laughed softly.

The observation wasn't wasted on Annalisse. She did love her aunt's brashness. It reminded her so much of her little sister's feisty ways. When Ariel had used her outspokenness to get what she wanted from their parents, Annalisse had envied her courage.

"I can think of someone else who's pretty darn direct." Chase pointed at Annalisse while rounding the hall corner with Alec close behind.

"It's a family curse," Kate said.

"Not a curse. Perfection." Alec put his arm around Annalisse's waist. "Curses don't stand a chance in his house."

"Why'd you sneak off?" Annalisse pushed memories of Ariel aside.

"This." Alec presented her with a pink-and-red rectangular box.

"Red Hots—candy?" she asked him.

"Read." He motioned at the bold red inscription.

Tears she'd held on to since Kate's arrival trickled down her cheeks as she scanned his words: I'm Hot for Ewe.

"This has to be one of the most silly and romantic—me too, Alec. Me too." She wrapped her arms around him, basking in the heady sandalwood overtaking her.

"And this." He stepped back and handed her a trifold document tied with satin ribbon and a freshwater pearl ring she immediately recognized, hanging from the bow.

Her heart swelled with so many emotions at the same time; she closed her eyes to steady herself. He'd found Kate's ring she'd lost somewhere between the hotel and the Italian Tower.

"Thank you," she whispered. "I thought it was gone for good. Where did—"

"Agent Mason found it in the Italian Tower during a search."

"When I broke the ties on my wrists." A tear fell on the ring. "It was so dark. I started to look— This ring means so much to me." Annalisse stood on her toes and held his face between her hands, gazing deeply into his silvery eyes. "A thousand thanks."

"Lambie, I would've found you another one." Kate's voice barely registered.

Alec ushered Annalisse to the couch and sat down next to her. "Open it." He untied the ring and slid it on her right hand.

Annalisse noted Kate's grin as she sank next to Generosa and hoped that her aunt wasn't expecting more meaning in Alec placing the ring on a finger.

Unfolding the parchment with a shaky hand, she found a yellow sticky note in his handwriting that said: She's yours. Annalisse pored over the seal and official-looking printed page.

"Alec... these are Jockey Club papers for Harriet; this is her registration to the association."

"Uh-huh."

She was stunned.

"I love her, but you shouldn't. You can't. I can hardly take care of myself, let alone one of your gorgeous mares. I may have to give up my brownstone if I can't find a job. Where would I keep her? Tie her up to one of the maples near the stoop?" She tried to give the paper back to him.

"Who better to take care of Harriet and her foal?" Alec asked.

"Foal? You said she's been open."

"I thought so. On a hunch, I asked Hank to preg-check her again after we left. She's due to foal in the spring."

"How wonderful." Helga clapped her hands together.

"I can handle two more mouths to feed at Walker Farm if you need a place to keep them," Kate added.

"Come here." Alec leaned over and planted a lingering kiss that heated Annalisse's cheeks. "Harriet can stay on Brookehaven. For as long as you want, babe." His deep laughter filled her ears.

"I can't pay for her board. Unemployed lady here."

"Not necessarily." Generosa threw off the quilt and looked at Kate. "You won't hear this from your niece, but I wouldn't be here without her. She threw herself in harm's way more times than I can count. I love her like she was my own. *We* love her."

As hard as she willed herself to stay stoic and strong, Generosa and Kate's beaming admiration mashed her heart to pieces. Annalisse dabbed at the steady stream of tears, remembering Generosa's endurance during the days following Frank's terror and Titov's captivity in the castle. All under the scrutiny of her own disgusting villa maid. It left Annalisse cold; how final the trip overseas could've been—for everyone.

"Annalisse, we can't let Chase have all the fun." Generosa sent a mischievous smile her way.

Chase blew on his fingernails and buffed them across his shirt. "Yeah, I'm the new Zavos Gallery Exhibitions Officer. We can't forget you. We're a team."

"My business has grown too large, *bambolina*. I need a partner of sound judgment and solid expertise. Someone like you to keep me focused and in line." Generosa smiled at Alec.

"Someone to keep me in line too." Alec rubbed her hand with his.

"What about the Westinn lawsuit and Peter? Gen, you've had enough bad press for a lifetime. Peter's out to destroy me. I can't subject you to that."

"Peter Gregory is in jail, Anna," Chase said.

"Honestly? I haven't pressed charges yet."

"Peter's been liquidating the gallery big-time since Harry's death. Illegally pocketing cash from the Russian Mafia— from commissioned as well as noncommissioned works. That Chesnokov guy spilled his guts to Mooney. They locked up the ogre when you were in Greece, and get this. Harry helped put him away."

"How's that?" Alec asked Chase.

"Harry had a legal affidavit in his desk, explaining what had happened with the appraisal for the Nelsons. And that he suspected Peter of stealing from the gallery but lacked enough proof to indict him. We have that proof now."

"Thank you, Harry." She turned her eyes on the ceiling. "Then there's only one thing left to do." Annalisse tossed her head back and burst out laughing. "Gen, you're so right."

"Did I miss something?" Alec's empty look was priceless.

"Go ahead. Tell him." Generosa winked at her.

"When in doubt, make baklava."

END

BOOKS BY
MARLENE M. BELL

Stolen Obsession ~ Annalisse Series Book One
Spent Identity ~ Annalisse Series Book Two
Scattered Legacy ~ Annalisse Series Book Three
Copper Waters ~ Annalisse Series Book Four
(Releasing Soon!)

Trading Paint ~ a short story, Volume 5 Texas Authors

Mia and Nattie: One Great Team!
A Children's Picture Book

ACKNOWLEDGMENTS

So many people, too numerous to mention, have contributed to my long and arduous eight-year *Stolen Obsession* journey. Thank you all.

Marlene Adelstein gives me the courage to cut most of my sub-plots and save them for future books. Because of her, I outline each book then write. It's such a time saver. Marlene also has a great first name!

Elizabeth Kracht of Kimberley Cameron and Associates guides me toward more suspenseful mysteries, points out flaws in characterization, and gently nudges layers of description for visual storytelling while using the senses. She's changed my writing in a good way. As a literary agent and editor, Liz knows how to ask the right questions to ensure mystery lovers have the best experience when reading my work. She's a gifted developmental editor and soon-to-be screenwriter! I'm so thankful to find Liz while attending the Texas Writer's Retreat.

Suanne Schafer is a writer who wore several cloaks during her critiques of the manuscript. Not only did she line and copyedit multiple drafts as they drifted through genres, she gave frank advice freely in every aspect of crafting fiction with a romantic flair.

Annie Sarac came to my rescue in the *Stolen Obsession* update after I rewrote the first advance reader copy. She flies through her copyedit and proofing duties while allowing my writer's voice to safely stay in place. Annie is one of the best in the deep sea of editors, and I'm thrilled to have her skills on the entire Annalisse series!

Patti Bulkeley, my closest friend and editor-warrior, came on board in 2009 when this story had a different title, fell into a different genre—and early drafts were nasty and unreadable. Always the optimist, Patti wouldn't allow me to get discouraged. Without her, this series might not have survived the long road taken to make it into print.

Vlad & Jade Erica of Steam Power Studios, Australia, designed the *Stolen Obsession* cover from scratch, including the design of the horsehead necklace to match the prose. This award-winning cover is truly one-of-a-kind. Vlad and Jade's overall concept encapsulates the story for the reader perfectly. My thanks to this talented husband and wife team!

Angie Dunnigan kept me sane and undaunted with her words of encouragement, while taking over promotion on social media so that I could get my book series out to the public.

Hugs and kisses to my husband, Gregg, for supporting my never-ending list of artistic ventures. Without you, my writing, drawing, painting and photography would only be a dream.

Any and all mistakes are my own.

ABOUT THE AUTHOR

Marlene M. Bell writes twisty mysteries and sheepish children's books with a caring message featuring Nattie, their bottle lamb. Marlene's an acclaimed artist as well as a photographer, using her talents to pay homage to the livestock they raise. Her sheep landscapes grace the covers of *The Shepherd, Ranch & Rural Living,* and *Sheep Industry News,* to name a few.

The catalog venture, Ewephoric, began in 1985 out of her desire to create personalized sheep stationery. She set out to design them herself and eventually added gifts from other artisans. Order Marlene's Ewephoric gifts and books online or request a catalog at TexasSheep.com.

Marlene and her husband, Gregg, reside in beautiful East Texas on wooded acreage with their Dorset sheep, a large Maremma guard dog named Tia, along with Hollywood, Leo, and Squeaks, the cats that believe they rule the household—and do.

Made in United States
Orlando, FL
24 May 2024

47144105R00163